BELONGING

BY

CAROL DARLEY DOW

... a novel ...

Title page drawing: The Luckenbooth Brooch is a traditional Scottish love token dating from the 17th century. The two hearts intertwined, topped with a crown symbolize love, friendship and good luck.

Belonging, Copyright 2025 by Carol Darley Dow

This book is a work of fiction. The characters, events, and places portrayed in this book are products of the author's imagination and are either fictitious or are used fictitiously. Any similarity to real persons, living or dead, is purely coincidental and not intended by the author.

ISBN: 979-8-9856551-2-4

Also by Carol Darley Dow

Window Friends

If we have no peace,
it is because we have
forgotten that we
Belong to each other.

—Mother Teresa

Chapter One
SARAH:
The Wedding

A multitude of flickering candles illuminated in the intimate stone chapel on this chilly December thirty-first, known in Scotland as Hogmanay.

"Who brings this woman to be married to this man?" asked the distinguished, portly gentleman with the rich baritone voice, who obviously belonged on the London stage.

He looked directly at twenty-two-year-old Sarah Duncan, who then turned toward her father, Richard, standing beside her. In unison they responded:

"We do."

Richard Duncan took the bride's right hand and placed it in that of Becket McTavish, internationally acclaimed theatre actor and brand-new wedding officiant. With a wink to the bride, Becket gently moved her hand into that of the groom. Declarations were made, vows were promised, and rings were exchanged. Becket allowed a dramatic pause to set the scene before he made his final proclamation…sounding very much like the Lord speaking from heaven.

"In the presence of God, and before these people, Seaneen Saundra McAughtrie and James Arthur Bradbury have given their consent and made their marriage vows to each other. They have declared their marriage by the joining of hands and by the giving and receiving of rings. I therefore proclaim that they are husband and wife. Those whom God has joined together…let no one…put asunder."

Stepping from behind Becket, a tall gentleman in traditional wedding chasuble attire addressed the church in a barely audible, squeaky, hoarse voice. The gathered assembly leaned forward to hear what the whispering vicar was saying.

"Let us pray. God the Father, God the Son, God the Holy Spirit, bless, preserve and keep you; the Lord mercifully grant you the riches of his grace that you may please him both in body and soul, and living together in faith and love, may receive the blessings of eternal life."

Finishing the prayer, Vicar Benedict Clark nodded toward Becket to continue. The stage actor came forward, smiling fondly at Seaneen and James, then announced, "Ladies and gentleman, I have the pleasure of introducing to you, for the very first time, Vicar and Mrs. James Arthur Bradbury." Turning to the groom he said in a loud stage whisper, "And, by the way, you may now kiss your bride."

Everyone in the small chapel burst into applause with cheers of good wishes. A bagpiper began his tune and the happy couple headed toward the back of the chapel to walk the quarter mile through the meadow toward the main house for the reception. Thirty or so guests followed, paying no heed to the light rain gently falling.

Sarah looked around the chapel, caught up in the wonderfulness of the moment. They had planned Seaneen's wedding in only six weeks, with the Banns of Marriage published in the newspaper very quickly according to tradition. Family and friends had been invited on short notice to celebrate the union on New Year's Eve and all had arrived safely. The only hitch in the plan was when Vicar Clark, best friend of groom James Bradbury, showed up with a nasty cold and laryngitis. It was evident he would not be able to conduct the entire ceremony and a mild panic ensued. A blessing arrived in the form of actor Becket McTavish, a former visitor to Leigheas and friend of both the bride and groom. He gladly stepped in to the relief of all involved. According to the Church of England's guidelines, a visiting minister can lead part of the service, as long as the official Church of England minister is able to conduct other parts. Technically, Becket wasn't exactly a man of the cloth, though he did play Friar Laurence in a very successful production of Romeo and Juliet in London's West End. Sarah hoped that would suffice.

With the crowd on their way to the reception, Sarah and her father lingered behind to blow out the candles in the chapel.

"By the way, you look quite elegant in your Duncan tartan kilt. It's the first time you've worn it?" she asked.

"It is. I'm becoming more Scottish every day," her father said, delighted she noticed. "Now, don't ask what I'm wearing under it."

"Not a chance," Sarah laughed, as she gathered up the candles.

"Well, I believe we have successfully merged the Church of Scotland, Seaneen, with the Church of England, James, in a harmonious union. Shall we Americans make our way to the reception and ensure sure all is well?" he asked.

"By all means," she answered, enjoying her father's sense of humor. "Nice to know your years as a diplomat haven't been wasted."

Father and daughter walked arm in arm across the meadow of Leigheas, their country estate located in the Scottish Borders, south of Edinburgh. The light rain was now a damp mist, but likely would turn into a downpour before long. In the distance, they could hear the nuptial party celebrating with the bagpiper playing a merry jig inside the manor house.

"Wasn't it the most perfect wedding?" Sarah asked. "It seems so fitting that the first person to marry in our chapel would be Seaneen. What would we have done without her these past six years?"

The question was rhetorical and faded into the night sky as both she and her father became lost in their memories. Shortly after Sarah's birth, twenty-two years ago, her mother, Victoria, deserted the family to pursue her own life. This left Richard to raise a child alone early in his career with the American Foreign Service. With the help of his widowed mother, Rosemary, the small family traveled the world for Richard's diplomatic job assignments. Changing locations every few years was the only life Sarah knew and it seemed quite normal. When Rosemary passed away, the bond between father and daughter grew even stronger as he tried to fill the void.

Six years ago they were sent to Edinburgh, Scotland when Richard was tasked with heading up the U.S. Consulate. Sarah was nearly sixteen and by then had attended schools in several foreign countries. From her view, it was pointless to try to make friends when another move was inevitable. Edinburgh's elite Campbell Manor School for Girls was just another temporary educational institution where she would never fit in. Naturally shy and studious, Sarah was far more content reading books and enjoying the companionship of fictional friends.

One autumn morning while walking to the dreaded school, a young man in a third-story dormer window waved to her. This innocent gesture grew into an unlikely friendship through writing notes back and forth and leaving them in the stone wall outside his home. For the first time, Sarah had a real friend. In the months that passed, Peter gave her courage, made her laugh and helped ease her dreadful routine at school. Naturally, she developed quite a crush on him, even though they had never met in person. He was her Window Friend.

Then came December, which to borrow a line from Charles Dickens, '*was the best of times, and it was the worst of times.*' In the beginning, the days leading up to the Christmas holiday were some of the happiest Sarah could remember. It had been a long time since she and her father had celebrated a traditional Christmas, but with the help of housekeeper Seaneen McAughtrie, who had become a grandmother figure, and Liam Morrison, her father's driver, they spent hours planning the big event. The house was wondrously decorated and the fragrant aroma of a picture-perfect Christmas Eve dinner filled the air. Even the questionable smell of Liver Koogs, a speciality from Liam's home in Shetland, didn't diminish the joyful day. After the memorable feast, they drove around the corner to Mayfield Church for the Watch Night service at midnight. Sarah recollected feeling all was right with the world, as she sat in the old candlelit sanctuary next to her father, Mrs. McAughtrie and Liam.

The scripture Luke 2:14 filled her thoughts, peace on earth, goodwill to men. She had no idea her life was about to be ripped apart.

Richard Duncan had chosen not to tell his daughter about the threat from the disgruntled man he replaced at the U.S. Consulate, nor had he told her that both Mrs. McAughtrie and Liam were security specialists hired to protect them. With no warning, two gunshot blasts hit Richard Duncan as they exited the church. Mrs. McAughtrie tended him, as Liam hastily put Sarah into the back of their waiting car and frantically drove away. Her worst memory was driving through the night and not knowing whether her father was dead or alive. Hours later, when they reached the north of Scotland, Liam stopped to make some telephone calls. The news that Richard Duncan was in surgery and very much alive was an absolute Christmas miracle. A short flight to Shetland Island for Sarah to stay with Liam's family until the gunman was found, changed the course of all of their lives. Once recovered, Richard traveled to meet Sarah in Shetland and as they say, the rest is history.

As they neared the manor house, Sarah voiced her thoughts.

"Have you ever considered how different our lives would be if you hadn't been shot?" she asked.

"Many times," he answered without hesitation. "Conrad Ratchford's attempt to kill me turned into quite a blessing. I met Lady Elizabeth Rose while recovering at Henley Manor, which led to learning I had a half-sister on Shetland Island, who turned out to be our own Liam's mother, Anje. We discovered family we never knew existed. You can't make up a story like that. So, thank you, Mr. Ratchford."

"Grandmother Rosemary would say it was divine providence, though it's hard to credit Conrad Ratchford for anything positive after what he did to you," Sarah said. "I wonder if you would've retired from the Foreign Service if it hadn't happened?"

"Probably not."

"And you wouldn't have bought Leigheas?"

"Probably not," Richard said thoughtfully. "It was only when I was recovering that I sensed it was time for a change. We traveled far too much of your young life and I began to understand the importance of putting down roots. I also saw first hand at Henley Manor, men who needed more than physical healing. Many were struggling with complicated life situations and wounded souls. My dream grew into finding a natural setting where we could offer relief from such difficulties, and restore a sense of well-being. The hope has always been for our guests to return to their lives with a renewed perspective and a spirit of joie de vivre, joy of living. You know, we chose the name Leigheas because it means *healing* in Scottish Gaelic. To be honest, I believe it has brought as much healing to us as to any one else."

"I think you're right, this house has brought joie de vivre to everyone. Having a real home is something I never knew I missed, but knowing this is ours forever has brought so much happiness, like we've found where we belong. I agree about the men who've visited here, as well. They always seem to leave with a spark of enthusiasm about the future. The idea of hiring Seaneen to oversee the house was one of your best in centuries. I love being related to someone so brilliant," Sarah said."

"I'm not quite centuries old, but thank you," Richard said.

"Which brings us full-circle to Seaneen meeting James Bradbury, a former Leigheas guest, and falling head over heels in love."

"Not to mention you and Peter reconnecting after all those years apart," her father added.

"And how about you meeting wonderful Kaitlyn? All because of that terrible Conrad Ratchford."

"Life is unpredictable at best, my lovely daughter. You never know what's around the bend."

They arrived at the side door of the house and entered through the kitchen, waking Maggie, their cocker spaniel, asleep in front of the Aga stove. Seaneen's assistants, Meara and Brennan were scurrying around getting platters of food ready to take out to the wedding guests. Sarah offered to help, but was assured they had it all in order.

"I believe you have a boyfriend who must be wondering what happened to you," her father teased.

The thought of Peter always made her blush and tingle with the anticipation of seeing him. Not to be outdone, Sarah countered, "Might you have a girlfriend who must think you and your kilt got lost in the fog?"

This produced a smile and slight reddening of her dad's cheeks. Meeting Kaitlyn Turning had brought a light into her handsome father's life which Sarah heartily approved of.

"Then, without further ado, shall we join the party?" Richard asked, offering an arm to his beautiful daughter.

Chapter Two

RICHARD:

The Laird of Leigheas

A large three-story manor house was the center point of the three hundred acre Leigheas estate. Among its many rooms, four were set aside for receptions, each beautifully decorated for entertaining as occasions arose. Tonight, The Elephant Room, nicknamed by Sarah due to its enormous size, had been embellished even more for the wedding reception and Hogmanay festivities. Floor to ceiling French doors were draped with white brocade fabric tied back with yellow satin ribbons. Tall vases of yellow roses, flown in from The Netherlands, were placed here and there, matching perfectly with the pale yellow silk wall covering. Several large dining tables were set with white linen tablecloths and sparkling silver candelabras. An immense fireplace roared with plenty of heat to keep guests comfortable as they mingled about. Richard stood alone in the doorway as the bagpiper finished his last tune. James slipped the musician a few coins, following the tradition of *'paying the piper.'* Sarah found Peter straightaway and they stood holding hands near the massive Christmas fir tree. At the far end of the room a local string quartet began playing soft background music for the dinner portion of the evening. Brennan and Meara were busy filling every inch of the long buffet table with traditional, time-honored Hogmanay cuisine. It was decided early on that the reception would be casual rather than a formal sit-down affair.

Scanning the crowd, Richard made eye-contact with Kaitlyn Turning, who smiled in return. He was still amazed that this lovely, bright woman seemed to like him as much as he liked her. What a stroke of genius for Sarah to have made her acquaintance on the train several months ago, and then arrange a meeting in Edinburgh a short time later. Life became far more intriguing the day he walked into Tuning Pages Book Shoppe and was introduced to the beautiful Scottish lass.

"A ha'penny for your thoughts, Richard Duncan," Kaitlyn said, quietly walking up to him.

"Oh, Miss Turning, they are worth at least a pound," Richard responded with affection.

She laughed with her lilting accent and promised to check her purse for such a vast sum of money.

Across the room, Sarah lifted a stemmed crystal wine glass and tapped it with a silver spoon to attract everyone's attention. Given the lively conversation and melodic music, this wasn't easy.

"Everything is served, please help yourself to the buffet table. Afterwards, there will be special Hogmanay celebrations."

A line formed at the sideboard with Seaneen and James leading. Before long all guests had dished up plates and were seated, enjoying their scotch broth, haggis with a side of tattlies and neeps, steak pie with skirlie, rumbledethumps, and stovies. When it was time for dessert, the girls delivered Black Bun and a large Tipsy Laird Trifle to a side table near the customary two-tiered wedding fruitcake covered in marzipan.

The Laird of Leigheas stood up.

"Ladies and gentlemen, if I may propose a toast," Richard said. "I've learned it is Scottish tradition for a speech to be given by the father of the bride, but I have been granted special permission to address you. Tonight we celebrate the union of Seaneen and James. As Laird of Leigheas…" he paused as this brought an appreciative laugh from the group, "I will take all credit for introducing them and nurturing their romance at every possible turn. I'm quite sure they couldn't or wouldn't have done so without my assistance."

Friends and family found the humor in Richard's exaggerated version of events very funny. Everyone knew the relationship between bride and groom blossomed when James ministered to Seaneen for months after she suffered a head injury from a fall. Looking directly at Seaneen, he continued.

"To be serious for a moment, I echo the words of my daughter, *'What would we have done without you all these years?'* You've brought wisdom, compassion and friendship to us through so may highs and lows, and in return, we love you as family."

There was a hesitation and moment of expectation as Richard turned his attention to James.

"James, you came to Leigheas in search of direction, and I think you found more than you ever imagined. You are a fine man and I have seen your devotion to Seaneen first hand. Sarah and I couldn't be happier for you both. However, Vicar Bradbury…" Richard raised one eyebrow in a mock-threat, "one wrong move and you'll be answering to the Laird of Leigheas."

James blushed and drew Seaneen closer to him. "You've no worries on that account, lad."

"Raise your glasses to Seaneen and James. May all your days be happy, and may health, peace and God's blessing follow you now and forevermore."

Richard ended his speech with a big smile, and the guests tapped glasses with hearty well wishes. The cake was cut and desserts were enthusiastically consumed. Tables were moved out of the way and the bagpiper returned to play a few Scottish reels before the clock struck midnight. It was an atmosphere of happiness and merriment as many took to the floor for Highland dancing. While there were a few who actually knew the steps, Richard wasn't one of them, and he purposely tried to fade into the background.

"I know you are hiding, but it's useless," Kaitlyn said with amusement. "I promise you everyone is so busy trying to follow their own dance moves they won't look at you,"

"I find it incredibly annoying that you read me like a book. Pun fully intended," he answered, while looking around for a way out.

"As Laird of Leigheas, you are mandated to dance," she said.

"You made that up," he shot back.

"How do you know?" she said mischievously.

"Because I've read the Ancient Laird's Handbook. It says, '*As Lord of the Manor I do not have to dance, even if tempted by a lovely Scottish woman with beautiful blue eyes.*' It's on page 321, third paragraph, fourth line down."

Her laughter was his reward, and thankfully got him out of making a spectacle of himself.

The Scottish reels were not unlike American square dancing, which he never mastered in his school years. In an effort to dissuade her from joining the dance, he inquired how she liked his toast.

"It was perfect. I was quite afraid you might use that dreadful one that was spoken at my brother David's wedding. '*May those who love us, love us; And to those who don't love us, May God turn their hearts; And if He doesn't turn their hearts, May He turn their ankles, So we will know them by their limping.*'"

It was Richard's turn to be amused. "Someone seriously said that?"

"They did. David's in-laws are an interesting lot."

"I've found all families appear normal until you meet them," Richard said with a smile. "Which reminds me, have you met everyone here tonight?"

"I've only had time for a quick hello to Seaneen's sister, Marjorie. Is that Marjorie's daughter in the green velvet dress?"

"Yes, that is Gwendolyn. She lives in Oban with her husband who is an archaeologist. I was told he is in the middle of an important dig," Richard said.

"In the middle of the winter?" she asked.

"All families appear normal…"

"Until you meet them.' Kaitlyn responded. "Well, it's lovely Gwendolyn could be here."

"I thought Marjorie also had a son, but he's never mentioned, so I haven't asked," Richard said.

They looked across the room as everyone danced, thoroughly enjoying themselves. It was hard to resist the urge to move in time to the bagpiper's happy tune.

"I see Stephen with his sweet son Henry, and Liam's family, and of course, Becket McTavish. What a nice, kind man he is," Kaitlyn said.

Richard chose not to remember how troubled Becket had been when he first arrived at Leigheas last year as a guest. It was just after a heart to heart talk with Becket that Seaneen had experienced her fall and head injury. All in all, it turned out to be a blessing, but at the time it was quite frightening.

"Who is the delightful gentleman in the kilt with the lady in red? They certainly know how to whirl their way through the Highland Fling."

"That is Robbie and Maeve Cavanagh, Seaneen's close friends and owners of Cavanagh's Antiques on Cockburn Street," he answered.

"No! Really? I thought they looked familiar. That is such a fascinating shop, though I haven't been there in ages."

"It is one of Sarah's favorites. We visit every time we're in Edinburgh," Richard said, then quickly added, "Second only to your father's book shop, of course."

There was a brief lull in the music while the bagpiper caught his breath. The large grandfather clock announced the Westminster three-quarter hour chime and everyone knew that meant it was nearly midnight. Thirsty from all the activity, most hurried to get quick refreshment, then gathered into a circle toward the middle of the room. Each person, even Richard, crossed their arms and held hands with the person on either side. Right on cue, the bagpiper squeezed the animal skin bag of his wind instrument and began playing *Auld Lang Syne*. Voices rang out, singing the familiar words of the Robert Burns classic poem about old friends and their memories that was traditionally sung at the end of each year. The fact that everyone present knew every word of all five verses brought chills to Richard, and tears to many.

Should auld acquaintance be forgot
And never brought to mind?
Should auld acquaintance be forgot
And days of auld lang syne?
For auld lang syne, my dear
For auld lang syne
We'll tak a cup o' kindness yet
For days of auld lang syne

As the final verse ended and the last strains of the bagpipe faded away, there was a moment of silence. Liam's father, Marcus, was the first to speak.

"Aye, that would-a made Rabbie Burns proud!"

This prompted much hugging with grand wishes for the new year, until the first explosion rattled the chandeliers. The tall French doors were opened and a nearby fireworks display lit up the night sky. It was mercifully short, as the air was quite nippy in the middle of the winter night in the Border country of Scotland.

With warm drinks to ward off the outside chill, and more good fun, the gathered group began to disband. Sarah and Seaneen had planned for everyone to have either a bedroom upstairs or a cottage to retreat to. Meara and Brennan had seen to the party clean up with help from a few village girls, and The Elephant Room was restored in short order. Though tired, Richard was reluctant to see the evening end. He and Kaitlyn settled down near the fireplace with Seaneen, James, Sarah and Peter.

"I cannot imagine a lovelier way to begin our new lives," James said, holding Seaneen's hand as though he was afraid of losing her. "My sincerest appreciation."

"Aye, Richard, how can I thank you for…everything?" Seaneen said. "It surpassed my dreams. Just think of it, now I'm Mrs. Bradbury, a vicar's wife!"

"Absolutely no thanks needed. It was my pleasure to launch you both into your new life, and besides the real work was done by you, Sarah and the girls. I just took all the credit," he laughed.

"As much as I am loving this day, I think it's time we retired to our cottage. Oh, I do love saying '*our cottage*,'" the bride said, looking lovingly at her new husband.

"I couldn't agree more," the groom replied with a mischievous smile.

"Good night, you two," Richard said. "And Seaneen, don't worry about breakfast tomorrow…"

"Oh, you scoundrel, Richard," she said, giving him a hug before they headed out the French doors, taking the shortcut to the cottage.

And then there were four sitting by the fire, all quietly basking in the glow of the marvelous evening.

"It is already two hours into the new year. Where does time fly?" Kaitlyn joked to no one in particular.

"A great two hour start to the new year, wasn't it? A brilliant evening altogether," Peter said, stifling a yawn.

"I don't know about you, but I think I'm too tired to walk upstairs to bed," Sarah said. "If anyone would like a cup of tea I might be able to make it to the kitchen and back."

"Thank you, Sunshine, but unless someone has a very good reason, I think it's time we all called it a day. Or a night. Or a morning."

Finding bedrooms for a party this size had taken a fair amount of creativity. It ended up with Kaitlyn upstairs next to Sarah's room, and Peter sleeping in a small bedroom at the end of the long hallway. Marjorie and Gwendolyn were sharing a large double room in the far wing with some privacy. Liam and his family had a cottage, as did Becket, who ended up sharing it with poor, sick Vicar Clark. The actor was none too pleased, muttering something about his play opening in a few weeks in London's West End.

The congenial mood was broken by a loud bang on the large wooden front door at the opposite end of the house.

"Someone must really want inside to knock that vigorously. Excuse me and I'll see who it is," Richard said.

The old fashioned latch on the heavy wooden door had not been locked. The truth was it was rarely secured as they lived in such a rural area. Approaching the door, he saw the handle turning. Slightly annoyed, he opened the door quickly.

"I am Richard Duncan, may I help you?" he said sternly to the gentleman standing outside the doorway.

"How do you do. My name is Frederick Hutton and I do apologize for my late arrival. I was told my aunt Seaneen McAughtrie was to be married tonight in this location. I've come from abroad and missed connections, so there you have it. I'm dreadfully late."

"Yes, you are. Nearly everyone has retired."

"I was afraid of that, but I had no where else to go. I had hoped to see my family and have a nights stay with them," Frederick said, nervously moving his large leather suitcase from one hand to the other.

It didn't take much for Richard to realize he couldn't leave this man standing on his doorstep at the crack of dawn on the cold New Year's Day.

"Do you have a silver coin, Frederick Hutton?" Richard asked impulsively.

"Yes sir. I believe I do," he said pulling out a silver shilling and handing it to Richard.

"Hogmanay tradition has it that if a tall, dark haired man is the first person to cross your threshold in the new year, good luck will be brought to the house.

Catching on immediately, Frederick answered, "That is called First-Footing. May I be the first to wish you a happy and prosperous new year?"

"Indeed you may. Come in and warm up. We will figure something out."

Still a little puzzled by such a strange entrance, Richard decided to welcome the man, after all he was Seaneen's nephew.

Stepping through the doors to The Elephant Room, Richard was surprised to see Seaneen had returned.

"I forgot my glasses," she explained.

Seaneen looked curiously at the tall man walking toward her. Richard noticed a slight hesitation in Frederick's step as he got closer to Seaneen. There was no sign of recognition on her face.

"Do I know you," she asked kindly.

"It's me, Aunt Seaneen, Frederick. Marjories's son?"

Seaneen sat down in the closest chair with a thud. Richard and Kaitlyn exchanged glances.

"What are you doing here, Frederick? No one has heard from you in over fifteen years. Not even when your father died."

"I'm quite sorry about that. Couldn't be helped. But I'm here now and I hear congratulations are in order."

In the light, they could see the man appeared to be in his late thirties and had once been nice looking, but now seemed to be slightly disheveled with well-worn clothes and a growth of whiskers. It must be that he traveled a great distance, Richard thought trying to justify this whole odd circumstance.

"It's good to see you, Aunt Seaneen," he said, then turned to the others in the room. "And who are you people?"

"Forgive my manners, this is my daughter Sarah, and our friends Kaitlyn Turning and Peter Michael-McGregor," Richard said, slightly taken back by the man's forward nature.

Without hesitation, Frederick focused his attention on Richard's girlfriend.

"Ah, Miss Turning, may I call you Kaitlyn? Such a lovely name," he said raising her hand in an effort to kiss the back of it, but to no avail, as she slipped it out in time.

"Nice to make your acquaintance, Mr. Hutton," Kaitlyn said without much sincerity.

"Frederick, what are you doing here?" Seaneen asked in her no-nonsense way.

"Actually, it's quite funny. I had just arrived in London from abroad and saw the Banns in the newspaper. I thought it was a grand opportunity to see my family. So here I am."

It was crystal clear to Richard that his old friend was clinching her jaw in anger and trying to decide the best course of action. It was time for the Laird of Leigheas to take control of the situation.

"Seaneen, I'm certain we can find space for Frederick. Why don't you head back to your cottage and your husband? After all, I believe your honeymoon has just begun. I see no need in waking either Marjorie or Gwendolyn. Morning light will be here before we know it."

The two shared a meaningful look, and she agreed.

"I will speak to you tomorrow, Frederick. Good night." Her parting words were said with no love lost.

"Dad, Kaitlyn and I have been talking and she's agreed to move into my room with me. I have a large bed and there's plenty of space. Mr. Hutton may use her room."

Without waiting for Richard to respond, Frederick accepted the offer.

"That sounds agreeable, and as it is rather late, would you show me to my room? What time might I expect breakfast?"

It would be hard to tell among those in the large Elephant Room who was the most offended by this strange intruder.

Chapter Three
SARAH:
A Bedtime Story

"I suppose he thinks he's charming," Kaitlyn said in a whispered voice.

"A legend in his own mind is more like it," Sarah answered, equally hushed. "It's hard to think of him being related to Seaneen in any way. I'm so sorry her wedding night ended on a bit of a sour note."

The two women crawled deeper into Sarah's large bed, grateful for the warmth of the down comforter. Even with the lights off, neither was ready to go to sleep. They kept their voices low knowing Frederick was right next door.

"You were generous to offer your room. I think I would have exploded if you weren't here to talk to. The audacity of that man!" Sarah said.

"Makes you wonder what his story is, doesn't it? I find it interesting Seaneen hasn't seen him in ages, and I gather neither has his mother," Kaitlyn said softly.

"I must say my writer's curiosity is piqued! Do you suppose he has any other family? A wife or children? We need to uncover this mystery. That should be our mission for tomorrow…or I guess it's today, isn't it?" Sarah said, as a yawn escaped.

"I'll have to leave the undercover work to you, I'm afraid. Your father is driving me to Waverley in the morning to take the train back to London," Kaitlyn responded wistfully. "It's been a lovely few days but I must get back to work."

"Oh, I'm so sorry you are leaving. Sometimes I forget you have another life away from us. I feel like you belong here."

It was so quiet in the large, dark room that Sarah wondered if Kaitlyn had fallen asleep. It's peculiar how embolden one becomes in the pitch-black of night. Without really thinking it through, Sarah decided it was a perfect time to appease her <u>inquisitiveness</u>.

"Are you still awake?" she whispered.

"I am," Kaitlyn responded.

Sarah turned on her side and raised up on her elbow.

"May I ask you a terribly personal question? And don't feel you have to answer," Sarah asked, immediately wondering if perhaps this might not be such a great idea.

"Sweet Sarah, you may ask anything you like. I'm not a big fan of secrets. What would you like to know?"

Another few moments of quiet passed before Sarah continued.

"It's just that I think you are about the most…complete woman I've ever met."

Kaitlyn laughed in that lilting Scottish way that Sarah had found so delightful the first time they met on the train.

"No, I mean it. You are beautiful, intelligent, loads of fun, clever, so kind and caring…" Sarah stopped before jumping into her real question. "Why hasn't some fabulous gentleman snapped you up? Not that I'm complaining, I'm thrilled my father is captivated by you." Sarah stopped speaking abruptly and covered her mouth with her hand. "Oh dear, I probably shouldn't have said that."

"Oh Sarah, no worries. I'm afraid your father and I have not exactly disguised our mutual attraction, but it is early days and we still have much to learn about each other. He is a brilliant man in so many ways and he adores his lovely daughter," Kaitlyn said.

"I am very glad you find my father brilliant, because he really is. I tease him a lot but honestly, he is a remarkable man."

"And I'm surprised, to put it in your words, he hasn't been snapped up by some charming lady," Kaitlyn answered. "But that doesn't answer your question, does it?"

They let the conversation rest for a few moments, before Kaitlyn spoke. "It's a wee bit of a long story, I'm afraid. If you're sure you won't be bored…"

"If I nod off, just nudge me," Sarah laughed. "No, there's not a chance I will be bored!"

The room was dark with only enough moonlight coming in so Sarah could see the silhouette of Kaitlyn's profile.

"Well, you already know I was born in Edinburgh, and the bookshop has been our family business for generations. After schooling, I stayed on and continued working there, partly because I thought they needed me, but mostly because I wasn't sure what else to do. Both Mum and Da were glad to have me, though always made it clear I was free to go another way if I chose. Remember, this was a long time ago and the opportunities for women were somewhat limited. One day, I saw an ad in a magazine for Pitman's Correspondence College–a place to learn all sorts of business skills. The subject that interested me was the secretarial program. The ad only pictured men, which was a wee bit intimidating, but I sent off for the free catalog anyway. A few weeks later, I was immersed in Pitman's Shorthand, New Era Edition," she said with humor. "For some reason, shorthand came easy and before long I received the Pitman's Shorthand Elementary Certificate proclaiming I had passed the examination. Years before, my grandfather brought a Remington typewriter into the bookshop for my grandmother to use. When I was a youngster I wasn't allowed to touch it, but as I grew up it was my favorite pastime and I became quite good at typing. Watching the keys strike the ribbon and leave a letter on paper was magical. Oh, I am getting lost in old memories…"

A noise in the hallway stopped the conversation.

"Was that a door closing?" Sarah whispered. "Who would be up at this hour?"

They were silent for a few moments before Sarah tiptoed across the room to her door and listened. All was quiet.

"It would be my guess if someone went out, they will come back," Kaitlyn whispered.

Sarah slowly opened her door and looked around the long hallway. Finding no one wandering about, she gently closed it and quietly walked back to bed.

"Maybe we just imagined it," she said, snuggling back under the covers. "Now, please go on. For the record, I've always been fascinated by typewriters, as well."

"I'll try to tell this story without so much detail," Kaitlyn said with her lilting laugh, "otherwise we will be here until next week."

"No, I love the details!" Sarah answered, adjusting her pillows.

"Well, with my new secretarial skills I set off to London for an appointment at Brook Street Bureau in Mayfair, which was and still is, a business that recruits skilled workers for secretarial jobs, especially women. The owner, Margery Hurst, was said to be very demanding when screening girls and I was terrified, yet naively confident. All went well on the long train journey to London until I got off at Kings Cross station. It had rained earlier so the streets and sidewalks were wet and the air smelled slightly of diesel fuel. It was exciting to be in the big city. I'd memorized the directions to the Circle Line on the Underground that would take me to Mayfair, and I was confidently walking that direction."

"You were so brave. Had you traveled alone before?"

"Never! I had been to London once but hardly knew my way around. I must have looked like easy prey because out of nowhere a large man came up behind me and tried to grab my handbag off my arm. I wouldn't let it go partly because it carried everything I needed and partly because it was stuck in the crook of my elbow. He kept pulling on it until he shoved me to the ground where I bumped my head fairly hard and scraped my arms and legs. I lay there while he ran off and left me in a rumpled heap…but I still had my handbag."

"How shocking! You must've been terrified!" Sarah exclaimed a little louder than she intended. "Were you badly hurt?"

"Everything was confusing and for a moment I was disoriented. Out of nowhere this very well-dressed couple, probably in their early-sixties, knelt down and helped me up. They gathered my things and the next thing I knew we were outside of Kings Cross station sitting in a Bentley automobile. The lady was gently tending my scrapes with her lace hankie and soothing voice. After a wee bit of discussion, I must have agreed to let them take me to their home and be examined by their private doctor. I've no idea how far we drove before we arrived at an impressive country home outside the city."

"So, let me get this straight. You've been accosted by a thug, knocked down, then rescued by two kind strangers who take you to their home. In a Bentley."

"Seems the Rolls Royce was in repair that day," Kaitlyn said with a wry smile. "I agree there is a little fairy tale quality about it, isn't there?"

"Then what happened?"

"The doctor said other than the nasty bump on my head, I was fine. He suggested I stay overnight with The Honourable Trevor Cumberman and his wife Miriam. Turns out my rescuer was a well-regarded retired High Court Judge and his wife was an accomplished pianist, and we were at their home in Oxfordshire about an hour from London. I protested, saying I didn't want to be an inconvenience, and told them I had an appointment at Brook Street Bureau to test for a job placement. Turned out the Honorable Judge was friends with Margery Hurst's barrister husband, Eric Hurst and one telephone call smoothed over my missed appointment and set up a new one. The evening was spent with my new friends, Trevor and Miriam, as they asked me to call them. They turned out to be fascinating people who mainly wanted to know about me. Being young and full of life, I'm quite sure I dominated the entire conversation with stories of my family and my fairly mundane upbringing. In hindsight, it all sounds a bit strange but at the time it seemed very comfortable and natural. Miriam saw me to my room when it was time for bed and shared that since her two boys were now adults they rarely came home and it was nice to have a young person in the house."

"You must have felt like a princess who found refuge in an enchanted land," Sarah said.

"It only gets better. The next morning when I went down to breakfast, they asked to have a word with me. I was convinced I must have done something wrong."

"I can't imagine you doing anything wrong," Sarah broke in.

"You must be president of my fan club," Kaitlyn laughed.

"Actually, that would be my father," Sarah said, "I'm sorry, I interrupted you."

"Well, it seems my rescuers called Margery Hurst directly and inquired about my skills. She said from what she knew, I was above average."

"Of course, you are," Sarah whispered enthusiastically.

Kaitlyn sat up in bed and settled in cross legged, as though she were fifteen instead of forty-two.

"Well, right there at the breakfast table they offered me a job working for them! The gentleman who previously held the personal secretarial position left to join the circus."

Sarah stifled a laugh. "The circus?"

"Actually I don't know why he left, only that the position was open and it was offered to me. I would live in the house, have ample time off and be well paid."

"And you took the job straightaway!"

"I did, and within a few weeks began to realize what a Godsend it was. Trevor and Miriam treated me as family, like a daughter. There was much to learn about being their personal assistant, but they were patient and I caught on quickly. I'd been there about eight months when we celebrated Miriam's birthday, though I never knew which birthday it was. She would always say, '*a lady never reveals her age.*' A large party was planned, and for the first time since I had been there both sons would be coming home. The oldest, Wilfred, and his wife Joyce, were the first to arrive with their three children. They lived in Spain where Wilford worked as an architect. They were lovely and very friendly to me. The second son arrived a few hours later. His name was Nigel."

Kaitlyn stopped speaking for a moment. Sarah could feel the spirit in her silence, and found herself holding her breath.

"Nigel was energetic and enthusiastic," Kaitlyn continued, "so full of high spirits. I had never met anyone quite like him. When he spoke, it was as though you were the only person in the world. He had the most gorgeous green eyes."

"And you fell in love?" Sarah whispered gently.

"In the first moment we met. It sounds a wee bit daft in the re-telling, but the feeling was overwhelming. He was dashing and worldly, and paid loads of attention to me. My innocence had not prepared me for anyone so charismatic. We got on well, as though we had known each other forever, and I honestly never expected to get involved with him."

"What was his life? Where did he live?" Sarah asked, totally caught up in the story.

"Well, that was a curiosity at first. From what I could tell he was an adventurer," Kaitlyn said.

"I have no clue what that means," Sarah responded.

"He traveled the world in search of…adventure. He would be gone for many months at a time, then come back long enough to prepare for the next excursion. When he was home he would regale me with stories about his travels and I would dream about one day going with him."

"What sort of adventures?" Sarah asked.

"Well, one trip took him across the Arabian desert by camel, another to Machu Picchu in Peru. After that, he became enamored by rivers and set off to see the Nile in Africa and the Amazon in South America. The one activity that became his obsession was mountaineering. It began on a trip to France where he climbed Mont Blanc with friends, then off he went to Switzerland to scale part way up the Matterhorn in the Alps. He even traveled to the Alaskan Territory and tried to climb Mount McKinley, but a dreadful influenza ended that trip. He came home for a wee time to recover, but soon went to Nepal for a climb in the Himalayas. Several of his climbing mates were able to secure the services of Sherpa Tenzing, the same man who was with Sir Edmund Hillary when they went to the top of Mount Everest for the first time."

"That's unbelievable! I can't imagine that kind of life. If you don't mind me being a little nosy, was he financially backed by his father? How could anyone afford to jaunt around the world simply for the fun of it? Did he ever have to earn a living?" Sarah asked.

Kaitlyn responded almost defensively. "Actually, he wrote books about his experiences. He would be gone for a time, then return home and write for a few months and be off on another journey. I would transcribe the manuscripts from his handwritten journals, and submit them to his publisher. I felt so close to him when I was typing his words, as though I had experienced things along side of him. If I'm not mistaken Da still has a few of Nigel's books tucked away in the book shop. They were very popular at the time." Kaitlyn said, softening her tone.

"I'd love to see them someday. What has he done lately, or is he still scaling mountains?"

Silence followed Sarah's question. It is hard to gauge someone's emotions when you can't see their face. Sarah watched Kaitlyn's head drop, and listened as she took a deep breath before continuing.

"The group arrived in Katmandu and met with Sherpa Tenzing to make the final arrangements for the ascent. I received a post card with this most beautiful exotic stamp on it, brimming with excitement about how he couldn't wait to tell me all about it when he returned home. He said this would be his best adventure yet and I better be ready to type my heart out. It was the first time he told me that he missed me and things would be different the next time he saw me. I was on cloud nine, already planning a future life with him in my mind. We knew this climb would take weeks so it was no surprise there was no communication. Everyday I would imagine what he was doing in such a far-away, foreign land, but I knew he was following his passion."

"I've never traveled to that part of the world but it must not be easy to stay in touch," Sarah said.

"No, it isn't. Telephone lines are minimal and postal service is understandably slow," she answered with her voice trailing off. "One day, weeks after his last postcard, Trevor and Miriam received a telegram saying, *'Nigel was injured, more to follow.'* While everyone was alarmed, it wasn't the first time he had suffered illness or injury on his adventures. He was a bit like a cat with nine lives. The next few days passed with a veil of normalcy, though there was a dark cloud hanging over the house as we waited to hear the extent of his injuries. Nearly a week later, the telephone rang just after breakfast and Trevor answered. Miriam and I were still at the table talking about some invitations she wanted me to respond to. Our first indication there was a problem was when Trevor dropped the telephone and just kept repeating, '*Oh my God. Oh my God...*'"

All the air left Sarah's lungs as she anticipated what was to come. Part of her wanted to stop Kaitlyn from having to relive the pain, though she knew instinctively it was too late.

"As you probably guessed, Nigel didn't survive."

Sarah reached out for Kaitlyn's hand, unable to say anything.

"It was a terribly difficult time. Trevor and Miriam retreated to their quarters and had very little contact other than with their son, Wilford. Meals were left at their door and more likely than not, returned only half-eaten. They would leave me notes on the dinner tray with a list of tasks. The first week I found myself in charge of making arrangements for the body to be sent home and cancelling all social obligations. Once the newspapers got wind of what happened, reporters were calling and showing up at all hours. It reminded me of a line from Alice's Adventures in Wonderland when she is in the rabbit hole, '*Would the fall never come to an end?*' Wilford arrived and the tension eased up a bit. He took over quite a number of things I was uncomfortable handling. A funeral needed to be planned, and an obituary needed be written, in addition to preparing a statement for the press. Poor Wilford was taking dozens of phone calls every day. Once Trevor and Miriam finally came out of seclusion, events happened quickly." Kaitlyn paused for a moment. "Unfortunately, that was about the time I learned that I was not the only girl in Nigel's life. Three of the current ones showed up at the funeral."

"You're kidding! What a rat!" Sarah said.

"As shocking as that was, life had to go on. Wilford stayed another month, before returning to Spain and we began a more subdued routine.

"How long had you been with them at this point?" Sarah asked.

"About ten years."

"So, you must have been practically family."

"Funny you should say that. One afternoon Miriam and I were going through some of Nigel's things when out of nowhere she said, '*Trevor and I were very much looking forward to you being our daughter-in-law.*' I think that was when everything really hit me. Nigel was gone, I was a thirty-seven year old single spinster, and my life suddenly seemed without direction. I, too, had expected to spend my life with Nigel. So many hopes and dreams," her voice softened. "It was a dark time, and by now my mum was beginning to fail as her cancer spread. Within a year she was gone as well."

Sarah could not summon any words to comfort her friend. Kaitlyn let a few moments of silence pass before continuing.

"It seems a long time ago, almost as though it happened to someone else and I was just an observer. But, as with all tragedies, wisdom is the consolation. I've learned there is a time to live…"

"And a time to die," Sarah finished her sentence. "And a time for every purpose under heaven."

"A time to weep and a time to laugh; a time to mourn and a time to dance," Kaitlyn continued on with the third verse of Ecclesiastes. "Neither Nigel nor my mother would want me to live in permanent grief and I know it's important to Da that I carry on. I have no complaints."

"You become more remarkable the more I know you. Thank you for telling me," Sarah answered feeling a little overwhelmed by all she had heard.

The grandfather clock downstairs began its Westminster chime, then struck four times, announcing it was very, very early into the new year. The young woman and the older one nestled down under the comforter, each lost in their own dreams as sleep came over them.

RICHARD:

The Morning Cometh

The first dawn of the new year arrived with heavy fog, or haar, as the Scots would say. It hung over Leigheas like a mysterious vapor obscuring all but the closest objects. Even with winter's chill, Richard was up early with Maggie, their doe-eyed cocker spaniel, enjoying a quiet walk about the estate. A feisty red squirrel crossed their path long enough for the dog to give chase toward a stand of old beech trees. The Laird of Leigheas marveled at how the little animal with the long furry tail could climb up the smooth, light colored bark of the tree so quickly. The squirrel stood perched on a high branch and chattered down at the dog expressing his annoyance at being interrupted. Maggie barked in response, with hopeful dreams of actually catching the squirrel.

When Richard became a land owner, he discovered a keen interest in nature. For example, he learned furry, red squirrels had lived in the British Isles for ten thousand years. Now, however, they are endangered because of the aggressive gray squirrels imported from America in the 1800's. Who knew squirrels had such a dramatic history? And wouldn't you know Americans would be to blame? Another area of fascination was the large variety of trees on the estate. He was especially intrigued by beech trees, also called Trees of Wisdom. In early days, their wood was sliced very thin and used as paper for books and letter writing. Beech tree trunks have long been considered a popular place for lovers to carve their initials, signifying unending devotion. Richard smiled briefly at the thought. Maybe he should bring Kaitlyn out here, along with his pocket knife.

This morning, however, his mind was troubled by the arrival of Frederick Hutton and the man's strange behavior. He didn't want to judge someone on a single meeting, but the circumstances didn't settle well–a prolonged absence, a sudden uninvited appearance, and obvious distrust from Seaneen, who was one of the kindest people on earth. Compounding his agitation, Richard didn't like the way Frederick made advances toward Kaitlyn. This was going to take some serious sorting out.

By now, Maggie had lost interest in the squirrel and was running toward a tall man who was headed their direction through the fog. For the briefest moment, Richard's muscles tensed thinking it was Frederick. A closer look showed unruly red hair and the friendly face of Liam striding toward him.

"I thought I might find you out here. Everyone seems to be sleeping, aside from my family, who have helped themselves to breakfast. We are leaving earlier than expected to make sure we catch the ferry to Shetland. It's a bit of a drive and I want to take it easy," said his nephew and former bodyguard.

"The mere mention of that ferry takes me back to that wretched experience the first time I visited Shetland. You people are made of stern stuff," Richard said emphatically.

This brought the expected laugh from Liam, who still felt guilty about not warning Richard about the very real possibility of experiencing motion sickness on the twelve hour boat ride. By now, it had become a family story to be told and re-told. Richard and Sarah now fly to Shetland when they visit.

"Do you have a moment, Liam? I'd like to run something by you."

"Of course."

The two men and the dog walked on through the forest as Richard related the odd details of Frederick's unannounced arrival.

"That sounds very dodgy, indeed," Liam said. "Would you like me to look into it? There are a few people I could ask to see if his name is known to the authorities."

"Yes, I would, thank you. I am sensitive about doing this without Seaneen's knowledge, but on the other hand, it was obvious she was not pleased to see him. There is something off about all of it."

"I've found it's always wise to follow your instinct. Let me see what I can find out."

"And we will keep this between us for now, if you don't mind. I don't like secrets, and I will share with Seaneen at some point, but not yet," Richard said.

"I agree, after all she's barely married twelve hours," Liam answered, looking at his watch. "We really must be on our way. Gathering our group is a bit like herding cats."

They shook hands, then spontaneously hugged one another.

"Thank you for making the journey to visit. It means so much to me and to Sarah to have family. And now you and Mairi have a little one to carry on the Morrison legacy."

"Aye, the bairn keeps us busy, but he is a wonder, like his mum."

"And his dad," Richard added.

Liam and his family left in a flurry of confusion, along with Becket, who was being dropped off to catch the early train back to London. Richard wished them well on their journey and promised to tell the others goodbye. Back in the kitchen, Maggie made a beeline to her bed near the Aga stove and Richard put the kettle on for tea. Before the water had a chance to boil, Peter came in with his overnight bag in hand.

"I'm heading home to Elibank, unless there is something I can do for you," he said.

"No, I think we are fine, but thank you for offering," Richard said, then looked around, and continued in a quieter voice, "I'm not sure what to make of Frederick and his strange entrance last night."

"It was an odd thing, wasn't it? Nothing about it seemed to really make sense."

The back door opened as Seaneen and James came through.

"Oh, Richard, I was hoping you were up and alone," Seaneen said.

The statement made Peter laugh, "No worries, Seaneen, I am on my way out."

"Peter, you know I didn't mean you. I meant…you know who," she emphasized glancing about the room to make sure Frederick wasn't lurking somewhere. "Have either of you seen him or Majorie this morning?"

"Not a sign of them and all is very quiet upstairs," Peter said, then turned to Richard, "I'm off then. Please don't hesitate to call if you need anything."

"Thanks, Peter. I'll let you know," Richard said, seeing the young man to the door.

Back in the kitchen the water was finally boiling and Seaneen had begun putting the tea things together.

"James and I have been talking and I think we should be the ones to tell Marjorie about Frederick being here. It is liable to come as a shock to her. To my knowledge, she's not heard from him in years.

"I'm of the same opinion. You are the closest to her and would know best how to present the situation, and James, you always have just the right words of comfort," Richard said.

"That's very kind," James replied.

Steaming hot Earl Grey tea was poured out, and the three friends sat at the large island table in the middle of the kitchen.

"Seaneen, do you have any thoughts about Frederick? You've known him his entire life," Richard asked.

"We were never very close, I must say. He was a smart, precocious little lad and not much of a pleasure to be around. Marjorie and Hugh did their best, but he was always a problem. As he grew into a young man, he became angry and manipulative. If I were to be honest, I think it was a relief to them when he left home. His final words of parting were, '*I've outgrown you people.*' Can you imagine such a thing? For several years he loosely kept in touch through his sister, Gwendolyn, but when that ended no one had the slightest idea of his whereabouts. It was particularly difficult for

Marjorie when Hugh died, and she couldn't find Frederick to tell him," Seaneen said sadly. "She really could have used his help and support."

James cleared his throat, "Would it be out of the question to give Frederick the benefit of the doubt and consider the possibility that he came all this way to make amends to his family?"

The look that Seaneen gave James was one of sheer adoration.

"Aye, James Bradbury, you are a fine man and I am humbled the good Lord chose to bring you into my life. I will try to follow your lead in thinking positively about my nephew, but I must confess I have a very uncomfortable feeling about him turning up here."

The kindly vicar held the hand of his new wife. "Remember ye not the former things, neither consider the things of old."

"Isaiah?" Richard asked.

"You are quite correct, Isaiah 43:18" James answered. "Well done."

"My mother would be proud," Richard said with a smile.

Seaneen began taking the tea pot and cups to the sink. She paused before speaking.

"Good thoughts, we will try to remember good thoughts, but I am dreading telling Marjorie…"

The door into the kitchen swung open and all three people in the room stopped what they were doing, including breathing, and looked to see who it was.

"Dread telling me what?" Seaneen's sister asked. "Has something happened?"

"Oh, pet, do sit down," Seaneen instructed, pouring more water in the kettle. "We've got a bit of news for you."

The gravity of Seaneen's demeanor caused Marjorie to find the closest chair and plop down.

"What is this all about?" she inquired of the three people looking at her. "What's going on?"

"I'm not sure how to tell you…" Seaneen hesitated.

"Oh, just spill it, sister. Nothing could be that troubling to cause your brow to wrinkle so."

James put his hand on his wife's shoulder as though giving her strength.

"Frederick showed up here last night," Seaneen blurted out.

So much for diplomacy Richard thought.

"What?" Marjorie stood up and demanded more from Seaneen. "What on earth are you saying? Here? Are you saying Frederick is here at Leigheas? Why? Where is he?" she asked looking around the room.

It was time for Richard to step in.

"He showed up early this morning while we were still enjoying the last remains of the festivities. When I opened the door he said he was Seaneen's nephew and had come from abroad to attend her wedding. Apparently he missed his travel connections and somehow found his way to our front door with no where else to go."

Marjorie's face held a blank expression. "Are you sure it was <u>my</u> Frederick?" She turned to Seaneen. "After all, you've not seen him for decades. Maybe it's an imposter. How would he know about your wedding? This is preposterous."

As Richard opened up his mouth to answer, Marjorie's daughter Gwendolyn came through the door, and all eyes looked at her.

"Gwendolyn, they are saying Frederick is here. Tell them that can't be."

The poor girl gave her mother a stricken look.

"I told Frederick about it, you know, the wedding and everything," she said looking guilty. "He wrote me a letter nearly a month ago and seemed so sad, I thought it might be a good time for us all to be together as a family."

"Gwendolyn! How could you not tell me? You've been in touch with him? This is too much," Marjorie exclaimed as she held her hand over her eyes as if to shut out the world.

It struck Richard that alike as the sisters were, he was very grateful Seaneen had not inherited the high drama gene Marjorie was exhibiting. Gwendolyn began crying and apologizing.

"I never thought he would come, and then when the wedding was over and he didn't show up, there wasn't need to say anything about it, was there?"

Somehow, there was a certain convoluted logic about her statement, but it was clear that neither Marjorie or Seaneen were amused by her attempted justification.

"You have betrayed me, Gwendolyn. Why haven't you said anything? You've known for weeks that your brother was alive, which is more than I have known. How could you keep such a secret from me? And then to invite him to a stranger's home without asking? This is just too much," Marjorie said.

"I'm sorry I didn't say anything. Really I am. It's just…" and without finishing her sentence Gwendolyn succumbed to sobs.

"I want to see that boy. I'm going to wake him," Marjorie said as she stood up, then realized she didn't know where he was. "Where is he? Please tell me where to find him."

Seaneen was biting her tongue, trying not to add to the discussion, and James kept patting her shoulder, probably in the hopes that she would continue biting her tongue.

This melodrama taking place in his kitchen needed to stop. Richard spoke in his most authoritarian tone.

"Frederick looked exhausted and I strongly suggest you let him sleep. There will be enough time to sort this out later. I will be leaving soon to take Kaitlyn to the train station, and if he has not roused by the time I return, perhaps James and I will awaken him. It is still early and I recommend you enjoy your tea and breakfast and lay this to rest for the moment. Have I made that clear?"

An uneasy silence permeated the room until Richard turned to his old friend.

"Seaneen, while I know you should be honeymooning, would you see to breakfast until Meara and Brennan arrive?"

"Aye, keeping busy is a fine idea," she responded quickly and began preparations.

As he left the kitchen, Richard could hear James suggesting perhaps a prayer in the chapel after breakfast might be a good idea. He knew the vicar would come in handy.

RICHARD:

Driving to Waverley

The fog had lifted and the winter countryside had a stark beauty about it, though neither Kaitlyn nor Richard seemed to notice. Their hour drive to Waverley station began with lively conversation about Frederick, and the morning fiasco with Marjorie and Gwendolyn.

"Isn't it interesting how one man can dominate all of our lives in such short order? From the little I've seen of him, and what I've just learned from Seaneen, he looks to be a rather unsavory chap, and that's putting it mildly," Richard said.

"I'd have to agree," Kaitlyn answered.

"And to top it off, I was not amused by how much attention he paid to you, Scottish lass."

With a laugh she bantered back. "Well, he is rather handsome in a shabby kind of way."

"So, that's the sort you are attracted to," Richard said in mock horror.

"And if I was?" she said.

"I believe the Laird of Leigheas would have to sock him in the nose," he answered.

They both laughed at the visual with humorous remarks about the outcome. With the topic of Frederick exhausted, Richard innocently asked if she and Sarah slept well or did they talk all night?

"We did chat a wee bit into the morning hours," she answered, not elaborating.

"I hope she didn't talk your arm off."

"Quite the opposite," was all she answered.

Rain appeared out of nowhere and the windshield wipers were having a hard time keeping up. Nothing more was said for several miles. His light and engaging friend seemed to withdraw. This was a side to her he had not seen before. Maybe she was sorry to be leaving him and Leigheas, or perhaps that was just wishful thinking on his part. Her mind seemed preoccupied and he fervently wished he understood more about women. Should he allow her some space and keep quiet or encourage her to talk? The dilemma of a grown man feeling insecure with a lovely lady sitting next to him was disconcerting. Ultimately, he chose to keep his silence, glancing at her every few minutes for reassurance. Many miles passed while she stared out the side window obviously lost in her own thoughts. The quiet allowed him to imagine all kinds of scenarios as to why she had become so distant. Thinking back, something triggered when he asked about her overnight with Sarah. Was she concerned about Sarah? Were there problems at her job bothering her? There was always the unthinkable–maybe she was going to stop seeing him. He looked her way again and noticed a sadness in her face. As they approached the fringes of Edinburgh, he had to speak up.

"You're very quiet."

"I'm sorry. Old memories swallowed me up," she answered, her usual smile returning. "Are we near Waverley already? How quickly the time passed."

Ha! Maybe it passed quickly for her! His imagination was worn thin trying to figure out what she was thinking and why she was so pensive.

They found a parking spot on a side street and walked down the wide staircase to the trains. Richard carried her suitcase in one hand and gently guided her through the crowd with his other hand on her back. He always felt train stations had a wonderfully romantic quality, and Waverley was his favorite. The Victorian structure was built in the 1850's in the valley between Edinburgh's medieval Old Town and Georgian New Town. It was designed with a thirteen acre glass roof to take advantage of the natural light and lend an airy atmosphere.

The booking hall had the famous massive stained glass dome in its ceiling, creating one of the most magnificent rooms in any train station. Regrettably, most people seemed to scurry through the station, never looking up or noticing what a grand place it was.

A large display board listed all departures, along with their assigned platform number. They were a little early which suited Richard's plan. The last few days he had been rehearsing words to tell Kaitlyn how much she meant to him. Even though they had only spent several months in each other's company, he knew there was something special between them and he didn't want to risk losing her. Given her contemplative behavior on the drive he was hesitant to speak, but something about the sentimental bidding her farewell at the train station gave him the nerve to continue. They stood together near her assigned train carriage on platform eight and he reached for her hand.

"Kaitlyn, you must know how fond I am of you," he said.

She interrupted before he got any further.

"Richard, we haven't been acquainted very long. You don't know me very well, you've no idea of my past," her voice trailed off.

Unfortunately, Richard could feel his ego spill out of his mouth and he couldn't stop it.

"Actually, I know quite a bit about you. You were born in Edinburgh, schooled in the same, began working for The Honourable Trevor Cumberman and his wife Miriam who reside in Oxfordshire. You've been employed with them for about fifteen years as personal assistant and had a close relationship with their younger son who was tragically killed in a climbing accident in the Himalayas five years ago," he answered almost triumphantly.

One look at her reddening face, he realized what he had done.

"How do you know all of this? Did Sarah tell you?" she demanded.

"Sarah? Of course not! She has nothing to do with this. She doesn't know anything."

"Yes, she does, but that's beside the point. How dare you have me investigated!" she said pulling her hand from his and planting it firmly on her hip.

"No, of course not…well actually…" Richard fumbled for words. "It wasn't me."

"Then who?"

This was not going at all as he had planned.

"Kaitlyn, I'm sorry. Let me explain," he said, then added under his breath, "though I really shouldn't."

He looked around making sure no one was paying attention to them, then leaned in close.

"Five years ago I retired from the American Foreign Service. It was time to start a new life, and while they accepted my resignation, I was asked to stay on in a unique position of consulting when they had specific issues. The only catch was that no one was to know, not even Sarah. Since the attempt was made on my life, every visitor to Leigheas has a modest background check. I had no idea they looked into you as well until your sheet came in with a stack of others. You can understand I couldn't tell you, can't you?"

Before she could answer, the conductor stepped toward them urging her to board as the train was about to depart. She picked up her suitcase and climbed the few stairs into the railcar.

"Can I ring you tonight?" Richard called after her, trying to maintain some dignity while feeling slightly desperate. He was suddenly afraid that she was leaving his life forever. Either she couldn't hear him or chose not to. All he got was a brief wave from the window as the train pulled out.

It would be a long drive home, and there was still the matter of Frederick waiting for him.

Chapter Six

SARAH:

Knock, Knock
Who's Not There?

Was the incessant knocking part of her dream or was there really someone pounding on the door? Struggling to wake up, Sarah heard her father in the hallway.

"Frederick, it's Richard Duncan. May I have a word with you?"

There was no answer.

Relieved she wasn't the one being roused out of bed, yet not quite curious enough to get up. She stretched and pulled the comforter up higher. The fuzziness began to leave her brain when she realized Kaitlyn had already left. Their enlightening conversation only a few hours ago echoed in Sarah's mind and she was reminded once again how everyone in the world had a tale to tell.

The knocking became louder, as did her father's voice.

"Frederick, I really must speak to you. Please open the door."

Silence again followed, then she heard James speaking to her father.

"I suppose it would be dreadfully rude if we opened the door," the vicar asked.

"It would, but I don't think we have a choice," her father answered.

This was getting interesting. Sarah tossed back the comforter and threw on her robe. She opened her door, startling both her father and Vicar James.

"What's going on?" she asked.

Her normally very controlled father looked slightly off kilter. Was it Frederick causing the irritation or was it Kaitlyn's departure?

"Seaneen and Marjorie want to see Frederick, and they want to see him right now."

"I gather he isn't answering," Sarah said stating the obvious.

Her father gave her an impatient look and instructed her to go back into her room. His behavior was strange given the situation and she had no intention of missing this excitement.

"I think I'll stay. You might need my help," she quipped.

Richard reached for the brass doorknob and gently turned the handle. He slowly opened the door, as if anticipating Frederick might attack him. When this didn't happen, he pushed it a little wider so they could all see in the room. It was fairly dark with rain pelting the windows and the heavy drapes half pulled across. James pushed on the round button light switch and to their complete surprise, there was no Frederick. Not only that, the bed hadn't been slept in and his suitcase was gone as well.

"What on earth…" Richard said. "Where did he go? I've been up since first light and I didn't see him. James, you and Seaneen have been here for hours and I know you haven't laid eyes on him."

"You don't suppose Gwendolyn is involved with his disappearance?" James asked.

"Anything is possible at this point. We had better have a word with her and tell the others what we found."

"Or didn't find," James added.

Sarah was confused, whether it was the lack of sleep or the shock of Frederick being gone, she had no idea what Gwendolyn had to do with anything.

"Gwendolyn?" she asked bewildered.

"Oh, Sarah, do put your clothes on and meet us in the kitchen. There's far too much to explain," Richard answered slightly cross.

Why was her father so ill-tempered with her? Some days were simply a little more complicated than others she decided. Hurrying to dress, she ran down the stairs, still adjusting the sleeves of her sweater. By the time she reached the kitchen, the tension in the room was thick and her father was speaking in his serious voice.

"James can attest, Frederick is not in his room, nor has he slept in his bed. He has simply vanished."

"Are you sure you aren't mistaken?" Marjorie asked. "Perhaps he tidied up the room and went for a walk."

Sarah could see Seaneen was beginning to lose patience, and Gwendolyn was sitting in the corner with a handkerchief wiping away tears and blowing her nose.

"Marjorie, it is clear that Frederick did not occupy that room," James said as gently as he could. "If you notice, it is raining quite hard, not the weather one would venture out in to take a leisurely stroll."

"Oh, Richard. We must call in the authorities," Marjorie spilled out, bordering on hysteria. "Someone must have taken Frederick and heaven knows what they will do to him. Gwendolyn, do you know anything about this? We must find him, he could be…"

"Marjorie! Please stop talking," Seaneen said sternly to her sister. "You are not helping."

The back door opened in a rush and everyone turned to see Meara and Brennan stumble through trying to keep the rain from following them in. The girls smiles faded when they looked around at the assembled group. Off came their boots, replaced by work shoes and on went their aprons. Seaneen took her familiar lead and began organizing.

"Meara, please take Marjorie and Gwendolyn up to the blue bedroom so they may have a lie down." Turning to her sister and her niece, "Go upstairs and we will let you know of any developments. Brennan, please fix a tea tray for them and run it up."

Watching Seaneen in action nearly caused Sarah to laugh. No one dared cross her when she barked out orders, not even her sister, who quietly followed Meara out the door.

"Oh, Lord. I don't know whether to be grateful or concerned that he is gone," Richard said. "Not meaning to offend, Seaneen."

"Believe me, no offense taken. That boy has been a troublemaker his whole life, and I'm inclined to agree with you. Good riddance, other than it worries me to see Marjorie so upset."

"Why don't we gather in the small reception room and light a fire," Richard suggested. "Perhaps we can sort this mess out. Brennan, would you bring us a tea tray when you have time?"

The young girl looked bewildered, but readily agreed.

Warmth from the fire filled the smallest of the four reception rooms. This was the one they used most often as it was a bit more casual than the others. There were probably more chintz, over-stuffed chairs than Richard would have preferred, but it made for a comfortable space. Today, however, it was anything but relaxed. Richard was the first to speak.

"Let's look at the facts. Frederick contacts Gwendolyn, she invites him to the wedding without telling anyone. He shows up in the middle of the night with the expectation of staying here, and it's Hogmanay to boot. We offer him accommodations, he accepts, then disappears without a trace. Have I left anything out?"

"I don't think so," Seaneen said.

"Perhaps we should examine the possibilities," James said. "There are only two explanations as far as I can see. Either he departed of his own will, which seems most likely, or he was taken away against his will, which is unlikely because it was the wee hours of the morning and someone would've heard something."

A small lightbulb went off in Sarah's head. She had remained quiet in the discussion so far with nothing to add until now.

"Wait a minute! Actually, Kaitlyn and I did hear something a while after we went to bed. We were chatting away when we thought we heard a door in the hallway close. I looked around but didn't see anyone and forgot about it."

"What time was this?" Richard asked.

"I would guess about three in the morning, more or less."

"Lass, wouldn't you have seen Frederick since he was right next door," Seaneen asked.

"Possibly not because it took me a minute before I got to the door. He could've been down the stairs by then," Sarah said.

"If that was around three, and I was up and dressed shortly after six, then we have established a three hour window. It was very foggy early this morning, but not raining, so he wouldn't have been hampered much by the weather," Richard mused. "And you didn't hear any commotion?"

"No, just the door closing," Sarah said.

"Perhaps we should check the downstairs windows and doors for any sign of forceful entry. That might rule out an intruder," James suggested.

"Excellent idea! Let's split up and look for anything suspicious," Richard said.

The four of them scattered throughout the main floor of the house and met back up with nothing out of the ordinary to report.

"I'm guessing for now that rules out foul play and no reason to call the constable. It leaves only the possibility that he left of his own volition," Richard said, "but why?"

"This is beginning to feel quite Agatha Christie-like. Maybe he simply didn't like his bed," Sarah said, trying to lighten the mood.

Her little joke landed like a lead balloon and was basically ignored, though she thought it was pretty funny. In fairness, she was a little sleep-deprived.

"Perhaps it was my fault. I wasn't very cordial toward him," Seaneen said with some guilt.

"I'm not sure he noticed. He seemed far more enamored with Kaitlyn and wondering what time breakfast was," Richard said drily. "Say, did anyone notice a note in his room?"

"None that I saw," James replied. "Unless it slipped under the bed or somewhere else."

"Hardly likely," Richard answered.

"I'm wondering if he decided not to make amends with his family and left before there was any further embarrassment," James said.

"Oh dear, then it would be my fault," Seaneen said sadly. "He's not my favorite, but I would not want to turn him away or make him feel unwelcome. Even if the circumstances of his arrival are a wee bit suspect."

The vicar reached over and held the hand of his new wife to comfort her. Before any more ideas were put forth, Meara arrived with a large tea tray complete with plenty of scones, clotted cream, plus toast and jam. Without wasting a moment, Sarah filled her plate with the delicious food. Apparently she wasn't the only one who realized breakfast had been skipped as the contents of the tray were gone in no time. Detective work must make people very hungry.

"Did anyone notice the size of his suitcase?" Sarah asked, wiping the last of the jam from her face. "He looked to be staying a while. I'm surprised he could lift it."

The color drained from her father's face. "Oh, no!"

James and Seaneen caught on quickly, and all three abruptly ran toward the door.

"What did I say?" Sarah asked her father who was halfway out.

"We must see what is missing," he called back to her. "How much could he put in that enormous suitcase of his?"

Chapter Seven

KAITLYN:

Playing Possum on the Train

The train carriage was nearly empty which suited Kaitlyn just fine. Her body was tired from lack of sleep and her mind was spinning with thoughts of Nigel, on top of her unfortunate quarrel with Richard. These two men should never be in the same sentence, but somehow they were. Her intellectual mind knew Richard hadn't nor wouldn't do anything unethical. After all, it wasn't as though he purposely inquired about her background, but she still felt emotionally betrayed. The consequence of trusting Nigel had left Kaitlyn with an overprotective wall concerning men. It had been years since she felt even the slightest interest in any relationship. Then along came Richard Duncan, and as Sarah said last night, he was brilliant and amazing. With his handsome good looks and easy, genuine manner, how could she not be attracted? More importantly, when she saw his devotion to Sarah and his sincere desire to help others at Leigheas, the more she found herself smitten. He really was an extraordinary man.

"I just wish he'd been honest with me," she said under her breath. Well, there was nothing she could do about it at the moment and stewing wouldn't help. Wrapped up in her warm camel wool coat, she let her head lean against the side window of the gently rocking train. The rain soaked, rural countryside passed by in a blur as her eyelids grew heavy. There would be many stops before she reached King's Cross station in London, and a little nap couldn't hurt.

Her body was nearly thrown from the seat when the rail car stopped abruptly. Whatever dream she was having departed the instant she opened her eyes. More people had boarded the train at every stop and the car was nearly full. She looked around with blurry eyes until her gaze settled on the gentleman across from her with a large suitcase.

"Frederick?!" she said, more as an accusation than a question.

"Yes, enchanting Kaitlyn Turning, it is. How fortuitous meeting you on the train. Did you tire of Leigheas and Mr. Duncan?" he quizzed.

Smart enough to not bite at Frederick's taunt, Kaitlyn questioned him back without hesitation.

"And what of you? I thought you were visiting family to celebrate Seaneen's wedding?"

"Well, it wasn't exactly a warm welcome, was it? I decided there was no point in staying simply to be insulted."

"Arriving unexpectedly in the middle of the night will do that to people," she said dryly.

There were so many strange things about this man, she couldn't put her finger on what she disliked most. Glancing around, all nearby seats were taken so there was no chance of an escape. She had no interest in further conversation no matter how much Sarah was intrigued by the mystery of his story. Unfortunately, he was too obtuse to notice her rebuff. She looked at the arrogant man in his filthy suit and shoes caked with mud and might've felt sorry for him if he weren't so obnoxious.

"Tell me, enchanting Kaitlyn, you and the Laird of Leigheas…are you a couple?" he asked.

"That, Mr. Hutton, is none of your business," she replied tartly.

"Ah, seems I've touched a nerve," he smirked.

"If you will excuse me, I'm going to rest now," she said, trying to be civil, though what she really wanted to do was slap his supercilious face.

"Yes, you rest enchanting Kaitlyn. I'm sure I'll see you again,"

She closed her eyes, and pretended to be asleep, half afraid if she opened them he would still be there, staring at her. His veiled threat was concerning as the last thing she wanted to do was involve her employers in this peculiar man's antics. The thought crossed her mind to call Richard as soon as she arrived at the Cumberman's. On the other hand, she wanted to cool off a bit before contacting Richard about anything. The train lumbered on, making stops along its way. She thought about peeking between her eyelashes to see if he was still there, but decided to *'play possum'* as Sarah once described pretending to be asleep. Before long her body relaxed and she dozed off again. The next thing she heard was the announcement that they were coming into King's Cross station, and Frederick was nowhere to be seen. A card was left on her lap with a hand scribbled note saying, 'See you soon, FH.'

Chapter Eight

RICHARD:

Stolen Goods

Serious crime in the Scottish Borders was minimal, though every so often something out of the ordinary occurred. Theft of priceless articles would fit that description. Several hours passed before the CID officers in their wool suits and hats arrived at Leigheas. As it was New Year's Day, the delay was understandable. Richard learned early on that CID stood for Criminal Investigation Department, a respected, hard working lot of officers. It was commonplace for them to put in long hours with a predictable routine— work in the morning, home for tea and a bite with the family, before going back to work, followed by evenings spent in the pub under the guise of cultivating informants.

Detective Inspector Alex Lawson and Detective Constable John Murphy followed Richard into the smaller reception room. There was a faint whiff of Scotch about them, so it was not a surprise when they declined a cup of tea. Richard suspected they might have accepted something a little stronger but he didn't offer. Seaneen, James and Sarah were sitting by the fire and introductions were made.

The protocol seemed to be DI Lawson would ask the questions and DC Murphy would write notes in his scrappy little book.

"From the message I received, time might be of the essence in apprehending the thief," DI Lawson said, "Can you tell us what occurred?"

Richard was the first to speak, explaining the series of events from the time Frederick unexpectedly showed up, to the discovery of finding him gone, along with a number of valuable articles. DC

Murphy wrote copious notes as DI Lawson asked several more questions before inquiring exactly what had been stolen.

"The most valuable item is the Pinner Qing Dynasty Vase from around 1740. It has been appraised in the millions."

"Not that it is my business, Mr. Duncan, but isn't that a rather valuable item to have accessible in your home."

"I don't disagree, DI Lawson. It was a gift to my mother from my step-father many years ago and as they are both deceased, it means a great deal to me and I enjoy having it around. I have toyed with the idea of donating it to the British Museum, but hadn't gotten around to it. Never in my wildest dreams would I imagine someone might steal it. The vase was in a locked, glass front cabinet in my office with the key in my desk drawer. Not a very clever place to keep the key I suppose, in hindsight."

"May I see where it was kept?"

"Of course. Follow me," Richard said.

Once the officers were satisfied the cabinet door had not been forced open and presumably the thief had found the key to release the lock, they returned to the reception room.

"And the key has not been found?" DI Lawson asked.

The occupants of the room looked at each other, a little embarrassed they hadn't thought to search for it. At that moment Brennan entered the room with a large tea tray, setting it down on the table in the center of the room.

"I thought you might be wanting tea after all," she said.

"Very thoughtful, Brennan, thank you," Seaneen replied.

The young girl reached deep into her apron pocket and pulled out a muddy metal object.

"I'm not sure if this is important, but I found it in the yard when I took Maggie out a

bit ago."

It was confirmed as the missing key, and DI Lawson began further inquiries.

"And what else seems to be missing?"

"Some large sterling silver spoons and forks from the butler's pantry. They are serving pieces to a very old, valuable flatware set.

I'm thinking they were taken in haste as the drawers where they were kept are still open. That was how we discovered they were missing," Seaneen said.

"Were they in a locked drawer, Mrs Bradbury?"

"No, we used the flatware frequently and never had a problem. This is all quite shocking."

"Please show me, if you don't mind."

When they left the room, Richard stood up and paced across to the large French doors and looked out across the meadow as light rain was falling. Staying calm in crisis was one of the first lessons he learned in the Foreign Service. While at the moment he was able to keep his exterior in control, his mind was in a jumble. He felt personally violated knowing Frederick had gone through their belongings and taken what he wanted. They had offered him shelter and he repaid their kindness by robbing them, and to make matters worse, the man was Seaneen's nephew! This was a fine mess. Of course, beyond despicable Frederick, Richard's last conversation with Kaitlyn was weighing heavily on his mind. At this point, he wasn't sure if she would ever speak to him again, and that was unacceptable to even think about. He realized Sarah was standing next to him.

"I'm so sorry about Grandmother's vase," she said quietly.

He put his arm around his loving daughter and pulled her close.

"I know, Sunshine. The important thing is he didn't hurt any of us. It seems he's a very peculiar man."

"Kaitlyn and I thought the same thing when we chatted last night."

Hearing her name caused him to flinch ever so slightly. Seaneen and the officers returned, deep in conversation about the best method to keep silver polished.

"I appreciate the advice, Mrs. Bradbury, and will pass it on to the misses, not that we have much silver to keep sparkling," DC Lawson said. Then turning to Sarah, he asked about the books missing from her room.

"They were gifts from my grandmother, as well. So far I've noticed three rather costly ones are gone, an early edition of *The Canterbury Tales*, a first edition of *Frankenstein* and a rare copy of *Audubon's The Birds of America*. The room he was sleeping in is a guest room where I keep my best books. He had hours to choose what he wanted."

"And none of them were locked up?" the officer asked.

"No, sir," Sarah answered.

Another half hour passed with the DI asking questions about Frederick Hutton and the DC writing notes. None of them really knew much about Frederick other than Seaneen's memories of what he was like as a child.

"Did you mention his mother is here in the house? Perhaps I might interview her?" he asked.

The others in the room looked at one another and stayed silent.

"Is there something I should be aware of?" DI Lawson asked, noticing their reaction. "I'm sure she could lend additional information."

"I suppose that would be appropriate," Richard answered. "You'll also want to speak to her daughter, Gwendolyn. We just learned she has stayed in loose contact with Frederick the past few years. A word of warning gentlemen, Marjorie and Gwendolyn are a bit prone to theatrics."

"Noted, Mr. Duncan."

"Why don't I fetch them?" Seaneen offered. "It would probably be best if I let her know why the officers are here and Frederick's possible involvement."

The teapot had been emptied by the time Seaneen returned with Marjorie and Gwendolyn.

"What is this about, officer? You cannot be accusing my son Frederick of stealing valuable articles. He may have his shortcomings, but he would never do such a thing."

DI Lawson interrupted in an effort to stem the tide of hysteria he felt was imminent.

"Mrs. Hutton…"

"That was my name before I married. It's Mrs. Harris now," Marjorie said.

"As I was saying, Mrs. Harris, we are examining all leads in connection to the missing items at this time, however it seems highly plausible that your son had the opportunity. I am gathering facts at the moment and we will follow where they lead. As I understand it, you have not seen Frederick in many years."

"He's a good boy…he would never do anything…how dare you accuse him!" Marjorie stuttered out as she dissolved into the feared hysteria and collapsed in a nearby chair.

"Mrs. Harris, can you tell me how Frederick knew you were at Leigheas?"

The sobbing woman only waved her hand at DI Lawson, indicating her inability to continue this conversation. All eyes turned to Gwendolyn, who was trying to be invisible. In an attempt to avoid a second woman succumbing to the vapors, DI Lawson asked his question again very gently.

"Gwendolyn, we have quite a mystery here and I need your help to sort it. Can you tell me when you last spoke to your brother?"

A few moments passed before she answered in a quiet voice.

"Two weeks ago."

"Now if you can, think about that conversation. At anytime was there mention of your aunt's upcoming wedding?"

"Yes," she answered, looking down at her tightly clasped hands.

"Good, good. Now, can you remember if you might have told him where the wedding was to take place?"

Tears began falling onto her hands, but no words came out.

"Gwendolyn, look at me, please," DI Lawson kindly said. "We simply need to know how Frederick knew it would be at Leigheas."

"Because I told him," the girl blubbered out. "I said it was so wonderful that Aunt Seaneen was getting married, and it was going to be at a fabulous estate and that Mr. Duncan was very rich."

Once Gwendolyn's statement was out, Marjorie began swooning again, complete with moaning. The officer gave Richard a pleading look for help.

"Perhaps it would be best if Marjorie could have a lie down in her room?" Richard said.

"Yes, of course. Come with me," Seaneen reached out her hand to help her sister up. When she wouldn't respond, Seaneen spoke firmly. "Marjorie, get up this instant and stop this behavior. You are not helping the situation."

The distraught woman immediately became compliant and followed Seaneen toward the door. Gwendolyn stood as though to follow. DI Lawson put out his hand to stop her.

"I have a few more questions for you. Please sit down."

Another half hour passed with the revelation that Frederick hinted at having a flat in London but according to what he told Gwendolyn, he moved around a lot. It was not uncommon for him to ask her for small amounts of money, which she was instructed to send to a postal box. Her mother knew nothing about her conversations with Frederick at his request. By the time the Inspector was satisfied she had told them everything, the poor girl looked pale and repentant. Her apologies were sincere and it was obvious she had been used by her brother with no knowledge of what he planned. James escorted her upstairs to join her mother and Aunt Seaneen.

"If it fits in your investigation, would it be all right if I called Marjorie's husband, Malcolm, to pick them up as soon as possible?" Richard asked the inspector.

Sarah spoke up for the first time since the officers had arrived.

"I think that is a marvelous idea, Dad," she said trying to keep the humor out of her voice.

"I quite agree with your daughter, Mr. Duncan," the officer said. "That is a marvelous idea."

The officers took their leave, telling Richard they would stay in touch. Walking back into the house, the grandfather clock struck five times. This had truly been one of the longest days he could remember. If only he could share it all with Kaitlyn, but he didn't dare contact her. Not yet anyway.

Chapter Nine

SARAH:

Henry's Zoo

A crumpled up wad of paper landed on the floor atop all the others. Nothing should be this hard. All through school at Cambridge she'd written short stories, essays, and articles for Varsity, the independent school newspaper. Her ideas always flowed like a rushing stream with no hindrance. As recently as few weeks ago, Sarah had a clear vision of what she wanted to write, even imagining what her first children's book would look like. Yet here she was, awake since dawn and unable to put two thoughts together that made any sense. Making it worse, she was beginning to doubt her ability. After her grand announcement of choosing to be a writer in front of God and everyone, fear was beginning to worm its way into her confidence. What if she couldn't write the stories she had in her head? What if she literally did not have what it took to be an author?

"Whose stupid idea was this anyway?" she thought to herself as she stood up from the antique desk in her bedroom. Her back ached nearly as much as her brain. Looking around, this truly was her favorite place to write, even if words were not coming forth today. The walls were painted a peaceful Ball and Farrow green-gray with the unlikely name of *Breakfast Room*. Whoever thought of all the funny names for paint colors obviously had a vivid imagination. The color was in contrast to white crown molding, designed with intricately carved vines and leaves. The tall bay window, small tiled fireplace and high four-poster bed made this a wonderful sanctuary. Too bad it wasn't offering her any creative inspiration at the moment. Outside, a dusting of snow was blowing around in a blustery wind. Maybe bears who hibernated until spring had the right idea.

The winter months had been quiet at Leigheas since the '*Frederick Episode*,' as it was now referred to. There had been only one telephone call from DI Lawson saying the despicable man might have been spotted boarding a train at Waverley on New Year's Day, but it wasn't a positive identification. Nothing had turned up regarding the stolen items, though he assured Richard the police were constantly checking their sources.

There was an uneasy atmosphere around the house Sarah couldn't put her finger on. Her father had been unusually withdrawn, spending the majority of time in his office. If she didn't know better, she thought he might seem a little down. Spring was still several months away, which meant it was too early to worry about the new group of guests. Maybe the theft bothered him more than she realized.

On the other hand, Seaneen and James were radiant in their own world, thick as thieves enjoying one another's company. Most of the housework and cooking was now taken care of by Meara and Brennan, who were more than up to the task. Seaneen continued to oversee the household and would shoo the girls out of the kitchen every so often to prepare something special. All in all, everything at Leigheas was fine–if it weren't for a slight sense of foreboding in the air.

The aroma of shortbread wafted through as Sarah came down the staircase to the main floor. She followed the fragrance as though in a trance to the warm kitchen where Seaneen was just taking a fresh batch out of the Aga.

"I will never tire of homemade shortbread," Sarah said snatching a piece from the hot tray.

"Good morning, pet. Have you had your breakfast yet?" Seaneen asked.

"Does shortbread count? No, I thought I might be in time to have it with you and Dad."

"I'm afraid he was in and out early this morning, but I noticed he was back in his office a wee bit ago. James and I had scones and tea in the cottage and are heading to the village for a few things. Would you like me to make you some tea and porridge?"

"Oh, goodness, no. You two be off on adventure. I will find plenty to snack on," Sarah said while taking another cookie.

"Would you do me the favor of taking shortbread to little Henry? Mind you, let them cool a bit before stacking or they'll stick together in the tin."

Little Henry was the ten year old down syndrome son of Stephen, the staff veterinarian. The two of them lived in a stone cottage in the meadow between the manor house and the stables. Everyone who met Henry fell in love with this happy, tender-hearted little boy. Sarah readily agreed to deliver the tin to sweet Henry…once the shortbread had cooled, of course. The thought of going out into the cold wasn't top on her list of favorite things, but she knew how much it would mean to the little lad.

After a cup of Earl Grey tea with its hint of bergamot orange and several slices of toast laden with orange marmalade, the shortbread was still too hot to pack. Her cocker spaniel sleeping by the Aga woke up and sniffed near the baking tray.

"Well, Maggie, it's just you and me," she said. The dog looked up with large brown eyes and wagged her little stub of a tail. "Come on, let's go bother Dad."

The office door was ajar as she and Maggie walked down the hall. Hearing her father on the phone, she hesitated before going in and shamelessly eavesdropped.

"And you're quite sure about this?" he asked into the telephone.

A few moments passed while the person on the other end of the line must have responded.

"Of course I understand the serious nature, but is all that really necessary?"

It sounded like estate business and probably not the best time for Sarah to interrupt. She and Maggie wandered around the house before the dog abandoned her to seek the warmth of the kitchen. Peter left a message yesterday saying he would be in Edinburgh visiting his grandparents for the next few days, but hoped to see her by the end of the week. Feeling a little at loose ends, she decided spending time with little Henry was exactly what she needed. The tin of cooled shortbread was packed and tucked under her warm coat, she slid on her wellies and was out the door. Thankfully, the wind had died down and the snow had moved on, leaving behind a sparkling landscape of ice crystals.

There was no answer at Stephen and Henry's cottage door, so she walked the short distance to the stables. The equestrian building at Leigheas was built to compliment the architecture of the manor house, as was the custom a hundred years ago. The stone structure had ten over-sized stalls and with only four resident horses, there was room for a veterinary surgery for Stephen and a space for any large animal in distress. In addition to the equine residents, the estate also had a nice herd of sheep and a few Highland cows for the vet to tend. Another empty stall became a home for small injured wild animals that were found on the property. Several years ago, Stephen, Marcus, the groundskeeper, and her father created an incredible sanctuary resembling the outdoors in the stall enclosure. The far two corners had several large potted live trees, lit by ceiling-high windows. Between the trees they built a long, wooden trough with a miniature hedgerow growing in it. It was surrounded by netting so animals who were healing in the trees couldn't bother the smaller animals healing in the hedgerow. It was little Henry's idea to re-create nature in the stall so the creatures would feel more at home. It became known as Henry's Zoo and the young boy spent hours naming and introducing one animal to another. His gentle personality resulted in unlikely friendships between creatures who would normally be enemies in their natural habitat.

The fragrance of well-worn leather greeted Sarah in the tack room, where Stephen was polishing one of the saddles perched on a saddle-tree. Wooden pegs lined one wall with various bridles and accessories hanging in neat rows. A large cupboard to the right was filled with brushes, sponges and buckets used to groom the horses. The other side of the room had a variety of English saddles on stands lightly covered to keep the dust off. The outside of the building was well over a century old, but the inside had been completely modernized. It was well-ventilated, cool is the summer and kept warm in the winter months. Overall, it was quite a pleasant place to spend time.

"Good morning, Stephen. I'm looking for Henry. His Auntie-Neen has sent me with fresh shortbread."

"Perhaps I should snag a sample before you give it to the lad," Stephen said with a twinkle in his eye.

Sarah pulled out a piece of the pure butter shortbread and handed it to him.

"I think that's only right," she laughed. "And where might I find the boy?"

"He's in Henry's Zoo," Stephen said, taking a bite of the crumbling cookie. "A few days ago we found a little Hazel Dormouse and already Henry has it playing with the others, most of whom would be predators in the wild. He really has a brilliant way with little creatures."

"It reminds me of the scripture where the lion lays down with the lamb," Sarah said.

"Do you remember how that scripture ends?" Stephen asked.

"And a little child shall lead them," Sarah recited, thinking back to Grandmother Rosemary's teachings.

Not wanting to disturb Henry as he quietly spoke to the animals, Sarah carefully opened the screened door and listened.

"Now, Mister Owl, you must be nice to Miss Mouse and you mustn't eat her. She has a hurt leg like your wing is hurt," Henry spoke softly to the small tawny owl perched on a branch.

He tenderly cupped the pocket-sized dormouse in his hands and carefully placed her in a cage lined with a soft cloth.

"You will be safe here, Miss Mouse. No one will hurt you," he said closing the cage door. "When you get a little better, you can play in the hedgerow garden."

"Good morning, Henry," Sarah spoke a little above a whisper so as to not startle the boy.

"Oh! Miss Sarah! Come see our new dormouse, but you must close the door so no one gets out by mistake."

Once inside the stall, she knelt down next to Henry on the straw floor. Several cages were on either side of the room, each containing a small creature. A few birds perched in the trees and a tiny hedgehog rooted in the hedge.

"My goodness, I had no idea there were so many animals in here," she said "And you take such good care of them."

"They all have names," Henry said beaming.

He then began introducing them one at a time to Sarah, finishing with the newest member of the group, Hazel, the dormouse.

"It's wonderful you have so many friends," she said.

"They are my family," the boy said earnestly. "We are a family of friends."

In that moment a light went off in Sarah's brain. A family of friends! That is exactly the book she wanted to write. A family of friends! She tried to hide her excitement and quelled the urge to rush away to get her ideas on paper.

"Henry, would you mind if I wrote a book about your animals?"

"No, Miss Sarah. That would be lovely," he said. "I can help if you need it."

"Thank you, I just might require your assistance," she said giving him a hug.

"Um…do I smell shortbread, Miss Sarah?"

"I almost forgot. Yes, Auntie-Neen made this just for you this morning."

"I love Auntie-Neen," he said taking a bite of the shortbread, "and I love you, too, Miss Sarah."

She sat with Henry and his animals for quite a while as he shared imaginary tales about his menagerie and their adventures. The spark of inspiration was intoxicating.

Chapter Ten

RICHARD:

*Keep Praying,
But Row Away from the Rocks*

The telephone connection was not bad considering the distance from Shetland Island to the Scottish Borders.

"Yes, I understand it is necessary, Liam. I really do appreciate your assistance with this. I suspected Frederick was dicey the minute I opened the door, but never would have guessed Scotland Yard and Interpol would be involved," Richard said.

"Apparently, he has run up significant gambling debts in three countries, the UK, Germany and Monaco," Liam said. "The last year and a half he has resorted to illegal and immoral methods of getting money to keep the wolves at bay,"

"He feels like more of a threat than Conrad Ratchford."

"Well, according to my sources, Frederick Hutton has stolen, embezzled, and intimidated with weapons, but there is no attempted murder on his resume. Yet."

"And that is supposed to comfort me?" Richard asked with a laugh. "He is a scoundrel of the first order. How many security men are you suggesting we will need here?"

"The ambassador suggested more, but I think two will be sufficient. Can you house them in one of the cottages? That way they can work more efficiently."

"Of course. I will speak to Seaneen and have a cottage ready for them. When should we expect them to arrive?"

"Tomorrow around mid-day I would guess. Their names are Giles Fisher and Mark Harris. Would you feel more secure if I came down for a bit?" his former bodyguard asked.

"While I always enjoy seeing my favorite nephew, I think for now the two security men should be enough. Kindly thank the ambassador for his quick response. I will gather everyone here and let them know what is going on. Do you know if Marjorie has any protection or even knows how dangerous Frederick might be toward her?"

"I've no idea, though I doubt she has the kind of money he needs to solve his problems. However, it might be wise to let her know. Better safe than sorry," Liam answered.

"Seaneen just came in and I'll mention it to her."

"I must go, my bairn is needing attention. I'll let you know if I hear anything more."

"Good-bye and thank you, Liam."

Richard motioned for Seaneen to sit down in the chair across the desk from him.

"Would you close the door? For the moment, I would like for this to be between us."

A flush crept across Seaneen's face as she raised her eyes to meet Richard's. For a few moments the only sound in the room was the crackling of the fire in the fireplace. His longtime friend and house manager finally broke the silence.

"Is this to do with Frederick?" she asked.

"It is, and I'm afraid it's worse than we thought. Far worse. Frederick has gotten himself into deep financial trouble by gambling and apparently losing quite heavily. The authorities surmise some nasty people are threatening him and he is desperate to pay them off. The case has been moved to Scotland Yard and Interpol because he is wanted on charges of stealing very valuable items and threatening to do bodily harm. His crimes are now on an international level. Needless to say, he is keeping a low profile and has been elusive enough that even global authorities haven't been able to find him."

"I'm guessing Liam is suggesting we have security so he must believe Frederick might return to Leigheas," Seaneen said, shifting away from her personal emotions to speak as a former security specialist.

"Yes, he reasons since Frederick has been here already and knows the layout of the place, it might be an easy target. We are a bit remote, which suits his desire to remain in hiding. There will be two security men arriving tomorrow afternoon. We will need to get one of the cottages ready for them."

"That's no problem. The girls and I will get on that this afternoon."

"Liam also mentioned you might want to contact Marjorie as soon as possible and fill her in on the severity of the situation in the off chance her son tries to make another connection with Gwendolyn."

"Yes, of course," Seaneen mused.

"Don't envy you that telephone call," Richard said wryly.

"Perhaps I'll write her a letter, and avoid her hysterics," she joked.

"If time wasn't of the essence, I might agree. Seriously, Seaneen, I respect your years spent in security and if you feel Marjorie and her family need protection, I'll gladly pay for it."

"Absolutely not, but thank you for the offer. I feel responsible for this dreadful mess. Marjorie and I will work it out. If you don't mind, I will telephone Liam later today to sort out some ideas."

"Of course. In the meantime I want everyone on the estate to be here for a meeting to alert them to what is going on. Have you seen Sarah?"

"She was delivering shortbread to Henry. My guess is she is in the stable."

"I'll head down there now and ask Stephen and Marcus to meet as well. Would two o'clock be convenient for you and James?"

"Yes. I'll have the girls prepare a small tea and make sure they attend as well."

Richard came from behind his desk and wrapped an affectionate arm around Seaneen.

"I am so angry at Frederick for causing you so much trouble, Richard," she said.

"We will get through this, you know. It could always be worse," he said.

A slight sniff and a damp cheek accompanied an up and down nod of her head.

"You're right. What is it your mother used to say?" she asked.

"Keep praying, but row away from the rocks," he laughed.

Chapter Eleven

KAITLYN:

Time is Long, But Life is Short

It's a curious thing about time. Man created a system for keeping track of the infinite in a very finite way. There are sixty seconds in every minute, sixty minutes in every hour, and twenty-four hours in every day…always. How can it possibly be that within this predictable, structured rhythm some days are so vexatiously long?

Kaitlyn had not spoken to Richard in over six weeks, though he had left two messages, neither of which she returned. Her heart hurt, but she couldn't bring herself to contact him. During sleepless nights, she recognized her overreaction to his confession of knowing her past, but it still left her feeling vulnerable and embarrassed. It wasn't as though she had anything to hide really, and in truth, would have shared most of it with him had he asked. Perhaps that was the problem. She would have told him what she wanted to tell him, rather than have every detail of her relationship with Nigel laid out for the world to see.

"What is wrong with me?" she said out loud, surprised to hear her own voice. "What is stopping me from calling Richard and apologizing?"

Her days had become painfully slow and her desire to talk to him almost overwhelming, but what would she say? She had painted herself into a bit of a corner with her sharp temper and wasn't sure how to swallow her pride. She wished she knew if he was as miserable as she was.

"Kaitlyn, dear, did I hear you speaking with someone?" Miriam Cumberbund asked, as she came in the drawing room.

"No, just thinking aloud," Kaitlyn answered, startled by the older woman's quiet entrance.

64

"I hope you are busy thinking of our social events coming up. I'm knackered at just the thought of organizing two parties. It has been an age since we entertained…you know since Nigel…" she didn't finish her sentence.

"I know, but I think they will both come off brilliantly," Kaitlyn reassured her employer with a false bravado, well aware it would take all of her energy and know-how to pull together these separate events several weeks apart.

Miriam reached out for Kaitlyn's hand and squeezed it.

"Whatever would I do without you, my dear?"

Kaitlyn blushed and the two ladies were silent for a few seconds. Opening her hardbound notebook, Kaitlyn began going down the list.

"Well, let's go over the first evening, Trevor's eightieth birthday. It's on Saturday, March 23, which is three weeks away. We have received RSVP's from all but four people, bringing the total guest list at this point to thirty-four including the two of you, Wilford, his family, and me."

"Will you be bringing that nice gentleman from Scotland?" Miriam inquired.

"No, I don't think so," she said. "He's very busy."

"That's a pity. I was looking forward to meeting him."

Kaitlyn went on politely ignoring the well-meaning comment thus diffusing any further discussion of Richard Duncan. The menu was reviewed, flowers decided on, musicians chosen, which left only the seating arrangement which they both agreed to hold off on until they heard from the last few guests. Flipping the pages in her notebook, they moved on to the second event.

"I must tell you Miriam, I am a wee bit out of my league with the reception two weeks later. Do we know why the King of Nepal and Queen Ratna are coming here? It seems extraordinary for them to take time from their short visit in England to request an audience with you and Trevor," Kaitlyn said, "not that you aren't lovely people."

"I couldn't agree more. The only thing we can fathom is something to do with Nigel. He enjoyed time with the Nepalese people, though never mentioned knowing Nepal's royal family. We have no other ties to that country other than our youngest son. We've never been there or even thought about going. Isn't it somewhere between India and Tibet?" she asked somewhat rhetorically before continuing on. "The communication we received only said they would be bringing something precious to us and we would be forever grateful. It is all frightfully curious, even Trevor is at sixes and sevens about the whole thing. Just between us, I've heard Queen Elizabeth and Prince Philip are not amused that King Mahendra and his family are interrupting their stay to come here."

"It is all very exciting, none the less," Kaitlyn said.

"Are you ladies discussing King Mehendra's visit?" Trevor Cumberman asked, as he sat down next to his wife.

"We are indeed," Miriam said. "And Kaitlyn is making wonderful arrangements. I'm sure it will be marvelous."

Kaitlyn flipped through a few pages of her handwritten notes.

"I found a Napoli chef who will prepare traditional Nepalese food. Chef Kamal recommended things like Dal Bhat, which is basically rice and lentils with a meat curry, and rice paper wrappers stuffed with vegetables and buffalo meat called Momos. We will have lots of fresh fruit and Yomari for dessert," Kaitlyn said checking her notebook. "And lassi to drink as well as kigali paani."

"While it all sounds exotic and delicious, remember from what I've been told they will only be here an hour or two at most." Trevor said. "It was specifically requested that only family be present. Of course, that includes you Kaitlyn."

"Well, no matter how long they are here, we must be prepared to serve them properly, so we will carry on with our plans." Miriam said. "Worst case we will have Momo leftovers for days and days."

As though answer to prayer, Kaitlyn's days became exceptionally busy seeing to the details of the upcoming social events. Her thoughts still wandered to Leigheas and the handsome Laird, wondering if he ever thought of her.

Wilford and his family arrived in a whirlwind several days before the birthday party and brought much needed life to the manor house. Wilfred's wife, Joyce, was occupied keeping the three children, ages five to ten, engaged and not underfoot, though the older Cumbermans appeared to enjoy the chaos. Wilfred's help with the last minute arrangements was invaluable and for the first time she caught a glimpse of the similarities he shared with his brother Nigel.

Trevor's eightieth birthday party was a rousing success and went off without a hitch. At the end of the evening the family headed to bed leaving Kaitlyn and Wilford in the kitchen to put a few things away and make sure all was well.

"Would you like a cup of tea?" Kaitlyn asked spontaneously. "I'm still so energized, I'm quite sure I wouldn't be able to sleep."

"Actually, yes, that would be nice," he said. "In fact, there is something I would rather like your opinion on and this seems a perfect time."

"Of course," she said filling the kettle and putting it on the burner. "You are welcome to whatever is left of my brain."

"Thank you," he said with a laugh. "This is a slightly delicate matter and I wasn't sure how to approach it or even if I should bother you with it."

"This is sounding very mysterious," Kaitlyn said.

Her heart began to beat a little faster and her mind raced. Oh, she hoped this had nothing to do with Nigel. She poured the hot water into the teapot and sat down across from Wilford at the table, trying to look calm.

"No mystery, just decisions about my future and which direction to choose."

Kaitlyn sipped from her teacup, quite grateful to not relive the Nigel years with his brother.

"To begin with, I am long overdue in thanking you for everything you've done for mum and dad. When Nigel died I'm sure you must have been tempted to leave, after all, there are reminders of him everywhere," Wilford said. "And before you deny it, I know how fond you were of each other. We all hoped for a future, well, you know."

"I know and I appreciate your thoughts, but it was not to be. Your parents have always shown me extraordinary kindness and I would never have left them when they needed me most. It was a dreadful time for everyone, and to see them finally getting on with their lives is most heartening. Was this what you wanted to talk about?" Kaitlyn asked, as she poured more tea into their cups.

"No, but I have felt remiss in never discussing that with you. Mum and Father understandably hold you in the highest regard and it occurred to me that you would be the ideal person to help me sort out what I should do. I hope you don't mind being my sounding board."

"I am happy to listen and offer my two-pence worth."

"Well, the day we were leaving Spain to catch our flight here, my company president called me in and announced they were opening a London office and wanted me to be the head of it. I was gobsmacked, I can tell you. We have grown to love our life in Spain and are quite settled in. On the other hand, spending time here this last week has reminded me how much I miss England and my family. I'm waiting to discuss it with Joyce and the children but decided I'd better think about how I feel about it first. There is so much to consider, it would be a big adjustment for everyone. You know my parents better than anyone and now that they are beginning to embrace life again, I'm afraid our being here might upset the routine they have established. Nigel and I were always a lot alike and I'm afraid my presence would bring reminders of losing Nigel all over again." Wilford drank his entire cup of tea in one gulp. "Does any of this make sense?"

It took Kaitlyn a few moments to answer. She had seen Nigel drink his tea in exactly the same manner as Wilfred. There was no denying the sibling resemblance. A smile twitched her lips.

"I think your parents would be absolutely over the moon to have you and your family close by. It would be the very best of everything at this time in their lives. They are not getting any younger and the opportunity to share time with your family would bring them the greatest joy." Kaitlyn continued, "And while it isn't any of my business, I would advise you have a conversation with Joyce as soon as possible. Women tend to not like being the last to know."

"It's a relief to share and you're right, I will speak with Joyce first thing tomorrow. It's only fair that she and I decide together. Thank you for your insight and for listening. How wise you are, Kaitlyn."

"Not as wise as I am experienced," she said. "You go on up and I'll wash our cups."

"Goodnight, then, and I hope you sleep well."

The kitchen door closed behind Wilfred and she was quite sure she would not sleep a wink. Visions of Nigel bombarded her mind and allowed the horrible '*if onlys*' to take over. If only he had lived. If only….

Chapter Twelve

SARAH:

We Have a Problem

It was nearly noon when Sarah left Henry in the stable, her mind spinning with all the ideas she had for her book. Rushing out of the building she ran headlong into her father.

"I've the most exciting thing to tell you," she said.

"I want to hear it, but not just now, Sunshine. We have a problem and I am arranging an immediate meeting of everyone here at Leigheas," Richard said.

"Ohhhhh….now?" she asked, sorely disappointed to not begin writing.

"Let's meet in two hours in the small reception room. It's very important and I need to alert the others," Richard answered, heading off toward Stephen's office.

She puffed out her cheeks in frustration and watched her father disappear into the stable, then exhaled. That gave her less than two hours to make notes and scribbles of her inspired musings.

For the first time in a long time Sarah felt like her fingers couldn't keep up with her thoughts. She was writing page after page of ideas and plots and characters and locations, totally lost in the process of creating. Not one piece of paper was wadded up on the floor. The loud knock rudely interrupted this almost spiritual experience.

"Oh rats!" She said out loud, as she got up from her desk and opened the door.

"Your father asked that you come downstairs now," Meara said. "Everyone is in the small reception room. Oh, and this came in the mail for you earlier."

70

With a heavy sigh, Sarah tidied up her desk and took the envelope from Meara, tucked it in her pocket and ran down the stairs.

"Excellent. I think everyone is here. What I am about to tell you is disturbing and important," Richard said. "For the moment, I prefer you keep this information to yourselves. It might render the situation worse if it became known,"

The assembled group of Sarah, Seaneen and James, plus Meara, Brennan, Stephen, son little Henry and Marcus sat with rapt attention. Normally, Richard was pleasant and easy-going, always ready with humor, but they all recognized he was deadly serious.

"It has come to my attention that our strange guest, Frederick Hutton, has a far more disturbing past than anyone imagined. Without getting into too many details, he has a frightening history of racking up massive international gambling debts and has some very dangerous people after him wanting their money back. Apparently, this has lead Frederick to steal, embezzle and threaten to harm people with serious weapons in an effort to extort money. Authorities have not been able to apprehend him and there is concern he may try to return to Leigheas. We are in a remote location, he knows the layout of the house and he is aware we have some valuable objects."

"Not as many as we used to," Sarah wryly thought to herself.

"Tomorrow, two security men will arrive and stay in one of the cottages. We will introduce you and give them time to ask questions about your daily routines. Please cooperate fully with them. On the off chance you should see Frederick anywhere–on the property, in the village, anywhere in this vicinity, do not approach him. Call me immediately. If for some reason I am not available, then call DI Lawson. I have written his name and phone number on these note cards for you to carry with you at all times. I am so sorry to burden you with this situation, but we are very vulnerable and this man is unpredictable at best. We want to keep everyone as safe as possible. Are there any questions?"

There was a stunned silence in the room. Finally, Sarah spoke up.

"What about Marjorie and Gwendolyn? Are they in danger?"

"I've just spoken with my sister, advising her of the situation and will call her again when she is finished with her hysteria," Seaneen said. "I doubt she will be bothered as Frederick knows neither she nor Gwendolyn have any substantial funds, though I thought she should be aware, just in case."

More silence followed. Meara and Brennen excused themselves and returned with a tray filled with treats. Little Henry's eyes widened when he saw the shortbread. Seaneen began to pour out tea and small talk began centering around the shocking news. Cup in hand, Sarah walked over to her father standing by the warm fireplace.

"I'm sure you've let Kaitlyn know what is going on. It is all so bizarre."

'I…haven't been able to get a hold of her," her father answered, not elaborating.

Sarah noticed a far away look in his eyes, but chalked it up to this dreadful situation they all found themselves in.

Back in her room, Sarah closed the heavy curtains across her large window. Daylight was quickly fading as it did this time of year in Scotland, and it was quite chilly. Living in an old house was charming, but could be drafty. Even with three lamps turned on, her room seemed dimmer than usual. This probably had more to do with her mood about the Frederick mess than the actual wattage of the light bulbs. Wrapping a long wool sweater closer around her body, she felt the envelope Meara had given her. How puzzling! It was from Peter from his Edinburgh address. She thought he would only be gone a few days. Why wouldn't he call rather than write a letter to her?

My Dear Sarah,

No doubt you are wondering why I am writing rather than calling on the telephone. As you can imagine, there is a story to tell. A few hours after I arrived here, my grandfather fell and broke his arm. It isn't a bad break, for which we are all thankful, but enough to keep him from doing things around the house to help my grandmother. For at least a week or so he will need assistance in pretty much everything. To add confusion to the situation, several telephone lines were cut by some workers and phones won't be operable for a bit. All this to say, it appears that I will be here for several weeks–far longer than I had planned.

I miss you already and it has only been a few days. After being apart for five years, then reuniting so recently, it is difficult to not have you close by. There will always be a divine factor in your Leigheas being so near to our Elibank, but right now Edinburgh seems far away from you. I'm afraid this is beginning to sound selfish, which is unacceptable as I have been substantially blessed. Just know I think about you daily and can't wait to see you.

While most of my time is spent helping my grandparents I have had a few opportunities to sketch in the city. There is an invigorating atmosphere in Edinburgh that lends itself to one being exceedingly creative. Speaking of...how is the book coming? I am most anxious to see what direction you are going and how I can contribute. A thought just came to mind! Why don't we meet a week from now at Turning Pages Book Shoppe? That will be Wednesday, say around noon? I will be going there anyway to pick up some books Thomas has set aside for me and I can happily hang around in case you make it. I do hope you can.

I must close and help grandfather get dressed. If the telephone service is restored I will call you straight away. Otherwise, I'll look forward to a letter or even better, seeing you at the book store.

Love always,
Peter

Isn't it funny how love can brighten a room?

KAITLYN:

When a King Visits

The King of Nepal was due to arrive any minute. The entire household was on pins and needles, even though an emissary from the royal family had visited them earlier in the week with instructions on proper etiquette. There were so many things to remember!

Early March had blessed them with a brisk, sunny day without a cloud in the sky. Yard crews had been brought in to insure the grounds of the Cumberman's estate were perfect, and additional help was hired to clean every nook and cranny of the house. Baskets of white viburnum flowers were placed throughout and tall Waterford vases filled with freshly-picked yellow daffodils were tucked in here and there. Kaitlyn had overseen all the details of the once-in-a-lifetime experience and was feeling exhausted and excited all at the same time. Adrenalin was in full force by the time the two long, black Rolls Royce motorcars drove through the gates. Trevor and Miriam were standing front and center with Wilfred, Joyce, and the children slightly behind. Trevor insisted Kaitlyn be part of the welcome, as she was considered family. The driver walked around the royal car and opened the passenger door, then stood at attention as the King of Nepal stepped out. He was dressed in a perfectly tailored three piece suit, of medium height with dark hair, clean shaven, very trim and wore black rimmed glasses. Trevor greeted him in the traditional Nepalese manner of pressed palms together above his chest and bowing his head.

"Namaskar," he said to the King.

"Namaskar," the King said in return.

In perfect English, King Mehendra introduced his petite wife, Queen Ratna, to Trevor, and the process continued with introductions to the rest of the family, with many Namaskar greetings exchanged. The King turned to his driver and gave him some instructions in Nepalese, then turned back to Trevor.

"I would like to speak with your family alone before anyone joins us," he said in his quiet voice.

"Of course. Please come in," Trevor answered, a little puzzled by the request.

They were led to the reception room beautifully prepared for the royal visit. Accompanying them was Major General Malla, chief military officer to the King, who carried a firearm in his hip holster. This was becoming odder by the moment. Joyce took the children upstairs before returning to the group. Kaitlyn indicated to Trevor that she would discreetly leave them to their business, but he shook his head and motioned for her to stay. The King and Queen sat on the long, dark green velvet sofa, and indicated for the others to sit as well. Major General Malla remained standing near the door, and Kaitlyn wondered if he was protecting those in the room or guarding it from those outside. It all felt very formal and awkward, with no one saying anything. They had been briefed that King Mahendra was shy and spoke in a very soft voice, and were assured he was a good and kind man. As she looked around the room, Kaitlyn could see the confusion on the faces of the family. After what seemed like an eternity of silence, the King spoke.

"May I offer my deepest condolences on the loss of your son, Nigel. While I only met him once at the wedding, he was a very engaging young man."

"Thank you, your highness. Your thoughts are very much appreciated," Trevor answered.

Another few moments of silence passed before the King spoke again.

"We were understandably surprised when Nigel married Devna. She was my daughter's closest friend and had been promised to a young man since birth."

That sentence had a far more profound effect on the people in the room than the King ever imagined. Kaitlyn became extremely lightheaded and fought not to faint. She watched Trevor and Miriam look at the King in utter shock, unable to speak. Finally, Wilford found his voice and chose his words carefully.

"Your highness, please forgive our reaction to what you have just told us. We were entirely unaware Nigel had married."

The King and Queen exchanged glances and were obviously at a loss as to what to say next. Major General Malla stepped forward and addressed the King in Nepalese, before stepping back to his spot by the door.

"It has been suggested that I tell you what I know of this story. I'm afraid I was unaware you had no knowledge of this…situation," the King said.

Queen Ratna reached out and touched her husbands arm, in a gesture of support for what he was about to divulge. The room was quiet as he gathered his thoughts. Kaitlyn was desperately hoping she would not throw up.

"For many years Devna was fascinated with the large Himalayan mountain we call Sagarmatha. I believe you call it Mt. Everest. Sherpa Tenzing was a close friend of her family and I believe he shared his love of climbing with her. From what I understand, Devna met your son sometime before his planned climb with Sherpa Tenzing. She had always shown a rebellious side and without a second thought, abandoned her family and lived with the group of climbers. According to my daughter, your son was handsome and passionate about life, which Devna could not resist. He felt affection for her as well and they agreed to marry before his climb. Devna's grandmother, her only living relative, was devastated by her disloyalty and embarrassed that she would have to explain to Devna's betrothed she had chosen someone else. Nonetheless, a wedding was hastily arranged and a few days later it was done."

As Kaitlyn and the family processed all of this shocking information, desperately trying to understand everything they had been told, Queen Ratna spoke up in her low voice, thick with a Nepalese accent.

"I'm afraid there is much more to this story. When Devna learned of Nigel's death, she was shattered and left Katmandu, returning to her grandmother in the remote village of Dhikur Pokhari, in the central western district of Manang."

The atmosphere in the room was stilled by fear of what was to come.

"Recently, it was brought to our attention that Devna's grandmother died of a fever illness, *jvaro roga* in our language." She paused speaking and looked at her husband, who nodded encouragement for her to continue.

"A short time later Devna died also. It has only been in the last few weeks we discovered she gave birth to a son some months after Nigel was killed."

"Nigel has a son?" Miriam said incredulously. "Are you quite sure?"

"I believe your son had unusual green eyes, did he not?" King Mahendra asked.

"Yes, he did," Trevor said, his voice quivering.

The room was starting to spin for Kaitlyn, and she quietly walked past Major General Malla on her way out the door. Not knowing which direction to go, she found herself outside in the walled garden, trying to breathe. Once the sobbing began, she was powerless to stop it. Before too long a men's handkerchief was gently tucked in her hand.

"I think you need this," Wilford said, sitting beside her on a bench. "Quite a predicament, isn't it? Fine thing for Nigel to leave us in such a mess. I loved my brother dearly, but sometimes his thoughtless nature inflicted havoc on those around him. I must say this tops everything."

Wilford stood and reached his hand out to help Kaitlyn up.

"Please dry your eyes. Mum and Dad need you. We must soldier on and meet Nigel's son."

"You're not serious! The boy is here?" she said. "The King of Nepal brought Nigel's son here?"

"Yes, he is in the car with his nanny in our front drive," he said.

"Without any notice to Trevor or Miriam or anyone?" She sat back down. "This is overwhelming. I'm not sure I can do this."

"Kaitlyn, this little boy has lost both parents, he was raised half-way around the world, brought to England and is suddenly told we are his only family," Wilford said, sitting down next to her on the bench. "Imagine his confusion."

"He is to live here?" she asked incredulously. "In this house?"

"Yes, that's the idea. King Mahendra had long arranged a trip to England and it seemed a brilliant opportunity to deliver him here. Of course, they had no way of knowing we were all in the dark about Nigel's life. I suppose to be fair, Nigel never knew he had a child. He died not knowing his wife was pregnant."

"So, this child will live here? With Trevor and Miriam?" she asked.

"We are all blown to bits by this, but that seems to be the plan. Joyce, the children and I will move here soon. We've rented a townhouse not far away until we find a home of our own. I haven't had time to speak to Joyce, but I am guessing we will help raise Sanani," Wilford said. "Can you imagine how Mum and Dad must feel? To actually have a bit of Nigel in this child? It's pretty close of a miracle if you think about it."

She nodded in agreement, feeling as miserable as any human could possibly feel. The realization that Nigel wasn't in love with her, nor had any intention of having a future with her caused a storm of emotions to well-up all at once: embarrassment, betrayal, rejection, completely heartbroken, and truthfully, quite lost. Where did she belong now? Surely she could not continue to live under the same roof with Nigel's child.

"I must go back in, please come with me," Wilford urged. "This isn't about you or me or anyone else really. It is about a bewildered little boy."

Kaitlyn wiped the tears from her face and handed the damp handkerchief back. The depth of pain in her heart was crippling, but she mustn't grieve now.

"Of course, you're right, Nigel. This is certainly not about me. I'm sorry. Sometimes I must remember '*whit's fur ye'll no go by ye,*' what's meant to happen will happen. God has a plan."

Both rose up from the bench and Wilford put his arm around Kaitlyn's sagging shoulder.

"I'm awfully sorry, if that helps any," he said, "but it will all work out, you'll see."

Kaitlyn had very serious doubts, but chose not to voice them.

Chapter Fourteen
SARAH:
Dear Peter

Dear Peter,

I am awfully sorry to hear about your grandfather breaking his arm. That must be terribly painful. How frustrating for him to be so limited in his activities, though a blessing you happened to be there. Please give him my best for a quick recovery. Of course, speedy healing brings you home sooner rather than later! Selfish me!

You asked about the book and I've had a breakthrough with so many creative thoughts I can't wait to share with you. Since you will be home in a few weeks I'll save the substance, only saying I hope you can draw and paint woodland animals. I'm hoping to have a first draft by the time you return. I sure miss you!

Your idea about meeting at the book shop is splendid and I will make every effort to be there. If something happens and I don't make it, know it wasn't for lack of trying!

Life at Leigheas is fairly quiet, though there has been a slight problem which I will tell you about when I see you. It wouldn't be a good idea to put it in print. Doesn't that sound mysterious? To my knowledge, there hasn't been any new information on Frederick Hutton and his whereabouts nor the things he stole. Sometimes that whole experience feels like a bad dream. It has been especially hard on my father who has become a little distant the past few weeks.

I will close and get this to the post. If you think about it, bring some of your new sketches with you to the book shop. I can't wait to see what you are working on.

Always yours,
Sarah

Chapter Fifteen

RICHARD:

Monuments Men

A sharp wind blew against the windows in his office, making the glass panes rattle within their framework. In the six years Richard had owned Leigheas he couldn't remember a colder, more inclement late March. No doubt it was contributing to the unsettled mood he was carrying around. Working in foreign service for many years, his job had been to fix things and he had been fairly good at it. However, the past weeks he was finding it hard to focus on any given task, much less accomplish anything. The two middle fingers on his right hand began tapping the leather top of his desk in perfect rhythm with the ticking of the grandfather clock.

"What to do?" he kept thinking over and over. "What to do."

Obviously, he would have to postpone the group of men who normally arrive in late spring, which made him furious. The situation with Frederick Hutton made Leigheas unsafe and Richard couldn't risk having guests in any sort of danger. It was bad enough that Sarah and the staff were in harm's way. While these gentlemen were looking for tranquility and peace, it could likely be a circus with security men hanging about and everyone on edge. He was frustrated and discouraged. And then there was the tangled mess with Kaitlyn. How could he fix that wad of knots? His mother, Rosemary, would tell him to let the Lord work it out, however he was more than willing to offer the Lord a few suggestions. The ringing telephone caught him off guard.

"This is Leigheas, may I help you?" he answered.

"Richard, this is Ambassador Stevens. How are you?"

"Good morning, sir. I am well, thank you, and you?"

"Keeping the fort down, which somedays is a victory all its own. Allow me to get right to the point. It has come to my attention that you recently had a robbery of several priceless articles from your home. Is that correct?"

"Yes, that's true. A man showed up uninvited on New Year's Eve, claiming he was Seaneen's nephew. The next morning, several very valuable items were missing and we are fairly certain he absconded with them. They disappeared into thin air, as did Seaneen's nephew. Liam Morrison mentioned you suggested several security men live on our premises until the scoundrel is caught."

"You cannot be too careful these days and you've had enough ambushes for one lifetime. Have you received any information as to the whereabouts of your stolen items?"

"Nothing as of yet. The authorities continue to tell me they are diligently searching, but my hope is dimming as time goes on."

"Very interesting. Well, I may have an idea for you to consider. Do you ever remember hearing about the Monuments Men in World War II?"

"Of course. The story has fascinated me for years, though I don't know many details."

"Most people are unaware that Hitler decided to create a private museum in Austria to house the world's finest art collection. During the war, Nazi soldiers were ordered to seize all paintings, sculptures and so on of any significance from museums and residences," Ambassador Stevens said. "They were hidden away in salt mines across Germany and Austria as that offered the perfect temperature and humidity to be safely stored. In 1943, President Roosevelt approved the formation of what came to be known as the Monuments Men. I suppose you know the story."

"What interested me was that they were civilians with art backgrounds but no military training. Suddenly, they were saving the world's art treasures from Hitler," Richard said. "It's incredible. From what I remember, about two dozen went to the front lines to recover some stolen objects when two of them were killed. In the end, they were able to return over five million art pieces to their rightful owners."

"I am impressed with how much you know," the ambassador said. "There are still millions of pieces still missing and the search continues by a group today."

"I had no idea. That's fascinating," Richard said, not sure how this related to his problem.

"Well, it so happens one of the Monuments Men, Daniel Roberts, is a friend of my older sister. He was one of the youngest and when they disbanded after the war, he formed a small circle who have continued to search for artwork. Now and then, he offers his services to individuals who have lost valuable items. You can see where I am going with this."

"I certainly can. Do you think he would consider helping me?"

"I took the liberty of speaking with him last night. He lives in New York, but comes to London fairly often. It so happened we were seated next to one another at dinner and the topic of recovering stolen goods came up. I told him what little I knew about your theft and he was intrigued. When I explained your work at Leigheas he was even more interested and it was my impression he might want to come visit you in the Borders."

"He would be very welcome, more than welcome. This is the first encouragement I've had since it happened. I can't thank you enough."

"Let's see what he can come up with. My guess is if anyone can find your missing items, Daniel would be your best bet. I'll pass along your telephone number and let you work out the details."

After a few pleasantries about Sarah and the weather, the ambassador hung up, leaving Richard smiling for the first time in many weeks.

A huge clap of thunder accompanied by howling wind, caused Maggie to come running into his office and hide under the desk. The dog was followed closely by Sarah, who was either out of breath due to the chase or because the loud noise scared her, too.

"Did you hear that?" she asked.

"One would have to be entirely deaf or entirely dead to have missed it," he laughed. "I'm sorry it frightened you…and Maggie."

The dog looked up at him with her large brown eyes and wagged her little tail.

"We weren't frightened. Well, maybe a little," she answered.

It had been a long time since his adult daughter had run to him for protection from a storm. As proud as he was of her as an adult, sometimes he missed his little girl.

"Your grandmother used to tell the tale that thunder was the sound of hoofbeats in heaven."

"I remember that so well. I would ask where they were going and what their names were." Sarah smiled at the recollection. "She used to regale me with details of each horse and what adventure they were on. Within seconds, I wasn't even aware there was a thunderstorm outside. I miss her."

"You always had a curious mind, Sarah Sunshine," Richard said. "I think you must have inherited her creative gene as well. She loved telling you stories. I miss her, too."

Another clap of thunder, followed a bright flash of lightening, prompting Maggie to leave her hiding place and jump into Sarah's lap. Hugging a furry dog was a sure cure for just about anything.

"How is Kaitlyn?" Sarah asked.

The innocent question caused the now-familiar pain in his heart to resurface. He knew there was no point in hiding the situation any longer from Sarah. He had hoped their relationship would've been healed by now, with no one the wiser.

"Truth is, we haven't spoken in several months. Before you ask, it was entirely my fault and yes, I've tried to contact her but she isn't responding."

"Oh no! I'm so sorry. Should I ask for the details?"

"Not at the moment. I'll tell you another time. Right now, I'm very sad. I've lost my best friend."

"I understand," Sarah said softly, recalling her own grief when she thought she had lost Peter. "Life is perplexing sometimes, isn't it?"

"That, my sweet daughter, is the understatement of the century. Now, what are you up to on this stormy Scottish day?"

"I was wondering if you would like to go to Edinburgh tomorrow? Peter is staying there for a time while his grandfather recovers from a fall and we are trying to meet at Turning Pages Book Shoppe. Maybe with the situation with Kaitlyn, you'd rather not."

"Actually, that might be a fine idea. At least it would give me the opportunity to ask Thomas Turning about his daughter. You know, just see how she's doing."

"And if she misses you," Sarah said.

Richard smiled, "Well, yes, that, too. Let's make a day of it and have lunch at Jenner's. Peter could join us."

"Not that it's any of my business, but I hope you and Kaitlyn can work things out. She is such a wondrous person."

"I couldn't agree more. On another note, tell me about your writing. Is it coming along?"

As the wind and storm continued outside, Sarah shared with her father all about her visit to Henry's Zoo that led to the inspiration for her book. She knew generally what she wanted the story to say, but was having difficulty getting it on paper. Watching his daughter speak passionately about her project was very satisfying.

"When I was with the Foreign Service, I constantly wrote reports and letters and such. It was annoying that it took so many rewrites until it was correct. One of my senior colleagues advised me that all first drafts were garbage. Apparently, that's just the way it is, so don't be disheartened. The important thing is to not stop writing. There's a great quote by novelist Louis L'Amour, '*Start writing, no matter what. Water doesn't flow until the faucet is turned on.*'"

"Before I try turning on the writing faucet again, I think I will go to the kitchen and find a snack. Would you like anything?" she asked.

"Might there be shortbread involved?"

Chapter Sixteen

KAITLYN:

Namaste

With the excitement and upheaval of Nigel's son, Sanani, and his nanny, Aasika, taking up residence in the Cumberman house, it was easy for Kaitlyn to become busy and stay out of everyone's way. For all her brave words to Wilford about God having a plan, she just couldn't bring herself to meet the boy.

One afternoon while holed up in her office near the back of the house, the immaturity of her actions felt overwhelming. Hiding was not a long term solution to her anxiety surrounding this innocent little boy. Not only was she letting Miriam and Trevor down, but she was disappointed in herself as well. It was time to face reality. The memory of Nigel she carried in her heart was not who he really was. Sadly, it was who she desperately wanted him to be. He was not a bad sort, but in hindsight, it was easy to see how egotistical and self-centered he was. His charm masked a life of doing exactly what he wanted, no matter the consequences or who got hurt in the process. It was time to take one last look at her relationship with Nigel, then pack those memories away, tie a ribbon on that box and put it high on a shelf. He was part of her history, and it was time to look to her future. Peeking out the window, the spring day beckoned her to leave her self-imposed exile, stretch her legs, breathe in a little fresh air and celebrate a new beginning.

The Cumberman estate consisted of five acres, most of which was covered with a wide variety of trees, shrubs and flowers. There were no formal gardens or really much rhyme or reason to the landscaping, except for a hidden spot where a glass pavilion was tucked away amongst some trees. Early April was always a welcome transition between winter and spring, though it was never wise to go for a walk unprepared. Dark clouds and showers could suddenly crop up at anytime, which is exactly what happened. Out of nowhere, a storm gathered and enormous drops of rain filled the previously blue sky, soaking everything it met, including Kaitlyn. The glass pavilion was within sight and far closer than returning to the house. She ran through the muddy trail, slipping and sliding, and nearly fell when opening the pavilion door. What a surprise to find she was not the only one seeking refuge from the rain.

Beautiful green eyes looked up and caused Kaitlyn to catch her breath. Before her stood an adorable five year old boy, with palms together, bowing his head.

"Well, hello," she said.

"Namaste, Miss Turning," the young boy said with a slight Nepalese accent.

"Namaste, Sanani," she responded, wondering how he knew her name.

A grin lit up his face. Kaitlyn had learned 'namaste' was a more informal derivative of 'namaskar' and was pleased he chose to address her this way.

"Did you get caught in the rain, as well?" she asked.

"Yes, I did," he answered. "May I ask, where does rain come from?"

Racking her brain for anything she could remember from school about evaporation and clouds, and how to explain it all to a five year old, Sanani interrupted her thoughts.

"Does it come from the sky?" he asked earnestly.

"Indeed it does," she laughed at the simplicity of his answer. "That's exactly where it comes from. Would you like to sit on the bench with me while we wait for the storm to pass?"

"Yes, thank you. I would like that," he said, gently reaching up to hold her hand.

The unlikely pair sat close together while rain pelted the glass, neither saying a word. Kaitlyn's mind ran in circles being so close to Nigel's son, holding his small hand in hers. It felt odd but strangely comforting. This engaging little person, so innocent and bright, and so wanting to be loved and accepted. How would he adapt to this new world he had been thrust into? What would Nigel think if he could see her with his son?

"Do you think the rain will stop soon, Miss Turning? I promised Aasika I would not be gone long. She might worry," he said.

Kaitlyn realized she had been staring at the boy this whole time as if in a trance. Much as she hated to admit it, Wilford was absolutely right–none of this was about her. The miracle of God allowing her to meet Nigel's precious child was almost overpowering.

"Sanani, I'm so glad to know you. A long time ago I knew your father and he would be so proud of you." She paused as she watched his face break into a smile so reminiscent of Nigel. "And I think the rain has stopped. What if we walk back to the house together?"

The little boy jumped up, still holding her hand, and they ventured out into the woods.

"Miss Turning, I am very glad to know you, too," Sanani said.

At that precise moment, Kaitlyn's heart was humbled with a joy she wouldn't have thought possible. A verse from the Psalms came to mind, '*Behold, children are a blessing from the Lord.*' Her mother used that phrase when praising her own offspring.

By ten o'clock that evening everyone had retired and Kaitlyn was headed up the grand staircase to her part of the enormous house. She couldn't remember a more extraordinary day. Little Sanani stayed close by her most of the afternoon, other than Aasika taking him away for a nap. At dinner he quietly asked if he could sit by Kaitlyn, raising the eyebrows of the rest of the family. It was obvious they were relieved at the budding relationship between the boy and their personal secretary. Once the meal was finished, he whispered so only Kaitlyn could hear.

"Can you call me Sanni?"

"Of course," she whispered back.

"It's what my mother used to call me."

At the top of the grand staircase, one hallway went east and the other west. Being directionally challenged, Kaitlyn referred to it as left and right. She reminisced about the first time the Cumberman's brought her to the east wing of their manor house. They proudly opened the door and announced this three-room suite was to be hers for as long as she wished to remain with them. Miriam had it beautifully decorated just for her, with lovely pale pink wall coverings and fine antique furniture. It became Kaitlyn's private retreat with a comfortable sitting room, spacious bedroom and bath, complete with an enormous English tub. Two large windows overlooked the rear garden all the way back to the tall trees in the distance. There was comfort in having her own space, especially tonight when she had much to ponder. The connection with Sanni felt as though it brought a real closure to her feelings for Nigel. Best of all, she was relieved.

After a hot bath, she crawled into bed and thought about Richard Duncan. Is it possible she ruined their friendship because of a contorted sense of loyalty to Nigel? Or was it her fear of commitment and a lack of trust? At the train station when Richard was sharing his feelings, she began to panic which made no sense because she was crazy about him. When it turned out he knew all about her history, including Nigel, there was an excuse to run away. What was wrong with her? Richard embodied every wonderful quality in a man: integrity, kindness, intelligence, sense of humor. His affection for Sarah, and the compassion he demonstrated toward the men who came to stay at Leigheas, spoke volumes about his character. First thing tomorrow morning she would call Richard and tell him how sorry she was. Just the thought of hearing his voice and sharing their playful banter warmed her heart, until serious doubts began to creep in. What if he's moved on and doesn't want any part of her? What if she has ruined the best relationship she's ever had? *Oh, sleep, please come quickly and save me from negative thinking.* Finally, she drifted off with thoughts of the Laird of Leigheas. At least a girl could dream.

The first sensation was smelly, hot, sour whiskey breath in her face, followed by a large hand over her mouth. Opening her eyes, there was only pitch black. Then a familiar voice spoke.

"If you utter a sound the sharp knife in my other hand will pierce your ribs and make a dreadful mess. Do you understand?"

Kaitlyn nodded her head up and down, feeling the tip of the knife in her midsection.

"You are to do exactly as I tell you without saying a word. Get out of bed and dress in your warmest clothes. I will wait in the other room with the door ajar. I warn you, do not try anything."

Frederick lit a candle, set it down on a nearby table and left her bedroom. Her heart was racing, adrenaline pumping hard through her body. She looked around madly for a way out, but fear told her to do exactly as he said. Within a very few minutes she had thrown on several layers of clothes, including long socks, trousers and boots. Grabbing a wool scarf from her closet, she knocked down several others in her haste, but this was no time to pick them up. Gloves and a knit hat were stuffed in her handbag and she carried the candle to light her way into the sitting room. Frederick was perched on the small love seat, barely visible in the low light.

"Sit down at the desk and find some writing paper," he instructed in a husky whisper.

Trying to do as she was told, she rummaged through the desk drawers but couldn't find anything to write with.

"Find a pen or we will write it in your blood. It's your choice, Kaitlyn," he seethed.

She dumped the drawers out with wild abandon, most of the contents ending up on the floor. Toward the back of the bottom drawer she found several pens, only one of which worked. Opening her mouth to speak, Frederick put his hand up and silenced her.

"We will be writing two letters. Write exactly what I tell you. I won't hesitate to hurt you if my directions are not followed. The first one is addressed to your employers."

He rose up and stood over her as she wrote, his foul breath far too close. With all her might she tried to keep her hand from shaking. The silver knife blade glinted in the light from the candle. It was pointed at her right arm.

"Tell them your father is quite ill and you have gone to him. You are sorry for short notice, but it couldn't be helped. Say you will be in contact soon, and sign it."

When she did as she was told, he instructed her to put it in an envelope, and write Miriam and Trevor's names on the outside.

"Now, this letter is a little trickier. I've been thinking how we want to word it so there is no doubt in Richard Duncan's mind that you are in a life and death situation. I see your hand is trembling. You should be frightened, my dear. I am in a very dangerous situation and you are my only way out. My life depends on your ability to squeeze money from your rich boyfriend. Without it, chances are we both will die."

Kaitlyn's whole body began to shiver uncontrollably and it was all she could do to focus on what Frederick was saying.

"Begin with '*Dear Richard, I find myself in a dreadful bind…*' Start writing NOW," he commanded.

She gripped the pen with all her might, but could not hold it to the paper. Her hand was shaking so badly the marks on the stationery were illegible. In a flash, the knife point pierced the top of her hand and blood began to trickle onto the paper and the desk. She looked up at the wild-eyed man wielding the knife, who began to laugh wickedly.

"Oh my, you are good, Kaitlyn. A drop of blood on the paper is precisely the message I want Mr. Duncan to receive. Now, write what I tell you!"

She followed instructions and wrote exactly what was dictated. Her mind was racing trying to come up with some kind of clue for Richard so he would understand she was doing this under duress. Whether she lived or died she wanted him to know Frederick was the culprit. The opportunity came at the end of the letter.

"Now, sign it as you usually do," he told her, then walked away and began putting on his coat, obviously preparing for them to depart the house.

Strangely enough, she had never written Richard a letter. How could she tip him off? Frantically, she settled for, '*Fondest Heart, Fair Hero, Forever Honourable*' in the hopes that he would decipher the initials being those of Frederick Hutton. It was a long shot but was the best she could do. Folding the letter, she placed it in the envelope and sealed it before Frederick had a chance to notice. The envelope became smudged from the blood on the desk.

"Address it to Richard Duncan at Leigheas and give it to me."

The still bleeding cut on her hand began throbbing. She dabbed it with a hankie and followed Frederick to the door.

"I advise you again to not make a sound," he said in a hushed tone, displaying the knife for her to see. "Walk in front of me down the stairs and out the front door."

SARAH:

A New Day

Yesterday's storm brought a brilliance to the new morning. Low mist still hung near the trees but a hint of sunlight promised a bright day. The drive from the Borders to Edinburgh was always a bit of an adventure with her father driving. Age-old hedges bordered both sides of the narrow road and there was barely room for one car, much less another on-coming vehicle. Sarah smiled, thinking of Mr. Toad from the book, *Wind in the Willows*, and how his notorious lack of driving skills landed him in the water. While her father was a fine driver, he had only learned to motor on the left side of the road when they moved to Leigheas. So far, Sarah had yet to get her driving license, though both her father and Peter offered lessons. Maybe someday.

Traveling by car to Edinburgh was a visual delight seeing hundreds of sheep grazing in the spring-green meadows, and the River Tweed running alongside the road. A series of ancient towns and villages, each with a fascinating history, kept the ride interesting.

"Did you know Walkerburn was originally built to house workers for the tweed mill in 1854, but its history goes way back to the iron age?" Richard asked, as they drove through the first little town.

Sensing her father was making a game of who knew the most local knowledge, she easily joined in.

"Really? Well, I bet you didn't know Innerleithen was founded by an itinerant monk named St. Ronan in AD737, who arrived on the River Tweed in a coracle, which is a small, round, very lightweight boat, and Sir Walter Scott wrote about it in his 1924 novel, St. Ronan's Well."

Hearing her dad laugh was heartwarming. They both shared a love of history and found Scotland a treasure trove of captivating tidbits. She enjoyed being with her father, whether is was because they had so much in common or because the trauma of nearly losing his was still fresh.

"That was a good one, but we are nearly to Peebles," he said. "You know, of course, that it is located where the River Tweed and Eddleston Water meet. What is the nickname for the Eddleston Water river?"

"That's an easy one. It is known as '*The Cuddy*.' Did you know that Peebles was made a Royal Burgh in 1152 by King David I of Scotland? And the oldest building in Peebles is St. Andrews church, founded in 1195? However, King Henry VIII destroyed it during the Reformation leaving only the tower standing," she said. "One thing I've never understand about the Reformation is why they destroyed all the magnificent buildings. I know a little about Martin Luther in the 1500's, but wasn't that basically a split within the Catholic Church and the creation of Protestantism in Germany and other parts of Europe?"

"It's a bit complicated. Henry VIII jumped on the Reformation band wagon not because of a great interest in the theology, but rather more as a way to divorce his first wife, Katherine of Aragon. She didn't produce a male heir and by then Henry was smitten by young Anne Boleyn. When Pope Clement VII refused to grant an annulment to his marriage to Katherine, Henry formally broke off with the Roman Catholic Church so he could marry Anne. Then the English parliament passed an act that denied the Pope any power in England and recognized King Henry VIII as the Supreme Head of the new Church of England. He was given full authority to bring reforms to the church, so he brought on Thomas Cromwell to lead it. Cromwell became far too important and head strong and thus began not only closing the monasteries, but destroying them, often killing the monks and others sympathetic to the Catholic Church. There is much more to it, but that is the gist."

Sarah looked at her father with her mouth agape, having no idea he was so knowledgeable about the Reformation and Henry VIII.

She had an sudden epiphany that perhaps there was a lot about Richard Duncan she didn't know. Imagine that! As they turned north at the outskirts of Peebles, he interrupted her thoughts with the continuing travelogue,

"It's thirteen miles of countryside to the town of Penicuik…" he offered in his best tour guide voice.

"I used to call it '*Pen-a-chuck*,' Sarah laughed, "until Kaitlyn corrected me that it was pronounced '*penny-cook*.' I'm still trying to get the hang of some of these Scottish names."

Her father winced a little at the mention of Kaitlyn's name, but carried on.

"Penicuik is the mid-way point between Peebles and Edinburgh, and did you know that Penicuik was first mentioned in print in 1296AD? The town itself was developed in the late 1700's by Sir James Clerk to become a planned village."

"You win Penicuik," she laughed. "I don't know too much about it."

Both were quiet for a few miles. The next village was Glencorse and she racked her mind to think of something about it to stump her father. He beat her to the punch.

"Do you know that Glencorse was named after a chapel that is now submerged in the reservoir that supplies Edinburgh with wa-ter?" he said.

"I wasn't aware of that. But I just remembered Robert Louis Stevenson attended a parish church in Glencorse and used it as an inspiration for several of his novels, *Weir of Hermiston* and *The Bodysnatcher*," she said.

"Leave it to my clever daughter to know the literary side of things."

Before long they were passing through Newington, the suburb of Edinburgh where they first lived in a two-story townhouse when they arrived in Scotland. So many memories–exchanging letters with Peter on her way to and from that horrid school, Christmas with Seaneen McAughtrie and Liam Morrison, and of course, her father getting shot. They never went back to the house after that and she wondered who lived there now. Life had taken so many twists and turns in the years since it had been their home.

"I can't wait to see Peter," she said. "He might bring some new sketches. I've missed him so much and he's only been gone a week. What time is it?

"Nearly ten-thirty. What time does the bookshop open?" Richard asked.

"Around ten. Kaitlyn used to say it opened whenever her father arrived. It will be good to see Thomas, as well. I have some questions to ask him about my book. He is very knowledgeable about all aspects of writing, and what he doesn't know, he will find the answer to in one of his books."

Another silence followed. Sarah recalled her father had his own mission in coming to Turning Pages Book Shoppe.

"Do you have a plan?" she asked. "You know, how you are going to bring up Kaitlyn to her father and sound nonchalant?"

"Not yet. I had hoped the good Lord would have given me one on the drive here. The best I can come up with is being honest and see how that goes."

"Honesty sounds like a good plan," she's said, slightly amused.

They found parking in Lawnmarket, walked through Upper Bow to Victoria Street and arrived at Turning Pages Book Shoppe before eleven o'clock. Peter was waiting out front, all smiles when he caught sight of Sarah. Richard stepped around them with a brief nod to Peter and walked through the door with its tinkling bell into a world filled with a wonderous array of reading material.

Chapter Eighteen

RICHARD:

Don't Touch Anything

"Aye, lad, I can see you are in a conundrum. My Kaitlyn can be a wee bit tricky from time to time. You say you've tried to contact her?" Thomas Turning asked.

"Yes, several times. I've left messages, but she hasn't returned them. I even wrote a letter, but never sent it. My ego might have gotten the best of me. If she didn't want to speak to me, why was I forcing it?"

The elder gentleman appeared to ponder all that Richard told him, which mainly was the fact they had a disagreement—no details of the event. It was new territory for Richard to open his heart and be vulnerable, but the thought of never seeing Kaitlyn again was incentive enough.

"The past few months have been busy for my Kaitlyn girl, I know that for a fact. She mentioned she had something important to tell me but wanted to wait until she came for a visit. This has been the longest she has stayed away and I miss her. Why don't I try calling her while you are here? To be truthful, I'd like to hear her voice."

"I'd like that very much," Richard said.

"Let me look through my cluttered desk to find the telephone number, I know it is here somewhere…"

Gazing around the book store, Richard reminisced about his first visit. It felt as though it was years ago, when in fact it had only been months. The attractive blonde with the lilting laugh and engaging personality had captured his attention immediately. The more he got to know her, the more he found to like. She was smart, a gifted listener, empathetic, and a tireless encourager. Miraculously, she appeared to like him as well. The relationship was moving along beautifully until that fateful morning at the train station. If only he could have a do-over and keep his mouth shut. Words of his mother echoed in his brain, '*Everything happens for a reason, son. God is in control. Lay it down.*' Far easier said than done.

"I found it! " Thomas said, interrupting Richard's thoughts. "Let's give it a try."

They waited impatiently as the line connected, then it began ringing. And ringing. And ringing.

"Perhaps no one is there. We can try again later," Thomas said, about to hang the receiver up.

"Oh please, give it just a few more rings," Richard implored.

"Aye."

Several seconds passed when Thomas finally heard someone pick up the phone.

Richard waited with anxious anticipation. He could faintly hear the person on the other end of the line say hello.

"Good morning, this is Thomas Turning. I would be Kaitlyn's father. Might she be about?"

"Mr Turning? Are you quite sure you are Mr. Turning?" the woman asked.

"Why, yes, I am quite sure. Is this Mrs. Cumberman I have the pleasure of speaking with?"

"Yes, it is, but you don't sound terribly ill? Have you recovered? We have been quite worried about you," she said in a concerned tone.

"I'm absolutely tip-top, nothing to recover from, dear lady."

"I'm very confused. Kaitlyn left a note in our entry night before last saying you had an emergency and she had to go to you at once. Mind you, she left in the middle of the night, and we assumed you to be near death. But you are not, are you?"

"Most assuredly I am fit as a fiddle."

Richard made a motion for Thomas to cover the mouthpiece of the phone.

"Might you hold the line for just a moment?" Thomas asked.

In a hushed voice Richard requested Thomas to ask if anyone had been in her room since she left. Thomas, not completely understanding, handed the telephone to Richard.

"Mrs. Cumberman, this is Richard Duncan, a friend of Kaitlyn's. May I ask if anyone has been in her room since you found the note?"

"Not to my knowledge. Kaitlyn has her own suite in the east wing and housekeeping only comes weekly. What is this about, Mr. Duncan?"

"I'm not sure, but would you mind checking her room to see if anything is amiss? I caution you not to touch anything. We will wait on the phone while you look."

"I'll put the telephone down while I check."

He could hear her footsteps fade away. None of this felt right. There was no plausible explanation why she would leave in the dead of night unless she was forced. Patience was not his strong suit and anxiety was building every minute Mrs. Cumberman was away from the phone. Thomas stood as still as a statue, not uttering a word, but watching Richard as if his life depended on it. After an eternity, the voice on the line returned.

"Oh my! Mr. Duncan. Her normally tidy room is a dreadful mess, and....there is blood on the desk and the door. What is going on?"

"Mrs. Cumberman, please listen carefully to what I say. Do not under any circumstance let anyone in her room. Do you understand?"

"Yes, I understand," she said with a tremor in her voice.

"We will call the authorities. Please keep this telephone line available. As soon as we know anything, one of us will telephone you. Is your husband home?"

"Yes, yes he is. Would you like to speak with him?"

"If I may," Richard said. Without missing a beat, he had taken charge and was relying on things he had learned when serving in the Foreign Service.

While waiting for Judge Cumberman to come to the telephone, Thomas touched Richard's arm.

"What's happened?" he asked.

"It would appear that Kaitlyn might've been kidnapped," Richard said.

"Why would anyone kidnap my daughter? I don't understand."

"That is the big question. It could be someone who had a problem with Judge Cumberman. Often people who come before the court feel they've been treated unfairly. I can't imagine Kaitlyn having any enemies."

Judge Cumberman came on the line, sounding very distressed.

"Mr. Duncan, my wife is all to pieces. Can you enlighten me to what is going on?"

The explanation was simple enough and the Judge grasped the implications immediately.

"I cannot fathom off the top of my head anyone in my sphere who would do this. I will contact my former secretary and inquire if she can think of anyone. Did Miriam say you would be calling the authorities?"

"Yes, with your permission, sir, unless you prefer to notify them. It occurs to me you would have more contacts with the London police."

"There is a gentleman in the Met I could telephone," the Judge said. "He is quite high up and would understand the gravity of the situation."

"That sounds very good. I am currently in Edinburgh but will be leaving momentarily for my home in the Borders. May I give you my telephone number? I would appreciate any news you can share. Kaitlyn Turning is very special to me," Richard said.

"And to us, as well, Mr. Duncan. I will be in touch."

The call ended after Richard gave the judge his telephone number. The gravity of the situation landed on a distressed Thomas Turning.

"What shall I do? I've never had anything like this happen before."

"My instinct is for you to stay here at the store given the possibility Kaitlyn or her kidnappers may try to contact you."

"I think I'll call my employee, Jacob, to come in. Just in case…" Thomas said, sounding a little muddled.

Richard saw Sarah and Peter at the back of the book shop sitting near the quaint fireplace. He would make one more telephone call before interrupting them.

"May I borrow your phone?" he asked.

"Of course, of course," Thomas said.

Dialing the familiar number, Richard waited what felt like an eternity until Seaneen answered, a bit out of breath.

"Hello, Leigheas."

"Hello, it's Richard. We have a situation. Is everyone at Leigheas accounted for? Do you know where each person is?"

"They are all in the dining room. I made Scottish Stew and invited the staff to share. This must be serious," his friend answered.

"We think Kaitlyn might have been kidnapped. It has just been discovered and there are no details as of yet. Please ask the staff to stay put until Sarah and I return. We will be leaving shortly."

"Hold just a wee moment," Seaneen said.

He could hear conversation with one of the housemaids before she came back on the line.

"I'm sorry, Richard. Brennan just informed me that a sealed envelope was hand delivered for you by a young boy on a bicycle about eleven this morning. I am holding it in my hand and there is no indication who it is from."

"Please put in on my desk and I will look at it when we arrive home. Probably a note from one of the local stores where we order goods. I've no need to tell you to keep a watch on things."

"Yes, and Richard, I'll be praying for Kaitlyn."

The silence on his end of the line was only because he felt like a fool not asking for God's guidance and wisdom in the first place.

"Thank you, Seaneen. How thoughtful you are. We will see you shortly."

Neither father nor daughter said much on the way back to Leigheas. Gone was the cheerful chatter about village history and who could outsmart the other. Sarah tried to fill the air with small talk about Peter's brilliant drawings, but Richard's thoughts were with the lovely Scottish lass and her safety. He was caught in a difficult situation as he wanted to be involved in searching for her, but she refused to speak to him. The authorities would question what interest he had in finding her and it would be a bit embarrassing to say she was a friend who wouldn't take his calls. For the moment it was a moot point as Judge Cumberman and the London Met would be on the case. He would go home and make himself crazy with worry and constant prayer.

Chapter Nineteen

RICHARD:

The Letter

Dear Richard,

By the time you read this I will be held captive against my will. If you ever want to see me alive, I need you to deliver £50,000 in two days time. DO NOT go to the police or my life will end. This is not a joke.

Instructions are as follows. The cash is to be in £20 used notes, not new money, English pounds not Scottish pounds, and placed in a leather satchel. You are to take the bus to The Cross Keys pub in Peebles and leave the satchel in the red telephone box across the street. You must come alone and deliver it not later than 16:30. Once you have delivered the satchel, you are to get on the next bus and go home. When my captor has seen you board the bus and the money has been checked, you will receive a telephone call at Leigheas regarding my whereabouts.

> *Fondest Heart, Fair Hero, Forever Honourable*
> *Kaitlyn*

He read the letter twice before dialing Liam in Shetland. His heart beat furiously with every unanswered ring. It was early afternoon and Liam was probably busy on the farm, but someone must be around the house. After five long minutes, he hung up and went in search of Seaneen. She might be his house manager now, but her early years were spent in the security business.

Why couldn't he find anyone when he needed them? He finally resorted to calling out Seaneen's name, then Sarah's name. No response. Brennan, the younger house maid appeared from the butler's pantry.

"I'm sorry, Mr. Duncan, if you are looking for Mrs. McAughtrie. She and Mr. Bradbury just left for Walkerburn. Oh! I mean Mr. And Mrs. Bradbury. I still can't get used to using her married name," Brennan said embarrassed.

"Was it you who received the note from the boy on the bicycle?" Richard asked.

"Yes, sir. It was most strange. When I answered the front door, this wee lad of about ten years thrust the envelope in my hand and said, '*You must give this to Mr. Duncan immediately or else,*' then off he rode on his old bicycle as fast as you please as though a dragon was chasing him."

"What time was this? Did you recognize the boy?"

"Right around eleven because I heard the big clock chime just before he knocked. No sir, he didn't look familiar."

"Have you seen Sarah since we returned?"

"She said she would be in her room writing. Would you like me to get her for you?"

"No, no. If you see Mrs. McAughtrie, I mean Mrs. Bradbury, would you ask her to come to my office?"

"Of course, sir," Brennan said with a little curtsy.

He collapsed into the wing back chair in his office with a feeling of desperation coming over him. Kaitlyn's life was literally in his hands and he didn't know which direction to follow. For a man who spent decades making very important decisions, he was unable to think clearly. He'd try to reach Liam one more time. After the third ring, his nephew answered.

"Liam! Thank goodness. Are you free to talk?"

"Of course. Has something happened?"

At that moment Sarah walked in and Richard motioned for her to sit down.

"Yes, Kaitlyn has been kidnapped and a ransom note has been delivered to me requesting £50,000. It specifically says not to contact the police or she would be killed."

Sarah's mouth dropped open in horror but no words came out. She stood up and read the letter sitting on the desk.

Liam let out a long whistle as he gathered his thoughts.

"Do you have any idea who kidnapped her?"

"Not a clue," Richard said.

He filled in his security-specialist nephew on the details of how Kaitlyn had gone missing from the Cumberman's home, and traces of blood had been found in her room. Then further explained Judge Cumberman's connection to the London police and how they would be working on clues at that end.

"They know nothing about the letter I just received. It came by way of a young boy on a bicycle who left it with one of our maids. The fact that it is written in Kaitlyn's handwriting is very disturbing. I cannot fathom who is behind this."

Sarah spoke up abruptly and pointed to the note.

"The clue is right here. Look!" she said, pointing to the writing at the end of the letter. "It's in the closing… Fondest Heart, Fair Hero, Forever Honourable."

"I don't understand," her father said.

"The initials! Look at the capital initials of each word. F and H, Frederick Hutton!" Sarah said triumphantly.

"Do you suppose? Of course, you're right," he said. "Liam, what do you think?"

"I think my cousin, the writer, is absolutely brilliant. Frederick noticed your fondness for Kaitlyn and knew you would do anything to protect her. What are your thoughts about ringing the police? After all, the Met will be involved in London," Liam asked.

"That is one of the questions I wanted to ask you. We can't do anything to jeopardize Kaitlyn's safety. I don't know if the threat to kill her is valid, but can we take that chance?"

"According to the records, Frederick has not murdered anyone…" Liam said.

"Yet. But I'm thinking he must be in dire straights to kidnap her. I don't know. We can't let anything happen to her."

Sarah was examining the note, front and back, then the inside of the envelope flap.

"Dad, is this blood?" she asked pointing to several reddish-brown smudges.

The color drained from Richard's face.

"Liam, there is blood on the note and the envelope. First blood in her room, and now on the note. We can't call the police. I'm convinced he has already hurt her and his threat is serious."

"If I leave now, I think I can get aboard the last flight out tonight from Shetland to Inverness, then catch the overnight train to Edinburgh by morning. We can meet at Waverley station. I'll have Mairi call you with the arrival time once I've left. Are you able to arrange for the money with your bank and find a leather satchel? What is our timeline?"

"I am to be at The Cross Key Pub tomorrow afternoon."

"Dear God. That doesn't give us much time," Liam said, falling into security specialist mode. "Check the bus schedules for Peebles, and bring in Seaneen, Giles and Mark immediately and alert them to the situation. When you meet me at the train station have Giles accompany you in a separate car. I will need one of the cars."

Hearing his nephew taking command brought a small amount of relief, however it underlined the seriousness of the circumstances.

"Yes, I will take care of everything you mentioned. Please hurry."

"*Keep the heid - 'keep calm and carry on, everything will be okay.*' I'll see you soon," Liam said, hanging up without a goodbye.

"Thank you, Liam," Richard said to the dead phone line.

Chapter Twenty
KAITLYN:
Where Am I?

It was completely dark with an overpowering odor of mold and dampness. Her face was pressed against a rough stone surface and her entire body ached. She opened her eyes and blinked several times. Rope bound her wrists tightly together and stabbing pain ripped through her right hand. Struggling to sit upright, the sound of scurrying of rodents was far too close for comfort. A scream caught in her throat, but nothing came out. Wherever she was, it was terribly cold and frightening. Trying to pull her wool coat closer around her shivering body didn't help. Suddenly, what felt like a bat flew past, ruffling her hair with its beating wings. Panic rose in her chest causing her heart to beat double-time. Everything seemed jumbled and confused. If she could only remember what had happened. Her brain felt dull and woolly, allowing only fragments of memory to flash in her mind. Frederick. A knife. A long ride in an old, smelly car, driving in the dark. A long, uphill hike, blindfolded. There was a slight recollection of drinking something. It hurt to think. By leaning back, the rough stone wall gave little support to her aching spine. Maybe if she just closed her eyes for a moment, it would all come back to her. Yes, sleep would be good. She felt herself surrender to an unnatural slumber.

A robin's song came from high in a leafy woodland tree and sunlight warmed her upturned face. The sky was azure blue with hardly a cloud and the air felt soft. Heather flowers were blooming everywhere, their delicate pink blossoms atop tough, wiry stems. A sweet, floral aroma was all around her. Was that Richard in the distance coming toward her? She was happy, running to him through the heather. He was smiling with open arms. She loved Richard. She loved Richard Duncan.

A forceful slap on her cheek abruptly ended her lovely dream.

"Sleeping Beauty has finally awakened," Frederick said, shining a torch in her eyes. "I was beginning to think you were dead, though I was quite sure I hadn't given you enough sleeping draught to kill you."

The sight of Frederick and the sound of his voice caused nausea to nearly overwhelm her. It took all of her willpower not to throw up. Clinching her teeth tightly, she looked around at her surroundings for the first time. The dimly lit ancient stone cavern had a low rounded ceiling that met the floor. A small square window let in a scant amount of light and barely enough air to breathe. At the far end of the cavern she could barely see a meagre excuse for a doorway that one would have to crawl on hands and knees to go through. A piece of old wood had been shaped to the opening to form a make-shift door.

"Where am I?" she whispered in a hoarse voice. "What do you want from me?"

"Ahhh, another time, another place, my pretty Kaitlyn. If only we had met under other circumstances." He brushed the side of her cheek with his dirty, clammy hand. "For now you are merely a means to an end. I've found myself with a gap in my finances and you are the key to returning me to where I belong among the elite of society. I am but a victim in this latest turn of events, but will rise again to be admired and sought after. So good of you to assist me. And to think how you ignored me on the train. Who is the winner now, my dear? And who is the loser?"

His maniacal laugh indicated the man was clearly delusional and irrational. Her mind tried to reason how to diffuse him and escape. Maybe he would take pity on her.

"Frederick, I'm so very sorry for your troubles. I can understand your frustration," she said with a raspy voice. "At the moment my right hand is quite painful. Do you think you could untie it for just a moment so I might see if it is infected?"

"Do I look like a fool? Give me your hand."

She lifted up her bound hands and let the vile man touch her damaged skin.

"Yes, it looks to be quite infected. Too bad," he said, letting her hands drop back in her lap.

"Please get some medicine," she said, with a dawning realization of how dangerous the infection could be.

"What is the famous line from that American movie with Clark Gable? '*Frankly my dear, I don't give....*'"

"Please Frederick. You said you don't want me to die."

"You won't die from that infection, at least not today, but maybe tomorrow," he said mockingly. "Before the sun sets I will have my money and your fate will be in the hands of Richard Duncan. Will he find his fair maiden alive or dead? Quite a thought to ponder, isn't it? Very soon you will no longer be my problem."

It was clear sympathy was not in this man's vocabulary. Her hand was becoming more painful by the second, until vexation and anger overflowed into an uncharacteristic eruption.

"Frederick, you are nothing but an evil monster, tying up an innocent, injured woman in some kind of bizarre dungeon. Does that give you a sense of power? Do you think you are dominating me? Think again. The world sees you as a wretched, self-important, pompous man incapable of thinking of anyone but yourself. Your inflated ego and arrogance are pathetic. How dare you involve a fine man like Richard Duncan into your slimy scheme. What a fool you are! You need to release me right now! I hope you never get your money!"

She was spent. The outburst took the last of her energy and tears flowed in exhaustion. The tall, shabbily dressed Frederick came closer, hunched over because the ceiling was too low for him to fully stand up. Drawing near, she wondered if he really was going to untie her. Instead, he slapped her face hard enough to knock her body onto the cobblestone floor. The last words she heard echoed in her head before all went black.

"You have served your purpose."

LIAM:

A Satchel Full of Money

Liam arrived just in the nick of time to board the short flight from Shetland to Inverness. According to the train schedule, there should be just enough time to catch the overnight sleeper to Waverley in Edinburgh, and arrive early Wednesday morning.

True to excellent Scottish railways, the train left right on time. His small compartment was adequate, as was dinner in the dining car. He was far too preoccupied to even notice what he was eating. The highlands of Scotland passed silently by as he settled in for the night. It was time to formulate the details of the plan to deliver £50,000 to a known criminal, recover it, collar the criminal, get the money back and rescue Kaitlyn, the love of his Uncle Richard's life. Oh, and do it in less than twenty-four hours. Was it any wonder why he only did security work part time now, spending the majority of his time as a farmer on Shetland Island? With a wife, a little bairn, and another on the way he was quite satisfied with life on the family farm. His old security company would call him in for special cases every so often, but of course, this one was a family matter. Apprehension lurked heavily in Liam's mind after the fiasco nearly six years ago when Richard had been shot during his watch. After the internal investigation, no one blamed him, in fact he was lauded for saving both Richard and Sarah from further harm. While that was all well and rosy, he still felt responsible. Every now and again a sleepless night would bring shades of guilt, searching for how he could have done things differently.

"Liam! Liam! Over here," Richard waved.

Beyond Richard, Liam saw Giles standing slightly apart, scanning the crowd at Waverley train station for anyone who looked suspicious. Walking quickly through the throngs of people, they finally met just inside the station ticket hall with its famous glass dome. It was a little quieter, perfect for conversation away from the hustle and bustle.

"You made remarkably good time. We were not entirely sure you caught your connection, but here you are," Richard said, shaking his hand.

"That I am, and even early," Liam said. "Good to see you, Giles. Thank you for accompanying Richard."

"Of course, sir."

"I suggest we have tea in the Palm Court at the hotel and I will lay out my plan," Liam said with some authority.

"Lead the way," Richard answered.

The trio walked up the wide staircase to Princes Street and turned right toward the North British Railway Hotel. Even at this hour the main street in Edinburgh was vibrant with cars and buses going this way and that. A slight haar hung over the city making the old stone buildings and cobblestone streets look like something from long ago. It was easy to imagine a horse-drawn carriage rounding the corner rather than a modern automobile. The clock in the tower of the North British Railway Hotel showed it was only half past seven. Of course, everyone knew the clock was always three minutes fast so hotel guests wouldn't miss their trains.

It was a short walk to the hotel, world renown since originally opening for its extreme luxury and attention to detail. It was no wonder celebrities and politicians were frequent guests. Walking through the lobby toward the Palm Court, one couldn't help but be impressed by the sumptuous surroundings. They were seated in a discreet location, between two of the many lofty potted palm trees for which this famous room was named. Once tea and scones were ordered the conversation turned serious.

"Before you tell us your plan, allow me to fill you in on what we've accomplished. Sarah telephoned Cavanagh's and spoke to Simon, Robbie's nephew. They have an old school-boy leather satchel that should work. He will open the shop this morning at half-past eight for us to collect it. I talked with my banker, explained what was needed, while dancing around why it was so urgent. He reluctantly agreed and will open the bank at nine for us," Richard said.

"Do I want to know how you maneuvered that? You must be a highly regarded customer to warrant such treatment," Liam chided his uncle.

"Years in the American Foreign Service, and my short stint as consular general here in Edinburgh came in handy," Richard said with a slight smile before turning serious. "I need not tell you how important this is to me. If anything happens to Kaitlyn, I would never forgive myself."

"I'm here to help make sure we find her. I won't let you down. Were you able to find the bus schedule to Peebles?" Liam asked.

"Yes," he answered, pulling the sheet out of his pocket.

Tea was delivered, and once the server departed, Liam leaned in close and spoke slightly above a whisper.

"Given the time frame we are working with and the gravity of the situation, here is what I suggest. Giles and I will take your car and drive to the Cross Key Pub in Peebles and secure a good vantage spot where we can see you leave the satchel in the call box. It will need to be a location where we are not visible, yet have an unobstructed view. We must ensure no one tries to use the call box while the satchel is in there. It's to our advantage that Mr. Hutton does not know me nor Giles so we shouldn't arouse any suspicion. Obviously, it is imperative that we be able to apprehend Mr. Hutton once he is in possession of the satchel."

"That sounds good so far," Richard said hesitantly.

"Now, Giles, you will be on a bench outside the pub with a newspaper, looking for all the world like a Peebles resident. Watch for Hutton to enter the call box and leave with the satchel. Follow him at a discreet distance, but don't confront him."

"Yes, sir," Giles said.

"Richard, when we leave here take the car Giles drove back to Leigheas and wait until the appropriate time to leave in order to get on the bus that will deliver you to Peebles by 16:15."

"Refresh my mind, 16:15 is 4:15 in the afternoon, correct?" Richard asked.

"If you're an American," Liam replied, with a slight smile. "Once you've made the drop, leave immediately and walk back to the bus stop. Do not look around, just get on the next bus that arrives. Go straight to Leigheas and wait to hear. This should be fairly simple if Mr. Hutton follows his plan. However, as a back up, if you do not receive a telephone call from me by say 18:00, that's 6:00 pm American style, you'd better call your detective."

"We will have a lot of explaining to do to DI Lawson if it comes to that," Richard said. "Let me see if I've got this, if all goes according to plan you will handcuff and secure him, then call me. What if he won't tell us where Kaitlyn is?"

"If he does what he says in the note, he will call Leigheas," Liam said. "Giles and I will give him time to call before we apprehend him. My gut feeling is he is a desperate man, but resorting to attempted murder is not in his bag of tricks. It is in his best interest that she be found. Alive."

Liam could see the look of utter dismay on Richard's face.

"We are her best chance. Peebles is remote enough and the area is fairly rural, so Mr. Hutton won't be able to get far. Giles and I will be on him as soon as he has possession of the satchel," Liam said. "Before I forget, you'd better arrange for Seaneen or Sarah to be by the telephone when you leave Leigheas for Peebles, just in case Frederick calls before you return."

"I will do that," Richard said.

There was a long pause while the waiter refilled their tea cups, and retreated to another table.

"Liam, I'm entrusting Kaitlyn to you, Giles and God."

"That's a team I'm happy to be on," Liam replied.

As promised, Simon Cavanagh had the school-boy leather satchel ready and didn't ask any questions. The small antique shop on Cockburn Street was truly a treasure trove of all things old and wonderful, from relic costume jewelry to war posters to glass cabinets filled with vintage silver items. Giles stood watch outside while the purchase was made.

"Have you ever heard the history of the satchel?" Simon asked. "It goes all the way back to Scottish monks in 300AD who carried their Bibles in them. Even Shakespeare mentions them in *As You Like It*."

"That is fascinating, Simon, but I'm afraid we must go. Please give my best to Robbie and Maeve, and thank you again for opening the store early," Richard said, trying to sound as normal as possible. "This is a gift for someone special."

"Aye, indeed, Mr. Duncan. Give my best to Sarah," Simon replied. "I hope the recipient enjoys this old satchel and gives it more history."

Next stop was the bank a few blocks away. Liam still couldn't quite wrap his mind around how Richard managed to get £50,000 in used small denomination British notes.

Mr. Gladwell met them at a side door and ushered them into a beautifully appointed private office. A cloth bag sat on the conference table with a guard at the rear of the room.

"This is a most unusual request, Mr. Duncan. As you are a customer of substantial means we have been able to secure what you require. Would you care to count it?" Mr. Gladwell asked.

Richard looked at Liam who ever so slightly nodded affirmatively.

"If you don't mind, Mr Gladwell, I would like to briefly go through it."

"Certainly, sir. I don't blame you in the slightest. Please sit down."

The bag was opened and more cash money than anyone in the room had ever seen in one place was set before them.

"Each bundle has £1000, consisting of fifty £20 notes. There are fifty bundles," the bank president said. "All bank notes have been in circulation for at least three years."

The room was silent while Liam and Richard thumbed through the bundles. It took quite a few minutes for the cash to be checked.

"It all seems to be in order, Mr. Gladwell. I am very grateful for your assistance," Richard said, choosing his words carefully.

"It is our pleasure to serve you, Mr. Duncan."

Giles handed the school-boy satchel to Liam, who very carefully placed the money inside.

Mr. Gladwell reached out to shake Richard's hand.

"Mind you travel safely with that sum of money," he said uncharacteristically concerned about Richard's well-being.

"That I will. As you can see, my two companions are trained specialists," Richard said. "Again, my thanks."

The trio left before the bank president could subtly make any further inquiries.

FREDERICK:

Pompadour Blue
Ford Popular

There had been a few altercations in his life, mostly in one pub or another, and usually alcohol-induced, but slapping a woman was a new experience. To boot, he had slapped Kaitlyn not once, but twice. Surprising how easily it happened and how little remorse he felt. Why didn't stupid people obey him? All his life he knew he was far more intelligent than everyone around him, yet he got no respect. Part of that might have been his penchant for embarrassing people by exposing their ignorance. If only they would recognize his superiority. Oh well, he was in charge now, and whilst his scheme had been hastily put together, he was quite confident that by the end of today he would be in possession of £50,000 and on his way to financial freedom.

Stealing a nondescript old, beat up Ford Popular auto from a seedy neighborhood in London had been a brilliant plan. There were thousands of the cheap motor cars painted Pompadour Blue running around Great Britain, and no one took any notice of them when he'd kidnapped Kaitlyn. The downside was this tatty car had no heater, or turn indicators, the manual choke operating the carburetor didn't work terribly well and there was a slight odor of rotting fish permeating the interior. He laughed at how this car was well below his usual standard, but that couldn't be helped. After all, it was serving its purpose. The E-Type Jaguar would have to wait a little longer.

Adrenaline raced through his body just knowing the dreadful past months were about to come to an end. Driving the clunker away from Kaitlyn and her disagreeable outburst, he began to feel quite elated. The idea of showing up at Richard Duncan's house on New Year's Eve had been one of his best. However, simply pilfering a few items from the grand home hadn't brought the desired financial payoff he had anticipated. That absurd vase was more trouble than it was worth. Then it struck him! The connection between his host and the lovely Kaitlyn sparked the scheme of holding her for ransom. Richard Duncan was loaded with money and certainly wouldn't miss a bag full of circulated £20 notes to the tune of £50,000. Miss Turning was a valuable commodity indeed.

The rough, primitive lane he was driving on would soon give way to a paved, civilized road leading him to Peebles. The drive along the River Tweed in the late afternoon was exhilarating. He was already past the village of Walkerburn and only about eight miles from his destination, and all that money. He would park the Pompadour Blue car a slight distance from the Cross Keys Pub, just in case someone reported it missing. Once the leather satchel was in his possession he would drive to London, go into disguise, and fly to France on a British Airways flight, landing at Cote d'Azur airport in Nice. With a ticket in hand, no one checked names or identification to board those flights. From there, he would take the bus to Monaco and pay off the first of his debts. Yes, this was a fine strategy. Simple and straight forward.

A trifling thought crossed his mind. *'I wonder if Kaitlyn is still alive? Doesn't much matter now.'* He could almost smell his money.

Chapter Twenty-three
SARAH:

The Waiting Game

Sarah had been awake for hours worrying and praying for Kaitlyn. The list of evil, dreadful things Frederick was capable of swirled in her mind uncontrolled. She needed to get a grip. Faith over fear–she must remember that. Dragging herself out of a warm bed, she wrapped up in her coziest robe and bent down to look for her slippers. While on hands and knees, she noticed a folded note had been slipped under her door.

Sarah Sunshine,

I'm leaving early this morning to meet Liam and discuss his plan to rescue Kaitlyn. <u>Please do not leave the telephone unattended</u> in case Frederick calls with her location. I'm praying he will do as he said he would. Not sure why I'm banking on that, but it is the only lead we have to hang on to. I love you, and will hopefully see you soon.

Dad

Try as she might, anxiety began to overwhelm her. What if that dreadful man harmed her father? She absolutely mustn't think that way, after all life is not made up of '*what ifs.*'

After an hour of staring at the phone and drinking four cups of Earl Grey, she put the kettle on yet again. The back door flew open with a gust of wind followed by James and Seaneen.

"I'm awfully glad to see you," Sarah said, handing them her father's note. "Dad left this for me this morning,"

They quietly read it together and exchanged worried looks. James put his arm around his wife as she leaned on him for support.

"Oh, Sarah. It is beyond the bounds that my nephew has brought so much harm and disruption to this family. Kaitlyn must be found safe and Frederick caught and brought to justice. It is unthinkable. I suppose I must telephone Marjorie and let her know," Seaneen sighed.

"May I suggest you wait to call Marjorie? After all, we don't really know anything helpful to tell her, do we?" James asked.

"You're right," his wife answered. "I am frightfully frustrated and I suppose I want her to carry some of the burden of this mess as well. Not very Christian of me, is it?"

"You are the most wonderful woman in the world," he said holding her close, "but you are human. Let's not worry about Marjorie for the moment."

The forgotten tea kettle whistled and Sarah turned it off.

"If there is nothing I can do here," James said, "I believe I will walk up to the chapel and pray. If ever the Lord was needed, it is now."

"I couldn't agree more," Seaneen said, kissing his cheek. "Mind you, don't get a chill."

"I won't be gone long," he said, closing the back door gently behind him.

"He is really a good man. I'm so happy you found each other," Sarah said.

Her dear old friend beamed with the compliment.

"I'd never disagree with that," Seaneen replied, handing her a shortbread out of the tin on the counter.

"I've been praying most of the night," Sarah said with her mouth full, "but somehow when James prays I have the feeling it is main-lined straight away to God."

"We share the same thought, pet," Seaneen said.

"Would you mind watching the telephone while I run upstairs? After four cups of tea I'm about to pop. I'll get dressed while I'm there."

"Happy to, Lass. Lord help Frederick if he calls and I answer," Seaneen said, furrowing her brow.

"I couldn't agree more, but until Kaitlyn is safe, we'd better be agreeable."

"Off you go. I'll pour tea when you return."

Within ten minutes Sarah was fully dressed and running back down the stairs when the phone rang. From what she could hear, Seaneen's voice was far too polite for it to be Frederick. The call ended as she came into the kitchen.

"Lass, you just missed Peter's call. He is leaving Edinburgh for Elibank, and will arrive in about an hour and a half. The lad wondered if we had news about Kaitlyn. I explained we needed to keep the line open and you would ring him later."

For the briefest of moments, Sarah allowed herself to bask in the glow of her love for Peter–how far they had come in their relationship and how blessed she was. The telephone rang again interrupting her thoughts. She and Seaneen looked at each other, silently praying this was the anticipated call. Sarah reached for the phone.

"Hello, this is Sarah Duncan."

"Sarah, this is Thomas Turning. I'm dreadfully sorry to bother you, but I am most distressed about my daughter. Do you know anything? I'm all alone and quite worried."

The first thought that came to mind was not to mention the ransom note. That would only cause him more concern, yet she understood how heart-wrenching this must be for him. She must choose her words carefully and briefly. This phone line mustn't be tied up.

"Thomas, this must be terrible for you. My dad is working right now on a lead but I am not able to share any more information."

"Well…that's something then," he said with a pause. "Would it be too presumptuous of me to drive to Leigheas and wait there for news? My other children are all far away and sitting here by myself is about to drive me mad."

"Of course, you are welcome to come to Leigheas, Thomas," Sarah said without hesitation. "Please drive safely and we will have the kettle on. I must hang up now as we are expecting a call. See you soon."

A loud exhale escaped her.

"You did the right thing, pet," Seaneen said soothingly. "This must be quite troubling for him. At least here he will be among friends. Shall I make some breakfast porridge? Much as we would like, shortbread isn't going to sustain us in this long day."

"Yes, that would be…"

The shrill ring of the telephone interrupted her. Once again, they exchanged looks before Sarah answered.

"Hello, this is Sarah Duncan."

The voice on the other end of the line was silent for a moment. Sarah could literally feel her heart beating rapidly. She spoke again.

"Hello? Is anyone there?"

"I am looking for Mr. Richard Duncan. May I speak with him, please?" asked the older gentleman with a polished voice.

"He is not available. I am his daughter. May I ask who this is and if I might take a message?"

"When is he expected to return?" the gentleman inquired formally.

"I'm not sure, but I would be happy to let him know you called," Sarah said becoming a little irritated and wanting to free up the telephone line.

"Please inform him Judge Cumberman, Kaitlyn Turning's employer called and I have a bit of information he might be interested in."

Sarah mouthed the name '*Judge Cumberman*' to Seaneen who was hanging on every word. The older woman waved her hand in a circle motion as if to say, '*ask him more!*'

"Judge Cumberman, would it be possible for you to give me your information and I will then pass it on to my father the moment he arrives?" she asked. "I care very much for Kaitlyn and am concerned for her."

Something in her sincerity must have touched the Judge.

"Of course, young lady. Tell your father I learned this morning my five year old grandson woke up the night Kaitlyn was kidnaped.

He told his nanny he saw a tall man making her go down the stairs and out the front door in the middle of the night and thought he might've had a knife. Sanni has become quite attached to Kaitlyn, as we all are, and is quite distraught. I've told the London police this information, but thought your father should know as well."

Immediately Sarah remembered again to keep quiet about the ransom note. She couldn't breathe a word of it to the man on the other end of the phone line. Frederick threatened to kill Kaitlyn if authorities were called in. Oh, how she hated to lie or at least lie by omission, but there was too much at stake.

"How awful for your grandson, Judge Cumberman. I am so sorry. This is a frightful situation for everyone involved. I will pass your message along as soon as my father returns home. Thank you so much for calling."

"You're welcome. My best to Mr. Duncan. Goodbye."

And the telephone line disconnected. For now.

Chapter Twenty-four
LIAM:
The Red Call Box

Giles and Liam would have enjoyed the journey between Edinburgh and Peebles far more if their mission hadn't been so dire. By now, Richard was on his way back to Leigheas, biding his time until he caught the bus for Peebles later in the afternoon. Liam's nerves were on edge, but it was essential he stay in the moment and follow the plan.

The Cross Keys Pub was on Northgate Road just off of High Street near the center of the village. They drove by slowly, choosing the most advantageous place to park the car. A space was open in front of a book shop near the pub with a direct view of the red telephone box, and the bench where Giles would sit in the pub courtyard. Liam had made a handwritten '*out of order*' sign to be taped to the telephone inside the call box. His mind was busy reviewing the details again and again. They still had two hours before Richard was scheduled to arrive and leave the money.

"We've no idea where Frederick is lurking at the moment, so it's best we not be seen together," Liam said. "Why don't you walk down to the bakery and have a cup of tea. At 16:00, come back this way and put the sign on the telephone. I will saunter into the book shop and watch for Richard's arrival. If all goes as planned, he should drop the satchel right about 16:15 and walk back to the bus stop. Frederick's note said the money wouldn't be picked up until he saw Richard get on the bus leaving town. We need to focus on that red phone box until Frederick Hutton takes the money. If he does what he says, he should call Leigheas and tell them Kaitlyn Turning's whereabouts."

"If he's a man of his word, which I hope he is, for Mr. Duncan's sake," Giles responded grimly.

The two men sat quietly in the car, each mentally replaying their part in this operation.

"I'll be off for the bakery, unless you have any further instructions," Giles said.

"Don't get too comfortable in there. I've a gut feeling once this begins to play out it will go rather quickly," Liam said. "You've got good instincts, Giles, which is why I wanted you with me today. Richard Duncan is not only a client, he is also my uncle and one of the finest men I've ever known. If things don't go quite as planned, I trust you to know what to do."

"Thank you, sir. That means a lot. I won't let you down."

Light rain made the cobblestone sidewalks of Peebles slick. Puddles reflected the two and three story old Scottish baronial style buildings with rounded turrets lining Northgate. Liam walked down the narrow street, looking in the display windows of each store trying to appear nonchalant. Various shops occupied the lower floors of the buildings with rental apartments above. It crossed his mind that the village was quite appealing and maybe he would bring Mairi here for a visit someday—but this was no time for idle thinking. Tying his wool scarf around his neck to keep the chill out, he stopped in front of the book shop. For anyone watching, it appeared he was interested in the contents of the big window. Mainly, he was using the large glass as a reflection to see the comings and goings in the pub. All was quiet for the moment. After a short while, he went inside as though browsing. Books were everywhere, lining the walls, over the doors, and stacked on small tables. He must remember to tell Sarah about this shop. His thoughts were interrupted by a grandmotherly woman, with rosy cheeks, looking somewhat like Mother Christmas.

"May I help you find something special, young man?" she asked in a kindly voice. "It's easy to feel a wee bit overwhelmed on your first visit."

"You are right about that. This is quite a remarkable shop."

"Thank you, thank you. That is a lovely compliment. Now, what brought you in today?"

Reality struck Liam like a rock. He was there to peer out the front window in the hopes of catching a kidnapper–a thought he kept to himself.

"If you don't mind, I would enjoy simply looking around," he said.

"You'll not be disappointed. If I may be of any help, I will be down that aisle," she said cheerfully, gesturing toward a book-laden pathway. "We've a shipment of old books to unpack, though the Lord only knows where we will put them."

"Thank you," Liam answered, not revealing how anxious he was to get to the front window. "I will let you know."

If he stood to the left of the big display window, both the red phone box and the pub were in his line of sight. A check of his watch showed it was 16:00. Right on the button, Giles went in the red phone box, affixed the note to the telephone, and sat on the bench in the courtyard of the Cross Keys Pub. He opened the Scotsman newspaper and looked every bit like a Peebles native. A bell over the bookshop door jingled a few times as customers came and went. Liam watched carefully as a couple of teenage girls opened the phone box door, read the note and left. Giles had them in his view as well. Liam glanced around the book shop and no one was paying him any notice. He spotted the title of a poetry book by British author Violet Fane on the table in front of him, '*Good Things Come to Those Who Wait*.' How incredibly appropriate. Out of the corner of his eye he saw Richard walking down the street carrying the leather satchel they had bought earlier in the day. Dutifully, Richard entered the red phone box and closed the door. He picked up the telephone receiver as though making a call, waited a few moments, then hung up the receiver and exited, leaving the satchel behind. Never looking back, he walked to the bus stop and got on the waiting bus. Within two minutes, the big green bus lumbered down the narrow street. Liam tingled all over knowing Frederick Hutton was watching all of this. He searched in every window he could see and noticed Giles doing the same. In the meantime, the sidewalk was becoming crowded as people got off work and headed home or out for a pint. Groups of middle-aged men laughed good-naturedly as they went through the wooden pub door, and several young lads kicked a football down the road, avoiding oncoming cars. Silly boys had no fear. A young mother pushed her proper dark blue English pram to the phone box, opened the door and went in, but exited fairly quickly. She made a bee-line into the pub. She must have read the '*out of order*' sign on the telephone but was in dire need to make a call. Who takes a wee bairn into a drinking establishment? He waited another three minutes, but no Frederick. Giles was beginning to look around nervously. Liam's tingling was turning to sweat. Something was wrong. Another two minutes.

"Sorry to bother you, sir, but we are closing. Was there anything you wished to purchase?" a gangly young man with thick glasses asked Liam.

"Oh, sorry, no, not today. Thank you," he managed to say before walking out of the book shop.

Giles looked at him from across the street questioning what to do next. Liam walked quickly to the iconic red phone box and opened the door. Giles stood by his side. It was empty. The satchel was gone. Without saying a word they both ran into the pub, searching the smoke filled room for the woman with the pram. Finding her at the far end of the bar, Liam abruptly folded back the top of the carriage, only to find a baby several months old looking back at him with a toothless grin.

"Where is the leather satchel?" Liam quietly demanded of the young woman.

"He took it," she answered without hesitation. "He gave me ten quid to pick it up and put it in my pram."

"Where did he go?" Liam asked, trying desperately to claim some level of civility.

The mother began to cry. The noise level of the pub was rising as more alcohol was being consumed and it was hard to hear her.

"He took my car keys and left through the back door," she managed to say between sobs.

Giles immediately ran toward the back of the pub, and out the door.

"He's gone," Giles reported.

"He won't get far," the young woman sniffled, "the car is almost out of petrol. A mile or two at most is all he will go."

"What does the car look like?" Liam asked.

"A red Morris Mini-Minor…with a dent on the bonnet," she answered and dissolved in another round of tears.

"Did he happen to mention which way he was going?"

"I think he said something about being in London before dawn," she said, wiping her runny nose with the back of her hand.

Liam began barking orders to Giles loud enough to be heard over the din of noise.

"Bring the car to the front, and I will call Richard. Be quick about it."

When asked to use their phone, the bartender pointed to the pay telephone in the red call box outside the pub.

The irony was not lost on Liam.

Chapter Twenty-five

RICHARD:

Proverbs on the Green Bus

The green double-decker bus owned by the Scottish Motor Traction company rumbled along the cobblestone street, obviously in need of new shock absorbers. Both driver and conductor seemed to know the regulars onboard by name, though they were equally polite to new riders. It was immediately evident that the heater on the big bus was either out of order, or woefully underpowered.

Boarding without turning around to see if he could spy Frederick was one of the most difficult things Richard had done in a long while. It was an enormous amount of money to leave in a call box, but beyond that, what if Frederick didn't live up to his part of the deal? What if they never got the call about Kaitlyn's whereabouts? The window next to him was grimy and fogged up, which didn't matter as all he could do was stare straight ahead. His pent up anxiety was ready to explode. Accustomed to being in charge and solving problems, he'd never been the victim of an extortion scheme. Everything was out of his command. Here he was on a rattling bus in the Scottish Borders, sitting next to a large man who smelled faintly of garlic, while the woman he loved was who-knows-where at the hand of a man with no scruples, to whom he has just given £50,000. It was not a very good scenario any way you looked at it. What would his mother have told him? He closed his eyes, trying to calm his racing heart, and search his brain for words of wisdom. Within moments it came to him and he spoke out loud in a low voice.

"Trust in the Lord with all your heart and lean not on your own understanding…"

Mr. Garlic Breath finished the proverb without hesitation in proper King James fashion.

"In all thy ways acknowledge 'im and He shall direct thy path."

Richard smiled gratefully at the man.

"Me mum was a great one for the Proverbs," the large man replied, contributing a bit more garlic to the bus air.

The remainder of the ride passed a little easier. By the time he walked down the long driveway toward the manor house, Richard noticed several cars parked in front. Once inside, he could hear voices coming from the kitchen.

"I'm so glad you're home!" Sarah said throwing her arms around him, then whispering in his ear, "I need to speak to you in the other room. Now."

Seaneen was pouring out tea to James, Thomas Turning and Peter, who were all seated around the large table in the middle of the warm kitchen. Being raised with manners, Richard shook hands with all the gentleman, then excused himself as Sarah followed.

"First of all, do you know anything?" she asked, as they entered his office.

"No, I made the drop, got on the bus and didn't look back."

"Well, it has been a mad house here. The phone has not stopped ringing, but nothing from Frederick. Thomas called and needed a place to worry, so we thought it best for him to be here. Peter just returned from Edinburgh and wants to help. Then there was a rather strange phone call from Judge Cumberman saying his young grandson saw a tall man forcing Kaitlyn down the stairs the night she was kidnaped. The Judge alerted the police, but I didn't say anything about the ransom note," Sarah said.

"Good girl."

The ringing of the telephone cut short their conversation, followed by Seaneen running into the office.

"Richard! It's Liam. He says it's urgent."

The telephone on the office desk was an extension of the one in the kitchen.

"Liam, what's happened?" he asked, picking up the receiver.

"Frederick has the money, he tricked us, but we are headed after him. I'm quite sure he will abandon the auto he stole and go on foot following the river…"

The call was broken up by static before Liam continued on.

"…if you…on horseback by the river toward Elibank. If you hurry, we will nab him. Must go."

And the line was dead.

The bewildered listeners looked at one another.

"I think he wants me to go on horseback from this direction and he, Liam, will be coming from the other direction and we will catch Frederick in between," Richard said.

"It's not wise for you to go alone," Seaneen advised.

"Peter and I will go with you," Sarah spoke without hesitation. "It sounds like it's close to Elibank and Peter will be familiar with the area. I'll go change."

She was out the door with Richard close behind. He turned back.

"Seaneen, can you and James keep things going here?."

"Aye, we will, of course. Go on," she said. "And God be with you, lad,"

They drove Peter's old Land Rover to Elibank, where horses were saddled and they were on their way toward the river within minutes. The late afternoon would be growing dim soon, which added an additional element of distress.

"If you look upriver the meadow is fairly open with only a few trees here and there. We should be able to spot him from quite a distance," Peter said. "The river bends about four hundred meters ahead, where there is a stone fence to keep the sheep in. Let's head for that."

The horses were kept to a slow canter, giving each rider a chance to look for any sign of Frederick. Clumps of low bushes hugged the river bank, with a few outcroppings of large boulders. A startled Grey Heron flew out of the rocks and noted its displeasure with an ear-splitting *awk* squawk that lasted several seconds. Sarah's horse shied a bit, but she kept him under control. They slowed to a trot.

"Look, up toward that hill," Richard said, pointing to a woodland off to the left. "Is that something moving around? The leaves are rustling in an odd way."

"More than likely it is a large Tawny owl. Their wingspan can be a hundred centimeters wide," Peter said. "There are a lot of them in this area."

The uneasy feeling among the three of them was palpable. There was minimal conversation as every noise was magnified. A stand of tall trees ahead caught their attention and Peter indicated for them to stop, then spoke in a hushed voice.

"If he has gotten this far, the trees over there would be a possible hiding place. Follow me."

It was much darker under the canopy of oak, aspen and Scotch pines. They carefully guided their horses, single file past the bushes and brush along a rough path. Two red squirrels chased each other up a tree and chattered as they passed by. Peter stopped and quietly dismounted, handing the reins of his horse to Richard. He indicated to stay silent as he carefully stepped around the path and disappeared behind a huge hibiscus plant. It was eerie with only the sound of the river flowing in the distance. Even the horses seemed to be breathing softly so as not to disturb anything. Moment after moment passed and Richard could literally feel his heart racing in his chest. Where was Peter? He didn't dare even turn around to make sure Sarah was behind him. Of course, she was behind him. Counting the seconds to himself helped ease his anxiety. Peter finally emerged and spoke out loud.

"He's not here. These woodlands are the only hiding place along this part of the river. My guess is he hasn't gotten this far yet. Why don't you two stay here and I will go alone and scout his whereabouts? It is mostly sheep pastures for several miles on and if I ride along the high ridge that runs parallel to the river, I will be able to spot him," said Peter.

"That is quite a distance away. How will we know?" Richard asked.

Peter mounted his horse and thought for a moment.

"If you see me heading directly toward the river, it means I've seen him. Ride like the wind in that direction. If I stay on the ridge it means there's no sight of him. Does that work?"

"Yes…that makes sense," Richard said.

"Peter," Sarah said softly, "Please be careful. He's probably armed."

"He is on foot and I am on a rather large horse, giving me a bit of an advantage," he answered. "Keep your eye on me."

"Always," she said.

Father and daughter watched as he rode away through the opening in the stone wall and turned his horse up the shallow incline to the ridge. A low mist was developing over the river, bringing even more chill to the air. Richard was aware it would be dark before long but they must stay the course. Capturing Frederick and finding Kaitlyn was the only thing that mattered.

"Do you ever wonder what we are doing here?" he asked.

"You bought a house and fell in love," his lovely daughter answered.

"That I did. Guilty on both counts."

Sarah sat up straighter in her saddle and pointed to the distant figure on the ridge.

"Look! He is riding toward the river!"

"That's our sign."

They galloped in the direction Peter was riding and saw a man in the distance walking close to the river. It was obvious the man was watching Peter and had no clue Richard and Sarah were coming up behind him. Richard signaled for Sarah to slow to a walk alongside him. They were close enough to hear the conversation.

"Hello, sir. Might you be lost?" Peter asked solicitously.

"No. I'm not," was the terse answer. "Now, get out of my way."

"Actually this part of the River Tweed belongs to my family and you are trespassing."

Richard could tell Peter was stalling, waiting for he and Sarah to get closer. They were now within twenty feet. Frederick caught Peter looking behind him and turned to follow his gaze.

"What is going on?" he yelled furiously.

In one quick motion Richard dismounted and stomped angrily toward Frederick, who began to stumble backward. Anticipating this, Peter had positioned his horse so there was no way to go other than in the river.

"Get out of my way!" Frederick demanded. "You will NOT spoil my plan."

"It's over, Frederick. You're over. This evil game has ended. Give me the satchel and put your hands over your head."

The leather school-boy satchel was strapped across Frederick's chest. He slowly took a knife out of his pocket and cut the strap. Instead of handing it to Richard, he flung it into the flowing river.

"Find your precious money now, you pillock!"

Sarah screamed, while her father never took his eyes off of Frederick. Peter immediately ordered Sarah to follow him. They raced along the river bank, watching the satchel tumble over and over as it hurried downriver.

"Frederick, where is Kaitlyn?" Richard demanded, clearly losing his patience.

"Ah, you've lost your fortune and now you will lose that useless tart you think so much of. She's nothing but a common…." Frederick said, lunging toward him.

That's all it took for Richard's clinched fist to connect with Frederick's aquiline nose with a forceful punch that would have impressed boxer Archie Moore. Unfortunately, the knife found its target in Richard's forearm. Frederick scrambled around on the ground, bloody and dazed from the hit, trying to find his knife.

"Are you looking for this?" Richard asked, showing the knife still embedded in his arm.

Right then, Liam and Giles drove up through the sheep pasture and slammed on the breaks next to the two men.

"Well done, Richard. Remind me not to tangle with you," Liam said, as Giles tied Frederick's hands together and moved him toward the car. "Where is Kaitlyn? And where is the money?"

"The satchel is floating down the river with Peter and Sarah in pursuit. He hasn't told me where to find Kaitlyn."

"And I never will," Frederick shouted. "Your girlfriend is lost forever."

A crazed laugh caused Richard to charge the horrible man with the intent of punching him in the nose again. Liam forcefully held him back.

"Hold up there. Perhaps we should get the knife out of your arm first?" he asked while assessing the damage. "I'm fairly sure it's a flesh wound, but it's bleeding badly."

"There is a first-aid kit in the boot of the car," Richard said, becoming aware of the growing pain in his arm.

It only took a few minutes to remove the knife, sterilize the wound and wrap gauze tightly around it. A bit of blood soaked through, but nothing significant.

"Well. All right, then, all bandaged up," Liam said. "Giles has Frederick tied up in the back of your car."

"What do we do now?" Richard asked.

"Giles and I will haul Mr. Frederick Hutton to the Edinburgh police station and try our best to explain why they nor the London police were never in on this adventure. We will have the hour drive to figure some plausible story. By the way, since I have your car, are you fine on horseback?"

"Yes, but what about Kaitlyn?"

The conversation was interrupted by an approaching car, driving erratically over the bumps and valleys in the pasture, scattering sheep this way and that. It didn't take long for the driver to abruptly stop the vehicle and exit so fast he almost fell out.

"Stephen! What are you doing here?" Richard asked the resident Leigheas veterinarian.

"Seaneen sent me," he said panting and trying to catch his breath. "Said it was important. The bartender from the Cross Keys Pub called with a message. Castle."

"That's it? Castle?" Richard asked.

"Yes. He said a man wrote down the telephone number of Leigheas on a paper napkin along with the word 'castle' and gave him ten quid if he would call in an hour. The bartender forgot and just found the note."

"Castle? What could that possibly mean?" Liam asked. "Are there any castles around here?"

Two thundering horses came toward them with Peter in the lead and Sarah following, carrying a very soggy, dripping leather schoolboy satchel clutched to her chest.

"We got it!" Peter said.

"I'm quite sure nothing fell out," Sarah added breathlessly. "I am totally soaked."

"She was amazing," Peter added, "jumping into the water and grabbing the bag."

The riders stopped short, seeing Fredrick in the back of the car under the watchful eye of Giles, and Stephen standing by.

Richard anticipated their question.

"He refuses to tell us where Kaitlyn is, but Stephen said there was a phone call with the message '*castle*.' Do you know of any castles around here?"

"There is Neidpath Castle about a mile from Peebles, but it has been privately owned by the Wemyss family for over two hundred years and I can't imagine it being used to hide someone. I used to go there to visit friends of my grandparents," Peter said.

"Sorry to interrupt, but Giles and I need to deliver Frederick to the authorities. Uncle Richard, if I might have a word?" Liam asked.

The two men walked further away from the car so they wouldn't be overheard by its occupant.

"We will take Frederick to Edinburgh police, then make sure we connect with DI Lawson. I think I've an idea of how to present the story of why we apprehended the criminal without letting them in on it, but I'll explain later. You've got to concentrate on finding Kaitlyn. I will head back to Leigheas as soon as I can and fill you in on everything. God speed," Liam said, giving his uncle a firm handshake.

The car slowly drove away in the direction of Edinburgh. Night was quickly approaching and Sarah was beginning to shiver from the cold, though not complaining.

"And you're sure Neidpath Castle isn't something we should follow up on?" Richard directed his question to Peter.

The young man slowly shook his head, eyebrows furrowed with a distressed look.

"I just can't figure Frederick gaining access to the castle, nor can I imagine the Wemyss family not noticing him on their property."

Like a bolt of lightening, Peter looked up with eyes wide and couldn't get his words out fast enough.

"Good grief! We have a castle! There is a castle ruin in the hills above Elibank. It's remote, mostly tumbled down and hardly anyone goes there. That must be where he put her!"

Not wasting a moment, Richard got on his horse.

"You lead us, Peter."

"May I suggest we meet at my house, get Sarah in dry clothes and grab some torches? There is a rough road we can drive, much safer than taking horses up there at night," Peter said.

"Good idea. Sarah, you ride with Stephen and I will take the reins of your horse. Stephen, do you mind coming with us? Should we find Kaitlyn, we've no idea what shape she might be in and we could use your help," Richard asked briskly.

"Happy to, if you think I can be of assistance," the veterinarian answered.

Within ten minutes the group arrived at the Elibank manor house, and in less than twenty they were packed in the old Land Rover. At the last minute, Peter found several blankets, filled a thermos with water and grabbed a box of biscuits his mother had left for him. By now, night had fallen and it was completely dark. Only because Peter knew his family's estate by heart were they able to make their way up the primitive pathway. They were jostled around from side to side, rushing headlong into the night, the weak head-lamps flickering on and off, hardly lighting the way. The air inside the old Rover was thick with prayer.

Chapter Twenty-six

SARAH:

The Castle Ruin

Even borrowing Peter's warmest clothes, Sarah was freezing. Wet boots were not helping nor were her damp underclothes. She was trying to control her trembling so as not to alarm Stephen, who was seated next to her in the Rover. Perhaps her shivers were more a nervous reaction about Kaitlyn, having less to do with her chilled body. The fear of what they might find kept edging into her thoughts. Everyone in the Rover was quiet as Peter drove with her father sitting nervously next to him. Overgrown bushes and low hanging tree branches scraped the sides and top of the vehicle as it strained to make the uphill climb. Cresting the top, suddenly the castle ruin came into view. Barely visible was a crumbling high sandstone structure with small rectangular openings for windows. From what she could tell they were on a small plateau which must have an expansive view of the River Tweed valley below in the daylight. It was far too dark now to see much of anything.

"Mind how you walk," Peter advised when they got out of the car. "There are centuries of rubble to trip over and not even a moon to guide us."

They each carried a dim torch to light their way with Peter in the lead. Taking their steps slowly, Sarah wanted more than anything to shout Kaitlyn's name and hear her friend respond. As anxious as she was, it was hard to imagine what her father must be going through. They walked single file through tall grass to a wooden gate built into the ancient low stone wall. Up the hill they went, closer and closer to the castle ruin, ever afraid rocks would tumble down on them. They approached a low arched doorway at the very

139

bottom of a wall and stopped. Peter shined the light into the vaulted cavern. The screech of an owl echoed in the night and a few bats flew out in response to the torchlight.

"This area is divided into two chambers with loose stones and rubbish everywhere. Be really careful, it's awfully dark," Peter advised as he ducked his head down to enter. The others followed.

Torchlights lit both caverns sufficiently to see there was no one there.

"Bloody hell! I was certain she would be here. I'm so sorry, Richard," Peter said. "I'm so very sorry. I was sure we would find her here."

She could see her father was too stricken to speak, as his shoulders sank. Try as she might there were no words of consolation. Her eyes were becoming accustomed to the dark environment.

"What's that? Back in the corner," Sarah asked.

Without hesitation Peter went toward the far end of the left chamber. A loose rock was enough to unbalance his step and he fell face first on the rock floor. Sarah let out a gasp.

"I'm okay," he said, continuing to crawl toward the object in the corner. "It's a wool scarf, and smells of ladies perfume. It hasn't been here very long."

Stephen began to back out of the cavern, very deliberately, looking closely at the floor. He shined his torch back and forth across the entry floor.

"There is fresh blood here," he said, bending down and touching it with his finger. "I think Kaitlyn was here and has escaped. Either by her own will…or not."

Stephen's words hit her hard. Looking around this dismal, damp, disheveled ruin, Sarah was horrified. Seeing the blood on the ground, made her heart sink even more. Where was her lovely Scottish friend?

"God, we really need your help here," she said quietly.

Back out in the cold night air, the four of them stood in the dark not sure what to do next. Sarah watched her father clinching the woolen scarf tightly. His breathing was becoming ragged, and she fervently wished she had a suggestion. Finally, he spoke.

"I think we need to follow the theory that she has tried to escape on her own and is out here somewhere. It would be best if we didn't move the car, just in case. Peter, can we leave the headlamps on for a bit without completely running down the battery?"

"Probably good for about thirty-five minutes," Peter said.

"That will give us a little light. Let's split up into pairs. Sarah, you and Peter go to the left and cover the area from the castle down about a hundred yards, then head toward the back of the ruin. Stephen, you and I will do the same on the right. Yell as loud as you can if you find anything…anything at all. Let's go."

Richard and Stephen began the tedious task of walking down the hill and back up, searching the ground for any sign of Kaitlyn. They moved their torches from side to side over the rough terrain. This was repeated by Sarah and Peter on the opposite side. Up and down, back and forth. No sound other than an owl's warning hoots, and the twigs crushing beneath their boots. It was getting colder with a smell of rain in the air. Up and down, high and low.

"Over here! Over here!" Richard cried out. "She's over here."

Peter grabbed Sarah's hand and pulled her along toward the back of the castle ruin, about halfway down the hill. There was Richard cradling Kaitlyn's bloody head in his hands, while Stephen was checking for a heartbeat.

"Her pulse is faint and judging by her skin, she is dehydrated," Stephen said, "I've no idea how long she's been unconscious. Shine your lights over here, so I might see the damage."

"Kaitlyn, wake up. My beautiful Kaitlyn," Richard said stroking her forehead gently.

"Her head injury appears somewhat minor, but this wound on the top of her hand is infected. We need to get her stabilized," the veterinarian said. "And we need a real doctor to examine her."

"Edinburgh?" Richard asked.

"Too far. Let's get her to Leigheas and call Dr. McDonald. He lives close by and can be there in a matter of minutes. Let's lift her gently and carry her to the car. Sarah, you go ahead and get the car doors open."

With great tenderness Richard lifted her up in his arms. Stephen started to say something about helping him, but thought better of it. As they approached the Rover, Richard looked down and saw she had opened her eyes and was staring at him.

"Richard?" she asked tentatively. "I'm so glad it's you. But where is the heather?"

"My sweet Kaitlyn. Of course it's me. Hush now and save your strength," he answered.

"The heather was so bonnie…" she said before closing her eyes.

Everything was a blur after they arrived at Leigheas. The doctor had been called immediately and was on his way over. Thomas Turning watched in silent agony as his daughter was carried into the house. He reached out to touch her face, and she looked at him with a vacant stare. They settled her in an upstairs bedroom where Sarah and Seaneen cleaned her up as best they could. She was conscious, but listless and appeared to not have an ounce of energy left. James came upstairs and held her hand, saying a quick prayer thanking God for guiding her rescue and asked for complete healing of her body and mind. Kaitlyn gave the vicar a weak smile as he released her hand. She hadn't spoken a word since her conversation with Richard.

After what seemed like hours, but in reality was a very short time, Dr. McDonald arrived.

"Is that blood seeping through the gauze bandage on your arm," the doctor asked, reaching out to get a closer look at Richards injury. "What on earth happened?"

"I was stabbed earlier this evening, but it is Kaitlyn Turning who is upstairs that needs your immediate attention," Richard said.

"Well, I will tend to you later then."

"Doctor, I am the resident veterinarian here," Stephen interrupted, "and I was with Richard when he found Miss Turning."

"Your thoughts?" the doctor asked.

"Dehydration and possible infection from a stab wound."

"Another stab wound?" the doctor asked incredulously.

"Yes," Stephen said, choosing not to reveal anything about the crazy man with the knife. "In addition, she must have fallen and hit her head when she tried to escape, as there is a laceration on the right side near her temple. I suspect a possible concussion."

"Tried to escape? There must be quite a story to all this. Show me to the patient, please."

"Is there something I can do?" Richard asked, looking helpless.

"Not at the moment," Dr. McDonald said. "Seaneen, if you don't mind, would you show me the way. It might help to have a woman present while I examine Miss Turning."

"Of course, doctor," she said.

It was only last year when Dr. McDonald was tending Seaneen's injuries after a nasty fall. The two had become quite friendly during her recovery as she was always trying to do too much and he would use every threat he could think of to keep her resting.

It was nearly nine o'clock according to the grandfather clock and its Westminster chime, and no one had thought about food.

"Let's see if Meara and Brennan have something left of our forgotten dinner," Sarah suggested. "There is nothing we can do standing here."

Her stoic father led the way toward the kitchen, with Stephen close behind. Sarah noticed James putting a comforting arm around Thomas as they followed. The walk to the back of the house never seemed longer.

Tattie soup and warm beer bread satisfied the hunger of the people at the large table in the kitchen, but didn't help their sadness. Sarah was cleaning up the dishes when Dr. McDonald and Seaneen came in. All eyes turned to them and thankfully the suspense was short-lived.

"Miss Turning is in a dangerous situation. I have washed the knife wound with a saline solution and wrapped it with a sterile dressing but I can see it is deeply infected. This has caused a fever, which means her body is trying to fight off what ever is going on.

Between her high temperature, the infection, dehydration, a probable concussion and the overall trauma of what she has been through, she is likely to have some mental confusion. We must get antibiotics in her body as soon as possible."

"Should we take her to the hospital in Edinburgh tonight?" Richard asked.

"Unfortunately, that is not an option. There is an alarming number of influenza cases running rampant there now. We cannot risk exposing her to more germs. If it is possible, I would like to have her stay here."

"Of course. We can all take turns sitting with her," Sarah said.

"That won't be necessary if you don't mind my nurse staying here. I took the liberty of calling her and she is on her way with medicine and IV fluids. I mentioned bringing an overnight bag as well. I don't mean to be alarming, but this could take a turn and become very serious."

"Life threatening?" Thomas asked quietly with a desperate tone in his voice. "She's my daughter."

"Possibly, but let's not jump ahead of ourselves. The next forty-eight hours will be telling. Sarah, Seaneen will need your help for the next while keeping cool compresses on Miss Turning's head. We must try to keep her fever down. My nurse, Agnes, should be here within the hour and we will be able to administer her first dose of medicine."

"I will collect some towels and cut them apart, if you will prepare some large pots of ice water," Seaneen directed Sarah.

"Cool water will suffice, Seaneen. We don't want to shock her system too badly," Dr. McDonald said. "Now, Richard, may I take a look at your arm?"

The Laird of Leigheas reluctantly rolled up his bloodied sleeve and the doctor began cleaning the wound.

"Would you care to enlighten me as to why so many people are getting stabbed in this neighborhood?" the doctor asked.

Richard winced when the saline solution was poured over the open cut. Sarah was quite sure the pained look on her father's face had more to do with not wanting to answer the good doctor's question than with his physical discomfort.

Chapter Twenty-seven

LIAM:

Soggy Money

It was nearly dawn when Liam finally drove down the long driveway toward the manor house at Leigheas. Giles had been snoring soundly in the passenger seat since they left Edinburgh over an hour ago. The drive had been a bit of a challenge with torrential rain giving the windshield wipers a run for their money. Rounding the last corner, he was relieved to see several lights were on in the house. The events of the day had left him completely knackered and ready to collapse, but with all that had happened he was a tad wired. He woke Giles and sent him off to his cabin, then let himself into the manor house through the kitchen door. By following the light, he found Richard alone in the small reception room, sitting next to a fireplace with only a few embers left glowing. His uncle was lost in thought and hadn't noticed him coming in.

"Am I disturbing you?" Liam asked.

"Oh no, I was hoping to see you tonight."

"Actually the sun just rose. It's morning. Have you been here all night?"

"Most of it," Richard answered wearily. "We finally found Kaitlyn. Frederick had her tied up and dumped in a dark, crumbling basement of the castle ruin at Elibank. The stab wound on her hand has become badly infected, plus she suffered a concussion and is dangerously dehydrated. It looks like she tried to escape but only made it a few hundred yards before collapsing. When we found her she was barely coherent. We brought her here for the time being, but it's not looking good. Dr. McDonald has checked her over and his nurse is upstairs looking after her tonight."

"Why isn't she in hospital?"

"There is an influenza epidemic there and Dr. McDonald didn't want to chance it."

"Oh, mate. I am so sorry. Poor Kaitlyn."

Liam got a good look at his Uncle Richard and was stunned.

"You look dreadful. Worse than the time you took the ferry to Shetland."

"I could say the same about you," Richard replied. "I don't suppose you've had any sleep either."

"Not a wink in forty-eight hours, but I have a lot to tell you," Liam answered.

"Come in the kitchen and I'll put the kettle on. I am anxious to hear what happened when you delivered Frederick to Edinburgh."

The normally cheerful kitchen seemed dull and chilly as the rain continued outside. Liam related the events from the time they delivered Frederick to the surprised authorities to his conversation with DI Lawson. Richard listened carefully while pouring the boiling water into the teapot.

"Well, I'm glad you told DI Lawson the truth about what happened," Richard said, handing his nephew a cup of English Breakfast tea.

"By the time we arrived at the Edinburgh Police headquarters, I had come to the conclusion that while they may be angry for a bit, the mere fact that Frederick Hutton had been caught should calm the waters," Liam said. "And for the most part, that was how they took it. With two foreign countries, plus UK authorities after him, it's all a wee bit complicated. Each country's crime agency wants priority in convicting him and I've no idea whose charges will take precedence. As you can imagine, there are a number of people who want to speak to you and, of course, to Kaitlyn…you know…*if she is able.*"

A deep sigh was all Richard could muster.

"They will be looking for details to support their cases," Liam went on. "I asked they give you both some time to recover, though, of course, I had no idea Kaitlyn was critical."

"Thank you for everything. This entire situation blew up so quickly and I didn't know who to trust. I'm incredibly grateful for your help," Richard said, pausing to drink his tea. "I still can't get over Frederick taking it out on Kaitlyn. It's unconscionable. It would've been one thing to come after me, but why her?"

"She was far easier to kidnap and he knew you had the means and motive to save her. My guess is if it hadn't been Kaitlyn, it might have been Sarah, but let's not dwell on that now," Liam said. "I was thinking on the drive back, I don't have to be back in Shetland until the end of next week. Let me lend a hand here. As long as Kaitlyn is under your roof, you are going to be preoccupied with her progress. I'm sure there are tasks I can take off of your shoulders."

"Ordinarily, I'd send you packing back home–you've already done so much. But under the circumstances, I will gladly take you up on your offer," Richard said, relief visible on his face. "Honestly, I am feeling overwhelmed."

A knock at the kitchen door startled them and before either could get to it, the door swung open and a very wet Peter came in, making puddles with every step..

"I apologize for barging in so early," Peter said, removing his rain slicker, "but I felt I really must return this to you. I'm quite unaccustomed to being responsible for someone else's money."

The damp school-boy leather satchel was brought out from under his slicker and deposited on the large wooden table.

"Can you believe I actually forgot about the money?" Richard said.

"Let's just say your mind is elsewhere," Liam offered. "However, £50,000 is an awful lot to forget."

"Does it lose any value if it is soggy?" Peter asked.

"We will have to dry it out before taking it back to the bank. Either of you know how to dry money?" Richard inquired.

"I've heard of laundering money…" Liam laughed.

"I don't suppose the oven is a good idea," Peter added.

"Let's see how damp it is," Richard said, opening the satchel. "I hope I don't have to explain to Mr. Gladwell how his money came to be quite so…wet."

It took the three of them several minutes to pull out the fifty bundles of saturated cash.

"Should we make sure it's all there? Peter asked.

"Only two people have had extended contact with it, you and Frederick. While I trust you completely, I wouldn't put anything past that scoundrel," Richard said. "Let's clear the table and count it out. If we stoke the Aga and warm it up in here, maybe the bills will dry faster."

In all his years of doing security work, it was never lost on Liam how interesting life was with Richard Duncan. He couldn't wait to share this latest story with the family back on Shetland.

Half an hour later they were still separating £20 notes from one another. Several thousand waterlogged bills covered the table, the counters and even the chairs, all in great danger of the back door blowing open and scattering them everywhere. Liam took the precaution to lock it just in case.

"Now, no one sneeze!" he laughed, raising his arms up to emphasize his point.

"I think that is the last of it," Richard said, laying down a final damp £20 note. "Hopefully, it won't take long for them to be dry enough to count and re-bundle."

"Re-bundle what?" Sarah asked sweeping through the drafty swinging door into the kitchen. "Oh my goodness! I've never seen such a sight! So, this is what £50,000 looks like. Wow."

With her grand entrance about £10,000 in soggy notes went scurrying around the room higgledy-piggledy like a monetary whirlwind, and three grown men groaned in unison.

"Oops," she said sheepishly. "Sorry!"

Chapter Twenty-eight

SEANEEN:

A Snifter of Brandy

It was Richard's idea for her to use his office. Privacy for this phone call was probably a wise idea with Marjorie's recent tendency toward hysterics. Given the information Seaneen was about to impart, this was not a call she was looking forward to making, but it was important to share the news before the authorities contacted her. A silent prayer was sent up asking the Lord to keep Marjorie from dissolving into a fit. After three rings, there was a glimmer of hope no one was home. Alas, her sister's familiar voice answered on the fourth ring.

"Hello?"

"Good morning Marjorie, it's Seaneen. How are you?"

"As well as can be expected, I suppose. Are you well? I'm surprised to hear your voice."

"I've called because I have news of Frederick," Seaneen said, closing her eyes, waiting for the torrent to unleash.

"Oh, my poor maligned and misunderstood son. No one knows the misery I have gone through. I thought you, his aunt, would be more supportive," Marjorie began to lament, then stopped suddenly, "Oh no! Is he dead? Are you calling to tell me my son is gone?"

Then the wailing began and Seaneen could hear Malcolm, Marjories's husband, in the background asking what was going on. Words became unintelligible and Malcom took the telephone.

"Hello? Who is this?" he asked.

"Malcolm, it is Seaneen. Could you get my sister a brandy? There are things I must tell you both about Frederick and I cannot tie up the telephone line for long."

150

"Of course, hold on while I pour it."

"Better fill up the snifter," Seaneen said under her breath.

As the moments passed, Seaneen could hear Malcolm instructing his wife to sit on the love seat, sip the brandy and keep quiet. Malcolm Harris was a new hero. Anyone who could keep her distraught sister at bay was worth keeping.

"I'm back, Seaneen. Now, what is this about Frederick?" he asked.

"I'm afraid things have escalated greatly, Malcolm. In addition to Frederick being wanted by authorities in three different countries for a myriad of offenses, he kidnapped a young lady in London who happened to be a special friend of Richard Duncan. He held her in a barbaric place, withholding food and water and injuring her. His plan was to demand money from Richard for her safe return. He got his money, but stabbed Richard in the arm. Frederick is now in police custody. His victim is in very serious condition. That's the short version."

"Oh, blimey!" he said. "Will the young lady recover?"

She could hear Marjorie swooning in the background. Malcolm put his hand over the mouthpiece of the phone and instructed her to hush and drink more brandy.

"We don't know, Malcolm. If she doesn't, he will be charged with murder."

The even-tempered Malcolm gasped.

"She is here at Leigheas and has around the clock nursing care. As of this morning, her fever was still high which means the antibiotics have not yet addressed the infection. The doctor said if there is no improvement within forty-eight hours, which would be tomorrow, we will need to send her to London."

"And Richard? You mentioned he was harmed as well?"

"His arm should heal without a problem. The doctor saw to it soon after it happened and was able to properly treat it. However, Richard is beside himself with worry about Kaitlyn."

"What a dreadful mess. Is there anything we can do?" he asked sincerely.

"The reason for my call, other than to let you know what is happening, is Richard was concerned Marjorie and Gwendolyn might be contacted by law enforcement. It stands to reason they might want to interview the two of them. Frederick has created a massively tangled web of deceit which is in the process of being unraveled. We didn't want you to be caught unaware of the situation."

"That is most appreciated," he answered. There was a pause while he put his hand over the mouthpiece again before he came back. "Marjorie would like a quick word. I think the brandy has done its job. Do you mind?"

"Of course not. Put her on the line," Seaneen sighed.

It was a far more subdued, apologetic voice that came to the telephone. Gone were the hysterics of a few minutes before, obviously the brandy worked. Though not a big fan of alcohol consumption, Seaneen must remember this remedy when it came to her sister.

"Please forgive me," Marjorie said before hiccuping. "From what I could hear, Frederick has done some very bad things. My heart aches for those he has hurt–which seems to be everyone in his path. This must be all my fault. What kind of a mum raises a son who does such atrocities?"

"Now stop that," Seaneen said, softening in response. "You didn't teach your son to steal or gamble. Nor did you or his father ever condone such behavior. Both Frederick and Gwendolyn have the same genes, grew up in the same house with the same parents, teaching them the same morals. Your daughter is bright and loving, and all she should be. No, dear sister, you cannot take the blame for your son's actions. It is clearly the choices and decisions he made all on his own. Sadly, but appropriately, he will now pay the consequences."

"I feel so helpless. Where is he now? Should we be doing something?"

As briefly as she could, Seaneen related the information Liam had shared and told her not to be surprised if someone from law enforcement might want to speak with her.

"All you have to do is tell the truth, and Marjorie, try not to get too emotional. They will just want the facts."

Seaneen loved her sister and knew in her heart that Marjorie was deeply hurt and disturbed by Frederick's conduct. No doubt, she was very embarrassed, as well.

"Please give my apologies to Richard. What must he think of me? We will be praying for the young lady. She mustn't die..." Marjorie's voice was beginning to quaver and it was only a matter a time before she would begin to cry.

"I will tell him, but I must go now. There are others who need the phone line. I will call you soon."

The muffled response on the other end of the line was crying and sniffling before the call ended.

Chapter Twenty-nine

SARAH:

A Night to Remember

An earlier visit by Dr. McDonald confirmed Kaitlyn was not responding as quickly as he had hoped.

"If there is no change by morning we have no choice but to order an ambulance and take her to St. Bartholomew's Hospital in London."

"Has influenza reached there?" Richard asked. "You mentioned it was rampant at the Edinburgh hospital."

"As I said, we have no choice. It is not an ideal situation, but we can't take a risk of her declining without proper advanced treatment. I can only do so much. If you are praying people, I suggest this would be a time to engage your faith."

"O LORD, look down from heaven, behold, visit, and relieve this thy servant. Look upon her with the eyes of thy mercy, give her comfort and sure confidence in thee, defend her from the danger of the enemy, and keep her in perpetual peace and safety; through Jesus Christ our Lord. Amen."

Vicar James closed his well-used Book of Common prayer and bowed his head. Those surrounding the bed where Kaitlyn lay unresponsive with IV fluids pumping into each arm, followed suit. Sarah slyly opened one eye and glanced at her father, tenderly holding Kaitlyn's limp hand. Next to him stood Thomas, grieving silently for his desperately ill daughter. Seaneen tucked her hand in the arm of her husband, James, who patted it affectionately. Toward the back of the bedroom, in the shadows, Nurse Agnes made the sign of the cross.

At the end the prayer, Richard quietly asked everyone, including Nurse Agnes, to meet in the small reception room. The rain had stopped, but dark skies and a low mist made everything seem sad. Even the roaring fire did little to bring warmth to the room or to those seated. They were all looking to Richard for direction. Liam, Stephen and little Henry had joined the group, followed by Meara and Brennan, who brought in tea trays. No one was particularly interested in afternoon refreshment at the moment.

"Thank you, James for your prayer. I am choosing to believe that Kaitlyn will be healed," Richard said. "Nurse Agnes, at the moment you are the most important person in this house. As you have been awake all night, I think I'm speaking for everyone in this room, offering to take the overnight shifts. Each of us can stay with Kaitlyn for a few hours and, of course, awaken you if there is any problem."

"That is very kind of you, Mr. Duncan. I would need to get Dr. McDonald's permission first," Agnes answered. "However, a little rest would be most welcome."

"Why don't I call and see what he thinks?" Richard suggested, then looked around to the others. "Is everyone agreeable to taking a turn?'

Sarah watched as each one in the room, even Stephen and the maids, readily agreed without hesitation. The camaraderie was heartwarming–they were all in this together, and for some reason that made all the difference.

It was agreed that Stephen, being a medical person, would take the first three hour shift with Nurse Agnes, who would stay on for a bit to watch over things. Little Henry would be in the kitchen with Seaneen and James until Sarah and Thomas took the next shift. Then finally Richard would take the last shift before Nurse Agnes came back around seven in the morning. Liam was more than willing to take a turn, but was sent off to bed to catch up on two nights of missed sleep. Meara and Brennan would take turns making sure tea and food was available in the kitchen. It was destined to be a night to remember.

Chapter Thirty

STEPHEN:

The Vigil: 7pm to 10pm

Twenty-four hours ago he was searching the hills for a kidnapping victim, and now here he was watching over the same victim as she lay gravely ill in an upstairs bedroom in the manor house at Leigheas. It was hard to wrap his mind around everything that had transpired. Shocking, to say the least. As a vet he had experienced plenty end-of-life circumstances, but with everything that was in him, he was praying this would not be the case tonight.

It was interesting watching how efficient and caring Nurse Agnes was with her patient, carefully handling the IV's and gently cooling Kaitlyn's fevered brow. When asked if he would take the first three-hour shift, he was more than happy to help, though he couldn't remember the last time he'd spent time in close quarters with a woman as lovely as Nurse Agnes. She must be in her late thirties, and to a forty-eight-year-old widower, thirties seemed a lifetime ago. Far better he not let his imagination get the best of him. What on earth would a lovely lass see in him anyway? His life as a veterinarian and single dad kept him busy enough.

There was a soft glow from a lamp in the corner of the room and the open curtains showed the evening would soon give way to a dark night. The rain had finally stopped, leaving a chill in the air.

"What led you to nursing?" he asked, settling himself into the chair by the lamp.

"Medicine has always intrigued me," she answered in a soft voice. "My grandad was one of the few doctors up in the Highlands.

My sister and I spent summers with he and my Nana, and going with him on sick calls was my favorite activity."

"Didn't the midgies drive you crazy?" he asked.

"Ah, those pesky, biting bugs are a bother, that's for sure," she said, "but when you are young and having a grand time, it's of little notice."

"Where did you grow up when you weren't in the Highlands?" Stephen inquired.

"My family is from Aviemore in Cairngorm Park."

"Isn't that where the reindeer roam around?" he asked. "I am a veterinarian, so all animals interest me."

"Indeed it is," she said. "They are up at Glenmore."

Neither spoke for a few minutes. Kaitlyn moved around a bit in her sleep and Nurse Agnes continued applying cooling cloths to her forehead.

"Would you like me to do that so you can get some rest?" he asked. "After all, I am supposed to be helping."

"I'd like to stay for a wee bit longer. If only her fever would break, we would be out of the woods," she said. "Tell me about yourself. You're a regular James Herriot it sounds like. Why did you choose to heal animals rather than people?"

"Have you ever heard the old joke, '*If you locked your dog and your friend in a closet for the day, which one would be glad to see you once you opened it up?*'"

She covered her mouth with her hand to stifle a laugh. "I'd not heard that–a fine visual it presents!"

"Honestly, I've nothing against humans," he said with a smile. "My fondness just happens to be toward animals. They are fascinating creatures with such intriguing behavior. Once I learned there was an actual career in treating them, off I went to school. By the way, for the record James Herriot's real name is James Alfred Wight."

Stephen cringed as the words left his lips. Was he seriously trying to impress this young nurse?

"I didn't know that," she answered. "His books are my favorite."

Stephen smiled and hoped he hadn't made a fool of himself.

Nurse Agnes expertly changing the near-empty IV bag, then sat down in the other chair near Stephen. The light from the lamp revealed how tired she was, and just when he was about to suggest again that she retire to sleep, she interrupted his thought.

"How did you come to be at Leigheas instead of your own practice, if I'm not being too forward in asking?"

"Not at all," he said. "After graduating veterinary school in Glasgow, a small clinic in the south of Scotland hired me on as an assistant. I stayed in Dumfries for nearly ten years, became the senior vet and married a lovely lass. As we anticipated the birth of our first child, she began to have problems. Long and short of it, she died giving birth to my son, Henry."

"I'm so very sorry," she said. "Is that the young boy who was with you earlier?"

"Yes, that is my Henry," he answered with a slight smile. "It turned out single fatherhood and the demands of the practice were becoming too much. I wasn't able to spend the time with Henry that we both needed. About that time someone mentioned my name to Richard Duncan who happened to be looking for a resident veterinarian. We met and he offered me everything Henry and I could possible want. I can't imagine a more perfect environment to raise my wonderful son and do what I love."

She looked at him for a bit without saying a word.

"I hope I haven't bored you with my long story," he said, wondering if he had said something wrong.

"Oh my, no. I asked and I'm most grateful for you telling me," she said, pausing before continuing on. "My sister was down syndrome as well, and I would give anything if my parents had treated her as lovingly as you do Henry. They seemed ashamed and hid her away. It was hard to watch her mistreated in such a manner. That's why our visits to the Highlands were so important. Grandpa and Nana loved her unconditionally and she blossomed in their care. It was the only time she was allowed to be herself. Those are some of my favorite childhood memories."

"You used the past tense referring to your sister."

"She died several years ago."

"Oh, my condolences," he said, not knowing what else he could say to comfort her.

The dark room and unusual circumstance of being together watching over Kaitlyn had lent an air of intimacy he hadn't expected. Nor had he anticipated enjoying conversation with Nurse Agnes so much. They talked on comfortably for another half-hour.

"Well, it has been a long day," she said rising from the chair. "If you've no need of me, I believe I will try to get a little sleep. Should you be alarmed by anything, my room is next door. With your medical training, I'm sure you'll be fine." She held out her hand to shake his. "I've enjoyed talking with you."

The door closed softly behind her and she was gone.

Chapter Thirty-one

SEANEEN:

The Vigil: 10pm to 1am

"She has the face of an angel, doesn't she?"

"As do you, my lovely wife," James answered, watching as Seaneen gently placed a cool, damp cloth on Kaitlyn's brow. "You never cease to amaze me with your many abilities and soft heart."

The bedroom was completely dark now with only the lamp on the table casting shadows across the walls. Several candles on the dresser had been lit, giving the impression of warmth rather than adding light.

"Is her fever any better?" James asked hopefully.

"I'm afraid not," she answered. "Imagine what poor Thomas must be going through. Without a wife to turn to and from what Kaitlyn has mentioned previously, none of her siblings live close by."

"That's true. He was trying to get in touch with them earlier, but with time differences and how remote they are, he hasn't been able to track them down. The eldest, David, is in Hong Kong, Walter is in the army in the Middle East, and his youngest daughter Rachel is in a convent in Switzerland and can't be disturbed," James said

"My, aren't you a wealth of information?"

"I've spent most of the day with him. As a vicar, I've found people in distress tend to like having clergy around."

"I'm not in distress and I very much like having you around," she said warmly.

"For which I am most grateful," he answered.

Seaneen felt Kaitlyn's wrist to check her pulse, and adjusted the light blanket over her. It was nearing midnight and they both knew time was closing in. Without a break in her fever, the doctor would move her to London. It took quite a lot to discourage Seaneen, but she was beginning to fear the worst.

"I feel very guilty about all of this," she said wearily. "If we hadn't chosen Leigheas for our wedding, Frederick would never have shown up, Kaitlyn wouldn't be lying here close to death and Richard would still have his mother's Chinese vase."

She felt the tears about to make an entrance and couldn't hold them back.

"Now, now," James said tenderly, taking her hand. "The '*if only*' and '*what ifs*' of life are a waste of time and energy, my love. None of this is your fault. Let's take a look at the facts of the situation. Our choice of Leigheas was whole-heartedly endorsed by everyone and I'm sure Richard and Sarah wouldn't have had it any other way. Marjorie was innocent, she had no knowledge of Frederick's whereabouts, and poor Gwendolyn was unfortunately used by her brother to meet his own ends. No one is to blame other than your troubled nephew. I am reminded of the *Prayer of Serenity* by Reinhold Niebuhr. *God, grant me the serenity to accept the things I cannot change, the courage to change the things I can, and the wisdom to know the difference.* Let us ask for wisdom and not tarry with guilt, eh?"

Her husband's words were a comforting balm, calming the tempest in her soul. They spent the last hour of their vigil cooling Kaitlyn's brow and reading The Chronicles of Narnia by C.S. Lewis aloud.

It was indeed good to have clergy around in times of distress.

Chapter Thirty-two

SARAH:

The Vigil: 1am to 4am

The soft, cashmere blanket had been a Christmas gift from Jessica, Peter's mother. Sarah wrapped it close around her shoulders and wished she'd added a scarf. The doctor ordered the bedroom be kept cool as a measure to lower Kaitlyn's temperature. One of the tall windows had been opened a crack, letting in the chilly night air making the candles on the dresser flicker as they burned lower and lower. Thomas Turning sat quietly in the dimly lit room, withdrawn in his own thoughts as Sarah sat nearby silently pondering life. Had it only been a few months since Frederick had shown up and wreaked havoc in all of their lives? The ripple effect of one man's actions causing so much pain was frightening. Existence on this earth is awfully strange, she thought. The world just keeps going around and around, while every day, each person lives out their individual triumphs and tragedies, births and deaths. She was reminded of Shakespeare's quote, '*All the world's a stage, and all the men and women merely players.*' Everyone plays their part. Her philosophical moment was broken when Thomas cleared his throat.

"I've four children, you know," he said. "And I love them equally."

Sarah looked over at the grieving father, wishing with all her heart she could take his pain away. It wasn't so long ago that her own father's life hung in the balance.

"Aye, my Kaitlyn was always a special one, though," he continued. "Even when she was a wee bairn, she liked nothing better than following me around the book shop."

"I remember her telling me about it when we first met," Sarah responded fondly. "She said it was a perfect childhood."

"She had the run of the place, though I had to keep her off that blasted rolling library ladder. Customers enjoyed my bright-eyed, enthusiastic Kaitlyn and marveled at how clever she was and many books she had read."

The older gentleman became quiet again and watched helplessly as his daughter slept on. Sarah continued the same routine as the others, gently dabbing Kaitlyn's forehead with a cool cloth and touching her face to see if there was any change.

"Were you surprised when Kaitlyn left the book shop and Edinburgh to become a secretary in London?" she asked.

"Oh…I would have to say, we were a wee bit disappointed and missed her dreadfully, but would never have stood in her way. Even far away in London, she stayed in touch, sending us marvelous letters about her daily life with the Cumbermans. Of course, when my wife became ill, Kaitlyn would come home at least twice a month, sometimes just for a day or two. I don't know what I would have done without her during those times, it was mighty rough. After her mum passed, she would show up like clock-work every month, and stay nearly a week at a crack. It was always something for me to look forward to. Then there was that fateful day you and your father came into the shop," Thomas said with a slight smile. "Once she met Richard Duncan, I began to see a wee bit more of my lass."

For a brief moment they both meandered pleasantly through their memories of days not long past.

Kaitlyn began moving around in the bed, appearing agitated and restless, but never opened her eyes. About the time Sarah considered waking Nurse Agnes, Kaitlyn settled back down into deep sleep. Feeling her brow, Sarah was dismayed it was still burning hot. There was nothing left to do but wait and watch.

RICHARD:

The Vigil: 4am to 7am

It's a very odd thing waiting to see which side might win. Will life triumph over death? Will there be one factor that pushes it one way or the other? Looking at Kaitlyn's sleeping face, Richard was trying with all his might to compel her to grasp at life and not slip away. He lightly touched her arm with the tips of his finger as though infusing her with his own life force.

"Don't leave me, my sweet Kait," he whispered.

Closing his eyes to keep his tears in check, he began reciting the Lord's Prayer quietly. The stumbling block was when he came to *'thy will be done.'* He wasn't entirely sure he could sincerely pray that line. What if it was the Lord's will that she not live? How could he reconcile that? He thought of his mother and how faithful and brave she had been when her husband died. How he wished for her at this moment. The last sound he heard before dozing off was the beloved grandfather clock chiming five times.

He had no idea how long he had slept other than the crick in his neck was quite painful. Fine nurse he turned out to be. He lifted his head and looked around. His fingers still lay gently on Kaitlyn's arm. The room was less dark, with a dim light coming in from the window and the candlelight barely wavering on the far side of the room. It was just enough illumination to see one's way around without bumping into anything. He could hear Kaitlyn's unlabored breathing and leaned in close to touch her forehead to check for fever. Her face was wet with sweat.

"Hello," she said quietly, with her eyes wide open looking up at him.

"Hello," he answered, barely disguising the giddiness he felt.

"I'm afraid I am a wee bit…damp."

"Yes, you are and I couldn't be happier," he said with a smile that took over his face.

She struggled to sit up but collapsed back down.

"Hush and don't try to move about yet," he said, holding onto her hand, careful not to dislodge the IV needle. "You've been quite sick, my beautiful Scottish lass. We thought we might lose you."

"I'm awfully glad you found me," she said, closing her eyes. "Please don't lose me again."

She wasn't making much sense, but that didn't matter. He was looking at the woman he loved, no mistake about it, and she was going to live.

Chapter Thirty-four

Dr. McDonald:

The Happy Bug

Early morning sun filtered through the trees onto his windshield like tiny, dancing sparkles. Ordinarily, a sunny day such as this would be greeted with great anticipation. Today, however, as he motored down the driveway toward Leigheas Manor his heart was very heavy. No matter how perfect the day was, if Miss Turning had not improved overnight, the only hope was moving her to a hospital in London—and even then her future would be uncertain.

It was imperative he explain the seriousness of sepsis to everyone to underscoring the gravity of her situation. He recited the speech in his mind as he parked the car. '*Sepsis is a medical oddity that happens when a patient's body doesn't respond appropriately to an infection. Instead, the infection-fighting processes turn against the body and can become a frightening condition known as septic shock. Possibly fatal, septic shock causes the patient's blood pressure to drop dangerously low, creating damage to lungs, kidneys, liver and other organs.*' It was a frightening prognosis for any patient. As a physician, he had sworn the Hippocratic Oath to do his best. Sometimes, he wished he could do better than his best. Perhaps that was God's arena.

It had been long time since Dr. McDonald's spirit was so low. On days like today he wished he had taken up the plumber's trade instead of medicine. With the weight of someone bearing bad news, he knocked on the carved wooden door. The last thing he expected to see was Richard Duncan's face grinning from ear to ear, and the exuberant, almost giddy group that greeted him as a conquering hero. Seaneen threw her arms around him, proclaiming it was an all-out miracle, and Sarah, still in her dressing gown, praised his genius medical skill. Mr. Turning showed up with his shirt buttoned all wrong and untucked, and couldn't stop shaking his hand. It was obvious the highly contagious Happy Bug epidemic had hit Leigheas.

"Shall I guess our patient has improved?" he asked rhetorically.

"Her fever broke this morning, actually quite recently, about half past six," Richard said, hardly containing his joy. "She even spoke to me!"

The good doctor was humbled and grateful for the turn of events. While he knew the extent of his knowledge was vast, there were some outcomes simply out of his hands.

"Well, isn't that brilliant news? Thank you, Lord. Let me see our miraculous patient without haste."

Everyone trooped up the stairs behind Dr. McDonald. He stopped short at her door and asked if they would mind waiting outside while he examined her. They looked at each other in confusion, no doubt born of a significant lack of sleep, and agreed to meet him back downstairs in the small reception room.

Nurse Agnes was tending Miss Turning when he entered the large bedroom. The heavy drapes had been drawn back allowing the sun to pour in, and the previously open window had been closed. A chill still hung about the room, though a fire had been lit in the fireplace to warm things up.

"Good morning, Nurse Agnes," he said, placing his worn leather medical bag on the nearby table. "And a lovely morning to you, Miss Turning. You've given us quite a fright the past few days. How are you feeling?"

"I'm not sure. My head hurts a wee bit and when I try to think…it's all fuzzy. I can't seem to hold a thought," Kaitlyn answered, offering a slight smile. "My hand is rather sore as well."

"All of that is to be expected, given what you have been through. I'd like to check you over, if you're up to it."

She was agreeable and he carried out the routine of looking in her eyes with a small light, listening to her heart and feeling her pulse. All appeared normal, though her color was still pale, and she had obviously lost weight. The woman before him was a far cry from the one he had seen a few days ago with a dirt smudged face, blood-caked hair, and torn clothing.

"Nurse Agnes, would you assist me in removing the bandage on her hand? I want to see how the wound is healing."

"Of course, Doctor," she answered, already holding a tray with the instruments he would need for the examination before he asked for them. His capable nurse had been with him for five years and had proven to be a God-send. With her skill and intelligence, he often wondered why she hadn't attended medical school. There were more and more women doctors these days.

"The redness is gone and the wound is healing nicely. I believe the antibiotics are doing their job. Nurse Agnes, we can discontinue the intravenous drips and I will leave oral antibiotics to ensure the infection has been completely eliminated."

He carefully applied topical medicine to the injured hand and wrapped fresh gauze around it, then pulled a chair over beside the bed and sat down.

"We've been fortunate, Miss Turning. It is important for you to understand how seriously ill you have been, and while I anticipate a complete recovery, you must follow my instructions carefully. I want you to stay here in bed for at least a fortnight and rest. Let others tend to you for this short time. Of course, I will clear this with Mr. Duncan, but I'm quite sure he will be most agreeable to having you under his roof for a while," he said, slightly amused. "Nurse Agnes will stay another few days and I will be checking in often. We will take it one day at a time until I feel you are ready to rejoin the world. Even then, you will be restricted to very light activity."

"I don't like being a bother to anyone. Are you sure it will be that long?"

"Your healing is a marvel we don't want to take for granted. See all this grey hair? I earned it by years of experience as a physician. You are not completely out of the woods, and I believe a conservative plan will be in your best interest."

"I understand," she answered. "Thank you, Doctor."

Nurse Agnes had completed her task of removing the IV lines and was helping Kaitlyn sit up slightly.

"Perhaps you might be ready for a cup of tea, Miss Turning?" he asked.

"Yes, I would, very much," she answered, her voice still weak.

"Nurse Agnes, would you be so kind?" he asked.

"Of course, and tea for you as well, Doctor?"

"That would be lovely, thank you."

While his patient appeared to be healing physically, he was a mite concerned about her mental stability. He was seasoned enough to know he needed to tread carefully and not upset her.

"May I ask you a few questions about your ordeal?"

When tears welled in her eyes, he held her hand and wisely chose not to pursue the subject.

SARAH:

The Eternal Optimist

"Would you like to go fly fishing today?" he asked first thing when she answered the phone.

"With you?" Sarah teased.

"Duh!" he responded. "How soon can you be ready?"

"Give me twenty, no, thirty minutes. I'll have to find my waders and gear."

"Well, get a move on, lass. The salmon won't wait forever," he said with a laugh. "I'll pick you up in forty minutes simply because I know how your thirty can expand."

"Ha! I'll be ready, you'll see, smarty pants," Sarah answered smiling. "And Peter, I'm so glad you called. I've missed you."

"I'll be there before you know it."

In the five days since Kaitlyn's fever broke, the household had already adopted a new routine. Nurse Agnes arrived in the morning and helped her patient bathe, have breakfast and return to bed. Lunch was brought to her room by Richard, who was allowed only an hour, as the doctor was strict about visitors not tiring Kaitlyn. Thomas was granted the longest span with her at dinner time when trays were brought up for both of them. Every afternoon, Dr. McDonald came by to check on his patient and remind her of the limitations he had set. This left little space for Sarah to spend time with Kaitlyn, but twice she had snuck in, much to the patient's delight, and they enjoyed girl talk.

In the hours Richard wasn't with Kaitlyn, Sarah knew her father was busy catching up on business. Springtime was a team effort at

Leigheas that included the entire staff. There were lots of plans to formulate and decisions to make. In addition, DI Lawson was waiting impatiently to interview Kaitlyn. Dr. McDonald strongly suggested she not be questioned until her health improved. It was obvious to Sarah her father had a new spring in his step as Kaitlyn began to feel better. Liam stayed on and had become invaluable as Richard's right-hand man. The two men enjoyed each other's company and worked well together.

After many days at Leigheas, Thomas was ready to return to Edinburgh and the book shop. Relief at his daughter's recovery was apparent and his gratitude to the Duncan family was endless, but it was time he got back work.

As daily life was settling down, Sarah found time to continue writing. There were so many creative ideas she was anxious to share with Peter. Spending the morning fishing for salmon on the River Tweed at Elibank sounded like a perfect chance. Just the thought of being with him brought happiness that had not dimmed an iota.

"You know, I really can tie on a fly," she said, watching her boyfriend with his loosely curled hair, focusing his attention on threading the tiny filament line through the eye of the fishing hook.

"Hush. I've almost got it…ha! There it goes, now to tie the clinch knot, and…there you go," he said triumphantly handing her the long rod. They were seated on a rough wooden bench in the sheep field bordering the river.

"Fishing flies are really beautiful, but it does make me laugh that they are made to fool fish into thinking they are real insects. How hard can it be to fool a fish?"

"My girl, you have no idea how clever fish are. Creating a fly that is successful can take years to perfect."

"Why do they all have such peculiar names?"

Delighted she was interested, he lifted the little box attached to the lanyard around his neck and opened it to display an array of colorful, feathered flies.

"We call the act of fly tying, '*dressing flies*.' I've made most of these using well-known patterns that specifically attract salmon on the River Tweed. This yellow-green and black one is called the Posh Tosh, the creation of Iain Wilson of the Borders Gunroom in St. Boswells. Almost guaranteed to catch a salmon. You'll love this gorgeous red, orange, yellow and blue one, it's called the Sir Richard. The pattern was first tied around 1850 for Captain Richard Waldie-Griffiths of Kelso, who caught a 39 pound salmon with the fly on Tweed in November 1885."

"Sir Richard? Does my father know about this?"

"He does indeed. I gifted him several for Christmas and asked if he preferred I now address him as Sir Richard."

"Your knowledge is astounding. If you're trying to impress me, Peter, you've succeeded," she laughed. "What lovely feather beauty have you chosen for my line?"

"Ahhhh, for you, my fair lass, I've tied on the Eternal Optimist," he said.

"A perfect name for my less than stellar fly fishing ability."

"Not at all, it's the exact right fly for spring fishing when the Tweed is running a bit high. See the black and dirty green goat hair wing pattern," he said showing her the fly. "It was originally tied a long, long time ago to emulate the killing qualities of the Yellow Belly Devon minnows."

Peter gathered up their belongings and they walked toward the river, passing grazing sheep here and there. Wearing waders and boots they didn't have to be too careful about where they stepped. A fine mist hovered over the water, creating a mystical aura of other-worldliness. Who knew such contentment could be found clomping along a pasture holding the hand of the young man she adored?

The morning passed with Peter catching three large salmon and Sarah catching none. Though her fly had several bites, not one of the fish stayed on. If she were to be honest, simply being outside in nature, standing knee deep in the stream was satisfying all on its own. Watching Peter expertly cast his long line over his head, then gently guide it to land tenderly on the water with hardly a ripple, was a thing of beauty. His feathered fly perfectly resembled an insect touching down and sinking just enough below the surface to fool a fish into snapping it up. No wonder he caught fish and she only got bites. Her technique was far clumsier and something she was determined to correct. The next half hour was spent practicing her casting over and over, trying to copy precisely what Peter was doing.

"I've got one on!" she shouted, slowly reeling in the line and trying to hear all the instructions Peter was shouting back.

"That's it, keep the tip up, let him run out a bit to tire him. Good, good. You're doing great. Try to keep him from going behind that rock. That's it…now bring him in."

In a jiffy, Peter was beside her with the net, scooping up a nice, large fish. Sarah couldn't stop smiling. They really were a good team.

"Bravo!" Peter said proudly.

"Would it be all right if we let him go?" she asked. "He gave me such a thrill, but I'd like to think of him swimming around with his pals. Do you mind terribly?"

"Not at all. He will report back to the others that he was magnificently caught by a beautiful dark haired lass who spared his life. Off you go lad, live well," he said, releasing the salmon back into the water. "I'm starving and you must be famished. I didn't leave you much time for breakfast. There's a thermos of hot tea and a few scones in my pack, and a fishing hut around the next bend where we can sit for a bit. Actually, there is something important I need to discuss with you."

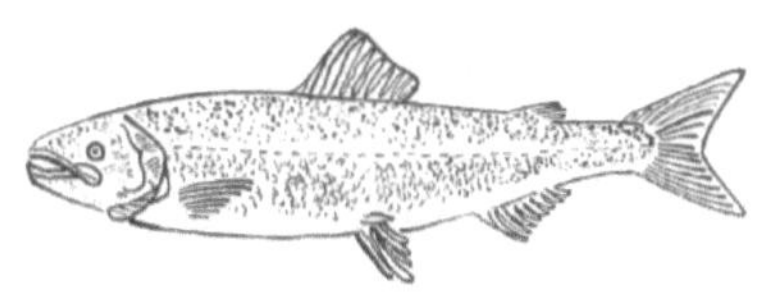

Chapter Thirty-six

PETER:

The Fishing Hut

The fishing hut had been his grandfather's idea. Basically one room with a door, a window and a tiny porch with a roof overhang. Inside were a few wooden chairs along with a small table and a very old worn broom. All the amenities a fisherman could ask for.

Walking across the pasture toward the hut, Peter kept mentally rehearsing what he wanted to say to Sarah. If he presented his plan right she might understand and not get angry. If not, she might storm home in her waders and not speak to him again. He had made some thickheaded choices in the past and didn't want to go down that path again, but this seemed to make sense and frankly, he was excited about it. However, if he acted too excited, that might put her off as well. Women could be quite complicated.

"This is really cute," Sarah said as they approached the hut. "I don't remember seeing it before."

"My grandfather built it as a refuge in case someone got caught in the rain whilst fishing. It has come in handy more than once," he said as they walked through the door.

"Not much in the way of a woman's touch, that's for sure," she laughed, looking around at the rudimentary contents.

"Not many good-looking fisher-ladies visit. We do sweep out the spiders and dead mice occasionally, so you've no worries."

Tea was poured and scones shared as they sat at the small wooden table. Everything felt so harmonious between them, he considered not even bringing up the subject.

"Was there something you wanted to talk about?" she asked, wiping away the last crumb from her mouth.

"Actually, yes," he paused before continuing. "Recently, my mum told me she and her friend, Lydia Mathews, had plans to open two small art galleries–one in Edinburgh on Victoria Street, if they can secure the lease, and possibly later on, another one in Oxford, about an hour and a half from London."

"I know where Oxford is, remember I went to Cambridge," she said smiling.

"Of course, silly me," he said taking a sip of the now-tepid tea. "Anyway, they are very keen on the gallery idea and ready to make the final commitment to doing it."

"What a great idea. Your mum is awfully artistic and enjoys being busy so it sounds like an ideal arrangement. Do you know Lydia Mathews well?"

"Yes, she previously worked in an Edinburgh gallery that once carried a few of my paintings," he answered.

"What could be better than that? She has experience running a gallery and is a friend of your mum's."

He hesitated searching for the right words. Finally, after his face twisted this way and that, he spoke.

"Well, here's the situation. They want my paintings to be the cornerstone in the galleries. I would be the featured artist, with a small rotation of art by others on a regular schedule. If it all goes well, in a year or two they would make me a third partner in the gallery."

She jumped up spontaneously and hugged him, her enthusiasm filling the room.

"I knew you were brilliant! This is amazing news! I am so proud of you," she gushed.

He allowed himself a few moments to relish her fervour as he was fairly sure it would be short-lived.

"Mum's thought is to open the Edinburgh gallery just before the Festival in August to take advantage of all the tourists visiting. They would hold off on the Oxford gallery to see how well this one does."

"That makes perfect sense," she said, still caught up in the whole idea.

"So…you see, I have five oil paintings in storage from before my Italian fiasco and the gallery would need at least twelve," he said, finishing his scone. "While I was in Italy I spent time learning new watercolor techniques and I've been experimenting with them the last few months, mostly thinking it would be appropriate for your book. As it happens, watercolors would be perfect for the gallery because it shows my versatility as an artist."

"And they dry much faster than oil paintings. That is an outstanding idea," Sarah added.

" You are already ahead of me," he hesitated. "It's a lot to think about and I'm concerned I won't be able to deliver."

"Once you are inspired, I'm sure you will be working day and night."

"That's what I'm hoping," he said, "But there is more."

Sarah didn't say anything, just watched him as he searched for what to say. He appreciated her patience and how she didn't quiz him, but quietly waited.

"The only way I can see this working is for me to go away for a few months and dedicate myself only to painting. A friend of my father's offered his retreat near Mallaig in the west Highlands. It's very close to the inner Hebrides Islands, Skye, Iona, Colonsay, Tiree, Jura, Staffa, Islay–you get the idea. I would use the place in Mallaig as a home base and visit the different places for inspiration and I wouldn't really be gone all that long…" he realizing he was talking far too fast in order to get it all in before she reacted.

He stopped because he ran out of breath, and by looking at her face, could tell the full impact had not hit her yet.

"Am I missing something?" she asked. "You are talking a mile a minute and acting a bit twitchy."

"No. Well, yes. Kind of. I think so."

"Well, that clarifies it," she laughed.

"Sarah, what it means is that I will not be able to do the art for your book for quite awhile."

"Oh," she said, her shoulders slumping and smile fading.

The weight of what he said clearly hit her.

"I haven't given my Mum an answer yet because I wanted us to talk about it first. This book is so important to you and it feels as though I am minimizing that by postponing my part. Nothing could be further from the truth. Working together has been our dream and I don't want to disappoint you. Just say the word and I will decline the gallery offer."

She didn't saying anything, just stared at him, her eyes looking dangerously full of tears. It took all his willpower to not hold her close and comfort both their broken hearts. After what seemed an eternity, the love of his life finally spoke.

"Peter, we have been through a lot in the past six years, but never, ever…"

He braced for the worst, visibly wincing.

"…ever have I been more proud of you or loved you more. Yes, my book is very important to me and creating it together is something we both look forward to. One of the benefits of writing a children's book is there is no time limit or expiration date. Both the book and its writer are happy to wait for you. In fact, it might give me time to edit and refine the words so it will be ready for you. Your sensitivity to spare my feelings and include me in your decision means everything. But Peter, my talented, creative, wonderful boyfriend, this is your time to shine. I am absolutely, completely thrilled. It doesn't take much to realize what an extraordinary opportunity has been offered. Of course, tell your mum a resounding *yes!*"

The huge breath he had been holding was released and he tightly hugged this marvelous woman who stood before him. What did he ever do to deserve her? Everything was right in his world. They sat for quite a while, bouncing questions and answers back and forth. They both agreed communicating by letter while he was away would be an interesting return to the beginning of their relationship. It was hard to believe the simple act of leaving a note hidden in the wall in front of his house in Edinburgh had brought them to this place.

"How soon do you leave?" she asked, packing up their thermos and cups.

"Next week, if all goes well. I will need to collect sufficient art supplies, paint, canvases and such, and confirm the accommodation. Mum is concerned I have proper clothes," he laughed. "Sometimes I think she forgets I am nearly twenty-six."

They walked across the field as little lambs gamboled together never far from their mothers. Peter was full of high spirits, yet if he were to be totally honest, there was a small nagging fear that he would make a mess of this opportunity like he did in Italy.

"I promise I won't let you down," he said suddenly to a surprised Sarah.

As though reading his mind, she took his hand and looked straight into his eyes.

"This is not Italy, Peter. I believe in you."

Enough said.

Chapter Thirty-seven

RICHARD:

A Look Through the Window

He stood at the long French window watching Sarah and Peter walk hand in hand toward the house. Laughter came easily and the bond between them was obvious. There was much to like about the young artist. He was kind, honesty, respectful, close to his family, and most importantly, absolutely adores Sarah. What's not to like? If there was one nagging issue that bothered Richard, it was how Peter would be able to support Sarah should they marry. While his daughter would inherit well, it was important her husband be able to provide for her. You never know what might happen.

"A man should be ready to support his wife," he said out loud to no one.

Turning back toward his desk, he was startled to see Liam standing in the doorway.

"Is this a private conversation or can anyone join?" his nephew teased.

"You are just the person I wanted to see," Richard laughed. "Come in, sit down. I was just musing about young love."

"Musing about Sarah or yourself?" Liam asked, still amused.

"Aren't you cheeky this morning? Sarah, of course. I'm hardly young."

"If you say so."

"I know you are about to head back to Shetland," Richard said, abruptly changing the subject. "When do you leave?"

"Early tomorrow morning. It's a four hour train to Inverness, late afternoon flight to Shetland, then home to my expecting wife."

"Expectant and expecting! When is the new bairn to arrive?"

"In a few weeks. Mairi is a wee bit anxious for me to be back in time."

"Understandable," he said. "If you are free for the rest of today, there are a few appointments I would appreciate you attending with me. Have I mentioned Daniel Roberts to you?"

"Aye, he's the gentleman Ambassador Stevens suggested. The Monuments Man?"

"Yes. He is coming for lunch today and I thought between us we could tell him all we know about what transpired. Mr. Roberts is quite interested in recovering the missing vase. Apparently, Frederick isn't talking, and is acting rather strange and mentally unbalanced."

"One wonders if Frederick is acting disturbed or if he really is disturbed. He's a slippery character, that one. No telling what he could have done with it."

"I won't argue with that. In any case, Mr. Roberts said he had a few ideas he wanted to share and was hoping to have a look around Leigheas."

"Sounds promising. Along those lines, I've spoken with Simon Cavanagh at the antique shop and he explained most of their inventory is found either at auctions or from individuals bringing objects directly to the shop to sell. Apparently, it's the same for most of the antique dealers in the area. He is in the process of contacting everyone he can think of from the Highlands to London to be on the lookout for the stolen items."

"Good, good. The Cavanagh's are a delightful family, and very old friends of Seaneen's. I'm grateful for their help. We must remember to tell Mr. Roberts of their involvement."

"Absolutely," Liam answered, making notes in his pad.

"Then, at four o'clock DI Lawson will arrive to interview Kaitlyn. I think it would be helpful for both of us to be there."

"I'm amazed you've been able to hold him off this long," Liam said. "Usually they want information as quickly as possible."

"I'd love to take credit, however it was Dr. McDonald who was the fierce bulldog. He was insistent no one cause her any distress.

The good news is she is recovering far faster than the doctor expected."

"And the bad news is that means she will be leaving Leigheas soon?"

"Yes," Richard answered sadly. "I'm afraid so."

"While it is none of my business, it doesn't take a genius to see how you feel about the lass."

"Is it that apparent?" he asked sheepishly. "I suppose there is no point denying it. I will miss seeing her every day."

"Have you told her of your feelings?" Liam asked.

"Dr. McDonald said in no uncertain terms to avoid any topic that might cause her stress. So, no, I haven't actually said anything, but I have visited her every moment I was allowed."

"Oh, Uncle Richard, for one so smart you can certainly be a dunce cap. Telling Kaitlyn you are keen on her would hardly be distressing. In fact, it might just be the proper medicine she needs. You've only a few days before she leaves."

"It's not that simple," Richard said, reflecting on the scene at the train station on New Year's Day. The sting of that rejection had not dimmed much.

"I've spoken out of turn," Liam said. "Matters of the heart are terribly personal and I've no business poking my nose in. Sorry."

"Liam, you are family. If you can't poke your nose in, who can? There is much truth in what you say and I will ponder it. On another note, did you have a chance to review the letters from the gentlemen who want to visit Leigheas this spring?"

"I have," Liam said, shuffling a small stack of papers. "Of the lot, there were three or four that seemed most interesting."

"Brilliant, thank you. Normally I do the choosing, but with everything going on I thought it best to have you and Seaneen share your thoughts. I'll compare our choices and see who we come up with."

"Happy to be of service," Liam said, with a casual salute.

"Honestly, not sure what I would have done without you. The past days have stretched me to my limit and your help has been invaluable. Not everyone grasps the complexity of running this place.

You have a marvelous ability to respond positively to every situation. I'm quite sorry to see you leave, but understand your heart is in Shetland with your, or should I say *our*, family."

"Interesting you mention that. I've been thinking about something I want to run by you, though I should really speak with my Shetland family first. Since I've been here…"

The sharp ring of the telephone ended their conversation.

"Hello. This is Leigheas," Richard said. "Good morning, Judge Cumberman."

He looked over at Liam, with an odd expression.

"Of course you are welcome to visit. I know how concerned you and Mrs. Cumberman have been. We are a bit tied up today, but why don't I see if tomorrow is agreeable? I will check with Kaitlyn and the doctor and ring you back. She is still a little weak, but improving every day."

Liam watched his uncle's eyebrows furrow.

"Well, I will certainly inquire if bringing your five year old grandson from Nepal would meet with the doctor's approval. Yes, I can understand he is quite attached to her. Yes, I will ring you back shortly. Good-bye, Judge."

KAITLYN:

Your Shoes Are Quite Nice

The sweet smell of heather, or *ling* as it is called in Scotland, surrounded her. Try as she might, she couldn't breathe deeply enough to capture the full fragrance. Far away in the distance was a wee cottage with a thatched roof set amongst trees with a wisp of smoke curling up from the chimney. Was that her grandmother she saw by the door waving to her?

The perfect scene began to fade way into a grey mist until it was gone. She felt something gently touch her cheek, and blinked her eyes open several times before she could clearly see Richard leaning in close.

"I'm so sorry to wake you," he said softly. "You were breathing deeply and seemed so content."

"The heather was beautiful and my grandmother was there," Kaitlyn said wistfully, "but it must have been a dream. She's been gone for ages."

Only then did she become aware that Richard was holding her hand. The wingback chair she had fallen asleep in had become dreadfully uncomfortable, but she didn't dare move. His warm hand on hers brought a flutter to her heart. Richard's daily habit of joining her for lunch was the highlight in her long days of near isolation. He was cheerful and funny and the perfect gentleman, though she couldn't help but feel there was a slight aloofness. Yet, here he was standing close, still holding her hand.

"I missed our lunch together today," he said. "Seaneen said she enjoyed her time with you in my absence."

"She is such a dear. James even popped in for a few minutes. Tell me about your visit with the Monuments Man? Will he be able to help you?" she asked, trying desperately not to move a muscle lest he release her hand.

"The short answer is yes, I believe so. He suggested a theory that could prove amazing if it holds up. There was much he didn't divulge as his investigation must be carefully handled. I'm sorry you didn't have a chance to meet him. His tales of tracking down art treasures after the war are intriguing."

"Honestly, I had never heard of them until you mentioned it." she said with a sigh. "Your brilliant daughter filled me in a bit about their history and how brave they were."

"Speaking of bravery, today is your meeting with DI Lawson. Are you feeling up to it? I'm not sure I can hold him off much longer. They are quite anxious to get your statement in order to proceed with prosecuting Frederick."

Simply hearing his name caused her head to ache. The last thing she wanted to do was relive the nightmare, or what she could remember of it. Her silence caused Richard to move his hand away. She looked up to his handsome face as her tears streamed down her cheeks. Without hesitation he tenderly cupped her chin in his hand.

"Oh, please don't cry. We will postpone the meeting. Nothing is worth upsetting you," he said. "You are all that matters."

This, of course, caused her tears to fall even more which had nothing to do with Frederick Hutton and everything to do with Richard Duncan. She adored him and had treated him so badly, yet here he was openly caring for her. Maybe all was not lost. He dabbed her wet cheeks with his white handkerchief, and the tears slowed until all that was left was an unladylike sniffle. She assured him she was ready to meet with the DI, and he promised to stay close by her side. They agreed she would come downstairs in half an hour, giving Richard and Liam a few minutes alone with DI Lawson, who was due to arrive anytime. Before leaving, he gingerly kissed the top of her head and stroked her cheek lovingly with his warm hand.

"I nearly forgot to tell you, Judge Cumberman called and wondered if you were up to seeing he and his wife tomorrow, and something about bringing their five year old grandson from Nepal who misses you terribly."

She couldn't hide the smile that overtook her face.

"Yes, of course, that would be lovely. Sanni is a delightful boy, I'm sure he will enchant you."

"Then, that is settled. I'll make the arrangements," Richard said, before closing the door behind him.

She couldn't help but be elated about seeing Sanni, yet wondered how Richard would feel meeting the son of her former love? *M'anam*, oh, my soul, she thought in Scottish.

Sitting by the pleasant fire in the small reception room, Kaitlyn felt a nervous shiver run down her spine. There was comfort looking out the window to the peaceful garden where the snowdrop flowers were in full bloom and the mighty crocus's were pushing up through the warming earth. Life truly was a cycle, she thought philosophically. This brought a smile, realizing perhaps she had been alone too much lately and it was time she rejoin the world. The door opened and Richard ushered in two policemen, with Liam, Sarah and Seaneen following behind.

"Kaitlyn, this is DI Alex Lawson and DC John Murphy. They have been involved with the case since Frederick's fateful visit," Richard said. "Gentlemen, please meet Kaitlyn Turning."

She could tell DI Lawson was obviously the one in charge. He was a thin man, average height, with dark hair beginning to grey at the temples, and he asked all the questions. The other officer, DC Murphy, was a large man, with ginger hair, dressed in a heavy wool tweed suit and Loake leather shoes. Such elegant footwear for the one who took all the notes and called DI Lawson, '*Boss.*'

For the next hour she relived the harrowing time with Frederick from beginning to end. Much to her surprise, retelling the event wasn't nearly as emotional as she expected, a bit like narrating someone else's story. After a few questions to the others in the room, DI Lawson rose from his seat and extended his hand toward her.

"Miss Turning, you have been an invaluable help. Your information should give us what we need to prosecute Mr. Hutton to the fullest extent. John, I'll meet you at the car."

Richard led the way toward the front door, having a quiet conversation with DI Lawson about the stolen items and Frederick's future.

DC Murphy shook her hand as well, "You're a mighty brave lass. We will raise our glasses to you in the pub tonight. Best o' luck to you."

"Thank you, Mr. Murphy, and by the way, your shoes are quite nice."

The large man beamed and left the room with a spring in his step.

"Oh, Kaitlyn," Sarah laughed, "it's so good to have to back! I've missed your humor. I'm off to write, but let's visit soon."

Seaneen and Liam took their leave as well, citing work to be done. Dr. McDonald came in as they left and was pleased to see his patient looking so well. She admitted having the police interview over was a huge relief. With a quick check of her vitals, he suggested she could get on with her life anytime she was ready.

"I'm confident you are out of the woods and everything is healing just as it should. Your bandages can come off in three weeks and any doctor can attend to that. If something should arise, you may always call me." The doctor stood before her for a moment before speaking again. "You've had quite an ordeal and come through it remarkably well. It must feel like a new beginning in some ways. I'm sure you must be anxious to return home, but please do take care of yourself."

She was left all alone and by now the fire had dwindled to ashes. Her mind rolled around the concept of going home. Where was home? Was it at the Cumberman's in London? Returning to their house and assuming her familiar duties seemed overwhelming. The thought crossed her mind that maybe they were coming to

Leigheas to give her the sack. Forty-two years old and no real home to call her own. Where did she belong? Maggie, the cocker spaniel, snuck through the door that had been left ajar and sat down close to Kaitlyn.

"Even you know where you belong, Maggie."

The dog looked up with big brown eyes and wagged her little stump of a tail.

Chapter Thirty-nine

RICHARD:

Here Comes the Judge

It was mid-afternoon when the Cumberman's arrived by taxi from Waverley train station. Yesterday had been quite long for Kaitlyn, and Richard wondered if she might be worn out, but quite the contrary. She was animated, cheerful and eagerly anticipating her visitors. They must feel like family after all the years she's spent with them. No doubt she was anxious to return to London and her work. A sad thought hit him—it would be wise to prepare himself for Kaitlyn leaving and rejoining her old life.

Judge Cumberman exited the taxi first. He was a tall, imposing man with a full head of white hair, looking every bit as formidable as his reputation. By contrast, his wife, Miriam, was charming, petite and rail thin. Holding her hand was a handsome, dark haired little boy gazing up at him with most unusual green eyes.

Richard led the visitors from the driveway into the house, settling in the more formal reception room. It was a lovely space with one entire wall being all windows looking out onto the meadow beyond. In the center of the room was an antique round table with claw feet, and a large vase of colorful fresh flowers. The joy of having your own greenhouse, Richard thought to himself. A large fireplace at the end of the room was unlit given the moderate temperature of the day. The guests chose to sit all together on the large leather Chesterfield sofa opposite a pair of wingback chairs. After a conversation about their train ride and how they hadn't been to Edinburgh in ages, an awkward silence filled the room. Kaitlyn had yet to come downstairs, and he knew Seaneen would be in the kitchen arranging a special tea service. Judge Cumberman cleared his throat to speak.

189

"May I introduce my grandson, Sanani Cumberman," the judge said. "Sanani, this is Mr. Richard Duncan. He is a good friend of our Kaitlyn's."

With the mention of Kaitlyn's name, the boy's face lit up with a big smile. A small hand was extended for Richard to shake.

"It is very nice to meet you, Sanani."

"You may call me Sanni, Sir Richard Duncan," the little boy said earnestly, "if you are a friend of Miss Kaitlyn's, that is."

Before he could answer, Kaitlyn appeared and Sanni ran to her without hesitation. There were warm embraces from Miriam and Judge Cumberman, who helped her sit on the sofa next to them. Before long, Sanni was in her lap, and they were all talking a mile a minute about things going on in their London world. It didn't take much to see the affection between them was genuine. Richard had to admit he felt a bit left out and unnecessary. This was a part of Kaitlyn's life he knew little about.

Tea trays were brought in carried by Seaneen and Sarah, and another round of introductions took place. He marveled how comfortable his daughter was meeting these people and enjoying their company. Yet, he stood apart feeling like an outsider looking in.

'Would you like to visit the stables, Sanni, and see the horses?" Sarah asked. "I have a very special friend there named Henry and he has all sorts of small animals I'm quite sure he would like to show you."

"Yes, thank you, I would like that very much," Sanni said. "Would it be all right, Grandmother? Grandfather?"

"That is a splendid idea," Judge Cumberman said. "Richard, perhaps you could show me the stables as well and we will leave the ladies to have a chin-wag?"

"My pleasure," Richard said.

Watching Sarah and Sanni skip across the meadow holding hands and twirling around gave Richard a slight idea of what a good mother she would be…someday. Time was passing far too quickly, and he wasn't ready to be a grandfather just yet. Judge Cumberman broke his reverie.

"I am very glad to meet you in person, Richard. Miriam has been close to Kaitlyn for many years now and speaks very highly of you. Plus, I still have a few friends in the police realm, and secretly, they are a bit in awe of you apprehending Frederick Hutton on your own. You're rather a legend."

"I certainly didn't do it alone, Judge," Richard said, a little embarrassed. "There were several of us working together, plus a fair amount of luck and a lot of prayer. Kaitlyn's life depended on it."

They walked together quietly as the late afternoon sun warmed them.

"You know, it has been a while since I've been on the judicial bench. I'd prefer you use my given name, Trevor. Sometimes, being Judge Cumberman seems like a life time ago. Another world," he mused.

"We have that in common. It seems like years ago that I was spending my days with endless matters to be resolved in the Foreign Service. It was a wonderful career, but life feels much more fulfilling now."

Trevor Cumberman motioned toward Sanni, as the little boy and Sarah neared the stables. "That lad has changed our lives. Don't get me wrong, we are thrilled to have him, but things are certainly more, shall we say, complicated now."

Richard wasn't sure how to respond to such an intimate disclosure and let it drift away. He had a feeling more was to come.

"I know you are very close to Kaitlyn. May I ask you a question?"

"You may," Richard responded, slightly unnerved by this line of conversation.

"I, well actually we, were wondering if you knew Kaitlyn's future plans once the doctor releases her from his care? It's not our business, of course, but you two..."

"I'm afraid I don't know her plans," Richard interrupted. "She has been through quite a traumatic situation and we have given her space to figure it out."

He knew his answer came out more abrupt than was polite, but of all topics he was not willing to discuss it was his relationship with Kaitlyn.

"Yes, yes. It's just we have a family issue, but we will sort it out. Forgive me for being so forward," Judge Cumberman said, then changed his tone. "Now, tell me about Leigheas. It is a magnificent property, and from what I hear you open it up every spring and summer to a small number of gentlemen who need to do some soul searching."

The remainder of their walk to the stables was spent talking pleasantly about many things other than the lovely Miss Turning. The old stone stable building was a large abbreviated 'L' shape with stalls on either side of a wide center aisle and the tack room on the short side.

"We used to keep six horses, but the past few years we found four is sufficient. This is Winston, Sarah's horse," Richard said, passing the chestnut gelding, "and this is Dasher."

"What a beautiful animal," Judge Cumberman exclaimed, stopping to admire the large stallion.

"Thank you, he is my newest horse. A lovely nature about him, but always ready to kick up his heels. I don't often let our guests ride him as he can be a handful."

By the time they got to Henry's Zoo, the two boys were fast friends. Sanni listened intently to everything Little Henry was telling him about a tiny dormouse. Sarah stood by the stall door watching with amusement.

"He looks quite at home here," the judge said quietly.

"You would think they've been friends forever," Sarah said. "Sometimes Little Henry can be shy with new people. Your Sanni is an endearing boy."

"I quite agree. He is all we have of our deceased son, Nigel. He was only brought to us recently, and what a gift he is."

Suddenly, all the pieces fit together. Richard realized for the first time that this little boy with the unusual green eyes was the child of Kaitlyn's former love. How stupid of him not to figure that out until now. No wonder she was so excited about seeing him and the family. Regardless of how much he cared for Kaitlyn, there was no way he could compete with a memory come to life in the eyes of a child. His head began to pound with this revelation.

It was late afternoon when the black taxi pulled up in front of the house right on time. With a four hour train ride from Edinburgh to London's King Cross station ahead of them, it meant the Cumberman family wouldn't arrive home until late that night. Their leave-taking lasted at least twenty minutes, with Sanni holding tight to Kaitlyn, telling her how much he missed her. Richard stood back from the group, not wanting to be in the way. Liam's words echoed in his brain, '*Have you told her of your feelings?*' He gazed at the Scottish woman who had opened his heart. Maybe it wasn't too late.

"So, we will see you in London in a few weeks," Judge Trevor Cumberman said to Kaitlyn, as he was the last to get in the taxi.

"You will," she answered happily.

Then again, maybe it was too late.

Chapter Forty

PETER:

Greetings from Mallaig

Dear Sarah,

Shakespeare got it all wrong. 'Parting is such sweet sorrow' is rubbish. There was nothing sweet about parting from you, and though I have only been in Mallaig for two days, I miss you already. It is late at night now and seemed like a good time to write, pretending we are sitting together having a conversation.

My accommodation is a small artist's bothy on the shores of a sea harbor. The front window faces the Isle of Skye across the Sound of Sleat. Behind the bothy is a dense woodland with an amazing amount of wildlife. Between the splendid landscapes and the charm of the small fishing village, I should have plenty of inspiration to start painting. Mallaig's location will be handy for short trips to the Hebrides islands and other nearby villages. All said, so far, so good. If only you were closer.

It was surprising how full the railway cars were on the journey here. This meant I had scant room to stow all of my art supplies and had to pile them around my seat. One downfall of living in a remote village is the inability to pop down to a shop and buy things I need. By luck, I found a seat by the window and enjoyed the passing Highland scenery. Feeling the clickity clack of the wheels on the rails was hypnotizing, however a cigar-smoking, Highland gentleman in a kilt sat across from me and talked non-stop. He was intent on telling me his clan's story–every detail of every battle. After several hours he finally ran out of tales and went to sleep. I settled in and reminisced about the last time I was on a train through this part of Scotland. It must have been at least twenty years ago on a trip with my grandparents. That was quite a big adventure for a little lad, and I remember it seemed like a long, never-ending journey. Surprise–it hasn't changed much! There must be at least twelve station stops along the way, maybe more. Towns and little villages such as Arrochar, Ardlui, Crainlarich, and Bridge of Orchy, are only a few. Once the railway begins to climb to higher ground, there is the hamlet of Corrour at nearly 1,400 feet above sea level, then Roy Bridge, Spean Bridge, Fort William and the larger town of Corpach. The most noteworthy part of the trip is Glenfinnan, made famous by a Jacobite uprising in the 1700s. There is a fantastic viaduct that is one hundred feet above the valley below, built entirely of concrete arches. A steam train follows the curving viaduct track in the most astounding way, delivering passengers to Mallaig. One day I must bring you here.

Tomorrow I start painting, should weather permit. There are several spots that appear to be ideal and I'm looking forward to unleashing my creativity. Yesterday was spent doing a few sketches and getting organized. I am quite enthused about it all.

How is your book coming along? I don't think I've told you how proud I am of you and your writing. You have a gift of weaving words together and conveying feelings beautifully. I've found your writing thought-provoking, humorous, and always striking the right emotional note. Would it be possible for you to send me some of your latest pages? That would give me a direction to think about in terms of illustrations.

My address is on the envelope and I look forward to receiving letters from you with all of the news. Please watch out for yourself and know I adore you. My best to everyone.

Yours forever,

Peter

After reading the letter twice and smiling each time, Sarah felt the warmth of his love through the pages. When they first began writing each other years ago, she would wait until she was alone in her room to devour his words and today was no different. Her first instinct was to begin a return letter immediately, but as it was quite late decided it would wait until tomorrow.

Life at Leigheas had become increasingly busy. The gentlemen guests were due to arrive soon, and lots of activity surrounded their visit. Cottages to be cleaned, food to be ordered, and menus to plan. It was also the time when maintenance of the estate shifted into high gear and the animals needed special attention. A number of sheep had already brought forth little lambs, and the Highland cows were due to calve before long. Springtime also meant the salmon run was peaking and it was not unusual to see her father join Colin, their fishing guide, throwing out a line to snag a large wild fish on the Tweed.

Longer days brought a welcome renewal of spirit with its rhythm and flow, a sort of exciting anticipation of things to come. For Sarah, this season held the hopeful expectation that '*the end*' was in sight for her book

Chapter Forty-one

THOMAS TURNING:

Back to the Bookshop

Much to Thomas's surprise, Jacob Silvers, his young employee, had done a fine job keeping Turning Pages Book Shoppe in order during Kaitlyn's recovery. There was comfort realizing the owner could be away and all was in capable hands. Thomas Turning felt sure he had underestimated the young man and made a mental note to give him more responsibility and perhaps a pay raise in the near future. It was good to be back surrounded by the aroma of old books and chatting with customers. This was where he belonged. For the moment, all was right in his world. A feeling of satisfaction was good for a man his age.

"Mr. Turning, an order of books arrived a few days ago," Jacob said. "Would you like me to unpack and inventory them in the back, or stay out front with customers?"

"Why don't you stay here and watch for Professor Newton. I've set aside two books he requested and added a third I thought he may find interesting."

"I don't suppose his first name is Sir Isaac?" Jacob quipped.

"You are a funny lad. Nor is it Fig" Thomas said with a laugh. "I believe his name is Nicholas. I'll unpack the books and write the titles in the ledger. It's good to keep my mind sharp. You know, there was a time when I knew the title of every book we carried, but not so much anymore. A written list is a wee bit helpful to a foggy old man."

Thomas enjoyed seeing the young man laugh.

A middle-aged woman approached the desk clutching a copy of Agatha Christie's *The Murder of Roger Ackroyd.* It was always hard for Thomas not to engage a new patron, especially regarding such a controversial novel. Sometimes he couldn't help himself.

"Are you a reader of Agatha Christie?" he asked.

"Oh yes," she exclaimed, "Though I'm embarrassed to say I've only recently discovered her books. I'd never seen this one."

"It is the fourth in her detective Hercule Poirot series and quite unlike any of the others. It has been cause for interesting debates over the years. You'll find it full of elegant twists that broke all the rules of traditional mysteries. I'll stop there before I say too much and spoil it."

"Not in the least, now I am seriously intrigued. Thank you for sharing," she said. "I notice you have more of Christie's books. I'll be back and you can tell me more."

"That would be lovely. I look forward to it," he said, as Jacob handed her the book wrapped in brown Kraft paper tied with string.

After the woman left and the dinging of the bell over the door echoed away, Jacob shook his head in amazement.

"Do you have a tale about every single book in this shop? And don't try to bamboozle me that you are a foggy old man. You're sharp as a tack, Mr. Turning."

"You flatter me, lad," Thomas said, with more pleasure than he let on. "I'll be in the back if you need me."

Once again, he was reminded how happy and content he was to own a shop in Edinburgh and be surrounded by interesting people and fascinating books. He liked both equally. He'd resumed his well-practiced routine of opening the shop in the morning, and often inviting a customer to sit in the back of the store by the little fireplace for a cup of tea. As the afternoon went on, he would close up early or let Jacob work the last few hours alone, if he grew weary. Yes, life was full and complete and he was fairly content. Thanks to the grace and generosity of Richard Duncan, his beloved Kaitlyn was safe and recovering. He had to admit, it crossed his mind that perhaps his daughter might want to live with him once she felt better, but he hadn't mentioned it for fear of putting pressure on her. After all she had been through, she would need time to sort things. How he would relish having her around, sharing their days together.

Nothing would please him more, but if she chose to return to her life with the Cumbermans, then better she fly free–even if it meant living four hundred miles away in London.

Chapter Forty-two

RICHARD:

What Are You Afraid Of?

"Meara, Brennan, I need you to give all the cottages a cleaning today and stock the cupboards with the essentials. The three gentlemen will be arriving in two days and we must be ready," Seaneen instructed the two housekeepers.

"With only three guests you want us to do up all five cottages?" Brennan, the younger sister asked.

"Of course she does, you silly goose," Meara admonished her. "What if one of the guests doesn't care for Bobby Burns?"

"How can you not like Bobby Burns? That is just…un-Scottish!"

"You can't go around calling people un-Scottish because they don't like a certain author, now can you?" Meara asked.

"Well, I can. He was a pure dead brilliant Scottish poet, and that's the truth," Brennan exclaimed.

"Girls! Miss Sarah and I chose the themes for each cottage to make them unique," Seaneen said. "Each was designed around a famous Scottish author—Bobby Burns, Sir Walter Scott, J.M. Barrie, Kenneth Grahame and Sir Arthur Conan Doyle. In six years, we've yet to have a complaint about an assigned cottage or the author for which it is named. Now, best you get along and get your work done—all five cottages."

"Yes, ma'am," they answered in unison and headed out the back door of the kitchen, still arguing the merits of Bobby Burns.

Listening to the banter amused Richard, but weightier things were on his mind at the moment. Two cups of tea and half an hour of pondering at the kitchen table hadn't brought any answer to his

200

dilemma. James came bursting in, full of good cheer and a hug for his wife.

"Hello, Richard," he said. "Isn't it a lovely spring day? The snowdrop flowers are covering the ground and daffodils can't be far behind."

Not feeling the vicar's enthusiasm, he managed a faint smile and let that suffice. He felt them both looking at him, no doubt waiting for an explanation about his sour mood. None was forthcoming. After a moment, James went on talking about his plans for the day.

"The latch on the door of the chapel has come loose and I believe I'll have a go at repairing it. A few other things need tending while I'm there."

"Richard, maybe you could lend James a hand?" Seaneen asked.

"Of course, I'm happy to," he said, laying his newspaper aside.

Given his current state of mind, he might as well get some fresh air. James found a few tools in the butler's pantry and the two men set out across the meadow towards the chapel.

"Is there something on your mind, James?" Richard asked, sensing there was more to this than met the eye. "I can't remember a time when you have ever requested my assistance to fix anything, not that I'm much help in any case,"

"For the record, Seaneen suggested your help," the vicar said with a laugh. "She's a mite worried and thought perhaps you would share with me what seems to be the trouble."

"I appreciate her concern, and slightly devious method of putting us together, but I'm not sure anyone can share this burden."

"If I may be so bold, might it have to do with Kaitlyn leaving tomorrow?" James asked gently, then let the silence lay as they continued toward the chapel.

The impressive antique brass handle on the heavy wood door to Rosemary's Chapel was indeed coming loose. A screwdriver and pliers quickly did the trick, securing it back where it belonged, insuring the door wouldn't swing open in a ferocious wind.

Instinctively, without saying a word to each other, they went inside the little church and sat on one of the polished wooden pews.

Sunlight poured through the brilliantly colored stained glass windows and rested on the wooden floor. The large cross at the front was a meaningful place to set your sight and feel peace surround you.

"May I ask you a question?" Richard asked.

"Certainly," the vicar answered.

"How did you know Seaneen shared your feelings when you were courting her?"

"Ah, lad, I've learned you never really know what a woman is thinking," James said.

"But you went ahead anyway?" Richard asked.

"Yes, I did. What was my alternative? I knew I didn't want to spend what was left of my life without her. Though I must say it was a bit of a leap, and there was ample prayer involved as well."

Richard leaned forward, resting his crossed arms on his knees in quiet contemplation. One of the things he appreciated about Vicar James was how he knew when to speak and when to be silent.

"Can logic and emotion share the same thought? I don't know which path to follow: what I know intellectually or what my heart is feeling."

"What are you afraid of, lad?" James asked gently.

In the stillness that followed, Richard replayed the past months he'd known Kaitlyn in freeze frame flashes–meeting in the book shop, long telephone conversations, dancing at Seaneen's wedding…then his faux pas at the train station. He shook his head as though trying to erase that memory, but it was replaced by his terror of Frederick harming her. Then lifting her near-lifeless body into the Rover and the weeks of recovery. And now she was leaving.

"I'm afraid of rejection and I think I'm afraid I won't be enough for her. My fear is she will walk out of my life forever. I'm at a loss how to go forward. "

"Have you spoken to her?"

"I've imagined a hundred conversations, but can't find the courage to actually speak to her."

"I'm certainly no expert on women," James laughed, "but my question to you is this: what are your options? If you say nothing, she will leave and no doubt go on with her life and you will be left always wondering. On the other hand, should you choose to be vulnerable and tell her your feelings, it will go one way or the other. She will either graciously send you packing or fall lovingly into your arms. At least you will know and won't be spinning around in circles in endless speculation. In my years of ministry, I've found it's always best to go to the source for your answer."

Before he could respond, he felt James's warm hand on his back and saw him lower his head in prayer.

"Lord, we ask your guidance for Richard. Lead him in the direction you desire and give him the courage and assurance to know you go before him. Amen."

"And I say to myself, what a wonderful world," he sung under his breath. mimicking Louis Armstrong. *"Oh, yeah."*

There were so many blooming spring flowers on his walk back to the house. And how beautifully the birds were singing. How did he miss that earlier? Perhaps it was the glimmer of hope courtesy of James. Without a doubt, his number one priority today would be to spend time with Kaitlyn. James was absolutely spot on, he wouldn't know until he knew. His reverie was interrupted by Brennan running towards him from the house.

"Mr. Duncan, Mr. Duncan," she yelled, nearly breathless. "There is an important telephone call for you. Mrs. McAughterie, er, rather Mrs. Bradbury sent me to find you. Do hurry, it's Mr. Roberts."

"I'm hurrying, Brennan. Run ahead and tell Mrs. Bradbury I'm on my way," Richard said, quickening his step, but not following the young girl at an all out run.

"Mr. Roberts, I'm sorry to have kept you waiting. You have news?" Richard asked a little winded.

"Quite possibly. Can you meet me at the Clovensfords Hotel in an hour?"

There was a hesitancy before Richard answered. Every part of his being wanted to talk with Kaitlyn as soon as possible, however

Daniel Roberts was spending his personal time trying to locate the missing Chinese vase. He calculated it was only a little after noon and Clovenfords was just a few miles away. It shouldn't be a problem for him to be back by early evening at the latest and Kaitlyn wasn't leaving until tomorrow.

"Absolutely, I will be there," Richard answered.

"Fine, fine. I'll be in the restaurant. Bring several flashlights, wear your wellies and rain gear. We'll be taking a long walk and liable to get wet. See you shortly."

Locating the vase was deeply important, and it would certainly be an all out miracle if they were able to find it. How could Frederick have known its value or was it just dumb luck? A heavy sigh escaped Richard's lips. It seemed a visit with Kaitlyn would have to wait until he returned home.

Now, where did Seaneen put the flashlights, or torches, as they call them in Scotland?

RICHARD:

Oh Lord, Show Me the Way

Only a few hundred residents lived in the picturesque hamlet of Clovenford. The old hotel, built in 1750 was the main attraction, with an enormous statue of Sir Walter Scott standing proudly out front. In 1799, Scott was appointed sheriff of the town and wrote that the Clovensford Hotel was his *'favorite watering hole.'* High praise from one of Scotland's best-loved sons.

The village was in a remote location surrounded by rolling hills and massive banks of rhododendrons and azaleas. The closest town of any size was Galashiels, about four miles down the road. It was curious why Daniel Roberts had chosen Clovenford, in fact, why he was even in the Borders was a mystery. The vase couldn't possibly still be in Scotland, could it?

After lunch in the hotel dining room, Mr. Roberts brought out a rolled up map from his large canvas bag. He spread it across the table and Richard instantly recognized locations from England all the way up to Edinburgh. Undecipherable notes and marks were scribbled all over map.

"I've been tracking our friend Frederick from the time he left your house on New Year's, which you said was sometime between two and six in the morning. The next possible sighting was at Waverley Train Station sometime between eleven and noon."

"Yes, he was on Kaitlyn's train headed for London, which left about half past twelve," Richard said.

"I lost track of him for several weeks after that I'm afraid," Daniel said. "But got a break when I contacted several high-end auction houses. A consignment specialist remembered Frederick coming in with a story about inheriting a valuable Chinese vase he wanted to sell. The specialist explained it could be worth an enormous amount but he would need to see the item in order to determine authenticity, condition, market value and establish ownership. Frederick said he didn't have it with him and suddenly became very agitated. The specialist immediately felt something was off and tried to detain him long enough to get some information, like his name and address, but he said Frederick practically ran out of the auction house. Shortly after that a colleague of mine spotted him in a rough area of the city at a cheap rooming house."

Daniel pointed to a particularly seedy part of London on the map.

"This was just before he took Miss Turning," he continued, drawing a pencil line on the map to the Cumberman's estate. "Then we know they traveled by stolen car to Elibank Castle ruin where he deposited her. My instinct tells me Frederick kept the vase with him the entire time with the intent of selling it on the black market in a foreign country. He couldn't risk selling it legitimately."

"I suppose no one in an underground market would care where he got it or how he came to have it in his possession," Richard said

"Exactly, it's all about the money, not the morality."

"As you know, when we caught Frederick he didn't have the vase on him," Richard said.

"Nor was it in the stolen car he drove. I checked twice with the police," Daniel added. "Once he left Miss Turning in the ruin, I'm quite sure he hid it somewhere intending to retrieve it after securing your ransom money."

Daniel Roberts went back to the map, drawing a circle indicating a radius around the castle ruin. "I've made a list of possible places we should look."

On closer examination, Richard saw a handful of locations marked in heavy black ink.

"And we will be visiting each of them today?" Richard asked, keeping the hope alive that he would still have time to see Kaitlyn before the day ended.

"It should only take a few hours. There are a few places where we might need to be a little…sly in exploring."

"Sly meaning a little trespassing?" Richard asked.

"Only a little," Daniel Roberts answered with a smile. "Not to worry, my experience has taken me to far more difficult places. I've narrowed it down to five locations, thinking we could begin at the furthest east and work our way back west."

Typical of the Borders, rain was now steadily coming down making large puddles in the road, causing huge splashes when their car drove through them. The first stop was Abbotsford, the historic country house of writer Sir Walter Scott, located south of Tweedbank village. The Scottish Baronial house was built on the banks of the River Tweed in 1877 and resembled a miniature castle with towers, battlements and thistle topped turrets. Hundreds of acres of manicured gardens and landscape surrounded the home. It had long been open to visitors and was a very popular tourist stop in the Scottish Border country.

"Sir Walter did indeed find a lovely place to live," Richard said, as they sat in the car waiting for a lull in the rain. "Where do we start looking? The house must be thousands of square feet."

"We are seeking a long-forgotten one room cottage surrounded by trees in the land between the main house and the river. If my research is correct, it was once used as an artist's studio many years ago. It is possible Frederick came here as a tourist and left the vase. It's a long shot but I think it's worth the effort. I saw similar hiding places during the war."

Mucking through the wet grass and mud, they found the cottage, but it proved to be empty and undisturbed. Only one Abbotsford employee stopped them and questioned where they were going in the rain. He seemed satisfied when told they were fascinated by the landscape and had simply wandered off the trail. They heard him mutter something under his breath about how absurd tourists were, out looking at flowers in a downpour.

Back in the car, off they drove to a parish church in the small town of Caddonfoot. In doing research, Daniel read several World

War I treasures had been found in this particular place. They met the rector, who was a kind man, but assured them the church doors were always securely locked when the building was unoccupied. He showed them inside, more as a matter of pride rather than actually thinking the vase might be hidden there. Built in 1860, the timbered dome chapel ceiling and unusual arch over the chancel, were a visual treat.

"Do you recognize the figure in the stained glass window?" Daniel asked Richard.

"Is it a depiction of Sir Walter Scott?" Richard asked.

"Yes, he was quite an influence around this area."

"Your knowledge is impressive."

"I do my homework," the Monuments Man answered.

After a quick look around, they thanked the rector and ran back to the car through the rain. The next stop was Ashietiel, a large manor house set amidst acres of soft curving hills. Hedges lined a trail that led them to the River Tweed. They parked well outside the entry gates, hiding the car behind an especially large rhododendron bush.

"Before our favorite Sir Walter Scott bought Abbotsford, he lived here from 1804 to 1812. He said it was the happiest time of his life, which must have been true, because he was at his creative best," Daniel said.

"How do you mean?"

"During the eight years he lived at Ashietiel, he produced several poems which broke all publishing records for poetry and made him very famous. One was *The Lady of the Lake*, which tells the story of King James V's struggle against James Douglas, and the other was *Marmion*, a historical romance set in the sixteenth century, which was so popular that JMW Turner painted a watercolor of Ashiestiel as an illustration for the *Marmion* book."

"You are a walking encyclopedia," Richard exclaimed. "Is your intellect specific to Sir Walter Scott or are you simply the smartest person I've ever met?"

"Before traipsing all over Europe with the Monuments Men group, I was a literature professor at a small university in Rhode Island. My speciality was nineteenth century British and Scottish authors–hence my knowledge of our friend Sir Walter Scott."

"You must have a chat with my daughter, Sarah. She's an avid reader and currently writing her first book," Richard said proudly.

"Nothing I would enjoy more–other than finding your vase."

"What is our target at Ashietiel?" Richard asked.

"A gardener's cottage. This one is slightly tricky as Ashietiel House is occupied by owners who I hear are not keen to have strangers on their property," Daniel said.

"You must think Frederick was ingenious enough to sneak in?"

"There is an area by the river's edge that is banked with trees, somewhat remote from the house. I'm told the cottage is in that vicinity. If he came up at night he might very well have stumbled upon it. I made a few inquiries and it is said to be in good condition, no missing windows or anything of the sort."

"How do we get there?" Richard asked.

"I can't say for sure, but we know where the river is. It will be dark soon, make sure you grab the flashlights."

Dense trees in the woodlands shut out what was left of the cloud covered daylight, as well as a good portion of the rain. Once past the West Lodge of Ashietiel, they set off to the left, careful to stay as inconspicuous as possible. It wasn't too long before the river was only a few hundred yards away and they caught a glimpse of the gardener's cottage to the right. The only problem was there was a wisp of smoke coming out of the chimney. Someone was already there. They waited and watched from a distance. Richard was hesitant to say anything to Daniel, but time was slipping by and his hope of speaking with Kaitlyn was ebbing away. Without warning, the front door of the cottage opened and a gentleman came out carrying a fly rod, heading toward the river.

"Couldn't have planned that better," Daniel whispered. "Come on, we will take a quick look around while he's gone."

The cosy cottage consisted of one main room and a bathroom. It took the two men about five minutes to determine there was not a priceless vase hidden anywhere. Richard's heart was pounding as they departed as quickly and quietly as they had entered. No one was the wiser. The rain had turned into a heavy mist, leaving their clothes wet and heavy. Instead of being discouraged, Daniel rubbed his hands together and spoke encouragingly.

"Well, all right then. We've marked three off our list."

"Where to next?" Richard asked, his pulse finally slowing down as the adrenalin eased.

"We're closing in on it, I can feel it," Daniel answered. "I'd originally thought we'd travel to either Kiran House in Walkerburn or a little further to Taquir."

"And now?" Richard asked, driving the car onto the narrow road.

With the map on his lap, Daniel looked closely at an area near the river, and muttered to himself before speaking out loud.

"If you'll indulge me, there is one place not far from here that isn't on our list, but it's on our way. I've got a hunch that maybe, just maybe, I have overestimated Frederick and he is lazier than I first thought."

Darkness was closing in and Richard was fighting the urge to call it a day and go home. Thoughts of Kaitlyn leaving for London without giving him a chance to speak with her weighed heavily. On the other hand, here he was with a famous man who was giving his time and expertise for the sole purpose of helping him. There was no choice at this point. They must go on.

"What are you thinking?" Richard asked.

"According to the map, right here," Daniel said, indicating a spot on the River Tweed, "there is a small island. Looks to be about a mile from here."

With the help of the flashlight, Richard recognized the area.

"I know where that island is," he said. "It's just east of Elibank. I've fished in that area with the owners of Elibank, but we never had reason to go onto the island."

"From what I can see, the river splits and flows around it. Will we be able to cross safely without waders?"

"Only one way to find out," Richard said, putting the car into gear. "Better hang on, the road is more of a path and can be a bit rough."

Several minutes later, the two men were walking in the mist beside the river searching by flashlight for a spot to access the island. An abundance of trees and bushes on the riverbank made their exploration more difficult.

"Daniel, over here," Richard shouted. "It looks crossable though it's hard to know how deep it is. If the water is over our wellies we could be in trouble."

A quick search located a branch that had fallen from a nearby tree. Daniel reached out as far as he could over the river, stabbing the branch into the water while Richard shined the flashlight on it.

"A trick I learned in Austria many years ago," he said, pulling the large stick from the muddy water. "According to this sophisticated scientific experiment we should be fine. It's only about a foot deep and wellies are nearly knee-high."

It was hard to not get caught up in the man's enthusiasm, so with only slight trepidation, they crossed the river to the wooded island. Two flashlights were barely adequate to light their way as night had fallen and the mist had once again returned to rain. Daniel was leading the way, tripping now and then over fallen limbs and brush. Richard followed closely behind single file with passing thoughts of what on earth he was doing on an island in the middle of the river in the dark. Without warning, his foot slid in the mud and he fell taking Daniel down with him,

"I'm so sorry," he said offering a hand. "I'm not sure what happened."

"Not a problem," Daniel said happily, brushing off the mud off. "Look! In that clearing ahead, there is a small building. I knew it! Come on."

Running out of the woods into the small open meadow, rain began pelting them unmercifully. Daniel reached the rickety structure first and easily pushed open the door. It appeared to be a rudimentary fishing hut about ten feet by fifteen feet with a wooden bench, and pegs on one wall to hang waders most likely. The smell was a combination of musty mold with overtones of rotting rodents. Discarded fishing things were in a box in a corner and a high shelf held three old willow baskets. No windows, no fireplace, no electricity, no warmth. None of this daunted the Monuments Man, who rubbed his palms together in excitement.

"Shine your light on those baskets," Daniel instructed, walking toward the high shelf.

Dusty spider webs floated down when he carefully reached up for one of the worn rectangular baskets. Richard followed him with the flashlight as he set it down on the bench. It was filled with old tools covered by more cobwebs. The second basket yielded only a dead mouse. No surprise.

"Think the third one is the charm?" Daniel asked.

He lifted the last basket and placed it next to the others. What looked like a burlap bag was tucked inside, concealing whatever it covered. Gingerly, Daniel pulled back a corner of the bag and revealed the contents.

"If I am not mistaken, I believe we have found your vase."

It took Richard a moment to fully comprehend. When he gently removed the rest of the coarse fabric bag, there was the vase in perfect condition, not a scratch or chip on it. The feeling was overwhelming.

"I don't know what to say. How can I thank you? This is a part of my life I never thought I would see again. You are an absolute genius," Richard said, his voice heavy with emotion.

"Hardly, my friend, but years of experience have taught me a few things. My reward is in having this treasure returned to you. I suggest we cover it back up and return it to the basket for the trek back to the car."

They left the hut as they found it, minus a priceless Pinner Qing Dynasty vase. Walking back through the dark woods, Daniel needlessly cautioned Richard to go slowly lest he trip on a root or a branch. He cradled the basket as though it were a precious child, paying no attention to the rain that was drenching them. As they neared the crossing point of the river, there was loud rustling noise on the opposite bank.

"Must be a deer," Richard said quietly.

Daniel proceeded ahead through the water to the other side with Richard close behind. They were met with blinding car headlights and a loud command.

"Stop where you are and put your hands up where I can see them," a voice in the dark shouted.

Daniel's hands shot up immediately, but Richard held onto the tattered basket.

"Did you not hear me? I said put your hands up," the voice shouted a second time.

"I am holding a very fragile article. I'm going to slowly bend down and set it on the ground. Then I will raise my hands in the air."

With this accomplished, two young constables approached them. One tall and lanky and the other shorter and rounder. Richard wasn't sure who was more afraid.

"We received a call about two suspicious characters trespassing at Ashietiel and we've been following you."

"And who are you?" Richard asked.

"Oh, right," the first young man answered stuttering and flustered, as though he was trying to remember the proper protocol he was recently taught. "Ehm...I'm Constable McHenry and this is Constable Jones. We are police officers."

"I gathered that. Now, what is it you think we've done, Constable? Was anything missing from Ashietiel? Any damage done?"

"Well, ehm...no, not actually. The owners were concerned and rang us up."

"Constable, we are two gentlemen who got a bit lost walking in the woods near Ashietiel," Richard said. "Nothing more than that."

Constable McHenry was taking a moment to process the explanation when Constable Jones stepped forward.

"So, what are you doing here on private property, in the dark, on an island, standing in the river, soaking wet, carrying a fragile item?"

All four of them stood silently in the pouring rain, but only the two with their hands up were trying to come up with an answer.

"This is all a wee bit fishy," Constable Jones said. "McHenry, put them in the back of the car. We're taking them to the station. And grab that basket."

That was the last straw. It was all Richard could do to hold his temper.

"Son," he said through clinched teeth, "do you know DI Lawson by any chance? Because I can pretty much promise that if you touch this basket and any harm comes to the contents your police career will come to a crashing end."

The two young police officers looked at each other in confusion. Obviously, Lawson's name had the desired effect and Richard took full advantage.

"If you allow me to carry the basket, we will come with you willingly and sort this out. I can assure you we are not criminals."

Sitting in the back of a smelly police vehicle, driving through the rainy night to a village police station had not been on Richard's list of preferred ways to spend this evening. He clutched the basket with his treasured burlap covered vase and thought about all he had wanted to say to Kaitlyn. At the rate they were going, by the time he got home she would be halfway to London, resuming her chosen life. He thought of an old gospel song his mother taught him—*Oh Lord, show me the way, I'm down here Lord and I need your power, show me, show me the way.*

RICHARD:

There's No Place Like Home

Hours passed until DI Alex Lawson could be reached to confirm the identity of the Laird of Leigheas. By then Richard and Daniel had sat on hard metal chairs in a small, stuffy room for the better part of the night–uncomfortable, damp and sleep deprived. Finally cleared of any wrongdoing and accompanied by profuse apologies, Constable Henry drove them back to Richards's car which was still parked near the island.

By now the sun was coming up and a few clouds floated by in the cerulean blue sky. The calm after the storm. Thankfully the car engine started right up and they were on their way. It made more sense for Daniel to spend the night at Leigheas before catching his train back to London. The road to the Clovensford Hotel to retrieve Daniel's belongings was deserted in the early morning, and the passing green landscape sparkled after last night's rain.

"I'm sorry this adventure was a little more dramatic than planned," Daniel said. "I must be getting old, normally I don't get caught."

Richard laughed out loud and his mood lightened.

"Daniel, you single-handedly found my cherished, irreplaceable Chinese vase that I thought was either gone forever or broken to smithereens. There are not adequate words to thank you. I am truly in awe of your deductive mind and how you tracked it down. For the record, that was the first time I've been held all night in a police station. Sarah will thoroughly enjoy this story."

By the time the wheels of the car crunched on the gravel driveway in front of Leigheas, it was nearly eight o'clock in the morning.

Richard felt like a teenager who had been out all night and was suffering the effects of exhaustion. He was sure he had missed Kaitlyn and would try to formulate Plan B to win her back, though at the moment all he wanted was to get Daniel settled in, take a hot shower and go to bed for a few hours.

"You must be proud of Leigheas, Richard," Daniel said, not showing any signs of fatigue. "It is a beautiful home in a marvelous setting. I look forward to exploring the grounds this afternoon. Thank you for your offer to stay here tonight."

"You're most welcome," he said wearily. "Come in and we will get your room arranged."

Once through the heavy wooden front door, the house was strangely quiet. The grandfather clock chimed eight times, echoing in the entry.

"Everyone must still be sleeping," Richard said, silently wishing he was one of them. "Let's leave your things here and go make a pot of tea in the kitchen."

At that moment, ladies laughter wafted down the wide stairway as Sarah and Kaitlyn appeared at the top landing unaware of the two men looking up at them. For the briefest moment Richard's heart beat wildly. She was still here!

"Dad!" Sarah exclaimed. "You look dreadful!"

Words a besotted gentleman rarely wants to hear.

She ran down the stairs dragging Kaitlyn's heavy suitcase, hugged her filthy father and introduced herself to Daniel Roberts.

"I've heard quite a bit about you," he replied shaking her hand. "Apparently we are both book lovers with unbridled curiosity."

Not a word of this conversation made it to Richard's ears. He had not taken his eyes off Kaitlyn and simply stood gazing up at her. She, in turn, had not moved either, looking steadily at him. The impasse was finally broken when Richard spoke, unaware of anyone else in the room.

"I'm very glad you are still here," he said with every bit of sincerity he owned.

"I'm very glad I'm still here, as well," she answered.

Silence followed.

"Kaitlyn Turning, I love you with all my heart and if you need to return to London and figure things out, that's perfectly fine as long as I have a place in your life."

He knew he was babbling but couldn't stop. "I understand your attachment to Sanni and the Cumberman family, but London isn't that far away and I can visit, and somehow we will make it work because I don't want to spend what's left of my life without you…"

A loud knock rudely interrupted his soliloquy.

Sarah was quick to answer it and greet Thomas Turning, who swiftly ascertained he was walking into an electric atmosphere. No one said a word. Neither Kaitlyn nor Richard had acknowledged anyone, just looked at one another. She descended the stairs directly into the arms of the damp, dirty Laird of Leigheas, still wearing his muddy wellies.

"I'll not be returning to London," she said. "I will be living in Edinburgh with Da and help with the book shop. My life is here with my father and with your family. It's where I belong."

"Indeed it is," he said, kissing her softly.

"*Tha gaol agam ort*," she said quietly, "I love you, too."

"Was someone at the door?" Seaneen asked, walking in and wiping her hands on her apron, oblivious of the grand declarations that just took place. "Richard! What are you thinking wearing those muddy boots in the house. Where's your head, lad?"

The happiness that filled the entryway spoke volumes of things to come.

Chapter Forty-five

SARAH:

Begin at the Beginning

Dear Peter,

To say it has been an extraordinary few days would be a vast understatement. Before writing to you, I tried to gather my thoughts as to where to begin. A quote from Lewis Carroll came to mind, 'Begin at the beginning, and go on till you come to the end: then stop.' I will try to do just that.

As I think you know, my father has been working with an American named Daniel Roberts to find the Chinese vase Frederick stole. Without telling anyone, he and my father went out on a search in the surrounding area. The incredibly, fantastic news is they found it! The downside was a constable thought my father and Mr. Roberts were thieves and they ended up spending the night at the police station. It took hours for DI Lawson to straighten the mess out. If you can imagine, Frederick had taken the priceless vase to a small island in the River Tweed on Elibank property and left it there in a fishing hut for 'safe keeping.' How Mr Roberts figured out where to look is still a mystery, but of course we are all thrilled. DI Lawson is a little cranky, but I think that's because he wasn't the one to find it.

The next miracle is my father and Kaitlyn finally admitted their affection for each other. This happened in a far more public way than I'm sure my father would have hoped, but all is well with them. Another bit of good news is Kaitlyn is going to quit her job in London and live with her dad in Edinburgh and help him with the book shop. Everyone is so pleased she will be closer. The last few weeks, she has been helping me edit my book draft. I believe it was my father who told me first drafts are always garbage and not to be discouraged. My mental pendulum goes back and forth between being extremely excited, then filled with self-doubt. Kaitlyn says it is called 'imposter syndrome' and is common with creative people. She said I am to completely ignore it and keep writing. Easier said than done. Do you struggle with this? As always, I wish you were here, but I'm quite sure God has a plan better than my selfish desire to have you near. I will follow your suggestion and enclose a few pages of the book. Hopefully, it will inspire your vision for the artwork.

You are in my thoughts every day as I wonder how your paintings are coming along. The train trip to Mallaig sounded fabulous, even with the cigar-smoking Highlander. I look forward to seeing all those villages with charming names. Glenfinnan viaduct bridge is familiar, though I cannot imagine how breathtaking to actually ride the train over it. Your artist's bothy must be a perfect location to create wondrous work. Plus it's free, which is a huge bonus!

In a few days the gentlemen will arrive for this year's spring/summer stay. I am proud of my dad for creating this opportunity and sticking with it. He has received lovely letters from previous guests telling him how it changed their lives. The fact that it brought you back to me might be another reason I'm a big fan, and it certainly altered our lives. It seems only right to share Leigheas with others when it has been such a blessing to us.

Time to close and turn off the light. My dreams will be filled with a handsome, curly-haired artist I cherish.

Love,

Sarah

RICHARD:

Looking Good in a Kilt

He smiled every time he thought about the scene in the entryway when he finally found the courage to come clean with Kaitlyn and tell her how he felt. Nothing like baring your soul to the entire household…while still wearing muddy boots!

A few days had flown by since Kaitlyn returned to Edinburgh with her father, and truth be told, he was still tired from his adventure with Daniel Roberts. He swiveled around in his desk chair to look again at the exquisite Chinese vase that was back where it belonged. DI Lawson's voice rang in his ears, scolding him for having such a rare object so readily accessible. One of these days he would donate it to a museum, but not yet.

Fickle spring was in full swing. After yesterday's rain, today was fair and glorious–ideal for a horseback ride around the property. He'd invited James along to discuss a few loose ends to tie up before the men arrived. The vicar had become a trusted friend and confidant, and Richard wasn't sure how they managed before he joined the staff.

Galloping across the meadow to the edge of the River Tweed, Richard and James slowed their horses to a walk. Sun peeked in and around passing clouds with only a slight breeze rustling the trees. It wasn't exactly warm, but far less cold than it had been.

"They should arrive tomorrow," Richard said, allowing his horse, Dasher, to drink from the river. "I want to make sure all is in order."

"Can you refresh an old man's memory? Which fellows did we settled on?" James asked.

"For the record, you are not old."

"Tell that to these tired bones," James laughed.

"Well, I try to bring together men with a variety of interests and personalities, hoping they get along. This year might be a challenge. First, there's Jeremy, in his late thirties, a very accomplished British equestrian with Olympic medals to prove it. From what I read between the lines in his request letter, he has issues relating to riding accidents which have left him short-tempered and quite unhappy. He's hoping time here will bring some peace and clarity in terms of his future. He may be a problem getting along with the others."

"Well, let's not plan on trouble until it happens," James said.

"Second gentleman is Hugh Thornhill, *the third*," Richard said emphasizing '*the third*.' "He is a Barrister, not a solicitor mind you, as he will quickly point out. He is in his mid-fifties, and married into a family of money, though I suspect a bit of marital discord. In addition, he has all the earmarks of being a British snob. He says he is burnt out, with a '*what is the point of everything*' attitude."

"You gleaned all that from a letter?" James inquired.

"That, plus someone I know from the Embassy in London is acquainted with him," Richard said. "His reasoning in coming here is '*Why not, I've got nothing better to do.*' My concern is the chip on his shoulder may rub off on the others."

"Again, let's not borrow tomorrow's problems."

"Because each day has problems of its own. My mother drilled that into me from a young age," Richard said.

"I think your mother and I would've gotten on famously. Who is the third member of the group?"

"Originally, it was a young doctor named Jeff, but when he found out Sarah was my daughter, he declined. Apparently they knew each other at Cambridge. When I asked her about him, she rolled her eyes and said something about him being an egotistical, self-centered idiot who didn't have a genuine bone in his body," Richard said, with amusement.

"Did you inquire to what she *really* thought?" James asked between gales of laughter. "I do find your daughter abundantly refreshing. However, from her description, Leigheas sounds exactly like what the doctor needs."

"So true. He was quickly replaced by an older gentleman with a little bit of a vague background. He is British, but has lived in New York for the past thirty years and recently retired, only returning to London of late. It seems he is interested in purchasing a country home with some land for his golden years. His children suggested he spend time with us to be sure it's a good fit. His name is Clive and his letter said he was here to learn and help out."

"Well, I like the sound of that. He might be the calm between two storms," James said. "It sounds as though it should be a very interesting several months. I'm looking forward to being part of it."

"You are a God-send, my friend," Richard said sincerely." Literally."

The next hour was spent going over plans and schedules.

The eight o'clock chime on the old grandfather clock made his pulse quicken. By then dinner was over, everyone had scattered to their evening destinations and he was free to go to his office, close the door and telephone the love of his life.

"Hello?" she answered with her lilting Scottish accent.

"Is this the beautiful lady I adore?" he asked.

"Could be. Are you the handsome man who owns my heart?"

"Yes, that would absolutely be me," he said.

"I'm so glad it's you," she said.

"I'm very glad it's me. How was your day?" he asked, settling in for a long chat.

"Really good. I am enjoying being in the shop. I grew up here and it's a wee bit like coming home." Kaitlyn said. "For the moment I am acting as bookkeeper, bringing things up to date. A low energy job for sure, though by next week I hope to take over a few of Jacob's shifts. That poor lad has been working nonstop for weeks and needs a break. Besides, it will be fun to roam among the books again. Now, it's your turn. How is life in the country?"

"Things are quiet here, mostly preparing for the guests tomorrow. Saturday will be spent familiarizing them with the place and making their acquaintance. It's always a fascinating few days as they settle in. Mostly, I miss having you here. Any idea when you'll be able to visit?"

"If everything works out I plan on coming down next week to help Sarah get her book ready to send to the London publisher. Has she let you see it yet?" Kaitlyn asked.

"She has not, though I've asked several times."

"Be patient with her. It's a very vulnerable time and fear of criticism can be crippling. It's a frightening thing to put your creative work out in the world to be judged."

"How did you become so perceptive?"

There was the lilting laugh he loved.

"More old than perceptive, I'm afraid," she answered.

"But I gather you have seen her book?" he asked.

"If you remember, I trained to be a typist and promised to assist her in preparing a final copy. Without letting the cat out of the bag, I can tell you that you are going to be very proud of her."

"I've always been proud of her," he said, "more so everyday."

"One of the things I most admire about you is your relationship with Sarah. It's a very telling thing about a man."

"While we are on the topic, is there anything else you admire?" he teased.

"You look quite good in a kilt," she laughed, "And that's very important to a Scottish girl."

Chapter Forty-seven

RICHARD:

Introductions

When he bought the house six years ago it was with full knowledge that it was a Grade B listed property. Long ago, both England and Scotland adopted a method of preserving old buildings with architectural or historical significance by assigning them a grade or category. In the case of Leigheas, Category B protection meant before any changes could be made to the outside, inside, or any structure attached to the building, it must be approved by planning authorities. Richard purchased the property from a family who had held title to it for three generations, and thankfully, had completed most of the modern improvements. The biggest change Sarah and Richard made was remodeling the oversized kitchen. They wanted it to be functional, yet comfortable–a place to gather for breakfast or a cup of tea. As long as they kept the character of the house in mind and passed inspections, all was good. Specialized workers were required who knew the ins and outs of these old houses, and were well worth the additional cost. When it came to the interiors, Colfax and Fowler, the oldest design firm in London, were given the job. The result couldn't have been better. Each room had it's own personality yet they all felt traditional, relaxed and inviting. The dining room was a perfect example with its pale sage green walls and white marble fireplace. Even with twelve foot ceilings and an oversized crystal chandelier, the room had a cozy atmosphere. An antique burled wood table in the middle of the room expanded to seat anywhere from six to twenty-six, depending on the guest count. Today it was set for ten to accommodate the new guests, and basic staff for a casual introductory lunch.

"On behalf of myself and everyone at Leigheas, welcome. We are pleased you are here and hope your time will be restful and well-spent. As you know, I am Richard Duncan, owner and Laird of Leigheas," he said, raising his eyebrow in amusement. "Believe me, it is an honorary title, nothing I earned. We tend to go on a first name basis, however if this is not comfortable for you, please let me know. Joining us today is Seaneen Bradbury, who runs the household and the one person you want to make friends with. Her husband, Vicar James Bradbury is seated next to her, and the two young ladies serving you are Meara and Brennan, who work with Seaneen. Stephen is our resident veterinarian and rules over the care of all of the animals here. Marcus oversees everything regarding the land and gardens, and last, but certainly not least, is Colin our expert fishing guide who can outfit you and share his wisdom of the River Tweed."

"Can you guarantee a large salmon?" Clive asked good-naturedly.

"We will sure give it a go," Colin answered. "I've got waders, fly rods and plenty of sure-thing flies. The variable are those blasted fish who are ravenous at times and prone to ignore the perfect cast and fly other times. Leave a note with Richard if you are interested and we will work out a time."

"Other than the hallowed activity of fishing, you are also welcome to meet with Stephen to arrange a horse for a ride." Richard continued, "In the packet you received is a map of Leigheas with locations of other buildings and trails for hiking or just roaming the grounds. The library is always open, feel free to find a book and settle in for a good read. Each Sunday Vicar James will conduct a short service in the chapel and you are most welcome to attend. Seaneen arranges for breakfast and dinner here in the dining room. As a courtesy, please let her know if you will not be here. Details of meal times are in your packet. You have each been assigned a cottage which is stocked with most things you might need. If there is something you would like, leave a note in the kitchen as one of us goes to the village nearly every day. Lastly, Vicar James and myself are almost always available if you care to have a private chat."

It was usual after the first meeting for the guests to gather infor-
mally with the staff and ask specific questions. Clive was interested
in everything, speaking to everyone and enjoying himself. The
equestrian, Jeremy, looked uncomfortable when James approached
him, but didn't bolt from the room. Their exchange appeared congenial, which was at least a start. Barrister Hugh Thornhill III stood
aloof from the group, looking bored and slightly haughty.

"Oh, Lord, this could be a rough few months," Richard thought
to himself.

With that in mind, he sought out Mr. Thornhill III with the
hopes of thawing the judicial iceberg. When inquiring about the differences between the British and Scottish legal systems, Richard
was given a mind-numbing, condescending explanation.

"Oh, what is the point? You're an American and have no idea
what I'm talking about. Get someone to show me to my cottage,"
the plump, white-haired barrister said indignantly as he walked
away.

Richard wasn't sure if he should be offended by being told he
was ignorant or being accused of being an American. Thankfully,
his mother had taught him finding humor in all things was a saving
grace.

After a quick stroll around the property to make sure all was
well with the new arrivals, Richard returned to the house ready to
tackle a raft of paperwork on his desk.

"Miss Kaitlyn telephoned for you," Meara said. "She said it was
a wee bit urgent."

"Thank you, I'll call her right away."

Scooping up some leftover shortbread on a tray with his cup of
Earl Gray, he headed to his office wondering what could be wrong.
Was she alright? Was it her father? No use speculating, just call.

"Turning Pages Book Shoppe, may I help you?" answered Kaitlyn.

"Yes, you may help me. I'm looking for a beautiful Scottish
Lass…"

"Richard, please hold on while I change telephones," she said. "Jacob, please hang up this phone when I pick up the one in the back."

A few moments passed while he anxiously waited.

"He is pleading not-guilty!" she said in a quiet tone so as not to be overheard. "Do you realize what that means? It will go to trial and I will have to testify in public. I don't think I can do that."

"How do you know this?"

"DI Lawson called a bit ago and told me. He said I would be hearing from a solicitor in a few weeks. Oh, Richard, how will I relive that horror all over again?"

"Let me do some checking and see what I can find out. Maybe there is a way around it. In the meantime, try to be calm and don't let it overwhelm you. James reminded me just the other day that we are not meant to rehearse tomorrow's problems…"

"Tomorrow has enough problems of its own," she said finishing his thought. "Just talking to you makes me feel better. Thank you for being there."

"You're not alone in this, my Scottish lass. I plan to be right with you at every turn. I'll call you tonight?"

"Yes, please. I would like that," she said. "Bye for now."

He hung up the phone and wondered if this Frederick mess would ever end!

Chapter Forty-eight

KAITLYN:

The Other Shoe Dropped

The Olivetti Lettera 22 typewriter was a beautiful writing machine, designed by Marcello Nizzoli in Italy. It had all the earmarks of sleek Italian artistry and was a joy to type on. Kaitlyn was delighted to be using her typewriting skills on this outstanding mechanical device.

When the last page was finished, she unrolled the paper from the rubber platen of the Lettera 22 and stacked the manuscript on the desk.

She and Sarah had spent most of the day going over what, hopefully, would be the final draft of the book. They made a few changes, caught mistakes and re-worded a few sentences to help the story flow smoother. Editing was not an easy process at best, though Sarah took most suggestions positively. They only disagreed on a few places and when at an impasse, decided to let Kaitlyn's father make the final call. He was due to arrive within an hour at Leigheas to review the book and join them for dinner.

"Time to take a break and go to the kitchen and celebrate," Sarah said stretching her arms over her head.

"Tell me about the publisher you're sending this to?" Kaitlyn asked, sipping her chamomile. "You've made their acquaintance?"

"Yes and no. After graduating from Cambridge, Mr. Dickenson of Carlyle and Bryer Book Publishing in London, hired me as a lowly Assistant Acquisitions Editor. He understood my desire to be a writer and saw promise in samples of my work. Our handshake deal promised he would promote my manuscripts within the company if he felt they were worthy."

"He must have thought quite highly of your writing," Kaitlyn said.

"We had an amazing relationship and he taught me so many things in the short time we worked together," Sarah said. "Unfortunately for me, and fortunate for him, he received an extraordinary job offer in Belgium he couldn't turn down and off he went. His replacement, Mr. Krabton, had little use for me and absolutely no interest in my writing. However, coincidently, I found out recently Carlyle and Bryer formed a small subsidiary called Puffin Press to publish children's books. I don't know anyone personally who is involved, but I still have one or two contacts at the main office. It seemed a good idea to send my story there since they are new and might not have signed too many children's authors."

"Sound reasoning. We will ask Da if he knows of them. I'm always astounded at the people with whom he is acquainted."

"Me, too. I was stunned when you both knew Peter. That was quite a fluke," Sarah laughed.

"And how is the wandering painter doing in Mallaig? Is it to his liking?"

"So far he is quite taken with the area, and says there are an infinite number of places that are inspiring him."

"Has he had time to do any drawings for your book?"

"I sent him a few pages to give an idea of the story. He should have received them by now. I'm anxious, but trying not to make everything about me. This is such a big opportunity for him–a gallery dedicated to his work," Sarah said. "Sort of a life-changing situation."

"He is immensely talented and I can see how much he has matured since his return from Italy. Not to mention, he is head over heels for you."

This brought a blush and shy smile to Sarah. The back door opened and in came Richard with Maggie trotting along behind, both covered in mud. His face lit up when he saw them.

"Hello! I wondered if you two were going to be upstairs all day typing away. Am I allowed to ask how it's coming along?"

"It might be finished," Sarah said. "Of course, that depends on what Thomas thinks."

"You don't sound as excited as I would have expected," he said, pulling off his dirty wellies. "Are you discouraged?"

"Oh no, mainly exhausted. I've written and re-written it so many times I honestly couldn't tell you how the story ended up. There is no objectivity left in my brain as to whether it is good or simply dreadful."

The kettle boiled again and Kaitlyn refreshed Sarah's tea and poured a cup for Richard.

"Well, I can tell you it is absolutely marvelous, and I mean that with complete objectivity," Kaitlyn said. "It is creative, meaningful, humorous, and exudes a message of kindness and love. Children's literature is one of the most difficult genres to write and you, Sarah Duncan, have done a masterful job. I can't imagine it not being successful."

"There you have it," Richard said cheerfully. "I suppose I will be allowed to read it one of these days?"

Sarah's response surprised both Kaitlyn and Richard when tears welled in her eyes.

"You both have been so supportive and I don't want to let you down. I haven't let you read it, Dad, because I'm afraid you will be disappointed and think it's trivial."

Without hesitation, he put his arm around his daughter and held her close.

"There is no way you could ever disappoint me. Ever."

Sarah just hiccuped.

"Mr Duncan, a letter just came for you," Brennan said coming in the kitchen

"Thank you, Brennan," he said, glancing at the odd handwriting. "Would you put it on my desk?"

"Of course."

Kaitlyn quietly began to clean up the tea things to allow father and daughter their moment.

"Maybe it would be a good idea if I lay down for a bit before Thomas arrives," Sarah said. "I'm dissolving into an emotional puddle."

She gave Kaitlyn a hug on her way out the door.

"Poor lass is worn out. Unless you've been involved in editing and re-writing you've no idea how tiring and brain-numbing it is," Kaitlyn said.

"You've had experience?" Richard asked, taking her hand.

"Yes, I used to help a friend edit books," she said, not adding any details.

"Have I told you how wonderful you are?" he said. "A woman with so many gifts."

She marveled how his touch warmed her and how secure she felt with him.

"I'm not sure we agree on that, but thank you," she said. "The thought of this upcoming trial is weighing heavily. How I wish it would just go away. It's like a dark cloud that won't go away."

"Have you heard anything more from DI Lawson?" he asked.

"No, but it is akin to waiting for the other shoe to drop. Every time the telephone rings, I pray it isn't more bad news. Being here has brought some distance to it, which is a relief."

"Do you miss London?" he asked. "The Cumbermans must be at a loss without you there organizing their lives."

"You know, I don't. It was the right decision," she said. "As it turns out their son, Wilfred and his family recently moved back to London from Spain, and his wife has been able to step in and manage beautifully. The Cumberman's are lovely people and we will stay in touch forever, but my time there was finished."

"And little Sanni?" Richard asked a little tentatively. "He is particularly fond of you and I suspect you will miss him."

Her face brightened at the thought of that engaging little boy.

"I will try to make time to see him when I have the chance. There is a sweet, sincerity about the lad that fills my heart."

There was no denying Sanni was a fascinating child, and Richard tried to not feel a twinge of jealously.

Seaneen and the girls bustled into the kitchen on a mission to begin preparing dinner for the group.

"Do you have an idea when your father might be arriving?" Seaneen asked.

"His plan was to leave after the shop closed, so I would guess around 18:00," Kaitlyn said.

"That's six pm to the rest of the world," Richard quipped.

"I know my 24-hour clock, laddie," Seaneen answered. "Now, you two go somewhere else. We have a meal to prepare."

Thomas arrived a little early, and after spending time with Sarah, joined the others in the dining room for yet another of Seaneen's delicious meals. Dinner conversations had become lively and comfortable as the guests got to know each other. The addition of Kaitlyn and Thomas Turning added even more sparkle to the evening. Sarah had declined dinner with the group, choosing a hot bath and a tray in her room instead. Richard mentioned that she had not yet met the three visiting gentlemen, but understood her desire for quiet time. She and Thomas had spent an intense hour reviewing the final draft of the book, which he declared a masterpiece. Thomas now appeared to be having a very good time engaging Clive in conversation about the history of book binding. Kaitlyn was amused knowing her father could make any subject interesting. Once dessert and coffee had been cleared away, Thomas was preparing for the hour drive back to Edinburgh.

"Are you sure you won't stay? We have plenty of room, as you well know," Richard offered.

"Thank you, but I must open the shop in the morning. I gave Jacob the morning off and my other help seems to be having a wonderful time here," Thomas said, with a wink to his daughter.

"I would like to keep her here for as long as possible," Richard said.

"And I'm sure she would be agreeable," Thomas answered.

"Da! I'm standing right here," Kaitlyn laughed.

"Oh, before I forget. I've a letter that came for you just as I left," Thomas said.

Her father reached in his pocket and pulled out an envelope. Looking it over, she noticed there was no return address and the writing was scribbled. When she tried to open the back flap, it was so securely pasted down that it ripped apart. A single paper, folded in half fluttered to the floor. Richard was first to bend down and retrieve it. When he handed it to Kaitlyn, she scanned the paper, let out an anguished moan, then dropped the note as though it was poison.

"What on earth…" Richard said, picking up the note for the second time and reading it.

'K, if you testify against me, I will have my people kill you. Do not involve the police. This is not a joke.'

Her entire body shook uncontrollably and her mind emptied of any coherent thought. Richard guided her to his office, with her father following close behind. A dram of aged whisky was brought to her lips, though she barely tasted the fiery liquid as it scorched her throat.

"Thomas, would you find Seaneen and James and bring them here?" Richard asked. "Also, I think it would be a good idea for you to spend the night as a precaution."

Watching Richard take charge brought the smallest bit of comfort, but she couldn't find her voice to tell him.

"My sweet love, we will get through this," he said gently. "I cannot imagine there is an iota of truth to his threat. He is a delusional man, scraping the bottom of the barrel to frighten you. Take another sip."

This time the whisky caused her to cough after she swallowed.

"I'm so sorry," she said, clearing her throat.

"You've nothing to be sorry for," Richard said. "You didn't ask for any of this. How I rue the moment I invited that man into this house. I promise to protect you and keep you safe."

Those words were a healing balm to her overwhelmed soul. She looked into the eyes of this extraordinary man who loved her and felt strength slowly returning.

"What's this?" Seaneen asked as she walked into the office. "What has that nephew of mine done now?"

James sat next to Kaitlyn and put a protective arm around her, as his wife read the note.

"He is despicable," Seaneen said, throwing it on the desk.

It was then Richard noticed the item Brennan mentioned earlier. Kaitlyn watched as he opened the well-sealed envelope, and his eyes narrowed. She could tell he was deciding whether to read it aloud or not.

"What does it say?" she asked. "It's from Frederick, isn't it?"

'*R, convince K not to testify or I will have you and your daughter killed.*'

"This has gone too far," Seaneen said.

"It went too far a long time ago," Richard responded. "I have a thought. You three stay here. I'll be right back."

James tightened his arm around Kaitlyn and quietly began to pray.

"Lord, we come before you in the face of evil and ask for your hedge of protection around Kaitlyn and this family. Keep them from harm and bring your peace that passes all understanding. In the name of the Father, Son and Holy Spirit. Amen."

Chapter Forty-nine

RICHARD:

The Business of Miracles

Upon closing the door to his office, second thoughts began to creep into his mind. In the six years they had welcomed guests to Leigheas, he had never approached any one of them with a personal matter, let alone a guest who was not especially congenial. In fairness, Mr. Thornhill III had unwound a little after spending time on the river fishing with Colin, however he still remained a bit frosty with Richard. The fact that Kaitlyn was being threatened drove him out into the night air toward Hugh Thornhill's cottage. He paused a moment before knocking to gather his thoughts.

"Mr. Duncan, to what do I owe this intrusion?" Hugh asked, when he opened the door scowling.

Mr. Thornhill had been given the Kenneth Grahame cottage, and the incongruity of this occurred to Richard ever so briefly. Scottish-born Mr. Grahame wrote the well-loved British children's book, *The Wind in the Willows*, portraying the thin guise of the snobby British boy's club mentality in the form of animals–Mr. Toad, Ratty and others. The overriding theme being the importance of friendship. With an oversized mustache and large eyes, Mr. Grahame's life was plagued with unhappiness and a failed marriage. Maybe Mr. Thornhill would discover the benefits of fellowship by staying in this cottage.

"Well, what do you want?" Hugh Thornhill demanded.

"I'm very sorry to disturb you but I am in need of some legal advice," Richard said.

235

"From me? You want legal advice from me? Have you any idea what I charge for legal advice? Especially after hours?"

"Actually, I don't have a clue and I wouldn't be asking if it wasn't important."

"What does this legal emergency entail?" the barrister asked.

For the briefest moment, Richard felt a slight melting of the arrogant demeanor.

"My dear friend just received a death threat from a man who recently kidnapped her and left her for dead. I received one as well from the same man."

"Well, that is an interesting scenario, to say the least. Always hard to resist a good murder threat. Where is this friend of yours?"

"She is in my office."

"At your home? She is here?"

"Yes, and for what it's worth, she previously worked for Judge Trevor Cumberman and his wife as their personal secretary. You met her at dinner, Kaitlyn Turning?"

Mr. Thornhill's white bushy eyebrows rose impressively.

"Well, let's not waste time. Allow me a moment to put on a coat."

On the five minute walk between the cottage and the house, Richard quickly recounted the main details of Frederick Hutton to the barrister. He listened attentively and seemed satisfied with the information Richard shared. Thornhill was well acquainted with Judge Cumberman, both legally and socially, and that seemed to be working in their favor.

When they entered the office, every seat was taken by James, Seaneen, Thomas, Sarah and of course, Kaitlyn. After a little shuffling and adding a few more chairs, Hugh Thornhill III slid into his professional mode, asking a number of pertinent questions. As he examined the two threatening letters, he inquired as to their authenticity.

"While it seems perfectly logical that these were written by Mr. Hutton, how do we prove that without a shadow of doubt?"

Seaneen spoke up, "Frederick Hutton is my nephew."

Thornhill's quick withering look at Richard silently spoke of *'why was this information left out?'*

"Frederick corresponded with his sister, my niece," Seaneen continued. "Perhaps we could get writing samples from her to check for the match?"

"Very good. Yes, please see to it they are sent immediately."

Seaneen and James left the office to call Marjorie and Gwendolyn. Richard didn't envy that phone call. Mr. Thornhill was deep in thought and asked for a pad and pen. He made some notes, wrote names and drew arrows across the page then finally spoke.

"Tomorrow I will make a few telephone calls to determine on what grounds he is pleading not guilty and who is representing him. My initial reaction is that this is a threat from a desperate man, as he's wanted for crimes in three countries. I seriously doubt he has access to anyone willing to carry out his threats. He would be the equivalent of a rabid dog–even in the criminal world. No one would want to be associated with him. That being said, I have learned you cannot be too careful when dealing with someone who is mentally unstable, which it seems Mr. Hutton clearly is."

The important London barrister turned to Kaitlyn and in a kindly voice explained his thoughts further.

"Miss Turning, if in fact these letters are proven to be written by Mr. Hutton, it would most certainly result in there being no trial due to witness intimidation. That alone is a serious offense that could result in a lengthly prison sentence for Mr. Hutton. My instinct tells me that is how it will play out. May I suggest you rest easy and try to not let it worry you."

Then turning to Richard, he continued on.

"And the same applies to you and your daughter, Mr. Duncan. Once I receive definitive information I will pass it along to you. Am I correct in assuming I may have use of your telephone?"

"Of course! Anything you require. Feel free to use my office. We are very much in your debt, Mr. Thornhill. Thank you."

"I thought you said we were on a first name basis here, Richard?" The barrister quipped.

"Indeed we are, Hugh, indeed we are," Richard answered.

As they walked back to the Grahame cottage, Hugh was uncharacteristically talkative.

"Interesting chap, Kenneth Grahame. He followed a rigid career, rose to the very top before quitting then found his creative side by writing *Wind in the Willows*. The story is about friendship of all things."

"I agree, it is a fascinating history. It reminds me a bit of my own path," Richard said.

When they reached the cottage door, Hugh shook Richard's hand and nearly smiled.

"I look forward to hearing more about your path and I'm glad to help your lovely lady. It's been far too long since I've had the opportunity to interact personally with a client. It reminds me why I studied the law in the first place. Good night, Richard."

"Good night, Hugh."

The door closed and Richard walked back across the meadow.

"God is still in the business of miracles," he thought to himself.

Chapter Fifty

PETER:

More From Mallaig

Dear Sarah,

The pages of your book just arrived and the story is absolutely marvelous! I am most anxious to see the rest of it. The woodland you describe sounds enchanting and your sketch of the tree is quite good–leads me to wonder which of us is the better artist. Armed with this information I will begin drawing and send off ideas soon. As always, I wish you were here so we could spend every day together.

Finding myself in Mallaig in the middle of May is proving delightful. The weather is warmer than usual and the days are beginning to be a wee bit longer, giving more time for plein air painting. The sun, the birds and the earthy feel of early summer couldn't be more inspirational for an artist. Everyday the sky is filled with meandering clouds causing changing moods to the scenery. Capturing it on canvas is a bit of a challenge but I find I'm enjoying it immensely. The early morning and late afternoon natural light is every artists dream and I'm taking full advantage of it.

Mallaig is a busy fishing port with the claim that they bring in more herring than any other port in Europe. Their oak-smoked kippers are very famous and sold in the factory shoppe near the harbour. As you can imagine, the salty sea air combined with smoking kippers can sometimes produce quite an aroma! Stinky might be a more appropriate word.

A few days ago I visited the Isle of Skye, not far from Mallaig. It is one of my favorite spots so far. The coastline is spectacular with cliffs hanging over the ocean and constant waves crashing onto the rocks. A strange mist hangs about the mountain tops, making it feel quite mysterious. Skye is part of the Inner Hebrides, which is a collection of islands that hug the west coast of Scotland. Beyond them are more islands, cleverly named the Outer Hebrides. This includes a bunch of islands, some inhabited and some not. Lewis and Harris is the most populated–in fact it is the largest island in Scotland and the third largest in the British Isles, after Great Britain and Ireland. I suppose that's enough of a geography lesson for now! One day we will return and I will show you this special part of Scotland with all its glorious history.

I sent off a package of ten watercolours to my mother and gallery partner Lydia recently. Not to brag, but I think they are quite good. I don't say that very often, so I'm anxiously waiting to hear if they agree. Several oil paintings are drying and should be ready to bring home in a month and a half. My time here is more than half-way over and as lovely as this area is, I'm ready to come home. Not to get your hopes up, but if things continue going well, perhaps I will be back a little earlier than expected.

You are the light of my life, as well as my first and last thought every day. Never forget.

My love,
Peter

Chapter Fifty-one

SARAH:

Mister Jeremy Fisher

One consistent fact about the Scottish people was everyone talked about the weather. If it was cold and miserable, you would hear the word *dreich*. If it was bright and beautiful, they would say *the sun was splitting the trees*, with an image of light filtering through branches in a forest.

Sarah woke up to the trees being split by rays of sunshine.

"It's a glorious day, lass, and time you set your foot outside in the fresh air," Seaneen said, handing Sarah a bowl of hot porridge. "You've been inside long enough. You'll grow cobwebs."

"You can't grow cobwebs," Sarah laughed, "they are woven on you by lazy spiders when you sit too long."

"I rest my case," Seaneen said. "Here's your brown sugar and raisins."

"Actually, I am planning on going to the stable this morning."

"Give me a wee bit of time and I'll stir up some shortbread for little Henry."

"Only if there are leftovers for the rest of us."

Richard came through the door like a man with a purpose. "Leftovers of what?"

"Never you mind," Seaneen answered. "Would you like porridge or are you in too much of a rush?"

"Never too busy to have a quick breakfast with two of my favorite ladies," he said, sitting down across from Sarah.

"We all know your first favorite lady is residing in Edinburgh," Sarah quipped, never missing an opportunity to tease her father.

241

"She is definitely in the top three of my list," he said.

"Aye, ever the diplomat," Seaneen said, setting down the steaming bowl in front of Richard.

"What are your plans today, my lovely daughter? You look like you're feeling better. That virus really got the better of you."

"My system was probably run down from the stress of finalizing the manuscript and getting it sent off. I didn't expect a week in bed, however. I actually sneezed so many times I began to say '*bless you*' to myself," Sarah laughed. "Did you know people in the middle ages believed when you sneezed your sprit left your body for a second, and by saying '*bless you*' it would bring you back to life?"

"Seriously," her father asked. "How do you know these things?"

"From spending a week in bed, reading the World Book of Knowledge from your library."

"I should've known. You realize that book is ancient," Richard said.

"Published in 1901," Sarah said proudly. "But it is chocked full of interesting facts."

"Interesting facts that were valid at the turn of the century," he laughed. "Back to my original question, what are you planning for today?'

"Seaneen is quite certain I'll grow cobwebs if I don't get outside, so I'll head to the stable and take Winston for a ride after a visit with Little Henry. He hasn't been out for a brisk gallop in ages.

"Little Henry or your horse, Winston?" Richard asked, amused at his own joke.

"I'm glad to see you can still laugh after those horrid death threats from Frederick," Sarah responded. "Weren't we lucky Hugh Thornhill was here to sort it all out?"

"No such thing as luck," her father said. "That was a pure blessing,"

"You sound like Grandmother Rosemary."

"That is a lovely compliment. And yes, we were fortunate Hugh was willing to get involved and bring it to a quick closure for all of us, especially Kaitlyn."

Seaneen stopped stirring the shortbread batter and spoke up in a weary voice.

"Are we certain this will put an end to Frederick in our lives? Are we truly safe from his beastly actions? I'm sorry for Marjorie, I truly am, but when I think of the damage he has done…it is unforgivable."

"According to Hugh, Frederick's solicitor is trying to convince him to plead guilty. The death threat charges on top of the original ones mean he could face decades in prison. One positive was Frederick confessing the threats were phony," Richard said. "My guess is he thought the court might go easy on him."

"In a weird way I feel sorry for him." Sarah said. "What a mess he's made of his life."

"It's the choices we make that often define our lives, Sunshine. Don't forget that," Richard said. "I'm meeting Marcus this morning about some dry stone walls near the cottages that need tending. Seems our borders and fences always need attention. You could run into one of our guests at the stable who mentioned he might be riding today."

"I promise to be polite," Sarah said, kissing her father on the cheek. "After all, the only one I've met so far is Mr. Thornhill. I'm sure they are all very pleasant gentlemen."

Sarah sat with little Henry on the floor of the stall, holding the tiny red squirrel kit.

"How old is this baby?" she asked.

"Father says she is about eight weeks old and has a hurt leg," Henry whispered.

"Tell me again what she likes to eat?"

"Nuts and fruits," Henry said in a hushed tone like it was a secret, "but green pinecone seeds are her favorite. We must remember not to let her get away. An owl or a fox or a pine marten could eat her."

She looked into the large eyes of this sweet little boy who was so earnest in telling her his animal secrets. He carefully placed the red squirrel back into her space.

"I almost forgot, Auntie Neen sent you this," Sarah said, handing him the small box of shortbread.

"Thank you, Miss Sarah. Would you like some?"

"You are very polite to offer, but no thank you. I'm going to take Winston for a ride."

"Mr. Winston is a very good horse," he said, shortbread crumbles falling from his mouth.

Stephen came out of the tack room as Sarah brought Winston from his stall to the main area. They chatted about the weather, of course, and he helped put both saddle and bridle on the ten-year old chestnut Arab gelding. Little Henry assisted by giving Winston carrots and rubbing his velvet nose.

"Winston is a beauty and one of the best tempered Arabians I've been around," Stephen said tightening the cinch on the saddle one last time. "He's a pleasure to have in the stable."

They were interrupted by a trim man who looked to be in his late thirties, wearing expensive well-worn riding clothes.

"I want to take a horse out. I do hope you have something better than a nag who can barely walk," he said condescendingly.

Sarah adjusted the reins on Winston and gave Stephen a knowing look. This must be the guest her father mentioned, though she would hardly describe him as delightful. The two men walked through the stable and looked at several of the horses, though none seemed to be to his liking. Finally, the visitor pointed to the horse in the last stall..

"That one will do," he said pointing to the large horse.

Stephen hesitated. "Are you sure? He's quite high-spirited."

"I assure you I'm more than capable," the man said in a superior tone.

Sarah put her left foot in the silver stirrup and swung up onto the leather saddle. She raised her eyebrow when the gentleman returned, followed by Stephen leading Dasher, her father's black stallion.

"Perhaps you can show me around," the man said to Sarah. "I'm a guest at Leigheas."

"What is your name?" little Henry asked in his happy, innocent voice..

"My name is Jeremy," the man answered curtly.

"Do you have a surname?" the boy persisted.

"Fisher," was his reply.

Henry pondered for a moment then his face lit up.

"Jeremy Fisher! Do you live in a slippy-sloppy house at the edge of a pond? I've read all of Miss Beatrix Potter's books."

"I most certainly do not," Jeremy said, as he went about seeing to the horse.

Henry followed him outside and began reciting the book:

"Once upon a time there was a frog called Mr. Jeremy Fisher; he lived in a little damp house amongst the buttercups at the edge of a pond. The water was all slippy-sloppy in the larder and in the back passage. But Mr. Jeremy liked getting his feet wet; nobody ever scolded him, and he never caught a cold!"

Sarah was finding the entire conversation quite funny and urged Henry on.

"Do you know more of the story?" she asked.

"Yes I do, Miss Sarah. Would you like me to say it?"

"I would, Henry. And I'm sure Mr. Jeremy Fisher would like to hear more as well."

This was met with a glare over the back of Dasher, however little Henry was glad to continue his animated recitation.

"He was quite pleased when he looked out and saw large drops of rain, splashing in the pond—I will get some worms and go fishing and catch a dish of minnows for my dinner." Shall I go on Miss Sarah?"

"No," Jeremy Fisher answered. "I am not a frog and that is quite enough. We are going for a ride. Out of the way."

While she would rather have gone alone, she promised her father to be nice so she let it go and they rode out together. He was obviously an excellent rider and galloped ahead of her. When they reached the woods they both slowed to a trot.

"I didn't expect a beautiful woman to be at Leigheas," he said. "I was under the impression it would only be men. What an exquisite surprise."

"This is my home, Mr Fisher. My name is Sarah Duncan. Richard Duncan is my father," she replied, somewhat taken aback by his forthright flirting.

"Oh," was all he replied. "How nice for you."

"You ride quite well," she said, trying to make small talk.

He stopped his horse and stared at her.

"Do you seriously not know who I am?" he asked.

"You are Jeremy Fisher and you do not live in a slippy-sloppy house near a pond," she laughed.

Obviously having no sense of humor, he ignored her reference to the Beatrix Potter character Henry had so perfectly recited.

"Miss Duncan, I have been on Team Great Britain for the last two Olympic Games. I've won equestrian medals all over the world," he said, waiting for her to be impressed, then went on. "Magazines and papers have featured me for years. I'm rather well known and quite sought after."

"Really?" Sarah said, with a slight mocking tone.

"I suppose it would be presumptuous of me to expect a silly young American woman, living in the Scottish countryside to know much about what goes on in the real world. Perhaps I can help educate you," he said moving Dasher closer to Winston.

Sarah bit her tongue and replied, "I suppose it would be greatly presumptuous of you, Mr. Fisher. Did I mention I have lived in four countries, was educated at Cambridge and graduated from Girton College? I'll not be needing any further education from you. Now, if you will excuse me, I will be getting back to my house."

"I didn't mean to offend, my little lass," he said, putting his hand on her leg and rubbing it gently. "I thought you might want to know me a little better. What do you say?"

"Thank you, I think I know you quite well enough, Mr. Fisher."

She turned Winston around and cantered off down the trail. Jeremy, not taking kindly to the overt snub, followed at a full out gallop, then rode up along side her, forcing Winston to veer from the trail into the bushes as he passed by.

"Your loss," he yelled.

Losing concentration for only a moment, she suddenly realized Winston was racing toward a fallen tree that blocked their way. Neither horse nor rider had ever taken any kind of jump before. Sarah had no time to panic, as Winston's front legs took off over the large limb, and his neck and back came up towards her. Instinctively she stood slightly in the stirrups and leaned into the horses mane. While the landing wasn't picture-perfect, she was elated neither of them was harmed…until Winston, already spooked, ran too close to an overhead branch and knocked his rider off.

It's astounding how large a horse looks when you are flat on the ground looking up. The thought of moving her body was overwhelming and it was hard to breathe. She hoped she would pass out so the excruciating pain in her arm would stop. Closing her eyes, she tried to move but her body screamed in agony. Maybe if she lay very still it would get better. Obviously, not a long term solution. After a few minutes, she tried again. With a loud audible moan, she used her right arm to propel her body to her knees. The woodland was spinning and her head ached.

"Keep breathing, keep breathing," she repeated like a mantra.

Crawling with one arm and two legs wasn't getting her very far and she collapsed.

Winston stayed by her side and looked on helplessly. After a period of time, her brain began to clear a little and she managed to gingerly stand up on wobbly legs. Carefully taking a step toward her horse, she was able to lean against his neck and grab ahold of the reins with her good hand. Somehow, together they hobbled out of the brush toward the stable. The blue sky had turned grey and mist was beginning to collect on everything. When they got within sight of the building, Stephen and little Henry came running out. Seeing her disheveled appearance, Stephen swooped her up in his arms and handed Winston's reins to his son.

"Henry, please put Winston in his stall and be sure to close the gate. I'm taking Miss Sarah straightaway to the house."

Every step Stephen took jolted her aching body, but she withheld making any sound, not wanting to alarm him. They entered the house through the kitchen and Seaneen led them directly to one of the unoccupied reception rooms. Instantly, her father was there barking orders–telling Meara to call Dr. Campbell, sending Brennan to make tea, suggesting Stephen look her over, and asking Sarah what the devil happened. She tried to smile and assure him she was fine, only to end up in tears for no reason. This in turn upset him all the more. Ever the capable vet, Stephen tried his best to reason with Richard.

"Most likely she is in shock from the fall. Let me take a quick look," Stephen said.

As gently as possible, Stephen felt her left forearm and shoulder.

"Her arm most likely has a bad sprain, and I think her shoulder is probably severely bruised. This elbow could be injured, it's already turning black. An X-ray will tell for sure," Stephen reported.

When he tenderly touched her ribs, she winced. "That really hurts."

"Could be either broken or cracked," Stephen said.

Seaneen appeared with warm water in a basin and a soft cloth to bathe the wound on Sarah's head. Dried mud and blood were caked on making it hard to clean.

"That must have been where I hit the branch that knocked me off," she said. "I've never fallen off a horse before."

"How in blazes did you run into a branch? You are an experienced rider and Winston is not a horse to spook," her father said. "You were all alone and ran into a tree branch, I don't understand."

"Actually, I wasn't alone," she said, flinching when Stephen felt the edges of her head injury.

"Thankfully, this looks to be a superficial wound," interrupted the vet said, "it will rise up into quite a hematoma and turn all sorts of colors as it heals."

In all the confusion, Dr. McDonald had arrived unnoticed.

"Stephen, if you ever want to treat humans rather than animals, I'll have a place for you. From what I've overheard, you are most likely accurate in your diagnosis of Sarah's injuries," he said, setting down his well-worn black bag. "Well, lassie, let me give a second opinion to your fine veterinarian."

It didn't take long for the doctor to confirm everything Stephen had suggested.

"We will need to put your arm in a sling for a few weeks. Your shoulder, while sore, doesn't appear to have bone damage. I suspect you have indeed sustained a deep bruise on your elbow as well. As for your head, there is no need for stitches, but it will require an antiseptic cleaning and dressing. I'll send Nurse Agnes over every few days to change the bandages. We don't want any infections, do we?"

The door flew open and a wide-eyed little Henry ran in obviously distraught.

"Father, Mr. Jeremy Fisher is in the stables and Dasher is really angry and rearing up and I got scared." the boy said, starting to cry. "What should I do?"

He ran into his father's arms and held on tight. Stephen turned sharply to Sarah.

"Did Mr. Fisher cause your accident?" he asked pointedly. "I saw he rode out with you.

"I guess," she said stuttering. "He was mad and galloped too close to me and pushed Winston into the underbrush. We were forced to take a jump over a big log, then I hit the overhead limb. Maybe I should have…I don't know what I should have done. It all happened so fast."

In the past, Sarah had seen her father angry, but never had she witnessed the look on his face as he processed the story she was telling. Even Stephen put his hand on Richard's arm to calm him.

"I will speak to Mr. Fisher right now," her father said between clinched teeth, his face beet red with anger.

"Henry and I will come with you," Stephen added quickly, trying to keep up with his boss who was storming through the hallway to the front door.

The last thing Sarah heard before the door slammed shut was little Henry.

"I don't think Mr. Jeremy Fisher is a very nice man, Father."

Chapter Fifty-two

RICHARD:

Don't Mess with Dasher

Barely aware that Stephen and little Henry were following close behind him, Richard stalked across the meadow, oblivious of the pouring rain. He couldn't remember being as filled with rage as he was at this moment. Part of him recognized he was close to losing control, however, the other part didn't care. This man, who he had invited into his home, had purposely harmed his precious daughter. What kind of dreadful man was he?

"Richard," Stephen said, finally catching up with him and trying to keep pace, "perhaps we should slow down a bit and think this through. You don't want to do anything you'll regret."

He stopped abruptly, causing both Stephen and little Henry to bump into him like dominos.

"Come not between the dragon and his wrath," Richard said with fury.

"King Lear, Act I, Scene I to the Earl of Kent," Stephen replied, trying to catch his breath. "…and that didn't turn out at all well, did it?"

Richard looked at his friend, the veterinarian, and the little boy who cowered behind his father, and remorse began to come over him. He had frightened the child and there was no excuse for that. The three of them stood in the rain, as though the cold water might diminish his red-hot rage. Slowly, his pulse slowed and his breathing became normal. More often than not, verbal lashing out was a self-centered, cowardly way of hurting another person to ease one's own pain. Words said in anger rarely solved anything. He had read that somewhere. Gathering his wits, Richard was embarrassed and grateful for Stephen's restraint.

"Henry, I'm sorry I scared you," he said kneeling down, speaking to the boy face to face. "Losing my temper is not acceptable and I will try not to do it again."

The boy's eyes met those of the Laird of Leigheas and with all the sincerity of a child, he spoke up. "It's alright, Mr. Richard. Sometimes grown ups make mistakes, too. I still love you."

"I love you, too," he said to the beautiful child. "And Stephen…thank you."

After a few seconds, Stephen spoke in a low voice.

"A long time ago I learned an old Chinese proverb, '*Not the fastest horse can catch a word spoken in anger.*' It's been a good reminder more times than I care to tell you. Let's go have a chat with Mr. Fisher before we are completely soaked standing out here in the rain."

Inside the large stable it was eerily quiet.

"Henry, would you go in the tack room and wait for me there?" Stephen asked.

"Yes, Father."

The two men walked down the main aisle of the building, looking in every stall. Each horse raised their head as they went by, then returned to munching on oats. Winston still had his bridle and saddle on, but wasn't bothered by it. At the end of the aisle on the left was Dasher's stall. The half door was gaping open and the black stallion was facing the other direction. He still wore his saddle and bridle as well.

"Don't approach him from behind," Stephen whispered to Richard.

The tension was palpable. The horse's ears were laid back against his neck, head raised and the whites of his eyes were visible. Even his teeth were bared–all signs he was enraged. Stephen began to speak soothingly.

"It's all right, Dasher. I'm here boy, everything is all right."

Beyond the horse, Jeremy Fisher stood pinned against the wall, not saying a word, with a look of panic in his eyes. Stephen very, very slowly started walking toward Dasher, making sure the horse could see and feel his every move. He continued speaking to him in a calm tone.

"There's a good boy, everything is all right."

It seemed to take forever for Stephen to get close enough to actually touch the horse's strong neck and stroke it gently. He spoke to Jeremy in the same even tone, never losing eye contact with the horse.

"Mr. Fisher, I want you to carefully inch your way toward the side of the stall. Don't make any sudden movements or noises."

The experienced equestrian did exactly as he was told. Stephen kept up his one-sided conversation with Dasher, then in the same monotone spoke to Jeremy again.

"Now, slowly make your way out of the stall."

Within a minute Dasher's ears turned to face forward, alert and relaxed. He even rested one hind leg, a sure sign he no longer felt threatened. Stephen moved to a position in front of the horse, serving to distract him, while Jeremy escaped.

"That's my good boy. Let's get that bridle off and find some oats for you," Stephan said gently.

Watching him defuse this situation gave Richard another level of respect for his resident veterinarian. However, it didn't take long to remember why they were there in the first place. The ember of anger reignited.

"Jeremy, I need a word with you. Now. Follow me, please," Richard said in a quiet, commanding voice.

When they entered Stephen's office, Jeremy immediately became defensive, shouting about Dasher's behavior.

"Why do you have such an unmanageable beast in your stable? What's wrong with you? I am an extremely experienced and talented equestrian and I am shocked. He was fine on the ride, then became vicious. He is a menace."

"Mr. Fisher, stop talking!" Richard said with force. "Less than an hour ago you nearly killed my daughter. At the moment, that is far more concerning to me than your sniveling about my horse. Not only did you cause Sarah's accident, you left her there with a concussion, a sprained arm and a gash on her head. I am trying exceedingly hard to contain my anger with you because, by the grace of God, she does not appear to be permanently injured."

"I have no idea what you are talking about," Jeremy replied contritely. "We did ride out together, had a few words and I went on my way. Perhaps your daughter was confused after her mishap."

"Are you seriously suggesting you were in no way responsible for spooking my daughter's horse and forcing them off the trail, as you recklessly galloped away? Please don't add lying to your list of offenses. I have invited you to enjoy all my property has to offer, and this is how you behave? Your lack of respect to me and my family is appalling."

The champion equestrian sat down in the nearest chair and was silent. He stared out the window for at least five minutes before speaking. Richard felt his patience being stretched to the limit as he towered over the seated man.

"I am sorry," Jeremy said in a barely audible voice, not looking up.

"I can't hear you. What did you say?" Richard asked.

"I said I am very sorry and you are probably right about everything you said," Jeremy said in a soft voice. "I honestly didn't know your daughter had an accident. She is a fine rider and last I saw of her she was taking her horse over a fallen log in good form. Had I known, of course, I would have gone back and helped her. I would never leave an injured rider alone. If you want to press charges or send me packing, I don't blame you."

The small office didn't allow much room to pace, but Richard went back and forth a number of times before fully gathering his thoughts.

"This is not summer camp, Jeremy. This is my home," Richard said. "I suggest you return to your cottage for the remainder of the day and ponder your options. I will do the same. We will meet tomorrow morning in my office at nine o'clock and discuss your future here."

"Yes, sir," Jeremy said quietly.

The equestrian guest went out into the rain, with his shoulders hunched up, and his head bowed down for the long walk back to his cottage. Whether he was dejected by life or simply reacting to the drenching rain, Richard had no idea. All he knew was Jeremy Fisher was a sad soul right now, and somehow that sucked out quite a bit of Richard's anger and frustration.

"Ahem…" Stephen said. "Sorry to say, I might've overheard your conversation."

"All of it?"

"Well, yes. I stayed close by in case you needed a hand with him," Stephen said a little sheepishly. "You made me proud, Boss. You handled it with amazing grace."

"With help from you and little Henry. Good thing to have friends who keep you on the straight and narrow."

"By the way, Dasher is fine and calmed down now. I suspect Mr. Fisher tried to remove the bridle, which I told him specifically not to do. I've no idea why that horse only allows me to mess with his mouth. That's something we'll need to attend to."

"Glad that's your department. I'm going back to the house and check on Sarah."

"Might I loan you an umbrella? It's coming down harder than ever," Stephen said.

"Yes, thank you. For your umbrella…and your wisdom."

The better part of the night, he wrestled with what the best course of action would be. By morning, he concluded his response would depend entirely on Jeremy's attitude when they met. Every guest was struggling with something in their lives and the whole mission of Leigheas was to help with healing. He needed to remember that.

The office door was left open on purpose in case Jeremy Fisher actually showed up. A new day gave fresh perspective and Richard wondered if his guest might not just escape into the night and avoid facing the music. One gnawing thought was that Jeremy had come to Leigheas of his own accord seeking something. How far should Richard go in helping him find the healing? In the meantime while he was waiting, there was paperwork on his desk to attend to.

The reliable old grandfather clock had just finished chiming nine times when there was a tap on the open door.

"May I come in?" Jeremy asked.

"Yes, sit down," Richard said, standing up and indicating a chair opposite him. "Close the door behind you."

"Thank you for sending Stephen to visit me last night," Jeremy said. "That was a very kind gesture, given the circumstances."

"Stephen paid you a visit? I'm afraid I had nothing to do with that, but he is a good man."

"Funny, he said the same of you. He also said you were someone I could trust."

The anguished look on the Jeremy's face made it obvious he was floundering with what he wanted to say.

"Mr. Duncan, I am a proper mess of a human being. My entire life has been focused on being the best equestrian in the world. My family were not of means and while they were supportive, I knew I would have to do it on my own. I worked harder than anyone else, and spent longer hours practicing; I studied horses endlessly and read every book and article having anything to do with riding and horses, even National Velvet. It didn't take long for me to learn that wasn't enough. I had to curry favor with horse owners and sponsors in order to make a living. I found myself agreeing to things I wasn't really comfortable with nor happy about. In the equestrian world, talent and hard work are just the tip of the iceberg. It takes enormous sums of money to compete, especially on an international level. My goal was to be an Olympic champion. To accomplish that, someone had to pay the bills to get there."

"You met your goal, am I correct?"

"Yes. Twice."

"That's quite an achievement."

"One for which I paid dearly. It was all I lived for. Everything revolved around my equestrian career. Once successful, I fell into a world of very wealthy people who pampered me like some celebrity idol. Looking back, it is amazing how naïve I was."

"You wouldn't be the first person to fall prey to that situation," Richard said.

"Believe me, I'm giving you the short version. I think I became the worst version of myself, completely self-absorbed at the expense of my relationships with family and old friends. I cut ties with most of them and burned a lot of bridges on my quest for fame. Jeremy Fisher was the darling of the equestrian crowd, meeting royalty and riding the best horses. Then, I had my first serious accident. One fall is acceptable, two or even three is not unusual. Like most riders, my body had sustained multiple injuries over the years—a fractured collarbone, sprained wrist, fractured ribs and patellar dislocation. By my seventh fall, it wasn't only my ego that was damaged, but concussions had triggered full-on migraine headaches. No one wants a rider on their exorbitantly expensive horse who is prone to temporary vision loss at any time. As you can imagine, owners began withdrawing offers, sponsorships went away, and no more magazine covers or telly interviews. My foray into elite equestrian society ended abruptly and here I am."

"That's quite a story. I imagine one you've not shared many times."

"Only twice. Last night and just now," Jeremy said, pausing before he continued. "I'm not sure where I belong or what to do. There's always been a goal, you know, the next Royal Windsor Horse Show, or World Equestrian Festival and ultimately the Olympics every four years. Now I have no place in the world, no purpose. By all rights I should have been able to ride successfully for decades, but my competitive riding career is over. It's all I've known and all I ever wanted. I'm afraid I've become a very angry man."

This confession was not what Richard had expected and he knew his response was important. He took his time before speaking.

"Are you familiar with the word areté?" he asked.

"No," Jeremy said, looking slightly confused.

"Areté was originally a Greek word about fulfilling your purpose in life with qualities of excellence: things like virtue, morality, courage, basically becoming your best self. The word was used by Plato and Aristotle, and even in the Bible, so I promise it's not something I made up," Richard said. "From what you've told me, your life has been very focused on one goal, and there's nothing wrong with that unless, at the end of the day, you are left questioning if that's all there is. I'm wondering if you've been so absorbed with achieving your desires you've yet to have an opportunity to develop your areté, your real purpose."

The face across the desk looked at him in puzzled silence. Richard wasn't sure if he had gone too far and offended an already fragile fellow. He wanted to tell Jeremy about his own life and how after the shooting, he too was lost, with no idea which way to go. With the help of Lady Rose and heartfelt prayers, he was now more fulfilled and purpose-driven than he had ever been. What could he say now to help Jeremy realize the most satisfying years could be ahead? The answer came from the young man himself.

"You've given me quite a bit to think about. I appreciate your being direct. In our chat last night, Stephen said something similar, though not quite so…elegant. His version was along the lines of getting my head out of…"

"Yes," Richard laughed. "I know how the rest of that goes. Here's my question to you– do you want to stay at Leigheas for your remaining time?"

"Absolutely," Jeremy answered without hesitation. "I know I don't deserve a second chance."

"It's not a matter of deserving. Leigheas is here for healing and restoration, and I think you qualify for that, don't you?"

"Yes, I do," he said sheepishly. "Do you think it would be possible for me to work with Stephen while I'm here?"

"I don't see why not. We will need to ask if he's on board with that."

"It was his idea," Jeremy said, with a smile.

"Good. We still have lambs yet to birth, and our Highland cows are due to have their babies very soon. Of course, the horses always need tending, so I'm sure he would welcome the help."

"Speaking of horses, I've been thinking about Dasher," Jeremy said, gathering a little confidence. "Stephen told me about the bridle issue and I may be able to help. Years ago I heard of a similar problem with a horse and there were several methods they tried until finally hitting upon one that worked."

"That would be remarkable improvement. Dasher is a wonderful horse, other than the fight to take the bit in and out of his mouth."

Both men stood up, marking the end of the conversation. Looking over Jeremy's head, Richard noticed the office door open slightly and saw Sarah standing there but didn't mention it.

"I want to be useful after all the trouble I've caused. My conduct toward your daughter was inexcusable and the reality of her being harmed is something I will regret forever. I'm afraid I don't have the words to adequately tell you both how sorry I am. Do you think I should write her a letter of apology?"

"That may be something best done in person," he suggested.

"She really is a beautiful girl," Jeremy said.

"And quite taken," Richard said emphatically.

"I should've known," Jeremy answered.

"As I've mentioned before, both Vicar James and myself are available for conversation anytime you would like. We may not have all the answers but we are good listeners."

"Your kindness is something I'm not accustomed to. Thank you," he said and turned to leave.

The door was still slightly open but Sarah was no where to be seen.

Chapter Fifty-three
SARAH:
Dear Peter, Hurry Home

Dear Peter,

The thought of you being home in less than six weeks is too marvelous for words. I can't wait to see your paintings and hear all about your latest travels. You make it sound magical and I so wish I was there sharing it all with you. Maybe not the stinky herring. Until we are actually together, I'll pretend we are having a picnic in a meadow overlooking the river.

The news here has been topsy turvy since you left. I will try to hit only the highlights, as full explanations would require more paper than I have. First of all, I had a riding accident but was not hurt as badly as I could have been. It was an unfortunate situation with one of my father's guests, who I now believe really didn't know the harm he caused. He is very penitent and apologetic, and not as unpleasant as I first thought. I'll save the details, but not to worry. Other than a pesky sling on my arm and a scary bandage on my head wound, I'm doing pretty well.

Shortly before the accident, Kaitlyn got word that Frederick was to plead not guilty, which could result in a public trial where she would have to testify. On top of that, she received a threat from that scoundrel, saying if she appeared against him in court, he would have her killed. My father and I also got similar death threats. Thankfully, a guest here happens to be a barrister and was very helpful in sorting it out. While it sounds dramatic in the telling, the barrister fully believes Frederick was just blowing smoke.

I've saved the best for last! My book has been sent to a publisher in London! It is a tremendous relief to have it completed, but

*also a very odd feeling to not be working on it. My fictional charac-
ters became like friends and I find I miss them. My mind goes back
and forth between worrying the story is not worthwhile, to thinking
it's quite good. In the meantime, I'm trying not to be overly anxious
about hearing back from the publisher. From my brief time working
in London, I know it can take a while. So I wait.*

*It is halfway through May and the hills are lush with wildflow-
ers blooming everywhere. The weather has been mostly mild and
the days are beginning to feel warmer and longer. I noticed Colin
out fly fishing with several of the guests and watched as they caught
a number of good-sized fish. What a delightful season in Scotland.*

*I will close now and take a walk outside and wish you were
here. You are always in my thoughts and I miss you immensely.*

Yours forever,

Sarah

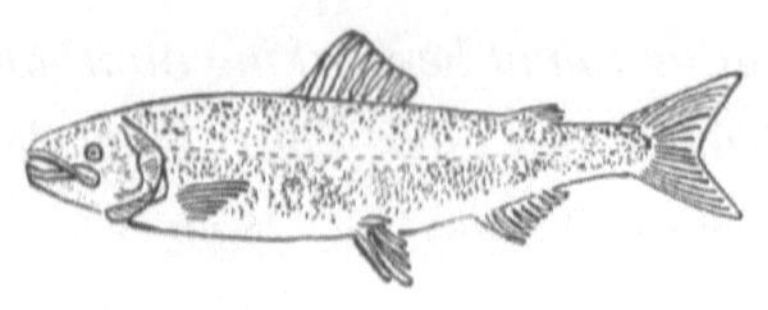

Chapter Fifty-four

COLIN:

More to Fishing than Catching

"So, let me get this straight. You are British and you've never been fly fishing?" Colin asked with some amusement.

"Hard to believe, isn't it? I'm afraid I was brought up in London, went straight from university to a corporate career and spent the last thirty years in the States," Clive said.

"To the best of my knowledge, there are a few streams in the new world, aren't there?"

"Not many in downtown Manhattan, I'm afraid," Clive answered with a laugh. "I'm a sorry Englishman with no fishing experience. On the other hand, think of me as a blank canvas, ready to learn."

The older gentleman was easy to like with an upbeat, cheerful personality. He seemed ready for a new adventure which was exactly the sort of chap Colin enjoyed teaching his love of the sport. Conversation was comfortable as they walked amongst the grazing sheep across the pasture toward the river. Sunlight drifted in and out through puffy, white clouds and a slight breeze kept the air fresh and clean.

"Fly fishing is a very old pastime, going back to ancient Rome, though I must say, the equipment has changed significantly since then," Colin mentioned. "The first book about fly fishing was printed in the 15th century with the unwieldy title of *The Treatise on Flysshyng wyth Angle*, basically meaning *'there is more to fishing than catching fish.'*"

"This is more interesting by the moment," Clive said. "Do go on."

There was very little about fly fishing Colin didn't know or like. The two exceptions being streams that were blown out with too much muddy water after a storm; and having to spend time with fishing clients whose egos were blown out with arrogance. He recalled with some amusement the obnoxious man who never stopped complaining. As subtle payback Colin made sure to help the man's wife catch a creel full of fish, while her husband got skunked on the opposite bank. Today, however, should be an enjoyable afternoon with a very pleasant gentleman.

They stopped at the small wooden fishing hut and put on their waders. Colin showed Clive his wide array of feathery flies, explaining the various patterns and how the fish perceived them.

"After the motion of a well-done fly cast, the tiny dry fly will land on the water with hardly a ripple and rest gently on the surface without sinking, imitating a real fly," Colin said. "And if you're really lucky, a hungry fish will saunter by and decide to make a snack of it."

"It sounds like a graceful dance. Why do I suspect it is far more complicated than your explanation?" Clive asked good-naturedly.

"You know, it really isn't. Of course, casting practice improves how your line lands. You don't want it to flump down and frighten any nearby fish, but like any sport, the more you know, the more you know. If you learn to tie on a fly, you have the advantage of changing it if the fish aren't interested or replacing it when you get your line snagged. Another lesson that comes with experience is figuring out where fish are most likely to be found depending on weather, stream conditions and time of year," Colin said as he readied the rods. "Patience and persistence are the basics to any successful fishing trip–if you're in a hurry or overanxious, the mystique will be lost. My father had an old joke, *'it is called fishing, not catching for a reason.'* I've found most days just standing in a stream, with nature is a gift all in itself. Watching a kingfisher flit about or a doe bringing her fawn to the river's edge for a drink are priceless moments. I can't think of a better way to spend a day."

The concept of time often slips by unnoticed when one is on the river. It was gratifying to watch Clive practice his casting and see the thrill on his face when his fly got so much as a nibble. It was late afternoon before they stopped for a snack and hot tea from a Thermos.

"Are you enjoying your time at Leigheas?" Colin asked, knowing it was off limits to ask why a guest was there or anything about their background.

"Very much. It is truly an extraordinary place and Richard Duncan has been a perfect host. I was sorry to hear about his daughter's riding accident, but she seems to be healing nicely."

"Yes, Sarah is quite a resilient young lady, and an excellent fly fisherman…or woman…or girl," Colin laughed. "I've watched her grow up the past six years and just heard she has written a book."

"Is that right? She is a delightful girl, I must ask her about it," Clive said, sipping his tea. "You know, I sought out a visit to Leigheas with the notion of purchasing a country home with some property, but now I must add a fishing stream to the list of necessities. Living only in big cities the majority of my life, I have recently found there is something in my soul that longs for the quiet countryside and the rhythm of creation. Does that sound daft and a bit idealistic?"

"Not in the least. I think there beats in the heart of every Englishman the desire to spend time in the country. A bit of warning in choosing your new property though, not all river front properties have private fishing rights. Be sure to ask about that. Can you imagine sitting in your garden and watching a proper strangers fishing yards away on your portion of the stream?"

"Oh my, no. Wouldn't that spoil the tranquility? Glad to know. I may have great knowledge about running an international corporation, but very little about how things operate in the country. I'm a widower with three children and six grandchildren and my hope is a small estate might entice them to visit me. Spending time at Leigheas was my son Oliver's idea, so I could see first hand what is involved before I spend his inheritance," Clive said with a laugh.

"Actually, all of my children have done well. It doesn't hurt that all three work in the family business."

Colin collected the cups and thermos then noticed Vicar James headed their way.

"Have you met our resident vicar?" Colin asked.

"Indeed, I have. What a nice addition to this beautiful place. It never hurts to have a man of God around."

"Gentlemen, how is the fishing?" James asked. "You certainly chose the proper day to be outside. Have you ever seen a more peaceful place than this?"

"Our guest is proving a very adept pupil. His casting is coming along and it won't be long before he catches a big one," Colin said.

"Are you a fisherman?" Clive asked the vicar.

"Let's say I am a work in progress. It is the perfect sport for a man of the cloth as fishing is not allowed on Sunday in Scotland."

"No! Is that right?" Clive asked.

"Technically, salmon fishing on Sunday is forbidden under an ancient Scottish law," James said. "As I recall, it was enacted for several reasons beginning with the church recognizing Sunday as the Sabbath and a day of rest. It was also thought to be a good idea to give the fish a day of rest, as well. Speaking from the ghillie's point of view, I'm sure it is rather good for you to have a day of rest, too, eh, Colin?"

"With all due respect, vicar, it would seem a pastime as harmonious as fishing would be encouraged," Clive said.

"That's a fact I'd agree with," James said with a laugh and changed the subject. "Are you finished for the day?"

"If Colin doesn't mind, I would like to give it a go for just a little while longer. I feel as though I am just getting the hang of it."

"Fine by me," Colin said, "Sunset isn't for an hour or so."

"Well, then I will leave you to it," James said, "Tight lines."

Either Colin was an excellent teacher or Clive was simply a natural student. There were a few fundamentals to a good cast, but Colin was of the mind that each fisherman would develop their own style. In a relatively short time, the Leigheas guest was raising his rod just right, gracefully allowing the line to form a nice loop, then putting energy toward the line releasing through the ferrels with the fly landing lightly on the surface of the water. It was a pleasure to watch Clive without the need to make any suggestions.

"I think I've got one on!"

"Keep the line taut, but let him run a bit," Colin said, reaching for the net.

"It feels like a whale on the line," Clive said, struggling a bit to keep his footing. "He must be enormous."

The fish raced to and fro across the river, obviously not amused at being snagged. Clive fought to keep with him, venturing further and further into the river.

"Now, slowly begin to reel him in," Colin directed from the shore. "That's it, slow as she goes, keep the rod tip up. You've about brought him in. Stay with him, that's it."

A lovely brown trout jumped out of the water in an effort to release the hook, but to no avail. He darted dramatically to the left in a final surge to get away.

It was stunning how big the splash was when Clive fell face first into the River Tweed. By the time Colin got to him, he had surfaced still holding the rod…which still had the fish on.

"Blimy, this is a great sport," Clive said, grinning from ear to ear. "Let's get this fish landed!"

With a little assistance, Colin helped him back to the shore where there was better footing. In less than a minute, the five pound Brown trout was cradled in the fishing net, with Clive looking like a proud parent. The barbless hook was gently removed from the exhausted fish and he was released to live another day.

Still soaking wet after changing out of his waders, Clive couldn't contain his exuberance. In the world of fishing guides, this day could not have gone better. Clive Middleton would be a fly fisherman for the rest of his life–not a bad day's work!

RICHARD

Hedgerows!

His fascination with hedgerows came on suddenly. Like most people, he took the iconic living fences for granted as they were such a common sight in Great Britain. It was only through a chance meeting with John Belmont, a longtime friend of Marcus, the head gardener, that he learned about the intricacy and skill required to create a hedgerow and the enormous benefits of having them.

"Aye, Mr. Duncan, you've a mighty old hedgerow on the far west side of your property which could use some tending. I was just telling Marcus the same," the small, whiskered man said. "Forty years and more it's been my trade to build and keep hedgerows in proper order around the Scottish Borders."

"I know the one you're talking about," Richard said, "over near the pasture where the Highland cows are. I've never really given it much thought, other than it kept the cattle where they belonged."

"That hedgerow has been doing its job for at least a hundred years or more. Beauty is they rarely need replacing, they are a true national treasure, they are. A countryside hero, I'd say."

"I had no idea they were so historical," Richard said, "and so extraordinary."

"That they are, though people are always confusing ordinary hedges, with a hedgerow which is a fair bit more complicated," Marcus said. "Some hedgerows are nearly ten feet wide and are made up of many sorts of trees and shrubs."

"You know, all manner of wildlife thrive in hedgerows," John added. "It's a place for nesting birds, and where hedgehogs, dormice and other wee animals spend the winter. Even beetles and butterflies call it home."

"After six years here, I've still much to learn," Richard said, shaking his head.

"Well, I'll tell you a little about hedgerows, lad," John said, pulling a pipe out of his pocket and lighting it. "It's thought they were first planted in the Bronze Age or perhaps even earlier. Maybe even in Neolithic times. Originally they were field boundaries, marking a landowners property, but as they were stock-proof and windproof they found use to contain animals and protect crops. They are sort of a living history, really."

"I'm on board! Marcus, wouldn't it be wise to add more hedgerows? I can't think of a better legacy to leave this property," Richard said, unabashedly impressed with John Belmont.

"Indeed it would, Mr. Duncan, though we must plan it out carefully to determine the best places as they will likely be there for a few hundred years."

"Are you available to help with this, Mr. Belmont?" Richard asked enthusiastically.

"Aye, always happy to work with my mate, Marcus. What do you say we take a look at your hedgerow near the coo's and I can point out some of the finer points?"

As they walked toward the west side of the Leigheas, Richard overheard John Belmont laughingly talking to Marcus.

"And we haven't even told him about wattle fencing yet."

The three men walked toward the hedgerow, and the coos began to amble toward them. It pleased Richard that his daughter was so fond of the Highland coos, as the cattle were called. She had done her research and informed him they are one of the oldest cattle breeds in the world. They are quite distinctive with their fluffy coats, shaggy bangs and long eyelashes that protect them from the elements. Beyond that, they are very docile and friendly, always looking for a little affection.

"Looks like you're about to have some wee Highland calves before too long," John mentioned.

"Yes, all four girls are due anytime, according to Stephen. He's planning on moving them to the open barn tomorrow."

"I wouldn't wait too long. You see the one of the far side over there?" John asked, pointing to a cow off by herself. "Watch how her back is arched and how she keeps getting up and down. Those are sure signs birth isn't far off."

"Good to know. I'll find Stephen after we've looked at the hedgerow and let him know. And about the hedgerow, when can we start?"

"We've just missed the time to plant I'm sorry to say. Ideal time is between November and the end of March," John said.

"Planting hedgerows is a bit of an art. The right plants, spaced correctly and put in at just the right time of year," Marcus added. "John here is one of the best."

"If you're still keen on more hedgerows, that gives us seven months to make a plan, and it'll take every single bit of that. I can work with Marcus and present you with some ideas in a month or so. In the meantime," John said with a twinkle in his eye, "are you familiar with a wattle fence, Mr. Duncan? I quite think you'd fancy it."

Chapter Fifty-six

RICHARD:

Tea and Coos

Tea time at Leigheas was more relaxed than at the fancy hotels in Edinburgh. Everyone was welcome to meet in one of the reception rooms each afternoon for an hour or so of relaxing conversation. Meara and Brennen prepared light pastries, small sandwiches and a variety of tea.

Today, Richard and James were deep in conversation about hedgerows, while Seaneen chatted with Hugh Thornhill about the goings on in London. Clive Middleton was relating the joy of fly fishing to Jeremy Fisher, while Sarah chose to spend tea time in her room writing a letter to Peter. The midday sun had surrendered to grey clouds and Richard could see through the French doors the threat of rain was not far off. Pretty typical weather for May in the Borders.

"I'm sorry to interrupt," Nurse Agnes said to the assembled group, "but no one answered the door and I have an appointment to change Sarah's dressing."

"Nurse Agnes, I'm so sorry. Please, come in. May I pour you a cup of tea?" Seaneen asked. "Though by now the water might be a bit tepid. Let me bring you a fresh pot."

"Thank you, no," she said. "Any idea where I might find Sarah?"

"Nurse Agnes, please excuse my manners," Richard said, rising from his chair. "Allow me I introduce you to our guests."

The attractive, red-haired nurse greeted each one with a nod of her head as they were named.

"Lovely to meet you all," she said. "Truthfully, Mr. Duncan, the only one to call me Nurse Agnes is Dr. Mc Donald. My given name is simply Agnes."

"You've been such a part of our household these last months, I'm afraid we've all adopted calling you Nurse Agnes as a term of endearment," Richard said. "We are forever grateful for your care of Miss Turning. Let's go find that daughter of mine."

At that moment Stephen appeared at the door, obviously distraught.

"Richard, we have real trouble. It looks like all four Highlands are going to give birth at once. I'm going to need some help. Immediately!"

This caught everyone's attention, with Clive being the first to respond.

"I don't know how to do anything, but I'm willing to help," he said.

"Likewise," Jeremy added. "Though I've aided a few mares deliver in my time."

"Oh Lord, this is what I get for a rest in the country," sighed Hugh. "Count me in."

It was only then that Stephen noticed Agnes standing by the door.

"You would be a tremendous help, Agnes, if you have the time."

"Of course. I'll do what I can," she answered, looking down at her dainty shoes and nurse uniform.

Seaneen immediately noticed the problem and instructed Agnes to follow her. In the meantime, the men left in a hurry following Stephen, who was practically running toward the far pasture giving them instructions as they went.

"Watch their horns, they are normally docile animals but will be hormonal and protective. If one seems to be having trouble, call for me. Mainly, I need you to watch and make sure things go smoothly."

There was an open-sided barn in the pasture with pens for the new moms and their calves. Unfortunately, Stephen hadn't had time to get them moved in there. When the men finally came upon the Highland cows, each animal had claimed an area away from the others preparing for the birthing process. Normally, Highlands have easy deliveries but these girls were young and on the small side. One in particular seemed to be struggling quite a bit.

"Jeremy, Clive, you oversee Daisy near the fence, and Hugh, keep watch on Honeysuckle over there," Stephen said pointing to his left. "Richard, you go out to Lady Macbeth by the tree."

By now, Agnes was running toward them in Sarah's wellies, with James and Seaneen following behind carrying towels.

"Agnes, please come over here," Stephen yelled. "James, go with Richard. Seaneen go with Hugh."

There was much mooing as the minutes passed and a group of nervous people, most of whom had no idea what they were doing there, waited. Twilight was upon them, but no one noticed. Sarah showed up, wondering where everyone had gone, just as Jeremy let out a loud whoop as his cow, Daisy, delivered quickly and easily. The mama knew exactly how to lick the newborn and within a short time the calf was on its wobbly feet ready to eat.

"Well done, Jeremy," Sarah said, caught up in the moment.

"Well done, Daisy," he replied.

"I'm concerned with Primrose here," Stephen said, "I've got a sneaking suspicion she might be with twins and that's always tricky…"

He was interrupted by Hugh, who with Seaneen's help was assisting Honeysuckle deliver a bonnie calf.

"This is incredible," he kept repeating. "Never been a part of anything like this, my, oh my. This is incredible!"

A short moment later, Richard was bellowing.

"Over here, we need some help!"

Without missing a beat, Jeremy and Clive ran over just as hind hooves were coming out of the reclining cow. They waited a moment to see if Lady Macbeth would deliver easily. When no progress was made, Jeremy made the decision they needed to assist. Hugh ran over to help.

"Richard, you stay at her head and talk to her, mind the horns though," Jeremy said. "Come on, Lady Macbeth, you can do this. Hugh, Clive, let's gently pull the legs when she has a contraction. One, two, three…"

That was all it took for new life to come into the world. The look on the faces of the four men was priceless. They were radiant, smiling and patting each other on the back, somewhat like proud parents.

Three of the four cows had successfully delivered what appeared to be healthy calves. Stephen's full attention was on calming Primrose who was mooing and moaning without much result. She would get up, lick her side then lay down and moo forlornly.

"I should warn you that if it's twins, it is liable to be difficult, possibly breach and either one or both calves may not survive," Stephen said. "It might be good to give her a little space."

Richard and the impromptu birthing team backed away and watched as the expert veterinarian pulled out the first one with Agnes's help. Within seconds the bull calf opened his eyes and began moving his legs vigorously trying to get upright. Primrose began licking him when yet another contraction must have hit. She let out a loud bawl and lay down again, obviously in great distress. Stephen worked quickly trying to free the remaining calf who was coming out backwards. With Agnes by his side, they would make a little progress, then Primrose would become agitated. This was the first time the Laird of Leigheas had seen his vet in this sort of emergency situation and was awed by his skill. Working together, Stephen and Agnes brought forth a small, ginger Highland calf. She lay motionless with no sign of breathing. Agnes quickly began rubbing her vigorously with a towel rag and cleaning out the little nostrils. Still nothing. You could feel the sadness in the air and hear a pin drop. Even Primrose was quiet. Stephen knelt down to help Agnes try to revive the little calf until they were both sweating from the effort.

"Sometimes nature deals you a hand…." Stephen said, rocking back on his knees.

"We are not done here yet," Agnes announced firmly, continuing to rub the chest of the wee calf.

Stephen's head drooped and he closed his eyes.

A little movement of the animal's legs caught Richard's attention.

"Look!" he exclaimed.

Within seconds the little lass opened her eyes and began to breathe on her own. A shocked Stephen carefully placed the calf next to her brother, close to Primrose, who began licking the new calf, with nurturing grunts.

With the last one delivered, the four new moms and their calves were gently coerced into the open barn not far away. Each had their own pen with food and water available, and fresh straw for the babies first sleep. Stephen would be busy checking them over with Agnes's help, before calling it a night. If the weather warmed, as it was supposed to, the coos would be let out in a few days to romp in the pasture to their heart's content.

Hours later, back at the house, the rejoicing and marveling at the miracle of new life was the order of the evening. Toasts were given to the new calves, their mothers, and each of the participants. Stories were told again and again, as every one of them relished sharing their part in the adventure. The camaraderie was infectious. Looking around the room, Richard felt a bit emotional at how this group had come together without hesitation to help one another. And in the end, they experienced a never-to-be-forgotten, once in a lifetime event. There was no better validation than this that Leigheas was fulfilling its purpose.

Chapter Fifty-seven

KAITLYN:

Rejection Loves Company

Tulips, crocus, and pansies bloomed in profusion across Princes Park in the heart of the city. She had forgotten how gorgeous Edinburgh could be in late spring. One flower bed had yellow daffodils as far as the eye could see, swaying in the breeze. Looming high above the lush garden was Edinburgh castle, built on volcanic rock in the year 1103. On the west end of Princes Park, the forty-foot tall Ross Fountain splashed 12,000 liters of water an hour into its enormous circular basin. Built in France in 1872 for a London exhibition, it was bought on a whim by Edinburgh resident, Daniel Ross, then generously given to the city. Unfortunately, the city didn't want it. It was an era of Victorian customs, and sculptures of bathing nymphs with bared flesh and voluptuous figures was not morally acceptable. It took ten years for tensions to ease and for the one hundred twenty-two piece fountain to be brought out of storage and assembled in its current place—bathing nymphs and all.

To the south of the city center was The Meadows, a large, flat park, notable for its spectacular spring display of blossoming cherry trees lining the walking paths. This was one of Kaitlyn's favorite routes to take to the book shop. Everything around her felt dipped in history, even the moss covered stone walls and ancient pillars and sundial. The air was crisp as she walked on the cobblestones up Victoria Street. Scented wisteria wound around window and door-frames, and hanging flower baskets graced many of the colorful shops.

"Good morning, Da. I'm here," she said, closing the door as the little bell finished its jingle.

"I'd be in the back, lass," her father said loud enough for her to hear. "Come join me for a cuppa before the day gets away from us."

Since returning to work at the book shop, morning tea together had become a ritual. Mainly, it gave them a chance chat and plan the day's activities. Tourist season had just begun and would only get busier in the months to come. June and July lead up to the crescendo in August when the traditional Edinburgh International Festival begins. Over a million people would descend on the city to experience the Arts Festival and Royal Military Tattoo production on the esplanade of the castle. The range of performances was incredibly diverse and sundry, but Kaitlyn had to admit the bagpipes and military bands were her favorite. If a Scottish heart didn't swell with pride at the haunting sound of a bagpipe, they must be as dead as Robert the Bruce. With all the festivities going on, business would soon be brisk in their wee store. Tourists were keen for anything Scottish and Turning Pages Book Shoppe wanted to be ready.

It was late afternoon when the last customer left and Kaitlyn turned the '*open*' sign around to read '*closed*,' and locked the door. The day was good with enough sales and customers to keep them occupied. Just as she finished tallying the days totals, the telephone rang. She hesitated before answering, after all they were closed, but it's awfully hard to resist a ringing phone.

"Good evening, Turning Pages Book Shoppe."

"They hated it and I am an idiot. I don't know what I thought I was doing. How could I be so stupid?" Sarah said on the other end of the line, ending the last sentence with a moan.

"Oh, lass, what has happened?" Kaitlyn asked, pretty much knowing the answer.

"The letter…just arrived…they rejected it…" Sarah managed to say in an emotionally choked voice.

"I'm so sorry. I don't understand. There must be an explanation."

Thomas was standing nearby, hearing only Kaitlyn's side of the conversation. He looked at her with concern as she silently mouthed she was speaking to Sarah.

"Can you come here…to Leigheas?" Sarah asked in between sniffs.

"I'm sure I can work something out," Kaitlyn said without hesitation. "I'll call you back in a little while with a plan. Try to be brave."

"Thank you…." Sarah answered tearfully.

"Let me guess," Thomas said. "Our newest author received her first rejection letter."

"Exactly. I'm not sure how I can help, but she has asked me to come to Leigheas. How can I turn her down?"

"You can't. She needs a friend, a female friend, to commiserate with and you are just the one to do it. Jacob and I will handle the shop tomorrow."

"Da, you are so understanding and wonderful," she said, giving him a hug. "I'll call her back in a bit and plan on taking the bus tomorrow morning. I'll not be gone long."

"Take all the time needed, lass. Bringing comfort to someone in need always comes first."

It was half past eight that evening when Kaitlyn finally dialed the number for Leigheas.

"Hello," a familiar voice answered.

"Richard?" she asked surprised. "For some reason I was expecting Sarah."

"Hope you aren't disappointed," he said. "Sarah has taken to her bed, feeling very discouraged I'm afraid. Did she tell you?"

"She did, and asked me to come to Leigheas."

"I can't think of anything I'd like better. When were you thinking?"

"My plan is to take the bus tomorrow morning and arrive about nine. Is that convenient?"

"I've a far better idea. Why don't I pick you up in Edinburgh at eight and we will have an hour alone on the drive back. I'm afraid once you are here, Sarah will want all of your time."

"Are you sure that's not too much trouble? It does sound like a lovely idea."

"My carriage is at your beck and call, m'lady."

"Kind, sir, I will look forward to the moment we shall meet," she said laughing.

"Seriously, your willingness to help is very appreciated. I'm afraid she feels she has somehow failed me which couldn't be further from the truth."

"Right now, it seems like the end of her dream but my father and I have a few ideas. Sometimes it takes someone who isn't family to help see things objectively."

"Not family yet…" Richard said teasingly under his breath. "Then I will see you bright and early tomorrow. Sleep well, my love."

"You too."

Typical of Scotland's weather, the morning dawned with a light mist in the air. Kaitlyn shivered under her clothes, thinking she should have grabbed a warmer scarf on her way out the front door. Richard was prompt as usual and thankfully the car was warmed up as they headed south for the drive back to Leigheas. They made one quick stop at Martin's Bakery in Newington, where the sweet scent of freshly baked goods was as impressive as the long lines of people waiting to get in. Richard had the clerk fill two bakery boxes with everything from jam squares to caramel flapjacks and rhubarb tarts. Kaitlyn speculated Richard hadn't taken time for breakfast. With two cups of tea in to-go containers, and a handful of paper napkins, they were on their way.

"Tell me your news," Richard asked between bites of a jam square. "How are you feeling these days?"

"Right as rain, I must say. I've gained my strength back, and apparently my appetite," she said, reaching for a caramel flapjack.

"Though Frederick's trial is always in the back of my mind, I try not to think about it."

"Not much information coming from Hugh Thornhill, though I know he has been in touch with Judge Cumberman."

"Which reminds me," she said a little cautiously, "Miriam Cumberman rang me a few days ago and wondered if Sanni could spend a few weeks with us in Edinburgh this July. Seems Wilford and his family are going on holiday, and she and the Judge will be in Ibiza. She offered the little boy several options, including taking him with them, but Sanni asked if he could visit us instead. I'm delighted, though not sure what we will do."

"What if you both spent some time at Leigheas? He gets on very well with little Henry and I am certain they would have a fine time together. The selfish bonus is I would have you around as well."

"You are kind and generous. Must be why I am so fond of you," she said, with her Scottish lilt.

"And I thought it was my dashing good looks, hair graying at the temple and a face full of smile wrinkles."

"Oh, all of that as well," she laughed. "I like the idea, I'm not sure if Da could do without me for too long. He's promised Jacob a week off during that time."

"I've every confidence you will sort something out," Richard said, wiping the crumbs from his face.

"On another topic, I had a thought about Sarah," Kaiylyn said. "What do you think about her coming to Edinburgh and working in the book store for a week or so? It would give her a change of scenery, and might get her mind off of her disappointment. She could stay with me, which I would enjoy immensely."

"She would love that, I'm sure. Might I join in as well?" he asked, with a laugh.

"I'm sorry, the Laird of Leigheas must have things to attend to in his realm. This visit would be girls only. Would you care for another jam square?"

"Agatha Christie had six consecutive rejections; Jane Austen waited fourteen years to get her first novel published; Rudyard Kipling was rejected by countless publishers and told he had no genuine talent; Kenneth Grahame was told *Wind in the Willows* was '*an irresponsible holiday story that will never sell*'; and our favorite, *Tale of Peter Rabbit* was rejected so many times Beatrix Potter published it herself. I think you know what a smashing success that was. So, while this feels like an enormous defeat, you are actually in excellent company."

"My goodness, I had no idea," Sarah marveled, wiping her tears. "To think I'm in the same place Beatrix Potter found herself in with her little rabbits."

For the first time in the past two hours, Kaitlyn was rewarded with a small laugh from Sarah. They had hidden themselves away in the library, examining the problem from all angles. So far, the conversation centered around the blow to Sarah's ego and confidence, in addition to the feeling she had let everyone down.

"Rejection sows nasty seeds of doubt that are incredibly hurtful and frustrating. It's as though you have been personally spurned, but in the writing world, rejection is part of the process. There is a phrase in Latin, *rejectio quadedam*, which means '*rejection is certain*.' So, chin up and let's get on with it," Kaitlyn said cheerfully.

The words found their mark and for the first time in twenty-four hours, Sarah sat up straight and blew her nose, a sure sign she was at least entertaining the idea of moving forward.

"No reason was given in their letter as to why they rejected it," she said, handing the letter to Kaitlyn.

"My insightful father said it isn't unusual for publishers to not give an explanation. Less than one percent of books written ever get published, leaving ninety-nine percent of authors wondering why. He explained there can be any number of reasons a manuscript is not accepted. First and foremost, it's important to remember publishing is a business designed to make money."

"You're right," Sarah said with a sigh. "I did learn a little from my short time in London with Carlyle and Bryer, but somehow I thought if my book was really, really good they would jump at the chance to have it."

"Might be they had too many children's book deals already in the works. Timing can be everything. Also, only a certain number of books can be published in a year, and you being a brand new author, they might've viewed it as a risky investment. Printing, distributing and marketing of books is very expensive. Also, keep in mind publishing companies hire editors who are all human with definite likes and dislikes. One favorite story my father tells is of a well-established author whose book was rejected because it was about a dog and the editor was a cat person."

"No! You are kidding," Sarah said.

"Absolute truth, even said so in the rejection letter. The book went on to be published elsewhere and sold millions."

"Do you think there is a problem with my story itself?" she asked a little tentatively.

"I do not, and neither does my father. It's well done and deserves to be shared with the world."

"Are you just being kind?" Sarah asked earnestly.

"I think we are well beyond that. If you recall, I assisted you editing and typing the final manuscript. I promise I would have brought up problems if I felt there were any. After a long chat with Da, I think we need to rewrite your query letter, fancy it up a wee bit and send it out to other publishing houses. We will include such things as why your book would be an excellent fit for their company, etc., along with a catchy tagline and short synopsis."

"Oh, hold onto that thought," Sarah said, jumping up and running out the door.

She returned shortly carrying a large brown envelope.

"I totally forgot to show you these," she said, opening the envelope. "They came in the morning mail, and Peter said they were little sample watercolors to make sure I liked them. I've been so busy wallowing in my pity party, I hardly looked at them. All I could think of was how to tell him I failed."

Six small watercolors easily slid out of the envelope, each one about six inches square. Kaitlyn examined every one intently before handing them back to Sarah. The two looked at each other in astonishment.

"He captured your characters beautifully," Kaitlyn marveled.

"Aren't they charming? Even better than I imagined when I wrote the story,"

"I knew he was talented, but these are brilliant," Kaitlyn said, "Looks like we'd better get to work and get this book out into the world."

The radiant look on Sarah's face said it all. If you could actually see courage and self-assurance grow in a person, Kaitlyn was witnessing it firsthand.

The door to the library opened slowly, and a cautious Richard peeked around.

"Are you ladies still alive? You've been in here over four hours without food or a fresh pot of tea. How on earth have you survived?"

"We are grand, better than grand," his daughter said, with so much enthusiasm he wondered if she had a fever. "However, I've had enough tea to sink a ship. I'll be right back."

On her way out the door, she stopped and planted a kiss on her father's cheek.

"I love you," she said in a low whisper, "but don't you dare mess things up with Kaitlyn again. I adore her."

"Me, too," he whispered back.

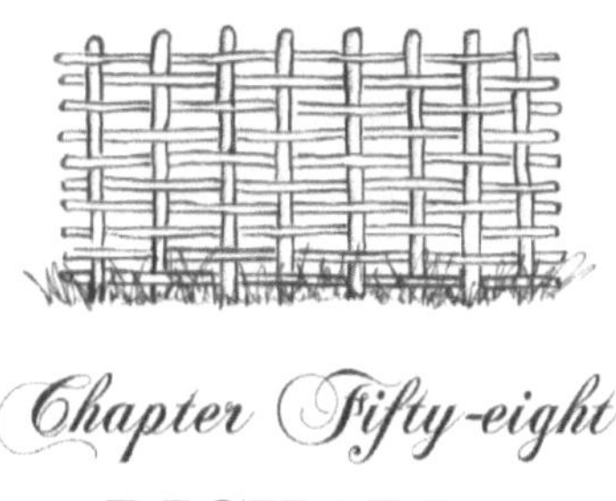

RICHARD:

Wattle Fences and Champagne

June would be here before long, bringing warmer temperatures and a bit less rain.

Everyone at Leigheas seemed enamored with Mother Nature and the anticipation of the new season. Since the birth of the Highland calves, the assembled group had all fallen in love with the little coos. At least two or three people visited the pasture every day to watch the wee ones cavorting about. The adorable furry creatures were quite friendly and enjoyed human visitors, though their mothers could be somewhat protective. Little Henry proposed naming them Flopsy, Mopsy, Cottontail and Peter in honor of Beatrix Potter, and somehow the names stuck.

Richard started the day early and was able to get most of his business taken care of well before Kaitlyn was due to arrive for lunch. The thought of making a quick tour around the estate struck him as a wonderful idea. He would saddle up Dasher and act as the Laird overseeing his land. Secretly, he knew this was unnecessary as the place ran like clock-work, but there was immense satisfaction in seeing it from the top of a horse.

First stop was the stable, where seeing Sarah in conversation with Jeremy brought a smile of gratitude for their reconciliation. Her arm was still in a sling, but it was obvious by the way she moved it around there was far less pain.

"Good morning, you two," he said.

"Dad, you won't believe this," Sarah said. "Jeremy has been working with Dasher and might have cured his bridle phobia. He was just about to show me."

"Well, lead on. This I've got to see."

They walked to Dasher's stall and as usual, the stallion went right to Richard, possibly because he carried several carrots.

"Hey, boy," Richard said, laying his hand out flat with the carrots on top.

Dasher gently nuzzled Richard's palm and retrieved them, chewing with gusto. When Jeremy approached with the bridle, instead of rearing up and baring his teeth, the large black horse took the bit in his mouth, and stood perfectly still while the leather headpiece went behind his ears. The broadband was placed on his forehead, and the throat latch carefully buckled. A unified sigh of relief caused the horse to look around curiously as though he had missed something.

"What a beautiful animal," Clive said, walking up to the group. "Not that I know anything about horses, but even I can tell he's quite a specimen."

"He's even more special now that Jeremy has taught him some manners. Never in a million years did I think he could be cured of his problem. Well done! Has Stephen seen this?"

"I showed him last night," Jeremy said modestly. "I've had a number of horses cross my path and picked up a few tips on how to correct difficult behavior. Horses are much like people. If you treat them with care and respect, you'll most often gain their confidence and they usually come around."

"I'm very impressed and I'm sure Stephen is as well," Richard said, reaching out to shake his hand. "Thank you."

"Thank you for treating me with care and respect," Jeremy answered quietly.

As Dasher was being saddled up, Clive and Sarah walked toward the front of the stable in congenial conversation. Richard couldn't help overhearing what was said.

"I understand you've written a children's book. Would you tell me a bit about it?" Clive asked.

Armed with self-assurance from her time with Kaitlyn, Sarah enthusiastically shared a synopsis of the book, described the characters, and explained the inspiration for writing it. When telling him about the brilliant illustrations Peter was doing, her eyes sparkled. Seeing her animated and excited about her project again brought joy to her father's heart.

"Would you allow me to take a look at it?" Clive asked.

"Of course," she answered. "I'll bring a copy to lunch. You are so kind to be interested. I'm getting ready to send it off to a few more publishers. I've already been rejected once, but I'm learning that's a badge of honor. Do you know how brutal the publishing business is?"

"So I've heard. I have done a bit of writing myself and it's always nice to meet a fellow author. Don't forget to include the illustrations," he said cheerfully. "I want the whole experience."

Since getting to know Clive the past few weeks, Richard found him a thoughtful, considerate gentleman with an engaging, positive attitude. He must've heard about Sarah's disappointment with her book and was going out of his way to encourage her. Lessons to be learned from a kind man!

It had been decided that John and Marcus would build a wattle fence near the sheep pasture. With all of their explanations and drawings, Richard still wasn't sure what he had agreed to and was anxious to see how it was coming along. He guided Dasher down a knoll toward the construction site and was astounded by a marvelous wonder of weaving artwork called a wattle fence. Strong wooden stakes were driven vertically into the ground about two feet apart. Long strips of flexible willow branches were twisted and woven between the stakes to create an intricate basket-like pattern. The fence looked as though it would be about five feet tall when completed and run for a distance of nearly forty feet. Richard was gobsmacked, as they say in Great Britain. An even bigger surprise was seeing Hugh Thornhill III working alongside John and Marcus.

"Isn't this a wonder? I can't believe they let me help," Hugh said. "It's the first time my creative side has come to light. My fellow barristers would be upended at the thought."

"Aye, and he's getting the hang of it, he is," John said smiling. "Might hire him for summer labor."

"This is absolutely incredible," Richard said. "I don't think I've ever seen anything like it."

"You'll find them all over the countryside, if you look. It's a centuries-old craft, you know. Been doing them all my life, and my father before me," John said.

"John and I have known each other since we were wee bairns," Marcus piped up. "And I can tell you, he's even better than his dad. A real artist, he is."

"Would you care to have a go at it, Mr. Duncan?" John asked.

"You know, I actually would," Richard said sheepishly. "You will probably have to redo whatever I touch."

"Not a bit of it. Now, take this willow branch…."

And for the next hour, the Laird of Leigheas was so thoroughly engrossed in the process of making a wattle fence, he lost track of time. A quick look at his watch reminded him he was due back at the house. He sincerely thanked John and Marcus for a most enjoyable morning, mounted Dasher and galloped home, hoping he would arrive before Kaitlyn.

The telephone was ringing in his office when he came through the door and he ran to catch it.

"Hello," he said, somewhat out of breath.

"Mr Duncan? This is Trevor Cumberman in London and I have news, though by all rights I shouldn't be telling you."

"Good morning, Judge. If this is concerning Kaitlyn, she will be here momentarily."

"It does indeed concern her, but I'm quite confident in trusting you. She will be contacted officially very soon anyway. So hard to contain good news, isn't it?" The judge sounded almost giddy.

The tension in Richard's body began to relax. He was very ready for good news.

"I couldn't agree more," Richard said.

"Well, that dastardly Frederick Hutton who pled not guilty forcing us all into sixes and sevens, has changed his plea to guilty!"

"You're kidding," Richard said, collapsing into his desk chair. "I don't believe it."

"Son, judges try very hard not to lie," Trevor Cumberman said, "though a few I've known might've…well, never mind. Yes, it's true. From what I heard Hugh Thornhill spoke to Hutton's attorney and shortly after, they requested an appearance in court with a plea change. There is enough evidence against Mr. Hutton to keep him locked up for decades. If you have any good champagne, my good man, today would be the day to uncork it."

"I do and I will," Richard said. "Thank you for sharing the news. I'll tell Kaitlyn the moment she arrives."

"Yes, you do that. Give her our best. We all miss her, especially Sanni. Good day, then."

Richard hung up the phone. What a difference a day makes, or sometimes an hour, or even a minute. This meant the nightmare was finally over for Kaitlyn and everyone else involved. The dark cloud of impending doom hanging over them was gone. It felt like a new beginning, a fresh breeze wafting through the room. He looked through the window to see his lovely Scottish lass walking toward the house and remembered Psalm 107, *"Oh give thanks to the Lord, for he is good, for his steadfast love endures forever!"*

Chapter Fifty-nine

SARAH:

A Cobblestone Lane in Old Town

Victoria Street is an enchanting, cobblestone lane in Old Town Edinburgh. The serpentine, narrow, uphill road was originally built in the early 1830's, as a much needed short cut from Grassmarket to the George IV Bridge. Renowned architect Thomas Hamilton was commissioned to design the unique five and six story Flemish-style buildings, featuring lots of peaked roofs and dozens of tall chimneys. On the street level, each shop has traditionally been painted a different vibrant color making them stand out against the muted stone buildings, and most have retained their original arch-shaped facade. Everything from tatted lace to curio establishments and cheesemongers are lined along the way, with a few pubs and tea shops tucked in between. Above the busy shops, charming, pricey residential flats are reminiscent of an earlier era and quite sought-after. Victoria Street is a rich world unto itself. Oh! How Sarah loved Scotland.

The wooden sign announcing Turning Pages Book Shoppe squeaked when the slightest wind blew through the curved street. It hung above the glass entry door, next to the display window which gave a view into the old fashioned shop filled with thousands of books, floor to ceiling. This fascinating emporium had been part of the Turning family for three generations. At the back of the shop the small fireplace with a carved mantle displayed several Turning family photos. Two well-used overstuffed chairs beckoned any and all to sit for a wee chat. Nearby was a cart with an electric kettle and everything needed for a welcome cup of tea. Sarah wondered if the comfortable ambiance had been one reason for its long-lasting popularity.

It turned out working with Thomas and Kaitlyn was exactly what she needed. They agreed she would fill in for six days while Jacob took a holiday to visit his sister in London. Before leaving, he was tasked with training Sarah in the finer points of bookselling, but the lad was clearly smitten with the young American girl, and more flirting occurred than actual teaching. Overall, she learned enough to be helpful and that kept thoughts of her perceived literary defeat in remission.

After stocking, dusting and selling books, Sarah was ready to sit down by the fireplace for afternoon tea. Kaitlyn returned from an errand with a box of treats from the bakery in Grassmarket and Thomas pulled up a stool. The three of them relaxed while there were no customers.

"You've taken to the shop like a duck to water, lass," Thomas said.

"I love being here. All the books and people who enjoy reading–it's definitely one of my very favorite places." she said, sipping her tea.

"Aye, spoken like a writer! I suppose I'm not objective, but this little shop is certainly where I belong. The opportunity to introduce a book to someone, at just the right time, can be life-changing. Why, some of our customers have been coming here for generations, and a few of them even remember my grandfather. They tend to think of it as their own private library," he laughed. "Very possessive, they are, and believe me, I hear about it if I dare change anything."

"Da has been a part of this shop since he was about five years old, isn't that right?" Kaitlyn asked her father.

"That's a true fact. When I was a wee one and no one was looking, I'd climb the library ladder and roll down the aisle, lickity split. Mind you, I was white knuckled, but it was marvelous," he said, reliving his childhood. "Oh, my father would be right mad, he would.

"You used to give me what-for when I went up on the ladder," Kaitlyn said.

"That's because I knew firsthand how dangerous it was," Thomas said, showing the scar on the back of his hand. "I might've slipped off once or twice and cut myself hitting a shelf on the way down."

"You never told me that," Kaitlyn said. "I suppose there is more I don't know, isn't there?"

Thomas rose from his stool and picked up a small silver frame from the fireplace mantle. It was a black and white photo of his wife, taken long ago.

"Have I ever mentioned how your mum and I shared our first kiss right over there," he said, gesturing toward a narrow aisle of books, "just under the works of Jane Austen."

"No! Really?!" Kaitlyn exclaimed. "That's terribly romantic."

"Aye, your mum was a great reader, and Miss Austen was one of her favorites," he said, taking his seat again.

"I can't believe she never told me that story," Kaitlyn said. "I know she used to come into the book shop when she was a wee lass after school to see you, pretending she was looking for something to read."

"Well…" he continued with a twinkle in his eye, "did she ever tell you I proposed marriage to her right over there?" he said, gesturing the other direction. "Right next to Elizabeth Barrett Browning's book, *Sonnets from the Portuguese*, the original edition written in 1850. '*How do I love thee? Let me count the ways…*" he trailed off, his face echoing a memory from a time long past.

The bell over the door tinkled and the spell was broken.

"I'll see to it," Sarah said, setting down her tea cup.

Greeting customers turned out to be much less scary and far more fun than she expected. Perhaps having the mind of a writer helped. Instinctive curiosity led her to be fascinated by stories shared by the wonderful customers of the book shop.

Walking to the front, Sarah didn't see anyone. Could they have left before she saw them?

Suddenly, from around the far book aisle a familiar face smiled and her eyes flew open.

"Peter! You're home! What are you doing here? How did you know where to find me?"

None of the questions were answered because the two were caught in a kiss only enjoyed by those who longed for this moment. He cupped her face in his hands and they were lost in each other. They held on without saying a word for so long that Thomas and Kaitlyn finally wandered up front to see what was going on.

"Peter, lad! It's good to see you," Thomas said, shaking his hand.

"Yes, it is," Kaitlyn agreed, "however, I think Sarah might be the happiest to get a glimpse of you."

"I only just arrived at Waverley this morning and mum insisted I come directly to her gallery, which by the way is on West Bow Street down at the end of Victoria Street," Peter said, still holding onto Sarah. "She will be your neighbor."

"That must be the shop with all the windows covered in brown paper. I've wondered what was going in there. Isn't that awfully exciting?" Kaitlyn said.

"She has done a bang-up job on the place. It's really coming along, but there is a lot to finish before the opening at the end of July," he said, then turned to Sarah. "I called Leigheas and Seaneen told me you were here. I couldn't believe my luck that you were in Edinburgh, only a short walk away."

"Tomorrow is my last day here, then back home," she said.

"I can drive you back if you like. I'm planning on spending tonight with my grandparents who are living here in my old house. I'm sure you remember where it is," he said, with a sly smile.

Sarah couldn't take her eyes off Peter, nor let go of his hand. If she had thought about it, she might've been embarrassed, but she didn't and she wasn't. Her face was flushed with pleasure.

"Actually my father is coming to pick me up, but I believe his ulterior motive is to have a few minutes alone with Kaitlyn," she said. "You are coming back to Elibank soon, right?"

"Hopefully by tomorrow afternoon. However, I suspect I'll be back and forth until the gallery opens. Now, tell me about our book deal, lassie," Peter asked innocently. "They must have loved it!

How could they not? I can't wait to hear all about it and I've got some new watercolors completed."

A stunned look of horror took over her face. She let go of his hand and covered her mouth where no words were coming out. How could she have neglected to tell him about the rejection letter? When the book was turned down, her disappointment was overwhelming, much like grieving a death. After pouring her heart into the book, writing and rewriting, editing and re-editing until she felt it was perfect, one letter had destroyed her confidence. There had been no word from the other publishers where she'd sent the manuscript and discouragement was creeping in. Maybe subconsciously she didn't want Peter to know she was a failure, but how unfair to let him continue spending his precious time creating brilliant drawings for a book that wasn't going to see the light of day. What a mess she had made of things. How could he ever forgive her?

Peter looked at each of them, a little bewildered, waiting for answers to his logical questions. No one said a word. At that moment, the shop door opened with its customary jingle and in rushed Jessica Micheal-McGregor, Peter's mother.

"Hello, everyone," she said, "I've just walked up from the gallery and I'm a bit out of breath. Lovely to see you. By the way, you are all invited to the gallery opening. What an undertaking! What was I thinking? Peter, you must come back with me immediately. The installation electrician is ready to place the lighting and he needs your guidance. Something about the glass on your watercolor paintings, the reflection is a problem. I'm sorry to tear you away, please forgive me Sarah, but the man is costing me a fortune."

"Of course," Peter said. "Give me a moment with Sarah first."

He pulled her outside the shop, away from the others.

"I'm guessing there is something I'm missing here?" he asked.

Seeing the tears slide down her cheeks, he had his answer. The others were still inside conversing the pros and cons of having a shop on this famous Edinburgh street, and thankfully ignoring Sarah and Peter.

"Whatever it is, it will be okay," he said brushing away her tears."

"I'm so sorry I haven't told you," she said. "The publishers hated it."

"That's absurd. It's fabulous. Do not let those buggers get you down."

"No, they didn't like it and have no interest in publishing it. I should have told you, but I was too embarrassed for you to know. Instead, I let you continue to create your exquisite watercolors….and kind of…didn't tell you. I am such a terrible person."

This produced a fresh round of inconsolable tears, as Peter's mothers came out the shop door.

"We really must go, son. Sarah, so good to see you," she said, oblivious to the hastily wiped cheeks.

"This conversation is not over," Peter said, kissing her on the forehead, then joined his mother walking rapidly down the cobblestone street. Rain began to fall, echoing Sarah's mood as she watched him disappear around the bend in the lane.

PETER:

Rejection Doesn't Define You

My Dearest Sarah,

Rejection is one of the most soul crushing experiences an artist can have. We expose our deepest, most private feelings for the world to judge and maybe the world is having a bad day. Criticism of our work is often a reflection of someone else's foul mood rather than an objective appreciation of our talent. These are not just idle thoughts designed to cheer you, but thoughts borne of my time with Mr. Antoneli in Italy. He stole my self confidence and I allowed his denigration to nearly ruin my life. My sweet love, one rejection does not define who you are as an artist. Far from being upset with you for not telling me sooner, I am absolutely bursting with pride at your accomplishment. I believe in you with all my heart.

LYF

Peter

The irony was not lost on him. Writing encouragement to Sarah was easy and he meant every word. If only he could now channel some of that positivity toward himself, he wouldn't be such a bundle of nerves. Arriving back in Edinburgh today he realized the pressure that lay squarely on his shoulders. The success of his mother's new gallery was dependent on how well his paintings were received. His reputation as a respected artist hung in the balance of the gallery's success. The offer to become part owner of the gallery, which would give him some financial freedom and independence, would be based on the favourable outcome of how many paintings sold. The press were becoming interested in the gallery and more pointedly, were asking to interview him. How would he slide past the fiasco years in Italy? And of course, he wanted Sarah to be proud of him and feel their future was solid. "Dear Lord, please calm my heart and my mind and help me remember you are the source of all strength," he whispered.

Thinking back, his time in Mallaig was exhilarating with constant inspiration. Every day he would paint plein air, then continue the project from memory well into the night in the bothy. It was as though a creative faucet had been turned on and it was all he could do to keep up. Overall, when leaving Mallaig this morning, he was pleased with his portfolio of paintings, however now being back in Edinburgh, he was assaulted on all sides with self-doubt and anxiety.

With a deep sigh, the note was put into an envelope and her name written across the front. Memories of doing this exact thing so many years ago flooded his mind. So clearly he remembered standing in this very room looking down at a beautiful young girl who was looking up at him. On a whim he waved to her and to his surprise she waved back. There was something melancholy in her lovely face that day that made him want to cheer her up. Thus began their exchange of letters getting to know one another through the written word. Little did he know then that it would be a long five years before he would actually speak to her face to face. Life was such an interesting adventure.

First thing in the morning he would push the envelope through the brass mail slot at Turning Pages Book Shoppe. Between now and then he must try to find some sleep—so much was at stake.

"Good night, my Sarah," he said turning off the bedside lamp.

Chapter Sixty-one

RICHARD:

Sitting in the Morning Sun

Every once in a while, a stunning phenomenon would happen in this little corner of the world. Sometime between July and August, without warning, a breathtakingly splendid day arises from the east, and graces the land so magnificently, that it defies words. Today was such a day. Gone were the heavy gray clouds and misty drizzle. The frequent wind was at a standstill and a divinely luminous day lay ahead.

Richard Duncan sat on the wooden bench outside the chapel, the sun warming his face all the way into his soul. His every sense was heightened by the majesty surrounding him. A meditative moment wafted over him, and he closed his eyes, silently thanking God for blessing him so richly. Breathing in deeply, the fragrance was like being in the forest, so fresh and green you wanted to inhale and keep it in your lungs forever. Overhead, in the tall trees, a multitude of birds chirped, one song overlapping another. Then all was quiet long enough to hear the low, sweet sound of the dove cooing. If you sat very quietly, it was easy to feel as though you were part of nature. Richard felt a sense of belonging in this land, as though he was right where he was supposed to be. The Scottish Borders were home.

"Are you sleeping, lad?" Seaneen asked, standing over him casting a shadow on his face.

"Yes," he answered, keeping his eyes closed but showing a hint of a smile.

"Then I will simply rest awhile on the bench and look at you until you wake up," she said sitting down. "Take your time."

The two old friends sat in companionable silence for a few minutes. Every so often Richard would slyly open one eye and glance over, then shut it quickly before she caught him.

"Do you suppose heaven is like this?" he asked.

"Aye, I do. Maybe even better," she said.

"Hard to believe it could be better," he mused. "I don't suppose you walked all the way up here to watch me commune with nature."

The huge wingspan of a golden eagle momentarily obscured the sun as he soared overhead. Landing gracefully on a high branch in a nearby tree, as though basking in the glorious day as well.

"You were the farthest thing from my mind," she said, with a laugh. "James asked if I would take a wee walk up here to see if we had any extra candle holders in the chapel. Peter called saying something about his mother in a bit of a panic about needing more for the gallery opening."

Richard took in the information without moving a muscle, eyes closed again.

"This gallery opening has become quite the event, hasn't it?" he asked. "When I was in the Foreign Service I attended many a gala and none seemed quite as elaborate as this soiree."

"And how many of those galas did you actually plan?" Seaneen asked pointedly.

"Good point, Mrs. Bradbury, good point," he said, stretching out his legs in front of him and blinking at the bright sunlight. "And, it is tomorrow, correct?"

"Indeed, it is. Mrs. Michael-McGregor was kind enough to invite everyone at Leigheas and to my knowledge, all are going. Hugh invited his wife, which I think bodes well for their relationship, and the timing worked perfectly for Clive to bring his son along."

"That's right, I had forgotten Oliver Middleton would be with us for a few days," Richard said. "I think Clive wants to show him the lovely property he's purchased not far from Melrose. It's twenty acres with a Grade B Georgian manor house on a tributary of the River Teviot. Everything he wanted, even stables."

"Then I'm guessing you've heard Clive inquired to see if Jeremy Fisher would consider coming to work with him?" Seaneen asked. "Seems Clive wants to buy a few horses and other livestock and thought Jeremy might be ready to settle down."

That news brought Richard to an upright position with a curious look.

"Is that right? He never mentioned a thing, but it might be a brilliant idea. Jeremy is a good lad in need of someone to look up to, and Clive is well-spoken and a good listener who could teach him a thing or two about life. Wish I had thought to connect them. Stephen mentioned just the other day how helpful Jeremy has been."

"As Laird of Leigheas, you've had an awful lot on your plate. I don't remember when so many people have been in and out of your office the last few days needing a bit of your time–Peter, Kaitlyn, Thomas, Stephen just to mention a few." Seaneen laughed. "I must say, looking back, this has been a rather enjoyable spring and summer. Things have gone along rather well, other than Sarah's arm in a sling and a concussion and her book being rejected."

"And Kaitlyn being kidnapped and almost dying," Richard added dryly.

"Well, all's well that ends well," she said with her usual bright optimism. "By the way, have you seen little Henry and Sanni? Those two have been inseparable since the boy got here."

"When Kaitlyn told me the Cumberman's asked if Sanni could visit for a few weeks this summer, I wondered how she would keep the boy occupied in a bookstore. It dawned on me he could come here with acres to explore. Little Henry was thrilled by the idea and Stephen was quite happy for his son to have a playmate," Richard said.

"I'm quite amused how Sarah has taken to Sanni, like a little brother. Can you imagine how different it must be living here, so far from all he knew in Nepal?" she said, looking over at Richard who was staring off into the distance. "Does it bother you that his father was once a special friend of Kailtlyn's?"

A quiet pause was interrupted by birds chattering in the overhead trees.

"No. I thought it might," Richard said thoughtfully, "but it would be like Kaitlyn resenting Sarah for being my child from Victoria. The lad is quite delightful and so curious about everything. It is clear that Sanni is terribly fond of Kaitlyn and vice-versa. In a way, it is a rare gift for her to have the best of Nigel in this charming little boy, much as I can look at Sarah and remember the good in Victoria."

"You're a good man, Richard Duncan." she said with a warm smile.

The tall man stood up and reached out his hand to help his dear friend rise, then wrapped his arm around her.

"Blessed by having friends like you to guide my path," he said.

"Me and the Lord," she chuckled. "You can be a handful, laddie."

"Who can be a handful?" James asked walking up. "Not our Richard, surely."

"Aye, you don't know the half of it," she said. "Did you give up on me ever returning with the candle holders? I'm afraid we got to talking about one thing and another."

"I always miss you, my love," the vicar said fondly to his wife. "Actually, Sarah was looking for you. The lass seems to be in some sort of dither about what to wear to the gallery opening and wanted your help. It might involve a trip to Jenners in Edinburgh with Kaitlyn."

"Then I'd better get back to the house," she said happily. "There is nothing more satisfying than being needed. Come to think of it, I might need a new gown. Gentlemen, I leave you to continue enjoying this magnificent morning."

"Take good care of my favorite ladies," Richard shouted after Seaneen.

"May I?" James asked, motioning to the bench.

"By all means," Richard answered, sitting back down. "Some days, doesn't it just feel as though the glory of God outdoes itself?"

"If you were to look for it, I believe you'd find the Lord's splendor in every day," the vicar answered thoughtfully.

Each man fell into his own thoughts as the warm, balmy air swirled around them–two friends silently sharing a meaningful moment in time.

"James, are retired vicars allowed to conduct wedding ceremonies?" Richard asked.

SARAH:

The Storm

It started in the middle of the night when everyone was fast asleep–a blinding light quickly followed by an ear-shattering boom. Sarah was disorientated being awakened so dramatically from a deep sleep. Before her wits were fully gathered, another jagged flash of light cut across the night sky. Again, followed closely by a resounding explosion and a loud, trailing rumble. An eerie silence followed. She held her breath waiting for the next round only to hear driving rain pelting the rooftop and smacking onto her windows with a vengeance. How could the spectacular weather of yesterday surrender to such a frighteningly powerful storm in such a short time? A not-so-subtle reminder that Great Britain was, after all, an island complete with spontaneous weather.

It was obvious sleep wasn't in her future. The grandfather clock chimed four times when Sarah passed by on her way down the dark staircase toward the kitchen. Maggie was asleep by the Aga and blinked sleepily when the light was turned on.

"What a funny dog you are. You didn't even hear the storm, did you?" Sarah asked, bending down to scratch the sweet pet.

"Well, I did!" her father said, standing at the open door in his robe. "I can't remember the last time thunder and lightening actually woke me up. For a moment, I thought England was attacking Scotland again."

"Tea?" Sarah asked, putting on the kettle.

"Please."

"Earl Grey or English Breakfast?"

"Do you know about the benefits of drinking Earl Grey?" Her father asked, then continued on without waiting for an answer. "It is made with bergamot, a citrus fruit from Italy, which can help reduce anxiety and depression. Plus, it improves digestion."

"Shall I take that to mean you'd like Early Grey?" Sarah laughed. "And how do you know all of this?"

"Kaitlyn found a book in her shop and was sharing some of the more interesting facts about tea. As you can tell, we have scintillating conversations."

They settled in at the large table in the middle of the kitchen with the tea pot brewing and a small plate of digestive biscuits between them. Holding up the sweet-meal cookie, Richard began to explain its history.

"And this biscuit, which originated in Scotland, was developed in 1839 by two doctors to aid in…digestion. As it turns out, it is perfect for dunking," he said demonstrating, "and comes in chocolate flavor, as well."

"Don't tell me, Kaitlyn has a book on digestive biscuits?"

"Same book," her father said, biting into the slightly soggy cookie. "What a treasure trove of information that woman is."

"Among her many other fine qualities," Sarah said. "I love watching you when she walks in the room."

"I suppose I have you to thank for bringing her into my life. It never occurred to me that I would meet such an extraordinary woman at my age. For the most part, the last few years have been quite good. I've been happy and fulfilled, but, one visit to a book store and WHAM–my life is turned upside down. I realized how much I missed having someone special to share things with."

"And it doesn't hurt that she is extremely pretty," Sarah said, pouring more tea into their cups.

"I might've noticed," her father said with a smile, "but it goes far deeper than that. She has a kindness and sweetness about her I find exceptional. She listens and really cares about what you're saying, plus she's bright, articulate, cheerful…I could go on and on."

"You're preaching to the choir, as Grandmother used to say. Next to you, I think I am Kaitlyn Turning's biggest fan. Not that it's any of my business, but if you were thinking of a more permanent, ah, situation," Sarah said hesitating, "I would be totally on board with it."

The range of emotions that crossed Richard's face was amusing and rendered him without a ready comeback. She couldn't help but laugh.

"My sophisticated father at a loss for words. It must be love," she said, delighted to have the upper hand.

A crack of lightening and a long roar of thunder caused the lights to flicker on and off. Even Maggie looked up and whined a little, before settling back down in her bed.

"Have you spoken with Peter lately?" he asked. "Tonight is the big event. He must be very excited."

"I think he's more nervous than anything. His mother has really gone all out, which I understand, but I'm not sure she realizes the pressure it has put on him. There are so many people invited! Family coming from all over, even flying in from the United States. I'm so anxious for him and wish I could help. He said the strangest thing a few days ago, something about the most important thing to him was that I be there. Isn't that odd? As though I would miss it!"

"He said the same thing to me, wanted to make sure I was attending. Must be nerves," Richard said. "You know, I'm very fond of Peter, especially the way he stepped up to help Kaitlyn. He is a good lad and if I'm not mistaken, he will have a successful future. You're both still young, lots of time ahead."

Sarah reached across the table and touched her father's hand.

"Thank you for liking him, even when I was mad at him. That really means the world to me. I quite fancy him myself."

The old grandfather clock struck six times as they cleaned up their tea things. If the sky hadn't been taken hostage by the raging storm, the sun would've been shining by now. As it was, between the heavy clouds and downpour of rain, it was barely light outside. The shrill sound of the telephone ringing startled them both.

"Hello," Richard answered. "Good morning, Liam. No, no bother, we were up. We are having some serious weather and the phone line is breaking up, but I can hear you."

There was a long pause as Richard listened. Sarah waited eagerly to know the news.

"Well, that is marvelous. You'll arrive this afternoon? I hope the storm won't be a problem. Yes, I know you Shetlanders are hardy folk." he said, "By the way, there is a gallery opening tonight for Peter and I'm sure you are all welcome. Yes, it's a bit on the formal side. Well, fine, we will look forward to seeing you before long. Cheers."

"What?" Sarah asked with excitement. "Liam's coming for a visit?"

"Even better! His sister has been accepted to the University of Edinburgh School of Divinity. Liam, his mum and Ava are coming to Edinburgh to locate a flat for her in the city."

"That's incredible! How perfect to have Ava so close. Aside from being my cousin, she became a good friend when I lived with them on Shetland. We'd better let Meara and Brennen know to get their rooms ready. Don't you love good news?"

The telephone rang again.

"It must be Liam with something he forgot to tell us. Who else would call at this hour?" Sarah laughed, as her father answered the phone

"Liam, was there more? Oh, sorry, Kaitlyn. I just hung up with Liam. No matter. How are you? Is everything all right?"

Again, Sarah waited somewhat impatiently to know what was going on.

"Oh my. I'm so sorry to hear that. And the power is out all down Victoria Street? You say Thomas is already at the gallery trying to help Peter's mother? Yes, it makes sense he would know how the electrical systems work in those old buildings, but if the outage is all over I wonder if there is much he can do. Of course, I will tell Sarah, and we will be careful. You're right, using the telephone in a lightening storm is not a good idea. I'll caution everyone to not bathe until the lightening has stopped. Will you call back in a bit and let us know what is going on?" Richard asked, then smiled and responded, "Je t'aime."

"You know I speak French, right?" Sarah said grinning from ear to ear.

"It seems there is no electricity in parts of Old Town, and Victoria Street seems especially hard hit," Richard said, ignoring his daughter's linguistic knowledge of French. "Kaitlyn's father has gone to the gallery to see what he can do. Apparently Jessica is in quite a dither but is determined the opening will happen tonight no matter what. I assured Kaitlyn we would both be there. No matter what."

By mid-afternoon the worst of the storm had passed. Huge puddles dotted the garden, and tiny rain rivers flowed away from the house toward the gravel driveway. Clouds remained heavy, but only a light drizzle fell. Most of the staff and guests at Leigheas had come through the house at one time or another, moaning about the storm and wondering if the gala at the gallery was still going ahead. Jessica telephoned Sarah with a plea for as many candles as could be found. She said the electricity was spotty, going on and off and decided to try illuminating the space as best she could with candlelight.

"I've no idea if it will work, but it's far too late to cancel. Do you think you and your father might arrive a bit early? I'm just short of a panic," Jessica said. "Poor Peter is trying to remain calm amidst this chaos. At least we haven't had any flooding yet. Victoria Street was awash in rainwater earlier."

"I promise, we will be there as soon as we can. Please let us know if there is anything else you need. Everything will be fine," Sarah said, trying to sound positive.

"Who was that on the phone?" Richard asked, walking into the kitchen.

"Peter's mother. She's always seemed so organized, it's interesting to see her all at sixes and sevens. She would like us there as soon as possible."

"Do you know where that expression came from?" he asked, holding out his arm and French cuff shirt sleeve so Sarah could attach the cufflink.

"From another one of Kaitlyn's books?"

"Exactemento!" he said with a terrible French accent. "It's from a French dice game called Hazard, something to do with French roman numerals. Thank you, here is the other sleeve."

She stood back and looked at her dad in admiration. He really was quite handsome in his formal wear, but then most men were.

"You'd better get dressed," her father said. "I'll find Meara and have her round up the all the candles she can find for Jessica. I hope her plan works."

Chapter Sixty-three

SARAH:

The Gallery Opening

The cobblestones glistened in the humid, misty air from the earlier storm. Sarah and her father walked up the narrow lane, each carrying a cloth bag full of candles, careful not to fall on the slippery uneven surface. When they came around the bend from West Bow to Victoria Street, they saw the gallery for the first time. The imposing storefront had been painted deep blue with towering floor-to-ceiling windows and a recessed paned glass entry door. Above the windows, in traditional gold lettering a sign read *Mathews • McGregor Art Gallery*. Several long planters of bright blooming flowers separated the first floor from the second. It was all very stylish and fit perfectly with the ambiance of the other colorful shops on Victoria Street.

Once inside, the refinement and elegance of the cream-colored walls with wide, white crown moulding, and dark hardwood floors was breathtaking. An antique carved desk was in the far right corner of the long main room where Jessica Michael-McGregor was giving instructions to several young women holding trays. To the left was an archway that opened to the actual gallery room, with a further archway leading to yet another room. All had been roped off, but a quick peek caused Sarah's heart to soar–the walls were filled with Peter's magnificent paintings. This was such a huge, defining moment for him and she couldn't have been happier. A tiny part of her wished they were celebrating a book deal together, but life was not about her right now.

In the center of the main room, a woman was tuning the strings of an impressive gold harp. The poetic, heavenly sounds filled the refined room creating an atmosphere of quiet elegance.

"Did you know sometimes performance harps must be tuned two or three times a day?" Sarah asked her father in a hushed voice.

"Sounds like a full time job," he whispered back. "Far better to pluck the strings of a harp rather than to pluck the feathers from a chicken."

"You are incorrigible," she said, stifling a giggle just as Jessica caught sight of them.

"Thank you so much for coming early and bringing the candles. The local shops are closed and you can see how dim it is in here with no electricity. Poor Thomas worked hours trying to remedy the situation, but to no avail. There are far too many people invited to cancel, so the show must go on. Forgive me, I'm running around like a chicken with my head cut off."

It was all Sarah could do to not burst out laughing. Far too many chicken jokes. Jessica took the candles and began explaining to the young servers where to place them. Within a few minutes the dimly lit rooms began to come alive with candlelight. While it was very romantic, it didn't show off the paintings very well.

"That helps a little, doesn't it?" Jessica asked. "Of all times for the power to go off."

"It looks lovely," Sarah said encouragingly. "I haven't seen Peter. Is he about?"

"He went home with his father to dress. I hope they hurry. Guests will be arriving soon. Do excuse me, I must go make sure the champagne is chilled properly. And Sarah, you look exquisite tonight."

Lydia Mathews, the co-owner of the gallery was busy adjusting more candles when the first guests entered. Thankfully, it was Kaitlyn and Thomas with Sanni in tow. Sarah watched as her father walked toward his beautiful Scottish girlfriend and handed her a small bouquet of heather, wrapped with a satin ribbon. Once Sanni caught sight of Sarah, he was at her side in a second.

"You are very pretty tonight, Miss Sarah," the boy said.

"Thank you, and may I say you look quite handsome yourself," she replied bending down to his level.

Young Sanni wore an English boys suit with short pants, knee socks and a perfectly knotted tie. He smiled brightly up at her and slipped his hand into hers. Thomas walked over, shaking his head in despair.

"For the life of me, I've tried every trick I know to restore the electricity, but nothing worked. I'm feeling quite bad, I'll tell you that. A dreadful time for this to happen," Thomas said.

"I'm sure you did everything you could. It is just one of those things," Sarah said, trying to console Kaitlyn's dad. "The candle-light is quite pretty."

People began arriving and the party was on. The harpist played a Welsh classic, '*Watching the Wheat*,' by John Thomas, which set the mood. Jessica and Lydia greeted each guest by name, made sure they had champagne, and introduced them to others. When the door opened and Peter walked in behind his father, Sarah's heart nearly pounded out of her body. He was dressed quite smartly in a black turtleneck under a black jacket with his hair curling a bit over his forehead. He didn't spot her at first as his mother was busy present-ing him to guests who quickly surrounded the young artist. It was odd for Sarah watching her shy boyfriend smile and nod graciously to the guests, every bit the picture of poise and confidence. Only she knew how timorous he was feeling on the inside. Observing the extraordinary young man who owned her heart, she forgot all about Sanni who was still holding her hand.

"Mister Peter looks quite handsome, too. Don't you think so, Miss Sarah?" the little innocent voice asked. "Oh, look, there is Henry. May I go see him?"

"Of course," she answered, giving his hand a squeeze.

Stephen waved to her as he guided Agnes and little Henry through the crowd. Sarah couldn't help but think what a marvelous couple they made, though she certainly hadn't put two and two to-gether until this moment. The Nurse and the Vet–sounded like a book title.

Hugh Thornhill arrived with his wife Cathryn together with Seaneen and James. They were followed shortly after by Jeremy, Clive and another man. It was great fun seeing everyone all dressed up and happily mingling. The circle around Peter grew larger, mostly with people she didn't know. After a few moments, he began looking around over the heads of the solicitous guests. When he finally made eye contact with Sarah, he politely extricated himself from the crowd and came her way. The man of the hour stood before her with an enormous smile across his face.

"You look gorgeous and I adore you," he whispered in her ear. "Shall we escape this mad place and find a quiet pub for dinner?"

"In your dreams," she whispered back. "The evening's only begun and you are the star attraction."

"That's because my paintings are all in those roped off rooms and no one has seen them yet. What if they are disliked and I am a failure?"

"I believe you recently taught me that rejection does not determine who you are as an artist. You are brilliant, talented and very handsome. Sanni even said so."

He wrapped his arm around her and pulled her close. The tender moment was interrupted by Clive Middleton along with a well-dressed man in his early thirties.

"Good evening, I was hoping to catch a moment with the two of you. May I introduce my son, Oliver?" he said. "Oliver, this is the author Sarah Duncan, and artist Peter Micheal-McGregor I told you about."

With introductions and handshakes made, Sarah couldn't help but notice the Cheshire Cat look on the faces of the two gentleman.

"It is an absolute pleasure to meet you, Miss Duncan," Oliver said. "My father was quite enamored with your manuscript and sent it to me straightaway. I must say, I share his enthusiasm."

"That's very kind. Thank you," Sarah said, looking confused. She had no idea Clive had shared her story with anyone.

Peter tightened his arm around her, as though sending a message to Oliver that she was taken. Apparently, the subtly was not missed by Clive's son.

"And you, Mr. Michael-McGregor, your watercolor paintings that accompanied Miss Duncan's book are perfection. The luck of being here to attend your gallery opening is almost as though it was fate."

This time it was Peter's turn to look confused. They all looked at Clive who seemed amused by the whole scene.

"Perhaps I should explain. You see, when I stepped back from being CEO of my international corporation, each of my three sons took over a division. I'm pleased to say every one of them has been outstanding at moving toward the future, while holding onto tradition. Oliver is my middle son and is in the process of expanding our publishing division from simply textbooks to mainstream, popular publications with an emphasis on children's books."

For the briefest moment, Sarah felt her head spin. Could this really be happening?

"Father, perhaps I can explain further," Oliver said. "Sarah, my team and I are terribly impressed with your story and we want it to be our debut piece into the realm of children's literature. You have captured meaningful life lessons about friendship and love in a way everyone can relate to, both children and adults. In this turbulent world, we want to emphasize kindness and compassion to young readers in the hope they will carry it forward throughout their lives. Your story fits perfectly with our mission. What do you think?"

"I...I'm not sure what to say," Sarah answered, a little tongue-tied. "It's a little overwhelming."

She looked up at Peter for reassurance. His expression said everything.

"I think Sarah would be thrilled to have you publish her book," Peter said.

"Yes, she would," Sarah laughed. "Yes, of course! Thank you, Oliver, Clive, I would be over-the-moon excited to have you publish my book. I'm in shock. Oh my gosh!"

"And Peter, about your illustrations..." Oliver said before he was interrupted.

"I need you over there next to Lydia right now, son," Jessica said, pulling him away. "We are about to introduce you. Excuse us, please."

"We can discuss details later, Sarah," Oliver said. "I'm so glad we were able to meet. You are as delightful as my father said you were."

They walked away toward the champagne server, and for the briefest moment she was left alone with her thoughts. Her mind was swirling with what just happened, but this was Peter's night and all the focus needed to be on him. She would resist the temptation to tell anyone about the book until after the party. A tiny doubt crept in concerning Oliver's words to Peter, '*About your illustrations...*' What could that mean? What if he didn't like them? That couldn't be possible.

The gallery lobby was now filled with lovely people, lit by candlelight with gentle harp music in the background. It was all quite impressive.

"Ladies and gentlemen, thank you for being here tonight. My name is Jessica Michael-McGregor and this is Lydia Mathews. We are the owners of this new gallery as most of you know. Our hope is to showcase the best and brightest of Scotland's artists in this space and be a vibrant part of the arts in Edinburgh. We are extremely excited to present a very special artist to you this evening. Forgive me if I sound a wee bit like a proud parent, but the fact is, our featured artist is none other than my son, Peter Michael-McGregor."

Peter stood next to his mother and nodded slightly in response to the applause, looking a shade embarrassed. A wash of nervousness passed over Sarah, realizing how vulnerable he must be feeling. Grandmother Rosemary told her to always go to prayer when she felt helpless. *Lord, guide him and protect him.*

"In addition to being an extremely talented artist, my son has added beautiful personal prose written on the back of each painting. We thought they made the art even more meaningful, so we printed his words on the tags next to each framed piece for you to read."

Guests murmured positively to each other before Jessica continued.

"Mother Nature threw us a bit of a curve with last night's storm, and I apologize for the lack of electrical lighting. While dreamy, it certainly isn't the best illumination for appreciating fine art. We will hand out individual candles when we drop the ropes to the gallery rooms. If you have interest in any piece or have questions, please feel free to find either myself or Lydia. In addition, Peter will be available to chat as well," Jessica turned to the young girls at the arched opening. "Ladies, please remove the ropes."

Unexpectedly, the electricity came back on as the ropes dropped, lighting the entire gallery with a soft , warm glow. The chatter amongst the guests stopped abruptly until someone said in a loud voice, "*Let there be light*," which was followed by another voice on the other side of the room not missing a beat, "*And there was!*"

Peter was swept up by guests as they made their way to the two rooms where his paintings were on display. A dozen large oils of Scottish landscapes graced the walls of the first area. Each painting had been placed in an antique gilded gold leaf frame which enhanced the art perfectly. The gentleman in charge of gallery lighting had outdone himself–the effect on Peter's work was breathtaking. Even the tags next to the individual paintings were well done with the title of the work, Peter's personal message, and the price. Once sold, a small red dot sticker was placed on the tag to indicate it was no longer available. A green dot meant someone was pondering. Sarah did a double take the first time she noticed the prices of the art work. She had no idea they fetched such a high figure. A little guilt crossed her mind when she realized how much the drawings for her book would've cost.

Among the guests admiring the art was an older man taking copious notes in a journal. She wondered who he was, but most of the guests were unknown to her. Looking around, she saw her father and Kaitlyn in an animated conversation with Simon Cavanagh and his lovely partner, Hazel. There was much back-slapping and smiling going on amongst the four of them. Seeing her father in love and being loved back warmed her heart. A few minutes later Liam, Anje and Ava arrived, full of news from Shetland. It was wonderful to visit with family, but Sarah was anxious to find Peter. She wandered through the crowd and noticed red dots on the majority of tags adjacent to the paintings. After all his fretting and insecurities, it looked as though the gallery opening was a huge success in every way. Her heart could hardly hold so much joy.

After viewing the oil paintings, many guests were now filling the second gallery room to view Peter's large collection of water-colors. It was a delightful assembly of woodland landscapes, beach scenes, village images and Hebredian islands. It was easy to see how his creativity was inspired by the west coast of Scotland.

"I'd no idea the boy was such a talent," Seaneen said, sidling up to Sarah with James right behind. "I'm a wee bit astonished to tell you the truth. He's such a humble lad, I had no clue."

"Isn't he absolutely brilliant?" Sarah asked, overflowing with love and pride.

"That he is, lass, that he is. By the way, did your father tell you Simon Cavanagh found the silver and your books Frederick stole?"

"You're kidding, really?"

"They turned up at an auction he and Hazel attended yesterday. He couldn't believe it."

"This evening can hardly get better, can it?" Sarah said happily.

Their attention was drawn to a young woman coming through the door, moving gracefully among the guests. She was a tall, thin, stunning blonde who appeared to have just stepped off a fashion runway in Paris. Her air of confidence and sophistication was not quite the norm in Edinburgh.

"Oh my," said James in admiration. "I wonder who she is?"

Without hesitation the lovely blonde spotted Peter in the crowd and went straight toward him. When he looked up and saw her they shared a long embrace that immediately excluded everyone around them.

This must be one of the women he met while he was in Italy, Sarah thought. She took in a deep breath and couldn't seem to let it out. Was she fool enough to think Peter only had eyes for her? How could she compete with this blonde goddess who just sashayed into the room? The thoughts running through her head must've been obvious to Seaneen.

"Steady, my girl. You don't know who she is," she said, reaching for Sarah's hand.

The wind in her sails rapidly departed, and the elation so recently felt, vanished. She was now looking at her future as only one of Peter's many admirers.

"I'm going to get some air," she whispered to Seaneen.

"I'll come with you," Seaneen offered.

"Thank you, no," Sarah said.

The mist had turned to a mild drizzle. Once outside, Sarah wasn't sure what to do next. Going home wasn't an option, but neither was going back in. She took refuge under an awning at the shop next door and tried to make sense of what she had just seen. Peter was obviously very excited to see this woman…this absurdly attractive woman. Well, fine! If that is what he wanted, then fine! Yet, for all her bravado, the tears were dangerously close to spilling over. What was she going to do?

Guests had begun leaving and thankfully paid no attention to her. The snippets of conversation she heard were all very positive about the gallery and Peter's work, no one mentioned the inclement weather or the electrical fiasco. So caught up in her woeful thoughts it took a minute before she realized her father was standing next to her putting his arm around her shoulder. Neither said anything. The increasing rain pitter-pattering on the canvas awning was the only sound. He held her close as she wept, no questions asked. After a few minutes, he handed her a folded white hankie.

"After the rain cometh the rainbow," he said.

"Oh really?? Well, what if it happens to be nighttime when the rain stops? Where is your rainbow then?" she challenged.

"It's called a moonbow," he said with a smile.

"You made that up," she said with a shuddering breath. "There is no such thing."

"You, my beautiful daughter, are wrong. They form just like a rainbow except the light source is the moon rather than the sun. It's rare, but aren't the best things in life worth waiting for?"

A few more guests left the gallery, nodding slightly to Sarah and Richard as they passed.

"We need to go back inside," he said, not giving her an option, instead opening the door and gently guiding her through with his hand on her back.

The entry area had dwindled down to family and close friends, all chatting amongst themselves. Peter approached her immediately, accompanied by the tall, lovely blonde. Before Sarah could gather her courage to be cordial, he interrupted with the introduction.

"I'm so anxious for you to meet my sister, Ainslee! She just flew in from San Francisco and came straight here. Ainslee, this is my Sarah."

"Your sister? Ainslee?" she said incredulously. "Oh my, Ainslee, I am so glad to meet you."

"Thank you. I am equally happy to meet you. Peter has been singing your praises forever and I thought it was time we met. I'll be here for a few days and will happily tell you all the tales of what a mischievous little imp he was growing up."

"I would love to hear it all," Sarah said, a little dazed at the turn of events. "Ainslee, the ballet dancer. Of course."

Jessica and Lydia were standing toward the back of the room, clinking on a glass to gain attention. The serving ladies continued to make sure everyone had a full glass of Dom Perignon champagne.

"Thank you all for your support, encouragement and presence," Jessica said. "We truly could not have had this successful evening without you. To our families who put up with the last few months of chaos, to our friends who rallied around us at the last moment when Mother Nature nearly knocked out our event, and of course, to my talented son, who's work speaks for itself. Lydia and I are grateful and humbled by your belief in our dream of creating this art gallery and we toast each of you."

Applause and cheers resounded from the small group as glasses were raised.

"Peter has one last painting he saved especially to be unveiled to this group," Jessica said, indicating a fabric covered painting on the far wall.

Sarah didn't remember seeing it there before, but much had happened and with so many people around, she must have overlooked it. Peter took Sarah's arm and led her to the painting, as the others followed. His hand was shaking when he reached for the fabric and he laughed nervously.

"I've never done this before," he said, releasing her hand and holding the corner of the fabric.

With a flourish, he pulled the canvas away, revealing a magnificent portrait of Sarah. Her face had an ethereal smile, not unlike a slightly happier Mona Lisa, looking directly at the viewer. Exclamations of wonder and admiration echoed through the group, with words like *sensational, fabulous, breathtaking*. Sarah couldn't take her eyes off of it.

"Please read the tag," he asked.

Sarah leaned forward to read the small print, saying the words softly out loud…it took a moment for it to sink in.

I will always love you
Today, tomorrow, and forever.
Will you marry me?

She quickly turned to Peter who was on one knee holding a ring up to her. Glancing over at her smiling father, who nodded in assent, her heart raced.

"Oh yes, a thousand times yes!"

He slid the ring on her finger, and right on cue, the harpist began playing Pachelbel's Canon in D. Peter gently cupped her face in his hands, and kissed his fiancé, much to the delight of those around them. He took her into his arms and slowly danced to the simple, elegant joyful Baroque melody. Never had life felt so right. She was exactly where she belonged. As they twirled in slow motion she could see the faces of all the people who meant so much–her father, Kaitlyn, Seaneen and James, Liam and family, finally, she looked into the eyes of the man she loved with all her heart, her Window Friend, and was overwhelmed by the grace and mercy of God above.

Chapter Sixty-four

GRAEME McPHERSON

One Reporter's Thoughts

Every once in a while there are events in life that take your breath away with their pure beauty. An invitation I received recently gave no indication what the evening promised, nor even the remotest possibility that it would restore a middle-aged man's belief in love. But, stop, you say. This is an art column written by a seasoned, cynical journalist. What would he know of love? My friends, even this old sot is able to discern the real thing when it appears, especially if it occurs in an art gallery. Alas, I digress. Allow me to proceed with my review of the actual event.

Six years ago, it was my pleasure to interview a talented young, local artist who set the art world on its head with paintings that belied not only his youth but the fact that he was self-taught as well. This artist had the honour of being given a one-man show by the Pure Arts Guild of Edinburgh. At that time, all of the paintings were simply signed PMM, with no one knowing the identity of the artist. Even without a name, the oil paintings were lauded and sold well. Sometime later, this same artist was invited by renowned Italian painter, Paulo Antoneli, to study in Florence. This prestigious offer was leaked to the press, probably by Signore Antoneli, and the unnamed artist became well-known.

Peter Michael-McGregor was in his early twenties when we first met. He was an articulate, interesting, young man about to embark on high adventure in Italy. As a gifted landscape artist, I found it peculiar he would want to study with a famous portrait artist, but Peter assured me he was open and ready to learn from the Master. Several years passed and not much was heard about Edinburgh's talented young man. Rumors swirled here and there, but nothing was substantiated, and in time the bright light of Peter Michael-McGregor dimmed.

My curiosity was aroused when the invitation I received a week ago was to the opening of the new Mathews-McGregor Art Gallery on Victoria Street. When I read the featured artist was none other than Peter Michael-McGregor, I was fascinated. What had become of the young lad with the abundant talent and glorious future?

When I entered the main door of the tastefully designed gallery, a number of invited guests mingled in a lobby lit only by candle-light. I was told the antiquated electrical system had been a victim of the dreadful storm earlier in the day. The candle glow had a lovely, calming effect on one's senses, heightened by the gentle notes from a harp being played in the background. I had the pleasure of a few moments alone with the artist who graciously recalled my previous article. He mentioned something about how it changed his life—a topic I will explore further with him on another occasion. It was a pleasant surprise to find Peter was the same humble, articulate, genuine young man I remembered. I inquired about his time in Italy and if he would follow in Paulo Antoneli's footsteps as a portrait painter, to which he shrugged and asked me to let him know what I thought after the show. Jessica Michael-McGregor warmly welcomed the guests and invited everyone to view her son's paintings in the adjoining gallery rooms. As though carefully orchestrated, the electric lights came on at that exact moment, highlighting each painting to perfection.

At the risk of appearing overly effusive, the latest artwork from Mr. Michael-McGregor is nothing short of magnificent. As with his earlier paintings, he draws inspiration from the romantic style reminiscent of British artist John Constable and Scottish painter Alexander Nasmyth in their landscapes. However, I found in both Michael-McGregor's oils and watercolors, an optimism and serenity with a dash of freshness and vitality. His style and choice of Mallaig as inspiration is a brilliant combination. Apparently, I wasn't the only one taken with his work, judging by how quickly the red dots appeared. It is well worth a visit to Victoria Street to experience Michael-McGregor's marvelous artistic impressions of our lovely Scottish countryside. I overheard there will be a tabletop book of his paintings published in the future by Oliver Middleton, including many of the works from the gallery opening. I will be the first in line to purchase it.

After several glasses of champagne, I departed the Mathews-McGregor Gallery, satisfied and quite pleased by the talent and success of the young Edinburgh artist. It was about halfway down the serpentine street when I realized I had misplaced my favorite fountain pen, a treasured gift from my grandfather. Like a salmon swimming upstream through the crowd of people leaving the gallery, I re-entered to find a vision I will long remember. Toward the back of the lobby a glorious portrait of a young lady had just been unveiled. Obviously, Mr. Michael-McGregor had learned quite a few things from his Italian mentor about portraiture–it was spectacular. As I admired the painting from afar, before my eyes Peter Michael-McGregor dropped to one knee and proposed to the very same lovely girl in the portrait. The exquisite Sarah Duncan flashed a look of surprise before saying 'yes' quite enthusiastically. Observing the genuine love that passed between them was nothing short of divine. Were I a religious man, I would say the presence of God was surely in the room at that moment.

In closing, my friends, it is a rare gift indeed when we are allowed a front row seat to a happily ever after story. Tha gaol mòr.*

** Love is grand*

THE END

Belonging

Character List

Sarah Duncan (early 20's): American girl who came to Scotland with her father, Richard, six years ago. She graduated from Oxford University, and returned to Leigheas, her father's estate in the Scottish Borders, to become a writer.

Richard Duncan (late 40's): American diplomat, who served as Principal Officer of the U.S. Consulate General in Edinburgh. Once retired, he bought an estate, Leigheas, and created a retreat center for gentlemen. He is jokingly referred to as 'The Laird of Leigheas.'

Peter Michael-McGregor (late 20's): A talented Scottish artist, who is Sarah's Window Friend.

Jessica Michael-McGregor (late 40's): Peter's mother and art gallery owner.

Kaitlyn Turning (mid 40's): Scottish woman, employed as a personal assistant to a retired Judge and his wife in London. She is Richard Duncan's love interest.

Thomas Turning: (early 70's): Kaitlyn's widowed father, owner of Turning Pages Book Shoppe in Edinburgh.

Jacob Silver (22): Employee at Turning Pages Book Shoppe.

Judge Trevor and wife Miriam Cumberman (late 70's): Kaitlyn's wealthy employers in London.

Sanani Cumberman (5): Grandson of Nigel and Miriam Cumberman.

Seaneen McAughtrie Bradbury (early 70's): Former security specialist, now house manager of Leigheas. Recently married to retired vicar James Bradbury.

Marjorie Hutton Harris (70's): Seaneen's sister, mother to Gwendolyn (20's) and Frederick (30's).

James Bradbury (mid 70's): Retired vicar of the Church of England, Seaneen's husband and works on staff as spiritual advisor at Leigheas.

Liam Morrison (mid- 30's): Security specialist and farmer from Shetland Islands. He is Richard Duncan's nephew and close friend.

Stephen Parker: (early 50's): Staff veterinarian and friend of Richard Duncan. Father of Henry.

Henry Parker (10): Down Syndrome son of Stephen, with a sweet, sensitive, loving personality. Nicknamed Little Henry.

Dr Ewan McDonald (60's): Physician in the Scottish Borders.

Nurse Agnes (late 30's): Accomplished nurse for Dr. McDonald.

Meara and Brennan (early 20's): Housemaids at Leigheas, who are sisters from a nearby village.

Colin Alexander (50's): Fishing guide at Leigheas, who shares his wisdom and good-humor, as well as proper angling methods.

Detective Inspector Alex Lawson and Detective Constable John Murphy (mid 40's): From the Criminal Investigation Department (CID) for the Scottish Borders.

Daniel Roberts (60's): Former member of the Monuments Men group from WWII.

Jeremy Fisher (late 30's): Guest at Leigheas, who was a former British Olympic Equestrian.

Hugh Thornhill III (mid 50's): Guest at Leigheas, who is a well-known London barrister.

Clive Middleton (70's): Guest at Leigheas, a successful British businessman, who lived in New York for several decades before retiring to Scotland.

River Tweed
Guest Cottages
Chapel
WELCOME
TO
Leigheas
Marcus
Stephen and Henry
Seaneen and James
Stables
The Loch
The Woods

Acknowledgements

The idea of writing a sequel to *Window Friends* seemed easy enough–simply carry on with the characters I had come to think of as dear friends and off we go. Not so fast, smarty pants. In addition to continuing on with the previous characters, the new book needed to stand alone and make sense to someone who had not had the pleasure of reading *Window Friends.* It was far more complicated than I first imagined. Thankfully, I was once again surrounded by supportive people who never stopped encouraging me. I'm forever grateful.

Living with someone who is writing a novel is not for the faint of heart. My husband, **Greg Dow**, has graciously coped with me being mentally absent during endless days of writing and months of editing. Often dinners were late and stacks of papers accumulated everywhere, but never a complaint. He's remained my rock when I've been discouraged and ready to quit, always lifting my spirits, giving me confidence and ready to hop a plane to Scotland at a moment's notice. Truly couldn't have done it without him.

Another person who has been in my corner from the beginning and whose faith in me has never wavered is my brother, **Chris Darley**. Knowing me from an early age…birth…gives him the privilege of teasing, cajoling and sharing his brilliant sense of humor, all the while encouraging me with wonderful ideas and perspective. His input on the book cover was invaluable. Bird is blessed with the best brother ever.

Three dear friends were prevailed upon to read and edit the book. Each helped with appropriate corrections that smoothed out the story immeasurably. **Jeannie Friehauf, Shannon Novakovich** and **Debbie Mushen**–I will forever be in their debt for the amazing gift of time, energy and willingness to walk a fine line of offering suggestions while keeping our friendship in tact. Thank each of you for the many hours spent on my behalf.

When a story is set in Great Britain, and the author lives in the United States, there is a lot of research in order to make the story genuine. There are only so many times you can visit Scotland, and the internet only takes you so far. Thankfully, two very special Englishmen and a Scottish couple contributed mightily to the story, lending expertise and marvelous personal anecdotes.

Colin Alexander is a fly-fisherman extraordinaire, former Detective Inspector at Hampshire Constabulary and a delightful human being. Over the years, our research phone calls (with an eight hour time difference) have often lasted well over an hour, and happily included not only Colin, but wife Teresa and family. Thank you, Colin, for your generosity in sharing hysterical stories, nicely correcting my mistakes, and for a lovely friendship that means the world. I would be remiss if I didn't mention their adorable grandson, Lawrence. However, I suggest you not call Colin if you have a plumbing problem. The curse of knowing a writer is you often end up in the book.

I met **Clive Middleton** at the British Motor Museum several years ago and turned to him when I need accurate information about a vintage bus. Not only is he a charming gentleman, but I do believe he knows almost everything about everything. He has done the most fascinating jobs from police officer to a double-decker bus driver in London. Our prolific email friendship has grown to include life events and our families, and I look forward to one day visiting Clive, his wife Elaine and their dog, Lucy. As I write this, Clive has no idea I wrote him into the book–I can hardly wait for his response.

As many of you are aware, Elibank in the Scottish Borders has become my favorite place to retreat. I've had the pleasure of getting to know owners **Eleanor and Adam Beatty** and mother **Rosemary**, during our visits. They graciously allowed me to use Elibank as a setting for much of the *Belonging* story, and when I needed specific descriptions of locations, Eleanor went so far as to take videos and send them. Huge gratitude for their help in bringing authenticity to the story. Look forward to another visit. Soon.

My unending thanks to David and Simon Cavenagh for permission to include their very special antique shop in the story. Without a doubt one of the most intriguing and interesting stores in Edinburgh.

About mid-way through writing *Belonging*, we visited Scotland once again. This time we traveled with close friends **Sally Hoganauer** and **Stuart Herman**, and they allowed us the privilege of showing them around Edinburgh and Elibank. Our time together sparked my creativity and was a terrific source of inspiration. I so appreciated our time together. "Which one of you is the senior citizen?" the train conductor asked, with a mischievous smile. In addition, Sally graciously agreed to be my medical advisor, answering endless questions for months.

To my daughters, **Christen Bagwell** and **Alex Stone**, thank you for always encouraging me and being proud of your mama.

To son **Ben Dow** and **Kahryn Campbell**, I'm so grateful for your belief in my writing and for the honor of *Window Friends* being on the shelf at Anelare Winery. Looking forward to doing a book signing for *Belonging* soon.

To **Aimee McGuire**, thank you so much for not only selling *Window Friends* in your adorable Moose Creek Bakery, but also for hosting two book-signings. You've left me with a constant craving for your pumpkin maple muffins!

To **Lonnie and Oscar Suarez**, owners of Novel Coffee and Tea, thank you for hosting my first book signing in my favorite coffee shop. Your support over the years has been so heartening. Is it time to sign a book for little Oliver?

To **Sully Sajjid**, one of the most remarkable young British lads it is been my pleasure to know. We met on a Virgin Atlantic flight to London years ago, and the friendship between our families has grown to frequent trans-transatlantic phone calls and visits. Sully has been a wonderful source of information about all things England, and a great tour guide (*countrytouring.com*) introducing us to places I never would've known to write about. His enthusiasm for *Window Friends* has become global as he often takes copies of the book to exotic locations, and sends me photos so I can brag about all the places the book has visited without me, often traveling first class! We tease his parents that we have adopted him into our American family.

To my two lovely tech savvy ladies: **Natilee McGill**, a wizard of social media sites and a wealth of common sense and great advice; and my extraordinary granddaughter, **Emma Molnaa**, who revamped my website to reflect the addition of the new book. Both of them are full of creative energy and so much fun.

To my BFF **Rozanne Tucker**, who has always been my cheerleader, sharing every facet of this journey with optimism, encouraging words and treasured loyalty. She just makes life better!

To **Chrissy Wolfe**, brilliant format editor, who once again agreed to make my words and drawings look really good. Thank you.

Thank you to the book clubs that have invited me to share with them. An author loves nothing better than talking about their creations.

And lastly, thank you to the wonderful readers who have stopped me in public to tell me how much they enjoyed *Window Friends*. Thank you to those who hated it and didn't stop me!

My hope is that my writing is graced by the spirit of God and a blessing to others.

May the Lord bless you and keep you;
May the Lord make His face shine upon you
and be gracious unto you;
May the Lord turn His face toward you
and give you everlasting peace.

9 798985 655124